SOME VISITORS FROM DOWN UNDER

The enemy had been met and defeated, and that enemy was no longer feared. For forty-seven years the seven great Hellgates were guarded, with guard duty being the most boring assignment anyone could draw. The dozen men and women at Gate One were but a few days away from the completion of their tour, and all would be glad to be free of the silence of Flux and the eerie crater of the Gate.

Suddenly a loud klaxon rang out three times and it sounded as if the end of the world was coming. Bandichar had been asleep but was quickly brought awake by the terrible noise. He stormed out of his tent, not looking like a powerful Fluxlord, but more like a man who had been caught with his pants down.

"Son of a bitch," Bandichar swore softly, "something's coming through."

SOUL
BOOK FIVE:
RIDER

Tor books by Jack L. Chalker

Downtiming the Night Side
The Messiah Choice

G.O.D. Inc.

The Labyrinth of Dreams
The Shadow Dancers
The Maze in the Mirror

Soul Rider

Soul Rider I: *Spirits of Flux and Anchor*
Soul Rider II: *Empires of Flux and Anchor*
Soul Rider III: *Masters of Flux and Anchor*
Soul Rider IV: *The Birth of Flux and Anchor*
Soul Rider V: *Children of Flux and Anchor*

SOUL RIDER

BOOK FIVE:

CHILDREN OF FLUX & ANCHOR

BY

JACK L. CHALKER

A TOM DOHERTY ASSOCIATES BOOK
NEW YORK

SOUL RIDER V: CHILDREN OF FLUX AND ANCHOR

Copyright © 1986 by Jack L. Chalker

Cover art by Dawn Wilson

A Tor Book
Published by Tom Doherty Associates, Inc.
175 Fifth Avenue
New York, N.Y. 10010

Tor ® is a registered trademark of Tom Doherty Associates, Inc.

ISBN: 0-812-52340-7

First edition: October 1986

Printed in the United States of America

0 9 8 7 6 5 4 3

*This one is for the female members of the Whitley clan:
Eva, who became First Editor when she married me,
and also Brigit and Lucy,
and even Mama Agnes who doesn't like this stuff.
For very different reasons, it's appropriate.*

To New and Old Readers of the Soul Rider Saga

This is the fifth, and probably final, novel in what has been labeled "The Soul Rider Saga." Faithful readers, and the books have created quite a large following, will probably wail, but they wailed when I ended my past long-form series as well, and I always have subscribed to Henny Youngman's advice to "always leave them wanting more."

The fact is, this book wasn't supposed to exist at all. The original novel as outlined, *Spirits of Flux & Anchor*, was to be it. One novel, broken into three volumes because of its length. These were published as *Spirits, Empires*, and *Masters of Flux & Anchor* by Tor in 1984. When completed, I discovered that my research and background material had an independent book all its own in it, and this was published as *The Birth of Flux & Anchor* (Tor Books, 1985).

While doing that one, a lot of things I'd wanted to put in *Masters* and could not because of that book's great length coincided with a lot of new interesting problems raised by the situation at the end of *Masters* and the new information provided in *Birth*. This book is the result. It is less a sequel to the original than a direct continuation. Familiarity with the first three books, and with *Birth*, is assumed, although the book will, I hope, stand on its own.

Readers new to the series, however, are urged to read the first four first to get the maximum benefit. They should be available where you bought this one; if not, your local bookstore has them or can get them quickly and easily (and don't let them tell you otherwise!).

Readers who have been faithfully following the saga will not, I think, be disappointed. If anyone gets through Chapter 15 and claims not to be very surprised, I guess I should hang it up. I will not, though. I'm already thinking up new characters and new strange places to go and new themes to explore, and I'm already working on them. That's what keeps it fun and interesting for both of us.

Melrose, Maryland
April 15, 1985   Jack L. Chalker

1

SOME VISITORS
FROM DOWN UNDER

For forty-seven years the seven great Hellgates had been guarded, and the guard duty was the most boring assignment anyone could draw. Mostly it was left to a few people in bad graces with one of the local powers charged with providing the rotating detail.

Gate One, in particular, was fairly remote from even the historical events that made the guard necessary. When, after twenty-seven hundred years, the Hellgates had been opened and the alien demonic enemy faced, that enemy had come through only three Gates, none of them this one.

All Gates, though, as well as direct access to the monstrous computers who ran and maintained them, had been closed by common consent after the crisis had passed. The enemy had been met, and defeated, at a great price in lives, but that enemy was no longer feared. They knew it now, what it was and what it could do, and they knew that now, at this stage, even an invasion at all seven gates could be met if need be. Then, and only then, the computers would automatically reactivate; the human-to-computer interfaces,

9

the Soul Riders and the Guardians, would activate with access to all the defense computers; and the powers that be on World would unite against a common foe.

Thus, the primary concern of those who'd fought the battles wasn't that any enemy would appear, but rather that some people would use the powers of those great computers to dominate or perhaps destroy World. Access to the computers had been terminated for that reason, although not before a tremendous amount of knowledge had been pilfered from it, some little of which was just now beginning to make sense to those who studied it. But only the wizards of World, those with the power, could command anything from those great machines, and they were as limited as always. None could again get into the great control rooms of the ancients nor speak directly to the tremendous thinking machines that ran everything automatically. The Gates themselves were almost an afterthought; they had been closed, and set to "outgoing," but they had been locked. Nobody really knew how they worked, or how to use them, and the computers had been strictly limited by the ancients so that even if they possessed that knowledge they could neither release or reveal it.

The huge dish-like depressions had been filled with debris based on the information that no one could use a dish for transportation if that dish was occupied, but there was uncertainty as to just how effective these measures were. If debris alone could stop an enemy, why had the ancients gone to so much trouble to seal them?

The Guardians, creatures with life created by the great computers out of Flux, roamed the system, beings of pure energy beyond human understanding, and kept things running smoothly and repaired properly. The Soul Riders, kindred creatures who alone possessed the codes that would open the computers to human command, rode as symbiotic things inside people all over World, many of whom were ignorant that they even had such things inside them.

The guard at each of the seven Gates was almost perfunctory and certainly not taken seriously by anyone. Everybody knew that if an enemy were to use any of the Gates, the Soul Riders would already be on station and the Guardians already in place. It was automatic. It had happened last time, when things had been in a state of ignorance. It would happen again.

Around Gate One were the four Anchors—Frinkh, Wahltah, Patah, and the one once called Holy Anchor and still referred to that way even though the great Church whose seat it once was now was no more.

Far beneath the former administrative centers of the Anchors, the "temples" of the old Church, the great control rooms and laboratories lay silent and deserted, access to them barred by command of those who had last been in them and had voluntarily left and surrendered their powers.

Now, though, in the transportation and communication centers of all four Anchors surrounding Gate One, lights automatically came on, and complex instrumentation became lit with flashing lights and digital readouts. A bell struck, and then some klaxons sounded, although there were no ears to hear, and then a woman's voice sounded in all four control rooms, the voice of the master transportation computer.

"Incoming, Gate One," the voice announced, casual and without real expression.

Guardians, taken completely off guard, rode the transmission lines down to check on things. This was simply not supposed to happen. An alert was suddenly sounded through the entire worldwide computer network, including the Soul Riders, but they were not yet activated.

The Guardians checked the information with their computer masters, then called off the alert. No one, in fact, was even aware that an alert had been called, least of all those in which bodies the Soul Riders lived. The defensive programs had never been designed to guard against Earth, but only against an alien menace, to block its progress towards Earth along the great strings of the Flux universe. This traffic was not inbound—towards Earth—and thus was not a threat by their mission and charge. It was outbound traffic.

The Guardians and Soul Riders of the Great War had been people of World: ignorant of high technology, backward, superstitious, and unable, really, to ask all the right questions or think of everything. They had been assured that the Gates could not be purged of debris by any invader's incoming signal without the joint consent of the Soul Rider and the Guardian. Their context, however, was defensive, and the types of computers and programs to which they had direct access were military in nature. These were the Forward Fire Base programs, modified thousands of years earlier to meet an unknown threat. By definition, though, incoming *from* the inbound direction was friendly; only incoming from the outbound direction was assumed hostile. The Gate locks had been absolute, barring friend and foe alike, but the Gates had not been re-locked. It seemed futile, since the codes to open them were now known but the means of changing them was not.

The Guardian assumed quite naturally that traffic from this direction was friendly, and the four Guardians of Gate One agreed and sounded the outer alarms for a purge.

The dozen men and women sitting in their camp at the edge of Gate One, reading or sleeping or playing games to amuse themselves, had been there for several weeks and had only a few days to go. Just a few days more to keep from going mad in the silence of the Flux and the eerie crater of the Gate. They all had some of the power and included a lean, hawk-nosed man named Bandichar who was a powerful wizard. Unlike the others, who were there because they were ordered to be, he was there because, by common agreement of the Fluxlords of each region, somebody powerful must be on duty at all times. Bandichar had been practicing some new spells and making everyone else nervous, but it was quiet now.

Suddenly a loud klaxon sounded three times, echoing across the crater floor and bouncing off its walls; it sounded as if the end of the world were coming, and guards jumped in startled fear, one woman rolling off her cot.

Bandichar had been asleep but was quickly brought awake by the terrible and unexpected noise and stormed out of his tent wearing only a pair of shorts. He certainly did not look like a powerful Fluxlord. He looked, in fact, like a man caught with his pants down.

"What the hell was *that*?" he demanded to know.

Atita Saag, a small, lean woman in an olive military uniform who was the officer in charge, shrugged and shook her head. "It came from the Gate." Suddenly the enormity of that statement hit her, and she yelled, "Everyone up! Full arms and packs immediately! Positions in view of the Gate but well back of the apron!" The apron, or lip, was a smooth area several meters wide that led to the depression.

"*Attention! Attention! Please remain clear of the Gate area until further notice,*" said a ghostly, amplified woman's voice from the crater's center. It, too, echoed eerily around the complex.

"Son of a bitch!" swore Bandichar. "Something's coming through! It had to be on *my* damned watch, too!"

There was a final warning buzz, and then the voice of the gate announced, "*Purging!*"

The small company of guards edged back as the entire Gate complex began to glow a sickly yellow-green. Then there was a roar that sounded like a huge volume of water coming down a pipe, but there was no water.

An incredible amount of junk had been thrown into the massive crater, from the remains of buildings to concrete and steel-like masses created out of Flux and allowed to flow in and harden. One could almost walk across the top of it.

Now that mass of junk glowed, was outlined in a crackling fire, and then vanished.

Atita looked at Bandichar, who was just staring, transfixed. If she didn't know better, she'd have sworn that the Fluxlord was as scared as she was. "I thought this couldn't happen!" she said, her voice trembling. "So what do we do now?"

"It couldn't! Wasn't supposed to, anyway," Bandichar

responded, his voice not sounding any better. "Still, that's why we're here. Just in case."

"Well, it's just in case! Now what? Anybody tell you 'just in case' of what?"

"We see what shows up, then if it's bigger than we can handle we run like hell and get help," he responded honestly.

"Maybe they won't come out here anyway, just go down the tube," she muttered hopefully.

"Uh uh. Even those furballs of fifty years ago couldn't get by that. It'd run another purge automatically, destroying them in the tubes, unless they knew the codes, and nobody that's not from here can know that code. No, they'll come out this way."

"Purge complete," the Gate announced. *"Stand by. Flag set to incoming. Incoming received. Gate flag reset to outbound. Transport personnel may now attend to offloading duties."* The glow died, and the silence returned.

Atita nervously stared at the Gate. "I don't see nothin'," she noted. "We should see it, shouldn't we?"

"I was there at Gate Two when they came the last time," Bandichar responded. "We should see a ship in there." Fear was being replaced by nervous curiosity. "What in hell happened?"

Nervously, expecting a trick, he walked towards the lip of the Gate, stopping just before it, so that he could see most of the crater. He made a simple hand gesture and materialized a pair of field glasses in his left hand, then put the glasses to his eyes and scanned what he could.

Except for the fact that for the first time in forty-seven years the entire dish was clear of debris and visible, there was nothing unusual. There was nothing in the dish at all. Frowning, his nerves more on edge from this than if the dish had held a huge invader ship, he walked forward to the edge of the depression itself and stared, first with his naked eyes, then with the glasses. Nothing. He focused on the small black hole in the center of the dish, the normal access to the Gate. For a moment he thought he saw the reflection of some internal light in there, but then it was gone. He stared hard through the binoculars, squinting because it seemed that something was blurry right by the access hole, but it was certainly nothing substantial.

He still didn't like it, but he couldn't help but give a sigh of relief. "There's nothing in there!" he called back to the soldiers. "Come and look!"

Slowly, apprehensively, arms at the ready, they did. "Now what in the name of anybody's heaven was *that* all about?" one man muttered, voicing the thoughts of the rest.

"Anybody see *anything?*" Bandichar asked, not able to believe what he wasn't seeing.

"Looks like a couple of little puffs of mist or something floatin' up over there," a woman noted, pointing. They all looked and spotted the two clouds or whatever they were—transparent, not terribly large, and rising to the rim about a hundred and fifty meters away from them. Bandichar realized that those were the indistinct blurs he'd seen in the glasses.

"Probably just some aftereffect of the Gate opening and closing," he told them. "Either that or the residue of whatever was sent."

They all looked at him, startled.

"This don't make any sense unless you think along the lines of somebody who wants in," he explained. "Say the fuzzballs check and find the Gates are open, but they got no report from their advance forces even after all this time. Maybe they just noticed after all the years that they were open at all. Now, after all those centuries, if I suddenly checked and found the Gates open, I'd send through something first to see if my senses or machines or whatever were lying."

"Well, what in hell would they send?" somebody asked. "Air or a bomb or something? It sure didn't look like much."

"Who knows how fuzzballs think?"

"Holy Angels!" somebody else swore, betraying a link with the old faiths. "Suppose it was some kind of poison gas or something?"

That started a mild panic reaction, but Bandichar shook his head. "Naw. Two little mist balls? If they were anything like that we'd be goners, and I think anything of that kind would be a lot bigger than what we saw. Anybody still spot the two little clouds?"

Everybody strained to look but nobody could. They had risen like the steam they resembled to the top of the dish wall and merged into Flux.

One middle-aged bearded man with a shotgun sighed and turned away from the dish and stopped dead, his mouth dropping, staring. Immediately behind the small group hovered two mist-like clouds, each smaller than a human and with no clear form, yet distinct from the Flux and flashing inside with a singular intensity of electrical activity. Suddenly the man raised the shotgun and shouted, "*Hey! Look—*" but he was cut off, frozen in mid-sentence and mid-gesture, just as the others started to turn and bring their own weapons up if they had them. They, too, were suddenly frozen in an eerie tableau.

The two clouds approached the statue-like forms of the guard and drifted among them, as if looking them over and trying to decide just who and what they were seeing. Had the guards been able to see and think and react, they would have discovered that the clouds were not clouds at all, but two dense, pulsing masses with a mathematical logic about them. By their movements, there was no question that the things were either sentient in some impossible way or directed by ones who were.

The "clouds" moved from the humans to their dwellings and animals, seeming to take a full inventory as if inspecting the premises before deciding whether or not to buy the place. The horses were not frozen, but ignored the things, although when they were almost literally enveloped by them, one at a time, they expressed not so much distress as annoyance.

Finally they moved out into the void itself, clear of all recently arrived beings and artifacts, and touched the soft, sponge-like floor of the world. Had Bandichar been able to view the scene he would have recognized immediately that the clouds were sending and receiving "spells" along the computer grid that underlay the entirety of the world. The spells were quite complex, too much so for any human, and entirely in the language of the great machines themselves.

Bandichar and the others might have been upset, even threatened, by this sight, could they have seen it, but they knew that whatever talked in this way was nothing more than a local threat. The great machines had taken their minds somewhere else almost three thousand years earlier, leaving only data and automatic programs to handle maintaining and nurturing the world and its people, and indiscriminate access even to the data was blocked by firm military-imposed and reimposed codes that not even another great machine like the ones buried in the Anchors of World could break.

The "clouds" themselves were discovering this, and were clearly agitated by it, pulsing and changing shape rapidly as their questions and commands were mostly refused or ignored. Clearly whatever they were they could feel anger, or at least frustration.

Finally they stopped, seemed to merge, and clearly had a heated discussion on what to do next and how to do it. Finally, they decided on something, at least, broke apart, and drifted back towards the frozen humans. Then, after giving a series of spells to the grid, they were away again into the void, quickly vanishing from view.

The humans unfroze. "What the hell . . . ?" the wizard muttered, looking puzzled. They *all* looked puzzled, or so it seemed, each one aware that something had happened, some time had passed, but unsure of whether or not the others felt the same or if they'd just gone a little bit mad.

There was a sudden crackling sound from inside the great dish itself, and several of them cried out and stepped back as the delayed program went into action.

As they watched, awed and more than a little scared, the dish gathered in sufficient Flux and transformed it into a precise duplicate of all the enormous volume of junk and trash that had been in the dish before.

Atita Saag turned white-faced to Bandichar. "*Now* what? There's not even any evidence anything happened. Who's gonna believe this *now?*"

"We'll report it," he told her. "They'll pick us clean but they'll be convinced that we all saw what we saw and heard what we heard. It's even possible that the incoming calls were heard in the Anchor temples. But we'll let wiser heads than ours figure it all out."

"Figure *what* out?" she wanted to know. "Just what *did* happen here?"

"Hell, ma'am, that's simple," said the old fellow with the rifle behind her. "Somebody just done stole our garbage, didn't like it, and dumped it back."

2

DISCOURSES ON SOCIOLOGY AND POKER

The air was damp and slightly chilled in the early morning light, the huge orb of the gas giant that provided World's illumination sending eerie ripples over the land as it rose. Two riders mounted on strong black horses made their way slowly down the well-worn dirt road, side by side. One was an older man with a full gray-black beard and long flowing hair of the same color, dressed in a long black suit coat and heavy black work pants, looking like the elder in some ancient and austere religious group. The other was far younger, dressed in a plaid flannel shirt and blue denim trousers; a man of medium build, clean-shaven and with dark hair cut very short. Only the most astute observer would see any resemblance in the two, or even guess a relationship.

They had now been two days together in New Eden, that vast Anchor area three thousand kilometers across, and still with vast empty stretches of land like the one they now traversed.

"I can't get over how little has changed," said the

younger man in a low, raspy tenor. "Forty-seven years, all the leadership dead, the women freed of their spell-enforced limits, and it all seems the same."

This was not the first time he had said it, but he still couldn't really believe what they'd found.

"It's not so odd," the older, bearded man responded in a rich baritone. "It's the way people in groups work, son. You take a bunch of lifelong slaves from some Fluxland. Something happens to the Fluxlord, and the slaves are suddenly free and they run off with one of them who's a wizard himself and set up their own Fluxland. Do they establish freedom and democracy and equality for all? Hell, no. They were born into a system with slaves and rulers and taught from the cradle that it was the system that was right, just, God's will, and whatever. They ain't been thinking of a different world—they don't know any other anyway. So they set up the same system with *them* on top and make slaves out of everybody else they find. Same system, only they're on top. You seen it again and again here, and I hear tell in the old histories of the ancients there's hundreds of similar things."

"Yeah, but this isn't like that."

"No? What's the difference?"

The younger man shook his head wonderingly. "I mean, O.K., it's one thing for the original New Eden. That far I'll accept your analogy. Coydt hated all women, and he got his men from matriarchal Fluxlands where they were on the bottom so naturally they set up this system. And when the Church the anchors all had been born and raised with, an all-female hierarchy, was shown false, there was some natural resentment there as well among some of the men. But they used Flux, after all, in the long run, to physically change the women so they couldn't read, write, do simple math, or fully control their emotions. But after the Invasion was beaten off—mostly by women, as it happened—and those brain changes were reversed, you'd think women would demand their rights."

The old man sighed. "Son, you sell old Adam Tilghman short. Like most of Coydt's hand-picked leaders, he was a brilliant man. He was actually born in Anchor, and thrown out under the old lottery system. Sold to some doddering Fluxlord goddess where he became one of her bodyguards and kept men, serving and servicing the underwizard women who worked for the old girl and ran her affairs. He had good cause to hate women, since it was women in the old priesthood who threw him out into Flux and it was in a Fluxland dominated by women that he was a courtesan, slave, and if need be, soldier. The fact was, though, he *didn't* hate women."

"I didn't know all that about him. So you mean he was just a product of his environment? When he got sprung by Coydt he just wanted to reverse things?"

"Well, you sell him a little short there, but not much. Fact was, he was a brilliant man who learned everything well. Even bright enough to understand what I'm saying about him. Trouble was, he was too human to accept that in himself, or see it in his own makeup. He felt comfortable with his new role and his new society, although not with its early brutality, but he felt a need to justify it all to himself. See, Coydt was honest with himself. He was out for revenge against women and he felt he had good cause. Old Adam, though, was too moral a man to be honest with himself. So he went through all of those fragments of ancient books Coydt had collected over the years, and out of it he built the religious foundation for New Eden. He was the New Eden theoretician, so to speak, and because he found that level of justification for all they were doing they accepted his conclusions wholeheartedly."

"Yeah, well, I know New Eden was the original name our ancestors had for the whole world when they came here, and I know they had a lot of religions, but I don't know if they led in *this* direction."

"Well, that depends. You read *fragments* and *excerpts* from holy books and it's taking things out of context. You can draw all the wrong conclusions. Then there was selectivity. He read lots of stuff from old religious texts—the Bible, the Koran, a couple of ones from a religion called Hinduism, and there he found what he wanted to find. The parts that didn't fit his vision he just ignored. Oh, I doubt if he knew he was ignoring them or being so selective; it was probably a subconscious editing. And remember his background—the old Anchor Church. You think the way you're raised, and even though he didn't believe in the Church he still thought in the same logic and context as the Church did. He couldn't help it. He read where Adam came first, then Eve was created second. That's in both the Bible and the Koran, so it's one good nail. Now, he figures evil couldn't corrupt Adam, so it worked on Eve and corrupted her. She was the one who disobeyed God and got punished for it, dragging Adam down with her. When two different religious books agree, that's holy writ. And when it becomes clear that the other beliefs were also basically patriarchies and that patriarchy was the rule for much of early human history—well, that cinches it. He's got God on his side.''

''But he's forty-seven years dead!''

''Uh huh. But think about this place. Only a handful of New Eden's citizens are older than New Eden. The vast bulk of them were born and raised in the system, and even the older ones lived under it for decades. It was always a collective leadership after Coydt was killed, and only Adam died. The rest just made him a saint and enshrined his system as holy writ. These folks have been born and raised in this in the same way as he was born and raised in the system of the Holy Mother Church. They don't know any other system, and they believe in their religion. Besides, they have no alternative system anymore.''

''Yeah, but doesn't your analogy hold? I mean, women are on the bottom here, so wouldn't they want a reverse?''

''You might be right—hell, there's Fluxlands founded for just that reason out there right now. You might be, but you'd ignore the other things. The Holy Mother Church lasted for over two thousand years and it was rigidly sex compartmentalized at the leadership level. The women set policy and interpreted it. The men carried the policies out, but the women had the veto. The one thing they all had was a fear of Flux. Anchor life was comfortable, and you always knew where you stood. Not everybody was happy with it, particularly some men, but the alternatives were all much worse. They gained safety and security from it, so they paid the price and griped. And the Church was smart enough to sort of borrow a little bit from the Hindu, and Adam was smart enough to keep it: the idea that we live more than one life, and that we live those lives as alternate sexes. It freezes the system. If everybody believes it, then there's no penalty for being on the bottom because in the next life you'll be on top, and you better be good while on top 'cause in the next life you'll be on the bottom. See?''

The younger man nodded. "Yes, I think so. It's a little hard to swallow, though. There's no outlet for the women here. There's still no schools for them except religious studies, where the rightness of their lot is pounded into them. They can't own property or inherit, can't get the training and skills to hold down a professional job, can't hold office, be a church official, or even get a divorce. An unmarried woman has less rights than a horse here.''

"Yep, it's crazy, all right, but it's also a secure system. It may be a waste and it may be wrong, but it works, just like the old Church system worked and like many of the crazy Fluxlands work. And, you got to think of the pragmatic side. Old Adam's system is really insidious, just like the old Church's.''

"Huh? What do you mean?''

"Well, think about it. Now, say you're a woman who feels this system's unfair, and there are probably lots of them. Lousy husband, or maybe you're bored or ambitious or whatever. So what can you do about it? Move out? Now what? If you take anything at all the husband can charge theft and they'll be out to hunt you down. Bitch to others? If anybody hears you who doesn't agree, you'll get charged with blasphemy and they'll send you to one of their conditioning clinics and you'll come back in six months or so a true believer ready to turn in your own daughters. You can't even hide it for very long, since those church meetings are required. I saw one once. They shoot questions at you so fast you don't have time to think, you have to answer automatically. Answer wrong, and the whole group turns on you so they aren't singled out. The husband's notified, and penalized, and is expected to discipline you. After a while, the only way to keep from getting caught in that trap is to start totally believing in everything and its rightness and purging all doubts and discontent from your mind. It's a technique taken from the old Holy Mother Church's method of indoctrinating novice priestesses, but I hear from folks studying the old records that it's a lot older than that. Works just as good on men, too, as some of the Anchors up north are proving.''

"*Sheesh!* I'd pack up and sneak out and try and make the border.''

"So? And what if you *did* make it? Outside of New Eden is Flux. You wind up a dugger, dead, or the slave of the first wizard you come across. You and me, we're children of Flux. We were born and raised there. We know it and its tricks and we can even use some of 'em. They can't. If you're going to make a run, you got to have a place to run to. Don't think the men got it any easier, even if they're on top.''

"Huh? Seems to me that would be what you wanted to be here.''

"Sure. But see over there—there's women in the field picking beans or something. Probably from a lot of farm families—they pick one, then the other. The system guarantees them the basics. Their husbands or fathers *must* provide for them. The Church makes sure you do, and those men go through their own indoctrination and reinforcement sessions. The system makes them a hundred percent responsible for all women and children in their families. All of it. *They are not allowed to fail.* If those women screw up the harvest, they're not responsible. He is. If he doesn't feed, house, and protect them even at the cost of his own life, *he* is held responsible. Hell, if his wife and daughters go off and rob a train, *he's* punished for the crime. And if his business fails, the Church will help out the women but he's left to starve in the gutter. The pressure's enormous. I've yet to meet a New Eden man who didn't have ulcers and whose hair wasn't gray while he was still relatively young. Very few of the women commit suicide—I don't think I know of one offhand. But a fair percentage of the men do.''

"Some system," the younger man noted dryly.

"Yeah. Yet there are folks, men and women both, who know the score and yet beg, borrow, or steal some stringer or friendly wizard to get 'em here. If you're willing to accept the system as a price, there's still land to home-stead here, protected from all wizardly magic and capricious Fluxlords and Anchor civil wars—stability and security. New Eden has contracts with the Guild to bring anyone here who wants to come, you know, and their missionaries have converted an Anchor or two far from here.''

The younger man nodded glumly and sighed. "Seems like we never learn. We get rid of one bad system, then trade it for another one that's even worse.''

"People will swap liberty for security every time, son. Right now old World's just living through a period like our ancestors did back on Earth long ago. Maybe still do, for all we know. We had it easy all those centuries, 'cause everybody traded for the same system and it worked. Now folks are trading for other systems that also work but are both equally unpleasant and mutually antagonistic. That's how bloody revolutions and wars come, and that always feeds the largest and strongest no matter how ugly it is. Somehow, I think Coydt knew that and planned it this way. He's laughing at us from someplace in Hell. By God, sometimes I wish I believed in this reincarnation business. It'd be real justice if he was reborn as one of those New Eden girls, now wouldn't it?''

"Yeah, but I never put much stock in that stuff myself. Who cares if we *are* reincarnated if we don't know it and can't remember our old selves? Might as well be dead, since without memory you're dead anyway. As you're fond of saying, there ain't no more justice in the world than in a crap game.''

"Yep. Life's a crap shoot, but it's more of a poker

game. You play the cards you have, and if you're good enough you'll win even if you were dealt shit. Win, that is, until you meet a better player than you. Most folks are bad players or never try the game. I learned long ago that the bulk of humanity are born victims, and no matter what you do they keep running back to being victims again.''

The younger man looked at the old one seriously for a moment. "Seems to me with that attitude you might as well just stop and blow your brains out.''

"Uh uh. Son, I been killed twice, once for real, and the cards kept coming back good. The purpose of life is to play the hands. You don't fold when you're holding aces, and you sure as hell don't quit the game when it hasn't beat you. One of these days I'll meet the one who's better than me, but not yet. If I check out now, I'll never find out what they're like.''

"Grandpa, you sure got a sick outlook on life.''

"Maybe. But I'm still here.''

The young man's tone changed and he pointed forward. "Riders up ahead.''

"I saw 'em. Most likely a patrol. Yeah. Look real smart in their shiny leather uniforms, don't they?''

They did not speed up to meet the oncoming riders, but let them come to them. The patrol consisted of a dozen men, all clean-shaven, muscular, and handsome, almost like a recruiting poster. They certainly didn't look very routine, though; while the officer wore a traditional revolver, the rest had submachine guns in their saddle holsters and a few appeared to have some of the new laser pistols as sidearms as well.

The old man nodded casually. "Morning, Lieutenant,'' he said pleasantly.

"Morning, gentlemen. I don't remember seeing either of you in these parts before. May I have your serial numbers and travel permits, please?''

"We're registered guests, Lieutenant, not citizens, but here are our papers.'' Both he and the younger man produced small packets in neat squared envelopes and handed them over. Neither could miss the fact that the two men in the rear with the clearest shots had their hands on their sidearms.

The lieutenant looked over the booklet and papers inside the first envelope. "You are James Patrick Ryan, Stringer's Guild, Retired?"

The old man nodded. "I am."

"This is not your first time here?"

"First time in a long time. I was here many years ago—during the Invasion—in the Signals service and helped on the railroad telephone project."

"Before my time," the lieutenant responded, but there was a note of respect in his voice. Very few stringers of the old man's day, and not too many even now, lived long enough to retire from the Guild. The officer opened and looked at the younger man's papers. "Rondell Hattori Akbar of Freehold. You are of the Freehold families?"

"I am," the younger man responded.

"Freehold is to the northeast. Why are you approaching from the west?"

"Colonel Ryan is an old friend of my family who we have not seen in quite some time. There is a war breaking out now between Atram and Tambaloo which he couldn't have known about. I went to make certain he came through New Eden rather than Flux."

The officer nodded and handed back the packets.

"May I ask why all the heavy guns?" the bearded man said. "These days this is the most peaceful spot on the whole world."

"Well, sir, most of it is, but we've had real problems with these border areas of late. A lot of the settlers here have pulled out and moved south, abandoning farms and fields and even a couple of towns. There's a nasty dugger gang that's been raiding of late out of Flux. We've got a whole army division up here trying to catch them but so far it's been like chasing smoke."

"From Atram?" Ryan was surprised.

"Well, geographically. We don't have much to do with them, but they keep to their side and we keep to ours mostly. Last few months, though, they began to have troubles with other Fluxlands and they pulled almost all their forces north and west for that. With the attention of those wizards on that war the gentleman here spoke about, the region bordering us has become something of a no-man's land. So long as this gang doesn't rock any boats up there, nobody in Atram cares much about 'em. That gives 'em pretty free reign.''

Ryan stroked his beard and thought about it. "I see. And you can't pursue into Atram because, with the war up north, they'll consider it an attack on their back and you'd face some world-class wizard power. Well, I sympathize, Lieutenant, and if we spot anything we'll get a message off.''

"Well, sir, if you take my advice, if you see 'em, you hide. If they see you, fight to the death and take some of 'em with you. They're a small army, well-armed and as vicious as any wild animals. They don't just raid, they torture and mutilate. They're wild savages.''

"Well, thanks, Lieutenant, we'll take precautions. I've had a lot of experience with duggers in my time, even this kind. Good luck.'' And, with that, the two groups parted and the pair of strangers continued on down the road.

"You heard much about this?" the older man asked the other.

"A little. Not much. You know how long it's been since I've been here. Almost as long as you. The stuff I heard, though, is pretty much the way the lieutenant there told it. Their leader's supposed to be a fellow named Borg Habib, who was a New Eden officer around the time of the Invasion who backed the wrong side in the revolt against Tilghman. Grabbed a couple of his girls and got into Flux one step ahead of the firing squad, or so it's said. Went wild out there, I guess. Word is he's not the world's brightest man, though, so he's never climbed above being a raider and a hired gun.''

Ryan nodded. "I heard of him now that you mention it. He's got some brains somewhere in his band or they'd have gotten him by now. This army's a pretty good one.

Somebody with fair Flux power, too. Nasty business. I wouldn't like to run into him out here.''

''Let's try not to,'' the younger man said, and checked his gun.

For almost twenty-six hundred years a unified culture existed among the twenty-eight Anchors on World, held together by a single religion and code of laws and social conduct and isolated by fear from Flux. At the same time, those in Flux even with great personal power were somewhat limited: the massive power tended to corrupt massively as well, and none of the truly great wizards who established their own Fluxlands could be considered sane. They were tyrants, some better, some worse than others, but all limited to what one mind, no matter how powerful, could create. None of the Fluxlands tended to be larger than five hundred kilometers square and most were substantially smaller. The power of even the best of them had created an understandable egocentrism and also a sense of paranoia, for they did not wish to lose what they had. They seldom if ever cooperated or even met with each other unless to meet a common threat, and then only for the duration of the emergency.

New Eden had shaken both Flux and Anchor to its core. Civil war within the Church for decades followed by its collapse in the face of the Invasion from the stars caused a total breakdown in the Anchors. The Church collapsed when met with incontrovertible evidence that it was false, leaving no social or cultural foundation. Everyone who ever had a grievance against the Church or the system and could find adherents tried to grab power; theory contested theory, and resulted in civil wars within the various Anchors themselves. These in turn broke down the always-fragile economics and caused massive death, destruction, and starvation.

New Eden had managed to capitalize on this in three Anchors near to it, supporting pro–New Eden factions there with arms and even some troops and eventually installing its system there. Others farther away had taken other tacks; a few were still in ferment, or divided into mini-states, but most had seen one or another faction win out and extend their own social and economic theories over their Anchors with increasingly totalitarian methods patterned after the successful New Eden methods but towards different ends.

In Flux, even the maddest of Fluxlords had been faced with the realization that his or her power came not from divine providence but from the remnants of the technology of an ancient civilization whose machines still worked— and that their power could be threatened by other technology being rediscovered all the time in ancient files and records. New Eden had once been four Anchors surrounding vast areas of Flux; technology had made it all Anchor, and in the process eliminated Fluxlands of some of the strongest wizards ever known.

Clearly Fluxlords who wished to remain Fluxlords had to unite or face ultimate attack from others who would or from new machines that could render them impotent to attack. They met and combined into multiple godheads with a single agreed-upon vision reinforced by Flux spells and some of that very technology that threatened them. Vast new Fluxlands, some extending a thousand kilometers or more, were formed with a hierarchy of gods ranked according to their relative Flux powers in a feudal system of gods and demigods.

A few independent and small Fluxlands remained, of course, but there was none of the ancient sense of permanence about them. The most independent and flourishing ones were in the broad gaps between the northern clusters, although a few, like the Freehold, were in the midst of the expanding states and held because they were sparsely populated regions inhabited entirely by families of powerful wizards.

Some of the new technology, however, was denied everyone. The big amps had been deactivated when the first settlements of the ancient ones collapsed; Coydt had discovered a way to tap the tremendous power differently and had used them again. Now, however, before the shutdown of the defensive computers, that loophole in physics had been plugged. The big amps would work no longer, and some of the other wondrous things that ran on the same sort of power were still nothing but useless junk. Some things, however, did work. The small handheld amplifiers used a different energy principle which might have been cut off but through oversight had not been. And New Eden was developing both steam and electric power once again, and also finding ways of actually tapping the raw Flux of the great Gate at its center.

Everyone had cheated for their own or their area's gain before the big shutdown. Vast numbers of program modules covering history, philosophy, economics, and technological wizardry had been removed or recorded before the great library was closed once more.

Many of the smartest men and women of World had prognosticated that New Eden would eventually dominate and perhaps swallow the whole of World no matter how abhorrent its system. It offered a curious mix of religion- and technocracy-based culture that provided stability and a sense of place in the cosmos to those of Anchor and those dispossessed by violence. Its system was so tight and so absolute that rebellion from within was next to impossible. Its lands were so vast and rich that no outside force could conceivably take it by attack, and its economic system, tightly state controlled but offering some independence at the producer and retail levels, worked. The state provided technological help and a guaranteed price to the farmer or manufacturer, so production was high. The state alone controlled all transport and wholesale trading, so prices were controlled. The Church fostered communalism; everyone helped you build your new barn, or repaint your house, and you did the same for them. If someone had bad accidents, or a series of reverses, and needed help, it came from the others.

At the same time, New Eden welcomed the refugees from anguished Anchors and paid the stringers to bring anyone who wished to New Eden. Civil and ideological wars elsewhere following the loss of more than a million lives in the battle against the *Samish* invasion had left much of World weakened and battered. New Eden remained pretty much intact and had a growing and thriving population. It was estimated that it might take a century or more for the rest of World to regain its former levels; by that time, New Eden would have a large enough army and technological base to take on or dominate both Flux and Anchor. Flux power was inherited; it was known that even now New Eden was in a breeding program to produce and train an army of powerful wizards all of whom would be true believers. And New Eden was patient, and would nibble bit by bit.

To a world whose people were shaped by a culture left static for twenty-six hundred years, New Eden, for all its faults, offered a powerful lure.

They didn't realize it, but they were following a classic pattern of human history which Tilghman apparently had deduced and which the new analysts now saw as well. It would not be the first time that people embraced a shallow and repugnant, even insane, system, turning a blind eye to all its faults and excesses and seeing only the stability, the power, and the glory of being part of an empire.

The mother in some northern Anchor, watching her children starve, does not think of the morality of a cultural system. Find the New Eden missionaries; get out, get down to the land of peace and plenty. . . .

The man who backed the losing side in the civil war knows that they will come for him and his family. Get out—get out or else. But where? What do high-sounding ideals mean when it's life or death? New Eden can't be as bad as all that, anyway. . . .

We die willingly for the greater glory of the Emperor! Banzai!

"Concentration camps? What concentration camps?"

"We had to destroy the village in order to save it."

"I will take the explosives into the heart of their camp. I shall die a martyr's death and God will be so pleased He will elevate me to the Paradise of the Martyrs. . . ."

Adam Tilghman may have been fragmentary and arbitrary in his knowledge of human history, but he got the mechanics right.

Almost four hundred kilometers of border had illustrated what the lieutenant had meant. The land was good, fertile soil and showed signs of cultivation and had buildings that seemed recently abandoned, but few had stuck it out. Now, however, they were far in from the border area crossing the top of the triangular northern tip of New Eden, a hundred kilometers or more south of the border, and things had seemed normal. The land was still less populated than most of New Eden, but that was due to the weather patterns which kept this small area very dry and made water difficult to come by.

Both riders halted as if one. "Smoke up there," Ryan noted.

"Think it's trouble this far in?"

"Can't tell, but my instinct says we better assume it is."

Both had 9mm pistols and Ryan also had a shotgun, but both ignored these and went into packs, bringing out pieces of metal and professionally clicking each part into place. Each took out long magazines of ammunition and put them in every pocket they had, then one in each of the new weapons.

The land swept up from where they were. It was more a rise than a hill, but it was sufficiently high to block their view. They approached it, then dismounted and went down on their stomachs, crawling to the top on their bellies.

They looked down on what had been a small ranch. The house and barn were now in flames, and several human figures were going from place to place, checking on things.

"The raiders?" Rondell asked the older man.

"Looks like some of 'em. I don't make it as more than a dozen, though. Probably a rear guard." Both clicked their sights to maximum telescope range and looked again at the sight.

The range was still too great to make out individual features, but there were clearly some dead bodies scattered around. The raiders themselves seemed a ragtag bunch, dressed in mismatched and outsized clothes that looked like somebody's refuse, but commanding nasty-looking weapons that seemed to be related to the two now pointed at them.

"Look at the horses over there. See anything odd?" Ryan asked the other.

Rondell looked. "Can't tell much from this distance, but they sure don't look like work horses or breed horses, either."

"Right. They're also out of the corral but are the most passive bunch I've ever seen with all that going on."

"Think they're the raiders' horses?"

"I do. But that's clearly a horse farm down there—I can make out the picture on the sign, and you can see the layout yourself. So where's the farm's horses and the other raiders?"

"*Whoops!* Looks like they're getting ready to pull out down there. I hope they don't decide to come this way."

"Ten to one they'll screw the road and take off overland to the northeast. Shortest route to the border and away from the roads and the army. How many horses you make down there?"

"Huh? Looks like sixty or more. Why?"

"They came in overland and probably pushed hell out of those horses. Bet they did a hundred kilometers without real rest just to get here by midday. They had it well thought out."

"A hundred is pushing it to the limit," Rondell noted. "You—oh, I get it. They knew this place was here and that it had a large number of fresh and broken horses. They came in, pushed everything to the limit, and when they got here the horses were spent. So they left a sufficient number of them here to move the horses out while they continued to ride off on the new fresh mounts. It explains some of it, but *they're* gonna be pretty damned exhausted after that ride and a fight."

"Uh huh, but they've had most of the day, and night will fall in an hour or so. They can afford a cold camp and some rest now. See, when the army gets here, or a posse is formed, they're gonna take off after this bunch here—northeast. Easy tracks off the road, at least for a while. In the meantime, the main bunch will be ahead of us, mostly on the road until they want to camp, then probably making a dozen cold camps just out of sight of the road for the night.''

"But the only thing up ahead is the Logh District—the old Anchor. The Sea starts in another twenty or thirty kilometers and runs right up to it.''

"Then that's what this is all about,'' the old man sighed. "A dozen or more raids up and down five hundred kilometers of Flux border, so you got two army divisions spread thin as blazes. No railroads up here yet, so it'd take 'em days to form into any sort of military unit and get here.''

"But you're saying that they're going after Logh Center! That's crazy! There's half a million people living there!''

"At least. But those half million don't know what this group's about, and we don't know how many more are set up to draw off the division guarding the old Anchor border. *Damn!* I just wish I knew what they were really after!''

Rondell sighed. "The only way to find out now is to nab one of them down there alive and make him talk.''

Ryan sighed. "The range on these babies is up to two thousand kilometers. My distance guide says they're seventeen hundred and forty-two meters away.''

"That's still stretching it. And we'll never take 'em all out.''

"Don't have to. Whittle them down and they'll have to come to us. They've burned most of their cover down there.''

"They could just mount up and get out.''

"Naw. They want to buy as much time as possible. They'll come for us if only to see who and what we are. That's all open ground between us and them, though. Single shots, in alternation. Wind's blowing our way. The sound might not carry down to them.''

The man known as Ryan carefully aimed his automatic rifle and pushed a series of small studs on the side. A little dot of light appeared in the scope and after a moment centered on the back of one of the raiders below. He pulled the trigger, having set it for a single shot at a time. There was a sharp, hollow sound as it fired, and the figure was suddenly propelled forward and lay twitching in the dirt.

Rondell fired, and a second figure was forced back against a fence rail and then collapsed like a stuffed doll.

They got four of them in under fifteen seconds, the amount of time it took for the others to see what was going on and react. The pair was able to get two more before the six remaining raiders, bewildered at where the shots were coming from, were able to identify at least the direction and take appropriate cover.

The pair's next five shots were not merely wasted, they told the defenders the general direction of hostile fire. Random shots began digging up the dirt all along the side of the rise facing the ranch.

"I can't make 'em out!" Rondell called, frustrated. "We got all the easy ones we're gonna get."

"Maybe not! Four of 'em are making their way behind the herd of horses. I think they're gonna try and stampede them up the rise, with them following. Good! Set to automatic, and when I tell you, fire right in front of the herd—close as you can. If you get a horse it's no problem."

"Gotcha!"

The bearded man watched until a tiny figure, moving too stealthily to get a shot at, made its way behind the horses. That was four, the most he could hope for. *"Now!"* he shouted, and opened up. He couldn't afford to wait until they started the stampede themselves.

Accuracy in automatic volley wasn't much, nor did it have to be, but a huge number of puffs of earth came up from in front of the horses and the nearest two suddenly whinnied in pain and started to keel over. That was enough for the rest of them, exhausted as they were. The horses panicked, began to jump, then roared off as a group away from the two shooters on the rise and right into the four just behind them.

They put new clips in their rifles and studied the scene. The whole thing had been over in seconds, and they could count two horses dead, one thrashing about on its side, and four very mangled human forms behind them.

Ryan chuckled. "I haven't pulled that one in fifty years. The old ones are the best."

The young man whistled. "They weren't kidding about you, were they? Now there's just two of 'em and two of us."

"Yeah. Now comes the hard part."

"If I were them, I'd make a run for it away from us. They got to know they'd be out of range almost immediately and some of those horses will stop pretty quick, being so tired. I can see a few just off there."

"That's what they'll do. They know we can't cross this area, either. If I were them, I'd have one of 'em make their way back and get a couple of horses, then bring them up behind that smoldering ranch house there. Then the other could make his way back to it.

"Yeah, that's what I'd do, but I wasn't given Flux orders, either, and I'm no butcher. Their decoy plan's spoiled, but they still don't know who or how many they're up against. They'll want to know to warn the main band. We've turned the tables on them, Grandson. Now *they* need one of *us* alive, so they can determine if we have sent off for the army or have communications equipment. If we do, that main group will have their backs to the Sea and be caught in a vise." He looked at his watch. "About an hour and a quarter until dark. They'll wait it out, knowing we have to come and get them."

"Do we?"

"Yeah, but not *their* way. Let's get back to the horses. I figure we can cut a pretty wide arc in an hour or so."

"You mean, come in behind them?"

"Uh huh. And with a little bait."

*   *   *

Two figures waited in the silence and the dark, one behind a watering trough, the other in the bushes between the front yard and what remained of the still-smoking ranch house. They were, perhaps, six meters apart, but they commanded a view of all approaches to the building, well, and remains of the structures. Anyone coming at them would be in the open as far as one or the other was concerned and a perfect target. They, too, had night sights.

"Why the hell don't they come?" one of them asked in an impatient whisper louder than a normal tone of voice.

"Shut up! Just means there ain't many of 'em. Maybe only one or two. Just hush. They'll come!"

There was a sudden noise and both turned and looked through their night scopes. It was just one of the horses—a saddled horse, at that—slowly ambling back. The scope didn't give a hundred percent night vision, but it was hard to miss the horse, the saddle outline, and the fact that it was riderless.

Both sighed and relaxed a little. "It's coming up on my side. I'll get her as she passes!" the first one whispered loudly.

The other nodded and looked back out at the darkened and deathly quiet desert. Suddenly there was a noise, a thud like the falling of some heavy body, and a small, aborted cry, and the one near the house suddenly turned and pointed the rifle at where the horse now was.

"*Renie!* You O.K.?"

There was no answer.

The raider looked into the night scope to see if anything could be made out, but the damned horse was not just standing there, it looked *tethered* now.

Suddenly there was a massive groaning noise behind the raider, and something fell and collapsed part of the roof with a crash and a roar. The raider, startled, stood up for a moment, and suddenly there was a cracking sound and something dropped down and coiled around the raider's body in a tight, painful embrace. The rifle fell and clattered on the ground, and then there was a tug and the raider, helplessly bound, crashed down as well.

"Got 'em!" Ryan called.

"Mine, too," responded the younger man. An electric torch flared. "Holy shit! It's a woman!"

A second torch went on. "Mine, too."

The one with the whip around her was screaming and writhing and trying to break the hold, but could not. Her rage was so strong she was mostly unintelligible, but she appeared to be mouthing and growling a lot of graphic obscenities. Still, the leather whip had cut through her clothes and the more she struggled the more it bit into skin. She was getting bloody fast.

Ryan pulled her up with an expert's move, and coolly rammed his fist into her jaw. Her head snapped back, then came forward limply. A trickle of blood came from the side of her mouth, but she was out cold.

He undid the whip; then dragged her over to a hitching post, using leather straps from bridles to bind first her hands, then her feet around the post. She hung there like some game tied in a hunting camp.

The other one they bound, face out, to a tall, deeply sunk pole. Only then did they begin to survey the rest of the scene.

"You did pretty good hanging on that horse's ass and side," Ryan told the younger man. "Glad you could. I'm getting too old for that stuff."

"Looks like you're pretty good to me," Rondell responded with more than a note of admiration in his voice. "Let's see—*God!*"

His light shone on one of the raiders' victims, a man who looked to be about thirty, although looks were deceiving, even in New Eden. He'd been shot twice, but then somebody had stripped him and castrated him with a knife.

There were two other males, one in his teens and one not that old, who had met identical fates. They found one other body not a raider, a woman, who'd been almost cut in two with a hail of bullets. She was so beautiful that it seemed almost sacrilege to have done that to her. She'd fallen with a shotgun nearby.

Rondell was clearly shaken, but he could still think straight. "I thought these Fluxgirls were passive."

"Ain't nothing meaner and more dangerous than a Fluxwife when she sees her family in danger," the bearded man responded. "Except maybe two of 'em going at each other over something. Come on. Let's look at the raiders. . . ."

Finally, Rondell sighed. "They're *all* women. Sure not Fluxgirls, though." *That* was an understatement. None of them, including the captives, were very attractive, and clearly none had bathed in weeks or longer. All had rough complexions, calloused hands, and scars here and there, and all had bad teeth, and all were dressed in rags that clearly had once been the clothing of victims. Two had missing fingers; one who might have been attractive was disfigured with a deep, old scar that ran from under her left eye almost to her mouth.

"A couple of 'em 'been shot twice," Ryan noted. "I didn't think we were good enough to fire only fatal shots. Not at that range."

"You mean the others killed them?" The younger man was already feeling sick.

"Looks like. They killed the survivors who wouldn't be any help and couldn't make it anyplace on their way, then dragged their bodies over here after dark. That's a nearly-full can of kerosene over there, too. After they got done with us, they were gonna burn the bodies. Maybe all of 'em. That way nobody could tell who was raider and who was rancher." He paused a moment. "What's the matter? You been around dead people before."

"I—I just noticed this little sack on the belt of the one with the scar. I—look."

Ryan looked and then spat. Inside were the three severed penises. "War trophies. Son of a bitch. Wonder what the hell she did with 'em?" At that moment there was a groan from in back of them. "Seems like the sleeping beauties are coming to. You're looking pretty bad, Grandson. You sure you got the stomach for what comes next?"

"I do now," Rondell responded, and they walked back to the nearest one, the one bound face-out to the post.

She watched them come, eyes filled with hate, lip curled in an animal-like sneer.

"How much time I take with this is up to you," the bearded man told her in an even tone. "Now, I know you can talk 'cause we heard you whispering a thousand meters off."

"Pigs!" she hissed, and spat at them.

"Now, we're not from New Eden and we don't have much love for 'em. We're from Flux," Ryan continued, wiping the spittle off and not blinking an eye or changing his tone one bit. "We also don't give a shit about their laws. It's Flux law here." He saw that she understood what he meant. There was no law in Flux except that power and brains ruled.

"Go fuck y'selves," she responded defiantly. "Go 'head 'n kill me. You ain't gettin' *shit* outta me."

"I'm not going to kill you," the bearded man told her. "I'm going to leave you here for the New Eden boys to really work you over. What I leave for 'em, anyway."

He thought he saw a gleam of fear in her eyes. "What you gonna do?"

He reached over and with his knife for aid ripped off her rags, leaving her mostly naked. "Back when I was a stringer and we got into a fight, no wizard around, I sometimes had to operate on people cold. Take off whole limbs with just a knife. Got pretty good, too. 'Course, before I could amputate a leg, it had to have a real bad wound in it." Slowly he removed his pistol.

"Who the fuck *are* you?" she demanded with real bravado, but her eyes were entirely riveted on that pistol.

"James Patrick Ryan's what I call myself these days, because that's the name I was born with. Strings don't give their born names, though, not even to each other, but I haven't been active for fifty years or more. Back then I called myself Matson."

Her eyes grew wide at the name. "You ain't Matson! He's dead!"

"Yeah, I been dead more than once. Once for real, way back when, but I got snatched back. Once again about thirty years ago so I could get some freedom of movement again. I come back to life whenever the stench gets too big. Feel conversational?"

"Go back t'hell!"

The big man fired his pistol into her right kneecap. She screamed in pain, and writhed on the post.

"Oh, my," the old man sighed. "I do forget the power of these things. Looks like I blew your lower leg clean off. Grandson?"

Rondell looked sicker than ever, but he tied a tourniquet around the upper leg and heated an iron to cauterize the wound. She passed out from the pain, and after she was tended to they went over to the other woman, the one hanging from the hitching post. She'd apparently awakened very early in the game and had been able to witness the whole thing.

"Much too slow and messy, Grandson. I'm really out of practice. We won't make that mistake with this one. Nice, neat little knife thrust into the lower spinal column here and we'll just paralyze her from the waist down. Then we'll do the same at the neck. A lot less messy, nobody passes out, and there's a lot less blood."

"You slimy son of a bitch!" she snarled, with difficulty. Clearly she'd bitten her tongue when he'd knocked her cold. "They'll get you. They'll get you both for this, and your kin, too!"

"Brave talk," Matson told her. "Stupid talk, too, from somebody who slaughters kids and then takes their cocks for trophies. Now, like I told your friend, I'm not gonna waste any time. I'm gonna ask you a few questions. You answer straight, and it's a clean out for both of you. You give me any shit and I'll leave you both here crippled and hung out to dry for the New Eden boys. They'll milk you dry with their machines, then take you into their little chambers at the Gate and turn you into good little Fluxgirls. Which'll it be?" He took out the hunting knife and made sure she could see it in the torchlight.

"You can't do nothin' noways anyhow. Ask."

"You're with Borg Habib's bunch?"

"Who?"

The knife came out again and he stooped down. "I might not hit it the first time from this angle. I'm out of practice and it might hurt a lot."

"All right, damn you! Yeah, Borg's chief. He and Ayesha."

"Ayesha?"

"Ayesha the Whore. She can't *do* nothin' but fuck, but she's his brains. You don't think a *man* could run this thing?"

Slowly the story came out. She didn't know much about their past, but Borg Habib's reputation as a man of direct action but not a plotter or planner was justified. When he'd fled New Eden, he'd taken along his regiment's whore, a Fluxgirl of incredible beauty who, for some reason, had not changed when the rest of New Eden was reset, but had been frozen as she was for all time. She appeared both passive and ignorant, but Borg at least knew she had quite a brain in that body, and she knew it, too. Because of her limits, and her needs, she needed Borg, who was incredibly well endowed, and he did pretty much what she told him because it always was right or it always worked. She got power and influence through him that she was incapable of exercising on her own, and he—well, among other things, he got Ayesha.

The gang was less a gang than a huge family, although its exact nature wasn't clear. A family that, except for Borg, was entirely female. It made a twisted kind of sense. If Ayesha was still under the old Fluxgirl spell, then she was at the mercy of men but could treat other women as equals, even as subordinates.

Their captive wasn't a family member as such, but had been a captive of a raid. Many if not most of the family had some measure of Flux power, none really tremendous, but combined they were a powerful wizard, powerful enough at least to convert captives. They had no wish to be unconverted, of course; they hated men in general, except

Borg, whom they considered a good leader but a stooge of Ayesha. All would die for Ayesha.

Matson had guessed correctly. The band, under Borg, about sixty strong, was headed for Logh Center to steal something of great value they'd learned about. The rest waited in Flux on the other side, ready to smooth a getaway. She didn't know what they were going to steal, or how, but she knew it had been well prepared and that whatever it was was going to give the family enormous new power.

There was little more they could learn. Calmly, but sadly, Matson put bullets through the heads of both women, then untied them and let them lie where they fell.

Rondell had been silent as they'd gone back to their horses, mounted, and started on down the road into the night. Matson wanted to get down to where the phone lines ran from Logh Center to the interior so he could tap in and perhaps give a warning. Finally, the younger man said, "It really doesn't bother you, does it?"

"Huh? What bother me?"

"Torturing, then shooting those women. They were creatures of Flux. They weren't the animals we saw, they got turned into them."

"Yeah, it rubs me wrong a bit, but I can't let it get to me. Listen, Grandson, suppose somebody nasty gives you an infection. A byproduct of the infection is that you go mad and infect everybody else, who in turn becomes mad and do the same thing. Now, it wasn't your fault, but you're dangerous and crazy all the same and you keep infecting more folks whose fault it isn't, either. You got to stop the crazy ones, kill 'em, so they won't drag more innocents down. You feel right sorry for them, yeah, but they are what they are and that's an insane threat. You save other folks that way, and you give them some merciful relief. If there's anything to a next life, they're a damn sight better off, and they won't ever hurt anybody else. Then you go find the bastard who infected them and get at the cause."

He sighed, reached into a coat pocket, took out and lit a cigar.

"There's always been folks who were bad," he continued. "And there have always been other folks making excuses for 'em. Their father was a drunk. Their mother beat them. They never got an even break. And all that might be true. But it was cold comfort to the victims being robbed and killed by the bad ones. So you treat the bad ones as bad ones, and then you go for the *cause* so you don't make any more bad ones, but you don't let those bad ones keep robbing and raping and killing other innocent folks because it wasn't their fault they went bad."

"Maybe. But you ever see anyplace that ever eliminated one of those causes?"

"Well, a Fluxlord can, and so can the New Eden system. Not in a society like the stringers', or in some of the open Fluxlands. Our ancestors came from a place that had no Flux, only Anchor. Must have been a hell of a mess. Bet they never cured it, either."

"Then what's the answer?"

"You treat the symptoms, Grandson. Always the symptoms. And then you weep for the eternal innocent victims and do the best you can and you play the hand and survive."

There was no reply. Finally, Rondell said, "I hope their target isn't old Vishnar's castle."

"Yeah, I hope the same thing. Still, what would the old fart have that would be worth all this?"

"Even so," the younger man responded uneasily. "I hope we can make our call."

3

WAR TROPHIES

Under the long reign of the old Church, there had always been a carnival in each Anchor before the sacrament of the Paring Rite, when excess population had been disposed of ruthlessly by sending children of age into Flux. The old Church, and its cruel rite, were long gone now, and, for a while, so were the carnivals, particularly from austere and fanatical New Eden. Now, however, they were coming back, and to New Eden first of all. The carney people had kept their extended families intact and plied their trades independently in Flux and whatever Anchors were interested, and now they were reestablishing themselves. This was in no small measure due to the Central Command of the Signal Corps, the military arm of the Stringer's Guild, who had fostered and protected the carney folk all those centuries because they were the best observers of Anchors—changes in various Anchors, changes in leadership and attitude, and changes in economic fortunes, all of which were of importance to the men and women who controlled the trade through Flux.

It had been Rasheed Vishnar's plan to throw the largest carnival ever on World and to reinaugurate the custom. Vishnar, Chief Judge of the Logh District, was an old-school New Edenite leader, one of the original set of leaders formed by Adam Tilghman in the times after the whole cluster had been turned to Anchor. He was a Tilghman man through and through, and had been placed under arrest when the Seven rebelled—a fact which gave him even greater authority and influence after the defeat of the rebellion and the invaders. He was an unreconstructed True Believer, but he was not an austere sort of man and he genuinely loved people, particularly children.

Vishnar had been the technical boss of Onregon Sligh, the brilliant scientific mind who'd deciphered the ancient records and machinery from Coydt's own researches, then joined the Seven. Vishnar himself was a scientist, and a good one, although he had nowhere near the intelligence of Sligh, and after purging or "fixing" essential Sligh men through Flux, he continued the scientific research, more administering than actually doing the work himself, since he was first and foremost a political leader.

He was a big man, a hundred eighty-eight centimeters in height and weighing in, with ample girth, at around a hundred thirty-six kilograms. With a round face and short, neatly trimmed full beard, dressed in the black cloth of a church elder, he looked both formidable and comical at the same time.

He had an enormous custom-designed home on the edge of the city, well away from casual traffic, and while most of the scientific research was done in the gleaming old temple in the city center, there was some done out at his place as well, particularly on things that simply couldn't fit into the Research Institute. His projects had paid great dividends to New Eden and continued to do so as they learned more and more about the old technologies and how to apply or adapt them to New Eden's requirements, and he was proud of that. He also loved showing off new things to visitors he knew and trusted, almost like a child proudly showing his new toys, and if he wasn't as up on the principles involved, he was well aware of all the ongoing projects and what they were about. It was because of this, too, that he maintained close ties to the stringers and to friendly forces in Flux, the only New Edenite leader who had no particular fear or dislike of Flux wizards if they were decent folk and respected New Eden's ways.

His love of children and his almost-childlike glee at his technological toys and things like the carnival made many people see him as something of a big child himself, but that was underestimating him. He had been there since before the start; he had been one of Coydt's hand-picked leaders, and had overseen the ruthless extermination of opposition in the early days of the takeover.

Still, when the stringers had talked of the old carnivals and the survival of much of the equipment and personnel to run them, his eyes had lit up, and he'd determined to throw the biggest, grandest carnival ever. It would only debut at Logh Center; after its ten-day run, it would move to various parts of New Eden, winding up at the capital itself. Out of gratitude, he'd invited some of the young children from friendly Fluxlands like the Freehold to be his guests at the opening. There had been much debate in the Freehold about sending *anyone*, particularly children, into New Eden, into a society where sexual differences were enforced from a very early age. The only one who had really wanted to go was, ironically, the oldest person in permanent residence there.

She knew it was wrong to feel this way, but it felt almost like a homecoming. Of all those who lived in Flux, she was probably the only one who viewed New Eden with anything near friendly eyes, and without any fear or real condemnation.

Certainly the place had changed for the better, and not just the technological end of it. The women seemed more at ease, less fearful, and there was a sense of fashion out there as well. The basic system remained, of course, and that system was wrong, but somehow, for her, it felt very—comfortable. Certainly she fit right in out there;

outwardly, she remained a Fluxgirl by choice, and after a day here she began to wonder whether or not it was strictly an exterior thing.

I'm the lost oddball that keeps bouncing back home, Suzl thought as she examined herself in the full-length mirror. The woman who looked back at her was short, pert, insufferably cute, and very, very sexy, with huge breasts setting off an otherwise perfect hourglass figure. The woman didn't look a day over seventeen, dark-complected with black, shoulder-length hair that was styled to flare out in back while ending in bangs in front.

She looked exactly as she had forty-seven years ago when she'd walked out of here after releasing the Guardian and shutting down the master defense system and direct computer accesses. The same as she'd looked for decades before that. Although a powerful wizard in her own right since reassuming control those forty-seven years before, she'd never even bothered to erase the tattoo on her rump that gave her first name and identifying New Eden number, although she'd changed the name to just plain "Suzl." She'd told herself it was to remind her of what things had been like here once time passed and memories became mixed, and to show the children what it was like, and it had certainly been used for that, but now, physically back, she wasn't so sure that was really it.

She'd been born and raised under the old system not forty kilometers from the big house in which she now was staying. She'd been short and fat and dumpy, and she'd known it, and she wasn't much better socially. She liked the company of men, which wasn't all that often, but she always seemed to fantasize about the really gorgeous girls that were around.

She'd been an indifferent—no, *lousy*—student, although she'd had a natural aptitude for math and had done well there because she never had to work at it. Books had never appealed to her; she had little interest in learning for its own sake, never had, and she'd never had any ambition, any clear aims or goals for herself. She barely passed most things, and checked off random blocks on the critical aptitude test at the end.

Then had come the Paring Rite, being sold to a stringer and thrown into Flux, and she'd been the only one there who found it something of an adventure. She hadn't had to make any more decisions or face any more stern lectures about her future, and her fate was out of her hands. She'd wound up getting stuck by a wizard's misfired spell with a penis, and she'd become a dugger and a freak and had reveled in it. Ultimately, though, she'd been turned into a true dugger, an inhuman monstrosity, with breasts a meter out and a prick almost dragging the ground, and she became a real lost ball. With flux power provided by Spirit and the Guardian she'd regained some normalcy, only to lose it again when she faced down Coydt van Haas. His cruel choice was to become a Fluxgirl or remain a monstrosity forever. She had chosen the Fluxgirl, of course, and had married Captain Weiz, the man who had invented Fluxgirls and the psychological conditioning methods by which New Eden maintained and expanded its control.

Now, she realized, that even with regaining her power and her self-control, she'd never really stopped being one. Once, as a teenager, in an all-too-successful attempt to shock the other girls, she'd opined that she thought the best job in the world was probably being a whore. You had your days free, all your basics provided, and at night people paid to have you lie on your bed, be sexy, and spread your legs and have fun.

Strange, she thought. *I haven't thought about that comment since I was sixteen.* Certainly she'd never really wanted to be one or she'd have tried it. All those strange, kinky men night after night. . . .

But what she had been, for forty years, was a Fluxwife. No responsibilities beyond household management, plenty of communal support in child care and rearing, and, because she'd been in the fringes of the upper classes (and ultimately at the top), some free time to just play around and goof off, even have a tumble now and then with women who looked and acted like her childhood fantasies.

She'd *fit*. For the first time in her life, she'd taken on a role she could do that was not freakish or antisocial. She had chafed under some of the restrictions on dress and freedom of movement and the like, but those were petty carps and she had learned to live with them, and get around them when necessary.

And, when the shutdown came and she'd gone with her younger kids and joined everybody else and *their* kids at Sondra and Jeff's Fluxland, Freehold, she'd taken up almost where she'd left off. She practically took over managing the place, supervising the staff, taking on an inordinate amount of time with the rather vast brood. She was better at it and she enjoyed it. Sondra had been forced into the Fluxgirl mold, and while she'd tried to maintain it for the kids' sake for a while, she really couldn't. She became interested in outside politics, and in trading, and in raising a herd of fine cows. And Cass—she really suffered. All those years of repression and all that guilt on top of everything just burst through. Matson was restless and she was going nuts, and they finally packed up his and hers and theirs and set off for the place that all good stringers who hadn't croaked went to retire.

And Spirit—she had a lot of catching up to do. As soon as little Morgaine was toilet trained they were off, coming back now and then but less and less frequently as Morgaine had grown into adulthood and begun the training that would give her her father's wizard's legacy.

She could have gone with either of them. She loved Cass more than she loved anyone else in the world, but Cass had Matson and Matson had more wives than he wanted or needed. Suzl knew right along that she just didn't fit.

Almost as much as she loved Cass, she loved Spirit, but the Spirit she'd loved was not the stunning and adventurous woman of the Invasion and Freehold, but rather the wondering and happy child-woman she had been. This Spirit needed neither wife, nor husband, nor close companion. She needed to be free, and Suzl had understood.

This wasn't the first time Suzl had had such thoughts.

Once she had confided some of these feelings to others, and had gone to see a wizard woman said to be a powerful doctor of the mind.

"Yours is not a complex situation to understand," the wizard had told her. "It is simply compounded exponentially by your longevity due to your Flux powers. You were always different, an outsider, and you really hated it, but to compensate you reveled in that difference and convinced even yourself that you liked it that way. Deep down, however, you knew the truth. Deep down, you didn't like yourself at all. It made you reckless, uncaring. You did not fit, so you stopped trying to make yourself fit. You stopped living and started *existing*, moment to moment, day to day. You measured success by what your friends accomplished, not you. Then came New Eden, and suddenly you were part of the crowd, one of the elite. You conformed for the first time to the social norms of a society, and it was one where little was expected of you. There was neither motivation nor means to resist. You had a place, and you fit in it."

"You make it sound like I'm a natural-born slave or something," she'd protested. "It's *wrong* the way they treat women there. Women are every bit as smart and capable as men in almost everything, maybe better in some. I'd like to see how a man would take the pain of labor and childbirth, or even twelve hours a day of wild kids with no break and eleven hundred poopy diapers."

"Yes, but, you see, that's at the heart of your problem. There's nothing evil or wrong about being a wife, a mother, or a homemaker. The only evil is that New Eden *compels* women to accept those roles and no others. Even now, that means little in and of itself on World. Anyone without a great deal of Flux power is compelled to take some sort of role. You have the power to avoid compulsion, and you feel guilty that you aren't using it to accomplish great things. Well, many with the power squander it or do very evil or foolish things. I rather doubt that the wife/mother/homemaker role would have been best for you when you were young. Then you would have probably been best as a major authority figure—a commune chief, or perhaps even a priestess in the old Church if you could have taken the indoctrinations. But fate forced you into that role, and it met your needs and requirements. We are also creatures of our environment, our experiences. You were a wife, mother, and homemaker for the majority of your life. That's what you are.''

The statement had startled and disturbed her. "You, a learned and powerful professional woman, are telling me I'm only cut out to be a wife?"

"Everybody has to be something, and it's the only something you've ever been where everything fit. Everyone can change, of course, but it is one of the curses of Flux power that we change the least once we find a niche. We live too long. Age never faces us in the mirror, and death is always remote. Still, as novice wizards, we are frightened and insecure. All of us. We must find a niche or the power will consume us, destroy us, or make us mad. Once we find it, if we do, it becomes a cocoon in our subconscious mind. We unknowingly weave our own complex spells to reinforce it. Just as Fluxlords get increasingly rigid, so do we. This is why your friends could not remain what they were, power or not, but reverted to the sorts of people they had been. They had previous niches, and they fell back into them as soon as they could.''

"You're telling me that if I live five hundred years I'm always going to be a Fluxwife because deep down I *want* to be?"

"In a way. Basically, you've been one so long you are beyond really changing the basics. When the Guardian lifted your binding spells, you had the most power anyone has ever had in this region. You changed yourself as little as your conscience and your duty would permit you. And, at shutdown, you walked away from New Eden into Flux, power intact, and you didn't change any more than that. You told yourself you were free and that you detested the system and the men who made it, yet you did nothing to change your direction. You felt like you should change, take off in new directions, but you had no direction to go and every alternative looked threatening to you. You made excuses to yourself. The children needed you. You were an object lesson. Sondra and Jeff needed you. And all of it might have been true, but it also reinforced that tight niche, that cocoon. You were afraid of becoming the drifting, aimless outsider again. The more you considered alternatives, the tighter the safe and warm cocoon gripped you. The same thing happened to me, only I was a professional woman, a healer. You have so many self-induced spells on you that they can't be counted, all reinforcing your safety image. So do I. So do Sondra, and Jeff, and the others. You must stop dwelling on what you could have been and accept what you are. You can accept it and find some happiness and comfort, or you can continue to reject it and remain miserable, guilt-ridden, and uncomfortable. But you will still be the same in either case.''

The terrible thing was, it explained so much, particularly about wizards. Why, even after centuries, wizards remained basically the same people, and why most of them feared changes. Why Fluxlands remained constant, and why, after half a century or so, they grew so negligibly.

The worst part had been after, when, in defiance, she'd really tried some radical changes on herself. She tried, she really tried, just to prove it false, to prove herself the exception to the rule. She tried changing herself physically, and succeeded, but all she got was a different looking Fluxgirl. Worse, she felt uncomfortable until she changed back into the old form again. Now, at least, she understood why Mervyn was always an old-man figure. It was his niche, his self-image. Oh, he changed himself into others at times, to carry out his purposes, but as soon as he could he always changed back again. She wasn't as strong a wizard as Mervyn had been, and she didn't have his motivations even for his temporary changes.

Worse were the changes *inside*. She had given up cigars years ago. They just didn't give her a charge anymore, and the idea of doing it now seemed, well, *wrong*. She used to cuss like a soldier, but somehow that had gradually faded away. It had just become, well, *embarrassing*, a word the old Suzl wouldn't even have known the meaning for. She liked personal privacy, but she didn't like being *really* alone. She'd gone off for a bit into Flux after the sessions, but she'd returned very quickly to Freehold. With others, fine, but out there, even with the power, she just couldn't stand being alone.

Even here, with servants to wait on servants, she had automatically and without even thinking about it made the bed, cleaned up any mess, and even wiped out the washbasin and tub with a towel. A smudge on the window that didn't even look out on much of anything had so preyed on her that she'd wetted a cloth and cleaned it off, then did the rest of the window so it would all look uniform.

Not that she was a true Fluxgirl, of course. She thought and acted independently, and could control her emotions at least as well as the old Suzl could, which wasn't all that much. She didn't believe for a minute the divine nature of all this. She was literate and did good math, although neither skill got much real use out of disinterest. It was still nice to send and receive letters and notes from faraway close ones like Spirit and Cass, but her own notes were stilted, phrased in simple sentences and written in block letters, and she read the notes aloud, one word at a time. When you haven't done something for fifty years it comes hard, and there was no incentive to improve. And, she was still pretty aggressive when she wanted to be. Any man who attacked her would find he'd attacked a tigress.

The bottom line was that she desperately needed someone to love and to love her, and that someone was not in sight, had never really been in sight except for all-too-brief moments in the distant past with people now far changed from that time. Not love as her friends loved her, or love as her children loved her, but real, personal love. She had never loved or been in love in New Eden, but it had been an easy, comfortable time, and the job and role was something she knew how to do and did well, unlike almost anything else. If anything, the one most important thing she'd ever done, being the Guardian, had humbled and frightened her. Such tremendous knowledge, such awesome power, such command of whatever skills were needed, seemed to her to magnify her unimportance in the scheme of things when not coupled with great machines. She would never really know, but would always suspect, that she was selected by the computers for the role not because she was superior at anything but because she was so unskilled and so insignificant that she posed no threat to the programs or to Flux and Anchor by having that role.

These dark depressions had been increasing in frequency in the past year, and so far New Eden hadn't helped. The wizard had warned her that if she continued to fight it or put off either taking command or finding a place for herself, she'd better get out of Flux, for the power within her would consume her, spinning spell after spell, turning her more and more into her own inner self-image, crushing and extinguishing her ego. The insane, deformed, animal-istic duggers were formed by the same process.

She sighed. Well, enough of that for now. Tonight she and the others were going to a carnival, a carnival in Anchor, and for a little while it would be all right to be a kid again. In a couple of days she'd have the pleasure of introducing some of the kids to the legendary Matson. After that—well, she wasn't so sure. She only knew that for her own sake she wasn't going back, at least not now, and she almost certainly wasn't staying in New Eden. She would return with Matson to visit Cass and the twins and their kids and maybe, with their help and the help of the best minds in the stringer organization, she'd find an avenue.

If Suzl had had someone for comfort and support, she would have been the ideal candidate for a permanent am-bassador to New Eden. Because she looked like a Fluxgirl and knew how to fit in, the men ruling the land neither feared her nor considered her a threat, unlike almost any-one else coming out of Flux. Because she was independent and World-wise, she made a good bridge between the two cultures, each of whom considered the other repugnant and dangerous. And, as a former wife of Adam Tilghman, the

Prophet himself, she was at the top of society always and could get away with much that none of the New Eden women would dare and be treated more equally by the male rulers than any other female except, of course, Cass— who wouldn't be caught dead here.

A Fluxgirl was waiting for her at the top of the grand staircase. "I am Sheva, my lady," the woman said pleasantly, "current head of the household staff. I am instructed to show you around the estate and grounds or assist you in any way."

"What about the kids?" Suzl asked. She had left them with the child care coordinator after getting in late the previous night. They'd been all in, anyway.

"They were up and about long ago," Sheva told her. "It did not seem necessary to wake you. They ate well, and then went over to see the final touches being put on the carnival before the grand opening today. We will all join them there when you like, although they are in good hands and the opening isn't for hours yet."

Suzl nodded. She'd brought only five kids, ages eight to fourteen, all her own grandchildren, and all picked because they were very good in strange surroundings and cultures. The two boys would have no problems at all here, but the three girls might, so the boys were told to watch out for them and they were a responsible group. There would also be a lot of toleration shown for them because they were her own grandchildren and *might* also be grandchildren of the Prophet. Only one was, but she hadn't told them which one.

"I'd like a little something in my stomach," she told Sheva. "Then you can show me around the place."

She had a hard time getting the girls of the house not to fix her a full formal breakfast. She wanted toast and coffee for now and that was all—with emphasis on the coffee. It might be an interesting, even enjoyable, day, but it was going to be a long one and she still felt the effects of a two-day horseback ride. She was sadly out of practice and she was only now relearning just what muscles were used only in riding.

Conversation with the "girls" only confirmed what she already knew: even as she was she'd be bored silly by this vacuous level. She might not be any brighter than they, but she had a wider world-view and a weight of experience. Some of them were probably in their thirties or forties—it was impossible to really tell with Fluxgirls—but to Suzl it was like being trapped in a crowd of fifteen-year-old adolescents. Worse, they were in awe of her as a wife of the Prophet. It was enough to spoil any breakfast, even one so spartan and basic. She was very polite and exited as soon as she could.

As she would be staying there several days at least, she accepted the offer to tour the place. Sheva seemed to have a good sense of propriety and wasn't as hard to take, and seemed genuinely pleased to show off the place.

And it *was* grand by anyone's standards: The Great Room, used for formal dinners and meetings, was as large as Adam Tilghman's old house where she'd spent several years. Sixteen bedrooms, not counting servant's quarters, two enormous kitchens, one at each end of the place, a massive library, a "cozy" den that seemed big enough to race horses in, and rooms especially made for displaying fine art and sculpture.

The whole place sat on a rise north of the city, with the entire area filled with green trees and brightly colored flowers and shrubs. It was more like a private park than the "front lawn" Sheva called it, and off in the distance could be seen the city itself, the old temple spires gleaming in the reflected rays of the great gas giant which gave World its light.

The rear area contained more formal gardens, a broad area used for some sports and entertaining, and even two grass tennis courts. There were even large stables for horses and a private exercise track. In fact, the only incongruity was a very large, round structure with a pointed roof far off to the rear. They'd done their best to conceal it with shrubbery and a dark green paint job, but there was no ignoring it. "What's that?" Suzl asked her guide.

"That is the private laboratory," Sheva replied. "None of

the household staff is permitted to enter there, so I can tell you no more than that. There is a road and a separate entrance that you cannot see from here where those who work there come and go. It is none of our concern.''

None of yours, you mean, Suzl thought, her curiosity aroused. *Men's work.* She remembered the time when she'd thought that way, too.

''Madame Suzl!'' boomed a hearty male voice from the vicinity of the stables. She turned and saw a large figure walking quickly toward them. She waited for him where they were. When he got there, he first took her hand and kissed it, then gave her a big, less formal hug.

''My apologies for not greeting you until now,'' Judge Vishnar apologized, ''but all this work plus the carnival has left me so little time. You slept well?''

''Fine.''

''And the children? Where are they?''

''Already at the carnival. They've never seen one, you know.''

''Well, neither have most people. But we'll show them what a good time one is, eh?''

The judge dismissed Sheva with a wave of the hand and took Suzl over to some lawn chairs in the garden. Both sat, and almost instantly a young and eager Fluxgirl was running out to ask if they required anything. Sensing from Vishnar's nod that it was not out of line to order, she asked for more coffee, and the judge nodded agreement. Inside of five minutes the girl was back with a pot on a silver tray, two exquisite porcelain teacups and saucers, and silver cream and sugar servers. This servile business made Suzl uneasy, but it was only her required conscience and she knew it. Given a choice of being server or served, the second was better every time.

''So, what do you think of the place?'' Vishnar asked her.

''It's most impressive,'' she responded, trying not to sound too much the country hick. ''I don't believe I ever saw or heard of anything quite like it.''

''It's based on a set of programs from the old records,''

he told her. "If our interpretation is correct, it's a good reproduction of the estate of the first military commander on World. Of course, that was up in Cluster One, in the Headquarters Anchor. It was actually of a prefabricated design. Fascinating. The method itself has saved us much misery here in New Eden, but no one expected something like this among the records. Goes together like a jigsaw puzzle, in fact. The grounds, of course, took much longer and are still in the process of development."

"It all looks fine to me," she told him truthfully. "I can't imagine what one might add to it."

"Oh, the original had several other features. I'm still considering the big swimming pool. Don't swim myself, but it's getting to be a skill needed in New Eden, what with the Sea and all. The trouble is getting instructors. Until I can, I don't want anything in which someone can fall and drown while we either stand about helplessly or drown trying to save them. Do you swim, by the way?"

She shook her head. "I'm from right around here, remember. It was never something we had to do. Oh, there were some nice ponds and small lakes—I guess they're still there—but it wasn't something you needed to learn."

He nodded understandingly. "The odd thing is, we owe a lot to this program. One of the other things it included in its grounds plan was an ambitious two-kilometer steam locomotive at one-tenth scale. It was from that alone, by simply scaling it up, that we developed our railroad system, which is the only thing that really makes such a massive Anchor area as New Eden work as one. The odd thing is, at their level, steam was an ancient and totally outdated method of propulsion. It was sort of like importing bows and arrows when you already had these computer-guided laser rifles. Or—am I boring you with this? I like to talk and sometimes I go on and on. Don't hesitate to say so if it's the case."

"No, I find it fascinating," she told him truthfully, although she knew his culture was battling his intellect now. "It was his—toy, then."

"Yes, yes! Exactly that! One marvels at what they must

have been like—to be able not only to travel vast distances here and build and colonize a world but to even indulge themselves by bringing such frills.''

She decided it would be pushing it too far to note that such things had always been and still were for the privileged elite only. The average settler or poor working slob, she guessed, probably got to bring two changes of clothes, a watch, and maybe pictures of his or her parents. All but a very few in New Eden would never be able to have an estate like this built and maintained, let alone the whole of World. "I assume that was also true of the carnival things?"

He gave a chuckle. "Oddly enough, from what we can find out, no. They were apparently built as basic amusements after the Betrayal by some people who'd escaped to the stringers. Oh, they are probably similar to carnival things the ancients had back on the Mother World, but it's not too clear. We've made them grander for this new carnival. Scaled them up, like we did the trains.''

"I'm looking forward to going. The last carnival I attended was here, too, when I was very young. In a way, it was the last innocent time I ever had. A few days later they picked me out of the crowd and sold me into Flux.''

He stared at her for a moment, then started to say something, stopped, took a drink of coffee, and decided to change the subject. He knew her history, at least up to the time she'd left New Eden. He decided he liked her. He wasn't sure he'd like all the girls to be this worldly or forward, but she was certainly entitled to be the exception.

"I understand you're not going home," he noted.

She gave a weary smile. "No, I'm sort of repeating history. Mr. Ryan's an old friend and his family are also old friends. Odd, though. It's almost like history coming around once more. I'm going to a carnival, then I'm going off and out of Anchor with a stringer—retired, at least.'' It was more than even that. She was going off with the *same* stringer who'd hauled her into Flux that first time, and she was going without regret because she was just as much an outsider and an oddball as she had been back then. "I hope it's a more uneventful and relaxing trip this time, though,'' she added.

"I dare say. Is this your first time back here since the Invasion?"

"No. I came back fifteen or twenty years ago—time doesn't mean much to me anymore, I'm afraid—over in the Bakha District with Jeff and some of his people to do some horse trading. Not in the city, though, and not for very long."

Vishnar looked at his watch. "Still three hours until the opening, two until I have to get over there. What say we walk over, through the city, and I'll show you a little of the town?"

"I'd be delighted."

"Would you like to freshen up or change before we go?"

"Do you think I should?"

"Oh, no, my dear. You look absolutely wonderful. Well, then—we'll have to go off the back way, here. I have to stop by the lab and check on something. Do you mind?"

"No, not at all. Do you want me to wait here?"

"Oh, no! Come along! Considering your background, you may be the only girl in New Eden who would be really interested in this."

She got up and followed him, curious and also flattered that he would permit her near his private preserve. She began to suspect that he was going to put the make on her sooner or later. She might be just different enough from these vapid girls to seem somewhat exotic to him. At any rate, he certainly seemed to be going out of his way to impress her.

The building proved more formidable looking up close than it had from afar, although if anything even uglier in the midst of all this beauty. The entry door was, like the building, thick and solid as a vault, and had an electrically encoded panel to gain entrance. She didn't know what would happen if you pressed the wrong code on the pad, but she suspected it wouldn't be nothing at all.

The place was *huge,* and almost entirely open, with just a few plasterboard offices around the base. That open area, however, was filled with an object she had never seen in person but which she recognized instantly.

"It's the ship!" she gasped. "The *Samish* ship!"

"One of the three," he responded. "Not the mother ship. That's being worked on down in the capital. This is the flying top, the part that caused all the damage beyond the gate. Useless to us as it was, of course. It was designed for those hellish creatures, not us, and also designed to be used in conjunction with their own master computers which are burnt out and not of any logical design we can find, anyway. Some of the best minds from all over World have been working on it and its two twins up north. Two different projects, really. We have always tried to find out how the damned thing could *fly.* No rockets, no apparent major power source like big engines, and it's as aerodynamic as an oak tree. But fly it did—and in ways even a creation of Flux could not."

She nodded absently. "I know. I remember."

He seemed slightly embarrassed for a moment. "Yes, of course you would," he coughed, then took a deep breath. "Well, the second thing was the weaponry. It carried an impenetrable and widening shield with it and it shot beams of something that was lethal to everything it touched. It's vital we understand them, in case we ever have to face them again. Even you will admit that we were lucky the first time."

Her expression was grim, remembering. "Yes. Very." But she wasn't thinking of a new encounter with the *Samish.* No one might ever know what had become of them, but if they hadn't shown up in forty-seven years they were no more likely to show up in the next century, if at all. She couldn't help thinking, though, of a fleet of these things, outfitted for humans, flying, spreading their impenetrable shields through Flux and Anchor, dealing out massive death and destruction. Outfitted for humans who would be in New Eden uniforms.

"Have you . . . had any success?" she asked him hesitantly, wondering how far again she could push it.

"For a long time, no. For almost twenty years actual work was abandoned, as it has been with the mother ships, because of a total lack of progress. Recently, though, two young lads at our own science university over in Babylon took a look at all the research out of curiosity and somehow cracked the core of the problem. It just had to wait until the genius was born and educated who could look beyond conventional knowledge. You know, this was something even our ancestors couldn't do, which was most likely why the other worlds were taken over. Broadcast Flux power. Like the radio. We've had some tests and it seems to work out. We're going for a full-scale demonstration in a week." He suddenly hesitated. "Uh—I'm sorry, my dear—that's all I can say and in fact that was too much. I'm certain you will understand that this is still confidential."

"Yes, of course."

"Excuse me, then. Wait here while I speak to my engineering chief and then we'll be off for fun and frolic, eh?"

She stood there, just staring at the thing. He *had* gotten carried away, and talked as if he were speaking to the Guardian. Not very long from now, though, if it wasn't already percolating in his mind, he'd see it as having spilled the greatest secret of New Eden to a mere girl. And girls, of course, couldn't be trusted to keep secrets. In fact, girls who were too smart for their own good and found out too much were downright dangerous. She knew, even now, that they could not let her leave. Particularly not with a stringer, retired or not. Before he left here, he'd make a call or two, and she'd be so tightly security-monitored she wouldn't be able to take a bath or a crap in privacy.

She might be able to give them the slip, even get out to Flux, which here, where the Anchor was pinch-waisted, was only a little over fifty kilometers away—but she knew she couldn't do it with five grandchildren. They would know that, too. For now, that was enough for them. They would still spend the afternoon and evening at the carnival, and the charade would be played out, but at some point they would figure out a plan and come for her.

She wanted to cry but wouldn't give them the satisfaction. At least, she thought, she wasn't wallowing in self-pity anymore. As usual, events had reared up and crapped on poor Suzl.

4

SECURITY PROBLEM

Matson grumbled in frustration. It had taken them half the night to reach a point in the line which hadn't either been cut or in some way disrupted every time he'd tried a splice—somebody on the other side was very good with communications him- or herself. The old ex-stringer had also been proud of himself for being able to manage a reasonable connection with the tools at hand after being so out of practice. He had never been a linesman, not of true wired systems anyway, and the old techniques that he had seen no use for that were drilled into his head time after time as a young trainee were slow to come back.

The small emergency box was only on one pole every twelve kilometers, and he'd had to break the seal and then assemble what he needed out of the parts kit inside. It wasn't easy, particularly with only a hand-held light. Not knowing where the raiders were camped, they dared not risk a fire.

The frustration was, after all that, and hanging on nervously from the top of a pole, Matson discovered that there were no central operators on duty between midnight and six in the morning at the interchanges along the route to the city. The phone service simply didn't work for several hours each night.

"We could keep going," Rondell suggested. "There's obviously a town between here and Logh Center or we wouldn't be having this problem."

Matson climbed down and sighed. "Grandson, that town might be right over the next rise, or the next, or the next, or it might be a suburb of the city which is still a day's ride away. We gave it our best shot, and I'm about shot, too. I'm going to turn in right here under this damned phone wire as soon as I can unpack my bedroll and bed down the horse. When I wake up, we'll make the call, and they'll have a lot less warning but they'll still have some. There's no way those raiders could make Logh Center tonight, and they'll need the day not only to get there but to blend in with the carnival crowds in small groups to avoid attention. They won't pull anything before tomorrow night. Probably around midnight, in fact, if they shut down the phones to the east as well."

Rondell sighed, actually grateful that he wouldn't have to push himself any more just to show off for his grandfather. "Well," he sighed wearily, "if they look like that bunch we took out they'll be pretty easy to spot."

"Don't underestimate 'em," Matson cautioned. "They got some Flux power, remember, and ten to one they all look like and will act like good, meek little Fluxgirls until the time's right. Smart idea, really. Hit New Eden right in its male-dominated blind spot. If none of 'em cause problems or have their numbers spot-checked—and in a carnival atmosphere with lots of out-of-town guests they'll be pretty lax—those poor boys won't even understand where the bullets are coming from as they fall. Nope, this is daring, all right, even chancy, so the prize must be something really big, but it's smart. No, you gotta figure that anybody saddled with that original Fluxgirl spell and a whore's spell on top of that who can build and run an organization like this is some kind of mind."

"The whore spell? I know the raider called their leader Ayesha the Whore, but I didn't think that meant anything specific."

"Oh, yeah, it sure does. It's a punishment spell, always doled out to men, for conviction of certain offenses. In civilian life, that means rape or incest with a daughter or something like that. She's military. That means a conviction for desertion, cowardice in battle, or treason."

"You mean—this Ayesha was once a *man?*"

"Yep. From the old days, since we know Borg took his unit's whore with him when he fled into Flux and it's almost certainly the same one. Must have been in Flux for some reason when the master program was reconfigured. There's some like that. She's under a lot of extra handicaps, and the whole program means she's always turned on and sex is like a drug to her. That's why she keeps old Borg around and won't permit any other men to get close. This is somebody who's real, real dangerous. She could be as dangerous as Coydt, and a hell of a lot harder to get close to. . . ."

The next morning he *was* able to call through, but he wasn't sure just how much was believed or passed on. The security clerk was very officious and bureaucratic, didn't like Fluxlanders much and trusted them even less, and could hardly take seriously an attack by a bunch of mere women. Matson became exasperated at trying to pound the danger into his thick skull over a less-than-excellent connection.

"Listen, we'll take your warning under advisement, I assure you," the clerk told him, obviously anxious to terminate the conversation. "Even if it's true, they'll not get out once they start something. There are two thousand policemen here, hundreds of security personnel, and along the border there are three divisions of troops."

Matson switched off and swore for several minutes. Finally he said, "That litany of power was the last straw. As if anybody capable of infiltrating a large armed force right into a district capital city wouldn't know that as well!

Hell—*six* divisions and an enormous, thick wall that surrounded the place couldn't keep people from coming in or going out when it was just the size of an Anchor!''

"We've done more than anyone could ask us to do for them," Rondell pointed out. "Let's just eat something and get on the road. About all we can do now is make our own way there and find out when we get there what they were up to. I gotta admit, I *am* a little curious." He stopped for a moment, struck by a sudden horrible thought. "You don't think it's just revenge, do you? Blowing up the carnival or something like that?"

"Uh uh. Oh, I wouldn't put it past 'em to come up with a hell of a diversion, but that's not what they're after. As you say, nothing more we can do about it. I admit to being kinda curious myself, though."

The carnival was gigantic, grandiose, wondrous—and the most miserable experience in Suzl's recent life.

Vishnar was the same, cheerful fellow as before, but she did notice a change almost from the start in his manner. Before, she'd been almost his equal; now he was treating her more like a high-rank Fluxgirl, talking down to her and also being pretty forward with his hands and other sexual gestures. In fact, when they got to the carnival and got to the dignitaries and official opening, he seemed to go out of his way to show her off while making sure she knew her place.

The kids were there, of course, all starry-eyed and full of fun and energy, but she found that there was a Vishnar household Fluxgirl for each one. A chance comment from Micah, the oldest boy, told her that there had originally been just two, and they had been different Fluxgirls. They'd been called unexpectedly back to the house for something. Micah didn't mind having his own Fluxgirl at his beck and call as well as for his guide. He was getting to be the age where hormones outweighed upbringing. He was not, unfortunately, in a mood or at a level of maturity where subtle signals that she had to talk to him registered. She tried with bravado to dismiss the attending Fluxgirls but they wouldn't *hear* of it, and their servile and deferential manner did not conceal their eyes. They knew why they were there, and they knew she knew as well.

As she began to tour the carnival with them and ride the various rides, some of which really were enormous and scary to boot, and play the midway games, she began to see openings where she could get messages across but she did not take advantage of them. For a secret like this, still at the stage where powerful outside forces might be able to nip it in the bud, they would not hesitate to do some harm to the children as well. Accidents, after all, did happen. She thought about trying to slip a message to some of the carnival people, all of whom were Fluxlanders connected to the stringers, but even if she managed, and nothing went wrong, she meant nothing to them, and they had orders to not interfere in New Eden in any way. It would surely go to the local stringer officer, who might or might not act on it, and if it were discovered by New Eden's internal security it could just as easily wind up getting a lot more people dragged down. The stringers wanted the carnival reestablished for their own reasons. They would hardly jeopardize a big project for one stranger who wasn't even a member of the Guild.

If it were just herself at stake, it wouldn't be worth any risks, but she could not shake her dark vision: The whole of World, Flux and Anchor, a gigantic New Eden. All the women, including her daughters, granddaughters, and the rest, reduced to servility and chattel slavery and held there, perhaps forever, by the old methods—Flux power, broadcast Flux power, maintaining the rigid New Eden dream against all possibility of breaking it.

Vishnar rejoined them at dusk for the fireworks. The kids were all already near exhaustion, and Suzl wasn't that great, either, from the nervous tension she'd been under.

At the end, the judge said, "Suzl, there's someone you just *have* to meet. I know you're tired but it won't take long. The kids are all done in, though. Why not send them back and we'll see they get tucked in tight."

"I really should go back with them," she responded, concerned.

"Oh, I must *insist*, my dear. Come, come."

"All right—let me just say good-night to them."

She went over, and as she gave Micah a big hug, she whispered, "I'm in trouble. Tell Ryan." He hugged her back and gave no sign amidst the noise that he'd heard her. She did it again with the next oldest, Robby, but he yawned and frowned and just nodded, "Uh huh." The other three she was a bit more public with, and said just the usual good-night things. Nobody seemed to have noticed. She felt bad putting them in potential jeopardy that way, but the stakes were just too high.

Still, she was certain the early whispers hadn't been noticed, or at least been made out by the others. A more troublesome worry was that neither boy had heard or understood.

Vishnar didn't want a scene with the crowds leaving, but he took her by the hand and led her back to one of the V.I.P. tents. There two leather-clad men with the lightning insignia on their right armbands were waiting for her.

"I think you know what this is about," Vishnar said to her, sounding really apologetic. "It's my fault and I feel guilty over it."

She just nodded and allowed herself to be led away.

They took her in silence in a closed coach down to the headquarters of internal security, a blocky, dull-looking building just off the old temple square. She couldn't help but think how ironic it was that she had once wielded absolute power over this and a quarter of New Eden from a spot probably no more than five hundred meters from where they were bringing her.

They bypassed check-in and took her to a small holding cell below ground level. She took a chair, and was left alone, but only for a minute or so. Then another man entered, a young-looking man, as trim and athletic as most of them looked, with dark brown hair and a matching, short-cropped moustache. He carried a thick file folder with him.

"My name is Major Verdugo," he said, taking another chair and seeming rather casual. "I'm sorry that this problem has come up—really sorry, considering your background and the trouble we've had to go through so far—but it's unavoidable. I'm afraid we spend a fair amount of our time covering up the judge's slips. If it wasn't for the fact that he really can manage to assemble groups who can produce results like what you saw today he'd have been nicely retired long ago."

"You'll understand if I don't sympathize with you," she responded cooly.

He shrugged and opened the folder. "These aren't all your records. We'd have several thick books if we had *them* all here. We've been going through here trying to figure out an easy way for everyone, including you, in all this."

"How considerate," she said sarcastically, knowing that the man meant exactly what he was saying.

"Let's not mince words. We've done a pretty thorough psychological profile on you, and we'll cut the kidding. You were a Fluxgirl here in the old days, long before I was born. You left, understandably, when your turn at Guardian was done, but you left still looking that way. You were a strong wizard, yet when you visited Yahbar Ranch sixteen years ago you hadn't even erased your serial number. In fact, you've barely physically changed at all, not even at home in Flux from our reports."

That startled her. They kept dossiers on people, and even updated their information, when those people were in Flux?

"You've been a Fluxgirl, not counting the past fifty years, longer than I've been alive," he noted. "When you went out there again after all that time, you couldn't shake the conditioning. You went dugger and froze yourself. We know it and you know it. That really makes it easy. You *belong* here."

"No," she told him firmly. "I guess maybe that was the real reason for this trip. I wanted to see if I did anymore, but I don't. Just today, for the first time, I really saw what I'd been like all those years as an outsider, an observer. I'm *old*. I've been too many places, know too many things. I'm a *woman*."

"We can take care of that. We've learned a lot since you left. A whole lot. We have devices now called Flux chambers, although they aren't really that at all. They're miniature programming centers, such as ones that were once inside that headquarters building. As you know, the Fluxgirl program was a module that Coydt van Haas discovered. We've got it down so well we can personalize it. It's amazing just how much of what and who we are is biochemical. Skills, talents, intelligence level, memory speed and access level, comprehension, *desire* to comprehend, love, lust, and all the rest. We really have documented that there are differences in the way men and women think based on these chemicals and the different balances in the bodies of the two sexes."

"There may be differences, but I don't know anyone who proved one way is superior to the other," she argued.

"As you know, we don't look at it that way. Different is sufficient to prove our case. Now, in the past we couldn't use this technique on individuals with Flux power because a wizard could turn the power against us. Not here. Makes no difference how much power you have— the process is strictly one-way. In your case we need only accelerate the process that's already begun in you. You will fit. You will *want* to stay. In fact, there will be no alternative but to stay when the process is complete. You would be helpless on your own. Then you can tell this with absolute conviction to your son and Mr. Ryan. Your family already knows of your problem. They won't be happy with it, but they'll accept it."

She started to object, but couldn't. Unless her message got through in time, there was nothing wrong with the plan. Sondra and Jeff, in fact, had been afraid that this was exactly what she intended to do.

"Why fight it?" he asked her. "You'll be happy. You were happy before, even if you won't admit it to yourself. And you'll be important, the most important woman in all

New Eden. Every big shot here will court the former wife of the Prophet. You'll be a social leader, fashion leader, have every luxury.''

"If it's so wonderful why aren't I anxious?" she muttered aloud. "And if it's so cut-and-dried, why tell me any of this? Why not just do it and be done with it?''

"Because we don't want you *our* way, we want you *your* way. We can program the modules and do it to our design, but it really wouldn't be you. If you voluntarily let it happen, just let the spells and tendencies inside you dominate without a fight, you'll be the way *you* want. Best for you, best for us, best for everyone.''

She sighed. "That's my only choice?''

"I'm afraid so. I—'' At that moment, the lights flickered, then went out, then came on again, but weakly. "What the hell . . . ?" Suddenly there were voices shouting all over the place.

Suzl had a momentary thought to take advantage of the darkness—what did she have to lose?—but it was absolutely black, and before she could do more than get up some of the lights came back on, low and flickering.

The door opened and a man stuck his head in. *"The carnival's on fire!"* he shouted.

"The *hell* you say!" Verdugo responded, and was on his feet in a moment. "You remember we have five young hostages up at the judge's estate!" he growled at her. "You stay here or somebody will pay!" And then he joined the mob running down the corridor.

Incredulous, Suzl found herself totally forgotten. She got up, went to the door, and peered out. There were shouting men above, but no one seemed to be on this level. She made her way nervously upstairs, past an unlocked gate and an unattended guard position, to the first floor, where there were quite a number of men, all on phones or looking over charts. None of them were paying the slightest attention to her.

There was a sudden series of explosions, well away from the center of town but strong enough to shake the building a little, and the lights went out again—not only in the security center, but outside as well. By the time some-body made it to the emergency backup generator down-stairs in the dark and managed to start it, bringing on the emergency lights, she was out the front door.

The whole city seemed plunged into total darkness, but out in the southwest, in the direction of the Sea, the whole horizon was ablaze with light. No matter what her own situation, she stood transfixed for a moment by the sight. The entire carnival area where she'd spent the whole after-noon and most of the evening was in flames! From the glow, although highlighted by the lack of city power, it was an *enormous* blaze. Had it happened just two hours earlier, she knew, it would have killed thousands.

She wasn't sure just what to do next. Verdugo was right about the children being hostages. If she escaped, *they* would go through his Flux chambers in her place, if only for revenge. That was the way these mean and petty men thought. It was simply not possible to consider abandoning them, even though it would be for the greater good of World. It was just not in her makeup. Still, it was a golden opportunity for her, a stroke of pure luck. Matson and Dell might already be at Vishnar's. Even if they weren't, or were off watching the fire as men would, the kids would be there. It was fifty-one kilometers or so to the Flux border. Not an easy ride, particularly for five dead-tired and confused kids. Still, there were forests to the south-east, places to hide in that weren't on the track they would expect her to take.

She took a look around and gasped again. There was fire in the southwest, too! And in several other places! It looked like somebody was trying to set the whole city ablaze!

Guardian, I'd love to have you now, she thought desper-ately. But, right now, she'd settle for a horse and at the moment the center city was the quiet and still eye of the hurricane. At least she knew her way. She kicked off her shoes and began to run as fast as she could. Fluxgirls had weak arms but real strong legs.

*   *   *

It was close to three in the morning when Matson and Rondell entered the city and made for Vishnar's estate. They were all in, and their mounts were no better, but having been close enough to actually see the telltale glow of massive fires, they could not bring themselves to halt even for a rest.

Still, it took the better part of another hour to make it up to Vishnar's place. Cities were not designed to be pitch-dark, and modern cities were mazes when they weren't designed for primitive ways.

The massive estate, too, was in total darkness, although it was not in flames, which was a great relief to them both. They went up the long approach drive, jumped down, then Matson put up a hand. "Get your gun," he said quietly.

Rondell did as instructed, but asked, "What's the problem?"

"That front door's wide open."

"Maybe they all just rushed out to help with the fires."

"Yeah, well, I think there's an arm on the floor just inside it. Bring the torches, but don't light 'em."

Cautiously, they approached the house, one on each side of the door. At a nod, Matson entered and dropped, and almost fell over the body of a Fluxgirl. He picked himself up, and stood there in the darkness, just listening. Then he reached back out and took one of the electric torches from Rondell, who continued his outside guard. Matson deftly switched it on and rolled it along the entryway at the same time. It didn't roll very far, but there also was no reaction to it from inside the dark house.

"Come on in," he whispered, "but be careful."

Matson picked up the torch and stepped into the entry hall. He wanted some light now, but he approached each doorway as if something lethal lurked on the other side of it. There wasn't, but there were bodies everywhere. A few men, a lot of women, none holding a weapon. Several seemed in death to have surprise frozen on their faces. Others were shot in the back and hadn't even known who or what hit them. Most were nude. The men, they noted, also had their balls cut off.

They examined the bodies. "Not warm," Rondell noted. "Some early stages of *rigor mortis,* but not much. I'd say an hour, maybe two."

Matson nodded. "The staff here was so big and changed so much they probably didn't even know everybody on it. Only reason there are so many dressed is that they probably got back late from the carnival. I'd say they hit just about exactly at midnight. Torched the carnival, probably with incendiary bombs, and blew the main power transformers. Set a bunch of other random incendiaries, too. Put the whole damned city in the dark in the middle of the night and drew everybody off in every single direction but this one."

"Then this was the target?"

"Almost certainly. There were only fifty or sixty of 'em. Figure half of 'em were needed to make sure all the diversions got done, and most of the rest went after whatever it is they were after. The few remaining got in the house and methodically finished everybody off. Who'd ever suspect some shy, demure little Fluxgirl?"

"My god! Suzl and the kids!"

Matson straightened up. "Yeah," he breathed, and they continued looking.

Vishnar was in the study, fully clothed. He'd apparently been going over something, although whatever it was was now gone. They had surprised him, of course, like the rest, although they hadn't killed him at first.

"Looks like they shot his limbs and then castrated him while he was still alive and kicking," Rondell noted, getting sick.

"Notice they're all laser pistol shots," Matson pointed out. "Real quiet. They might have finished off most of the help before they ever disturbed the old boy, since he looks like he didn't go quiet. Did it with one of his ornamental swords. Well, he's better off dead. He would never have been able to recover from the sight of pretty little Fluxgirls with laser pistols and swords doing in men and women alike. Probably refused to accept it even as they were killing him."

They made their way through the rest of the enormous house. Most had died in bed. Clearly the house had been terrorized before the diversions had started. "Probably needed the lights to make sure they got everybody," Matson guessed.

Many of the upstairs rooms were unoccupied. They found one and recognized Suzl's bag, but there was no sign of a body. Back down, they finally discovered where the children had stayed. They entered the room, but found no bodies. Although relieved, they were puzzled.

"What the *hell* was this all about?" Rondell wanted to know.

"I can tell you," said a voice behind them.

They whirled, guns up, electronic torches pointed.

"Suzl! My God, girl! I almost *killed* you!" Matson said, relief breaking in his voice.

She ran to them, sobbing uncontrollably for several minutes. They finally got her outside into the air and she did her best to get control of herself. Ultimately, her story came out.

"Everybody was already dead when I got here," she told them, quickly explaining why she hadn't been home in the first place. "My only thought was the children, and I entered through the back entrance there and didn't find anybody. I went up into the main house, couldn't see a thing, tripped over the first two bodies, and got back here. I was going to leave to see what I could do when I heard them out back. They were still here."

"Why did security take you in?" Matson asked her.

"It's what *they* came for. They were so afraid I was a security leak and all the time lots of others knew it." Quickly, she told them about the alien craft and Vishnar's scientists' discovery.

Matson gave a low whistle. "Yeah, that explains a lot. Maybe all of it. But how the hell could they move that flying top? Damn thing must have weighed forty or fifty tons."

"They didn't. Vishnar's men had gutted it long ago. I could see that much. It wasn't anything from the ship that they had. They just built it from what they learned. I never saw it. I don't know what it looks like, how big it is, or anything about it except that it was built in the labs out back and Vishnar said it worked. He was going to show it off to the New Eden brass next week. Big test."

"Makes sense," Rondell said. "They used the carnival to infiltrate, and they cut the timing so close they minimized the chance of any run-in with the law and registrations. They had to act now, because it would be moved under army security to an area near Flux any time now and they'd have had to fight an army to get it. Longer and it'd be out of here and being mass-produced by the New Eden brass."

"Suzl—you said they were still here. Did you see them?" Matson asked.

She nodded. "Some. They all looked like Fluxgirls in the dark. Is that *possible?*"

"It's how they did it. Now—this is important. Did you see them get away?"

"No. I only heard them. There's a separate road over there and the view's blocked by trees. Whatever it was it was big and made a powerful amount of machine noise."

Matson stroked his beard. "A lorry."

"A what?"

"Lorry. We have to keep up with things in New Eden or the Guild will be at a bad disadvantage. There aren't too many built yet, but it's like a big wagon only it has an engine instead of horses. They run them off some kind of alcohol they distill from corn, if you can believe it. They're big and noisy and not very practical, but they can carry tons of stuff. I guess it was here to help move the gadget or whatever it was, and they used it for just that—before the guard was on. Damned if I know how they managed to drive it, though, or even turn it on. It's a complicated contraption. It's something they got from the old engineering books. It's not anything in any program you can call up in Flux."

"Maybe they had practice—or help," Rondell replied.

"Some folks had to be in on this in advance—planning and finding out the schedules and everything."

Matson nodded. "Might have been as simple as four or five Fluxgirls down south where they have several of these lorries overwhelming a mechanic with sexy charm. *Ooooh! Neat! Will you take us for a ride? Please? Huh? Oh, you steer it like that. Can I squeeze over and try?* Then she's sitting in his lap and he's got ass and boobs and he's all turned on and all he wants to do is show off some more since he's the expert on this. Works elsewhere. Works here, too. Better here, since they just wouldn't think of a squealing little Fluxgirl as having a devious mind and ulterior motives."

"This—lorry. It's gonna stand out like a sore thumb," Suzl nodded. "How do they expect to get away?"

"Honey, those things with a full load can do thirty kilometers an *hour*, and the powers that be still don't know it's gone. Give 'em an hour-and-a-half start, and a predetermined route, and they'll be driving right into Flux in a matter of twenty or thirty minutes."

"You gonna tell 'em?" Suzl asked.

"Well, I think we'll try and find those children first, dead or alive. Then we'll decide on a course of action for the future." He frowned. "There should have been a *lot* of kids from the looks of that place, not just ours."

"Thirty or forty at least," Suzl agreed. "They *couldn't* have taken them all with them!" She had a thought. "I couldn't see very well, but there's no adult bodies, either. There were nannies and caretakers with the kids." She had a note of hope. "You don't think maybe they got wind of what was going on and got the kids out?"

"Damn it, I want to look for the kids, too—but don't you think one of us should tell *somebody?* I mean, that gang of cut-throats is getting away with the most powerful machine now around this world!"

Matson looked at him. "We got a bunch of very dangerous people with a real bad machine in Flux. In wizard and stringer territory. On the run, at that. One thing they can't yet know is just how to use it. It weighs a lot, and that truck can't run on Flux and can't be fixed on Flux, either. Yeah, I think both World and we are a hell of a lot safer if they make it.''

"Don't look at me," Suzl responded, regaining some of her spunk. "I'm a fugitive from internal security."

"That point, I think, is moot," Matson replied. "Now let's find those kids."

Incredibly, they found the children before security found them, and they found them alive. One of the nannies, a woman named Vena, had gone into the main house for something and had come upon the horror in progress. Not stopping to believe her eyes, her only thoughts were to protect the children. She managed to get back, rouse the others and the watch, and use a little-known service corridor to get them to a side exit near the big hedge-maze. Several of the women in there gave their lives to keep the door shut; it was their bodies that were found just outside.

The two Freehold boys, Micah and Robby, had been detained by security. The nannies didn't know where they were except that they hadn't even made it to the house.

The most amazing thing, though, was that the children did not escape. It was impossible to keep the littler ones from crying and some of the older ones had panicked. They found themselves boxed in the hedges.

"And then, it was crazy," one of the nannies, Clira, told them. "All of a sudden these girls shouted to us. 'We'll let you all live,' they said, 'if you stay right where you are and don't come out until you're found. Let you all live, that is, if you give us the Freehold children.' "

And they had done so. They had had no choice, considering that the raiders could have just sprayed the hedges with automatic fire and killed them all. They had given them the three girls, and were still amazed that they had not then all been massacred.

"They were very brave," Clira told them. "Even the little one."

After that, they waited until they heard them go and the lorry and a lot of horses ride off, and then they'd chanced leaving. They had gotten the last ones out while Suzl was meeting Matson and Rondell.

Matson sighed. "Well, I guess this makes it our fight. Can't figure out why they did it, though. They haven't raided in Flux, so they're pretty safe there. Now they deliberately went and alienated the biggest, most powerful family of wizards there. Don't make sense. Unless . . ."

"Those poor girls. With those murdering savages," Suzl sighed.

"I don't think they'll be harmed. Not just yet," Matson told her. "I think we might just be hearing from them. We—the family, anyway—has the power. They got the gadget, but only average power. Not a world-class wizard among 'em."

"You mean," Rondell put in, "that they're gonna hold the kids as hostages to get *us* to show them how to use it? Or get our expert help on figuring it out? Maybe operating it for them?"

"Something like that. Whatever it is, it'll be clever. This gang ain't no pussycat. They're gonna be rough as hell to take out. This stuff with the kids was deliberate. Not just taking ours, but sparing the rest. They showed us by the whole thing that they're clever, ruthless, that they'll kill kids with a smile, and yet by sparing those kids and nurses when they didn't have to—and killing might have bought more time—they showed they keep their word. That was a message for us."

"First we gotta get out of *this*," Suzl noted. "That sounds like an army arriving with full battle gear."

It took all night and most of the following day before they were able to spring the two boys and get some rest in a guest hotel in the city. Power had still not been restored to much of Logh Center, except the immediate center-square area which was fed by the transformers from the old temple and only needed some new wiring.

Still, Matson was almost a blur of action after they rested.

"Dell, I want you to get back to Freehold. Tell Sondra

to come here, in full old stringer regalia, understand? Just Sondra. I don't need a mob scene, and Jeff's got to run things and won't be a big help on this anyway. Tell somebody to get to New Pericles. Bring both Spirit and Morgaine if they can. Tell 'em we'll meet 'em at the old West Gate. All of them. West Gate in—oh, two days. Suzl, you stand by with me. Me, I'm going down to the stringer office now and fire off a message to Cassie she's not gonna like.''

Suzl was excited. "You're sending for *Cass?*"

"No. Damn it, she's totally immune to Flux. Totally. Anybody shoots her, all the wizards in the world can't stop the bleeding, or mend a broken arm. Up at the Guild redoubt she's got doctors for that. She's also lecturing in history at the Guild college, and doing a fine job raising prize horses and good beef. I'm telling her to stay put. *That's* what she isn't gonna like. But I want her standing by with a world-class Guild wizard, the strongest there. It's entirely possible we may have to fly her God-knows-where at a moment's notice.''

Suzl looked at him. "You've got a plan."

"A bunch of ideas. Can't have a plan until they make the next move.''

Rondell looked at him in wonder. "You're actually *enjoying* this! All these dead, three innocent kids out there in terror, a horror weapon in the hands of their kidnappers, and you're *enjoying* this!''

Matson sighed. "Son, last night five firefighters died fighting those blazes. It's a crappy, risky job that's ninety percent boredom and ten percent life on the line. They don't get much respect, but they're necessary. Ever wonder why anybody'd be one?''

"Huh? I don't see. . . .''

"There's some folks that just love fires. It's a thing in their heads. The crazy ones go around setting them, or just follow the firefighters and dote on 'em. Now, the firefighter's got the same disease, only he's a sane and normal sort. He doesn't want any fires to break out. He doesn't want anybody to get hurt, and he doesn't want anybody to lose property to fire. But, by God, if there's a fire, *he wants to be there!* Same with me. I hate this kind of shit for the damage it does to people's lives and futures. I really do. I wish there never was a bad crisis or a gang of murderers or a kid kidnapped or abused or invaders from another world or anything else. I like peace. Among my happiest times were the past few years. But I got a talent and I'm good at what I do. If there's some kind of trouble *I want to be there.* And, by God, here I am again."

At that moment a young security officer came in. Internal security hadn't been very friendly to them up to now, but because they were directly involved in this there was a certain level of consultation that was grudgingly given.

Suzl grinned sardonically when she saw the officer. Major Verdugo did not look pleased at being a messenger boy.

"Yes, Major?" Matson prompted.

"Verdugo, sir. Internal security. I've been assigned as your liaison in this unpleasantness so long as you remain in New Eden."

Matson's lips curled into a sour smile. "In case we get contacted by the kidnappers or something, you mean. I'm not a novice at this system, Major. You did what you did under orders, but your patron's dead now and your superiors have decided that it's all your fault because it can't be theirs. Your career depends on a successful resolution of this mess. All right—we can't avoid you at this stage. Have they found where the raiders crossed into Flux yet?"

Verdugo was not used to being spoken to like that, and he bristled. His eyes clearly betrayed his wounded ego. Matson had deliberately made an enemy of him.

"No, sir. No trace of the lorry or the others. It's most puzzling. We've had the army scouring every millimeter of Flux border along the eastern frontier and there's nothing. No sign at all, not even tracks."

"Uh huh. Then they didn't go out that way."

"But they must have, Mr. Ryan. They would certainly be conspicuous now heading either west or southwest along the route they came from."

"Then you've either missed them or they're still here someplace. It was well-planned and well-executed. There was excellent intelligence before the raid and good timing. They even knew that ranch would have sufficient horses for their needs. Any of the newer staff up at Vishnar's unaccounted for? No body, I mean?"

Verdugo seemed suddenly struck by the logic. "Yeah! Yeah! Just one. In the gardening staff. . . . Well I'll be damned!"

"Amateurs," Matson spat. "You're so hung up on your technology and controls that you consistently underestimate a determined enemy. All right—Dell, here, is about to take the two boys home and get some messages out to the clan. We're going down to the old West Gate to meet some people and decide what to do next. Nothing else we can do unless they contact us or until your folks find them."

"The *old* West Gate? You mean the old Anchor Gate?"

Matson nodded. "I mean exactly that. They're not going east, because that would take them through Assam, and the wizards of Assam were on very friendly terms with Vishnar and will be hell-bent, like all the Flux wizards, on getting that gadget for themselves in any event. If they go northeast they're going into Freehold territory. Hostages and gadgets or not, they're no match for Freehold if they even run into one of 'em by chance. At some point they have to go north, where they have good relations with the local Fluxlords and have the additional cover of a Flux war up there. The old Gate's a good compromise location. They have to break out sooner or later. I know they still have that little train going down that way, so we'll use it if we can. You can be a big help arranging it for us, including transport of our horses."

For now, the major was resigned to this. "I'll see what can be done. And you?"

"I have some messages to send, and I'm going to do some shopping." He turned to Suzl, who'd been ignored through all this. "You any good at barbering?"

"Yeah, sure," she responded. "You ought to be chief mommy to a hundred Freehold brats."

"No thanks. I'll want everything set up in the room when I get back, though. I want to pull out of here as early tomorrow morning as the schedule permits."

"I'll arrange the necessary permits," Verdugo broke in. "May I ask who we are meeting down there?"

"Oh, nobody you're going to like," Matson told him, and prepared to go out on his errands.

5

CONFLICTS OF INTEREST

Suzl had examined the packages Matson had brought with him, and watched as he removed a small wooden case from his pack. He did not open the case right away, but instead removed his old clothes and took a shower. Matson believed that showers were the one great thing New Eden had rediscovered, having always disliked baths.

He was quite hairy, a mixture of black and gray over most of his body, and still quite lean and solid, as he had been in his younger days. Suzl found his body extremely attractive, and couldn't help noting that his sexual equipment was at least as formidable as the rest of him. He radiated power, self-confidence, and strength at all times. With the fear element removed, as with her, he was a considerable turn-on.

He did not bother to dress again immediately but settled in for a haircut and a shave. "You know how I want it," he told her.

She was mixing the materials, but she had doubts. "Are you sure you want to do this? You went to a lot of trouble getting 'killed' that second time convincingly, and there's a statue of you facing outward from the temple not three blocks from here. It's like painting a huge sign."

"I know. That's just exactly what I'm doing. First, it'll cut through this New Eden bullshit, since, as Matson, I hold the titular rank of Field Marshal. More important, those women back at the ranch knew who Matson was. If *they* knew, then those above them know. I *want* to be easy to find. If we have to go through Flux after them, I'm going to be in a much better position as Matson to deal with the Fluxlords as well."

"Yeah, but everybody also knows that you don't have much Flux power. You'll be a sitting duck out there. Everybody likes their heroes well dead."

"Maybe. That's why I'm taking the rest of you along. It's a lot of Flux firepower if need be. As for Flux power, if I had a lot of it I'd be dead now. What good's it done you lately? The *old* Suzl, the one who worked dugger on stringer trains, now *she* didn't have any power at all, but I think she was a lot happier."

She began to cut. "You're right, I guess. Seems like everybody knows my problem. Even Verdugo."

"It's a natural deduction based on your own self now and then and knowing the way things work. You weren't cut out for this role; you're trapped in it. You should never have stayed at Freehold. You should've come with us at the start."

She stopped clipping for a moment, then continued. How could she ever explain to Matson that she'd been *jealous* of him? "It would have worked out just the same," she told him. "At least in Freehold I was needed for a long while."

"Then why'd you decide to leave now?"

She sighed. "Because first of all there are so many good parents there I wasn't really needed anymore. And, well, it was getting worse—faster. All my fantasies have been bondage fantasies. I only really feel alive, worth something, when I'm doing something like this. The rest of the time I'm either in deep depression or I just switch off, like downstairs until you turned to me. I've been alternating between acceptance, letting go, and killing myself.'' She stopped suddenly, feeling a bit embarrassed. Why was she going on like this? How could any man, let alone Matson, understand any of this?

''You don't have to have wizard power to feel like that,'' he told her. ''Lots of people get into things they feel they can't solve, that they're buried too deep, and get into that kind of mind rut. Most folks get into it without any effort at all on their own part. We now—all of us— were victims of outside forces beyond our control. That damned Soul Rider got all of us into a mess, including Cass, Sondra, Jeff, even me. The Guardian, now, sold you down the river for a mess of years. They not only *allowed* New Eden to happen, they actually gave it several pushes, since it served their own purposes. They didn't care about people in particular if it helped them guard people in general. It could have been done a lot cleaner than New Eden, with a lot less bloodshed and misery, but it was here, it was convenient, so they took it. Hell, that's the real legacy to the children of Flux and Anchor. For thousands of years people used machines. Now we're at the point where we're tools of the machine, to be used and used up and sacrificed or discarded when no longer useful or even if we're just in the way. That wasn't you over in the Master Control Room playing God. That was the Guardian doing what it damned well pleased and using you to do it because it needed you.''

That stopped her for a minute, while she thought it over. It wasn't the way she or anyone else had thought of things, but clearly Matson was right. She hadn't really *done* anything. The Guardian had picked her and salted her away here until needed and then used her as a conduit to connect it to some other computers. The original Fluxgirl spell Coydt had forced upon her, in fact, had been in machine-language code, far too complex for her to really follow—or anyone else. The same with Spirit's. How had Coydt gotten such codes together? Or had he? Had they, in fact, been furnished by either the Soul Rider or the Guardian?

"The way you say it, it's like we're in a zoo," she said thoughtfully. "Or some kind of laboratory, maybe. Being played with by our—owners."

"Yeah, I think that, too, sometimes," he admitted. "I keep feeling like there's an audience out there, observing us for its own amusement. Makes you feel sometimes like nothing's worth it. I get that way a lot, particularly now that I've grown so old and learned so much. You get to wondering what the use of it all is. Those things are so far in advance of us we can never understand them, and because we got no way to provide even the basics for ourselves without 'em we're stuck. The big difference between us and the animals is that we alone can know that we're owned and operated." He stopped, realizing he was getting her more depressed than ever, which hadn't been his intention at all.

"Now, look," he added, "this really isn't the end of it all. When I get too down I figure it's not much different in the long run between what we got and all those religions we clung to. We were always *somebody's* property—the gods, the goddesses, the wizards, whatever. O.K., so we now know who and what our gods are. So what? A wizard's spell is nothing more than a prayer to the gods for a miracle. Unlike most folks, that wizard usually gets the prayer answered. No big difference. So we do just what everybody in the past has done with their religions—we cope. We live our own lives and hope the gods won't notice us. And, if they do, we dance their tunes and play their games until they get tired of us and let us go again. We can't help it when the gods play tricks, but the rest of it is ours. Your problem was started by them, maybe, but it continues because of you. You said it yourself. Your own mind is doing it to you and you know it. You get the choice—become a sheep like most folks here, Flux and Anchor, male and female, or become one of the few who have control. Most folks don't have that choice."

She sighed. "I wish it was that easy."

"Being a sheep's the easy part. That's why New Eden works. And, the plain fact is, New Eden's just a bigger example of World itself. Oh, maybe the victims aren't the women, or just *some* women, or just *some* men and women, or maybe everybody at once, but it's all the same. Folks like Coydt and Adam, they were sheep once. They broke out and took charge.''

''Yeah—and look at the harm they caused.''

He chuckled. ''Maybe that's part of your problem. Coydt and the rest of the Seven took charge and caused a lot of evil and misery. Mervyn and the rest of the Nine led lonely, empty lives devoted to keeping all World down. The Fluxlords went nuts. With that much power, even Cass went nuts—living like an animal and leading armies of conquest. Now the whole world's gone nuts, with no real objective, no sense of the future, that's not pretty evil itself. New Eden built this super gadget so they could make the whole world into New Eden, and I saw that scared you. I kind of think that our raiders have a similar use in mind, but to make a different kind of world. I don't know what kind, but I have a sneaking suspicion that men aren't included in it.''

She was almost finished with him now. ''But I thought this Borg Habib was the leader. He's a man, I heard.''

''He's a puppet. Dangerous, but still a puppet. More dangerous because he's probably got an ego big enough not to even understand that he is one. No, the brains behind him is definitely his whore.''

She hesitated a moment. ''This—Ayesha. Anybody know what she looks like?''

''All I heard is that she's the ultimate and extreme Fluxgirl and she's under the original program. It's been too long for more, and most of the old records were destroyed by Habib when he left.''

She was finished now, and he stood and looked in the mirror and gave a nasty sort of grin. ''Looks like I never was away,'' he said approvingly. He turned to her, but saw that she was still deeply troubled and just sitting there on the couch, staring off into space. ''You all right, Suzl?''

''Huh? Yeah. I—I was just remembering. Thinking.''

She looked directly up at him. "Matson, I never told anybody about this. Anybody. I half forgot it myself. After we beat the *Samish*, and when we were still debating what to do next, we were all feeling like gods. All of us. It was impossible not to. I took time to order the computer to look up some folks. Family first, both old and present, and friends—what they had been before all this, if anything, that kind of thing. Seeing if I could give anybody a lift. I ran into my ex-husband's record doing that, and I found out that he was mostly responsible for making the New Eden system possible. He was real smart, maybe a genius, and he had a lot of access to the old records and old psychological texts. Coydt had assembled a bundle. He invented or developed the shock collars, the group sessions, the brain-mashing stuff that worked for awhile on me and worked even on Cass."

Matson shrugged."I didn't really know him, but somebody would have done it if he hadn't."

"Yeah, but when they attacked Nantzee he was given a combat slot because that was the only thing keeping him a junior officer instead of a big wheel. They told me he was killed in action, and I believed it. There wasn't a lot of love between us anyway—ever. It's just that how comfortable I was, and how much position I had, depended on how much he had."

"Uh huh. I understand."

"Yeah, well, maybe not yet. He wasn't killed. He was a bookish type who never even held a gun except at target practice. When he got put in a position where the odds were way against him, he chickened out. His troops mutinied and won anyway. You know what happens to officers in charge who turn into cowards?"

He began to see where she was going. "Yeah. I know. Got to talking about it just the other day. I told Dell that Ayesha had to have been a man once."

"Yeah, well, when I was there, in Master Control, and I thought of all those people dead and of my own sessions and Cassie's dad and all the rest, I got real mad. I had a search done and I found him—or her. Not in my quadrant, but way over to the east. The Guardian there was an old Fluxgirl, too. She understood. All I could think of was that he'd seduce some young wizard out in Flux after shutdown and be turned back into what he was. I looked at his readout and it was boiling with hatred. I knew if he ever got back he was fully capable of killing millions and enslaving more.''

"So when the master program was adjusted, you exempted him as the original had exempted Spirit, for example.''

"Worse. I wanted to pay him back for everybody as much as possible. I made him—her—into his own original inner fantasy for women. She's practically a thinking animal, designed for just one thing. She's immune to spells as such, but she draws from Flux. I—it's so complicated I can't even remember it all now.''

Matson stroked his now-bearded chin and thought about it. "And you think this might be our Ayesha. It fits, in a way. It might even explain it all. One item on their shopping list they missed at Vishnar's place was you. This'll make it pretty damned tough, if Weiz is as smart as you say, but she *is* vulnerable.''

Suzl was not so sure. "She might be destroyed— *might*—in Anchor, but never in Flux. Even if you beheaded her, she would be instantly re-formed. Unless she's reprogrammed by the master computers, she's the closest thing to an immortal we have on World.''

"That's bad,'' he admitted, "but not fatal. She's dependent. Right now, she's dependent on Borg. She absolutely needs him, and I think he knows that, which is why he's so confident himself. She knows it, too, so she's got to figure some way to get around it. We have to get her before she does, that's clear. A man must take her, but only a woman can get close enough. This'll be a real tricky one.''

"If she *is* Weiz, then she'll remember I once had a prick. Think that's the way out?''

"Hard to say. *You* wrote the program. The thing is, with this gadget, *she* can write everybody else's. With

Borg around, she has the luxury of being able to experiment. Whatever she comes up with, it's not going to be any nicer than Coydt's version of things.''

"Oh, boy! What a mess I always make of things! He was always a little kinky, even as a man. Of course, I was, too, so we fit pretty well. All I did was try and give a little justice and instead I made another Coydt!''

He went over to her and drew her to his naked body. "We all make mistakes," he told her gently. "Your mistake might still be for the best. We might never have stopped New Eden. Maybe you gave us a fighting chance.''

It was what she needed to hear, and tears came into her big, soft brown eyes. She very much needed to draw on his strength right now, and he was more than willing to provide it.

He had average desires, but she'd forgotten that his wizard ladies had given him nearly infinite capacity. It lasted for hours and through countless variations, and it was the best she'd ever had.

The hotel lobby was a buzz of conversation, filled with patrons both regular and visiting. Power was back on and everybody was celebrating a more-or-less return to normalcy, although nobody liked having to send to Flux to get fresh food and beverages, or paying what it cost.

The tall figure came down the central stairway almost casually, although it was something of a grand entrance. People stopped talking or doing whatever they were doing when they saw him and just stared, some open-mouthed. It spread across the lobby like a wave of silent awe, and it was both eerie and, to Matson, funny as hell.

He had purchased an all-black outfit, similar to, but a bit fancier than, what the stringers wore as their uniform. His boots, also new, were of shiny black leather and had silver spurs, basically ornamental but effective. He also had a new black felt wide-brimmed hat, the left brim hooked up in stringer fashion, although around the crown was a silver band of ornate design. On the upturned brim, he'd pinned the silver leaf and star cluster of a field marshal of the armies of New Eden, and under it the smaller, slightly tarnished eagle that marked him as a colonel, Signal Corps. That had come from the box he always carried with him.

Also from that box was the black leather belt, loose on the hips, with the worn silver design almost woven through it, and the well-worn buckle with the ancient symbol of the Pathfinder on it. A number of things in the case and out of it would attach to that belt as needed, but he had chosen to wear twin ancient pearl-handled revolvers, the outlines of rearing white stallions carved into those handles.

Everyone just stared, seeing this ghost from the ancient past come down the hotel stairs, not quite believing their eyes or knowing what to do or say next.

Finally the desk manager, a man of some practicality, muttered softly but loud enough for all to hear, "I'm sure *he* never registered. I would have remembered. . . ."

Matson, with his thick drooping black moustache and mean-looking eyes, surveyed the entire room like a king surveying his subjects. Then he said, in his best deep voice, "Don't let *me* stop your fun, people. I'm not going to be here very long."

Nobody had taken much notice of Suzl, who'd come down behind him, but she couldn't suppress a look of haughty pride and satisfaction. They all looked even sillier than she'd dreamed.

The grand entrance had been timed for Major Verdugo, who was just coming in the door and hadn't yet realized that anything unusual was going on. He stopped when he saw the people around him just staring, though, and he followed their gaze to the man on the stairs and his mouth dropped as well. "Oh, my God!" he breathed.

Matson saw him, and was all business, ignoring the others. "All right, Major. We have a train to catch, I think. Have somebody see to our bags." And, with that, first Matson, then Suzl, walked right by the major and out the front door.

Verdugo snapped out of it in a minute, but he wasn't thinking too clearly. He whirled and sped out the door after them. Matson was standing on the entrance porch,

breathing in the air and discussing the weather casually
with Suzl, just waiting for him.

"*You! You're not* . . ." the major began, trying to sort
it all out.

"James Patrick Ryan, Major," the big man in black
responded casually. "But I think we better use Matson
from here on in."

The major glanced down the street, as if to check and
see that the big statue of the legendary man was still
standing in front of the Institute and hadn't come to life
and walked down here. "Matson's dead!" he protested a
bit weakly. "It's against the law to impersonate him!"

"I'm impersonating no one, Major, and I think you
better show a little more respect and be a little less of an
asshole, if that's possible. In case you haven't noticed, I
have six ranks on you in the same army."

Verdugo came up close to him and stared. "Are you
really Matson?"

The big man sighed. "Son, unless you're a complete
idiot, which I doubt, you think it through. Either I'm
Matson, or his ghost, or somehow I got by all your guards
and went through Flux, did this, and then got back here
without breathing hard or any of your spies noticing. Since
I bought most of this stuff here yesterday, as you well
know, and since I spent the night right here in the company of this charming lady of old acquaintance, I think
you can figure out the rest."

Matson took out a four-pack of cigars, offered one to
Suzl who shook her head and declined, then stuck one in
his mouth and lit it with a safety match. He then pulled
back his sleeve and looked at his watch, the same watch
Ryan had been wearing. "It's getting on, Major. We're
going to catch that train. If our baggage and my horse and
one for the lady aren't on it as well, I will take great
delight in showing you how easy it is to make a eunuch.
Now *move!*"

The train was a small one, almost a toy by comparison
to the large locomotives that now went all over New Eden.

The original line was a prototype built from the old plans discovered in the ancient files; the track had been laid down along the main road between the old Anchor East and West Gates. It was still a prototype; now its power was electric, from a shielded third rail, and it was unusually smooth-running and quiet compared to the puffing steam engines on the full-sized long hauls. A nationwide electric system with sufficient surplus energy to run all the trains was not possible at the moment, but it was hoped that these sorts of trains could be used for the cities, and for city to suburban locations.

Matson sat back and watched the countryside go by. "Last time I rode this line it was night, I was stark-naked and manacled, and it was going the other way," he noted. It was just a memory. There seemed no bitterness or anger in his tone, and his thoughts did not dwell on the memories. "The country around here's gotten too built up. Not enough green showing anymore. It's a shame."

Suzl said nothing, but she certainly agreed with him on the way things had gone. The area alongside the train had gotten built up; farming had been reduced in the area to small truck farms serving the cities—chicken ranches and stuff like that. A lot of the trees had been chopped down, too, to make way for new villages and some small industry. She had been born and raised here, and had returned and lived in New Eden even longer when it was still just an Anchor, and she recognized few landmarks.

Matson sighed. "Well, Major, you've had me checked all out and you know I'm who and what I say I am."

"Yes, sir. I can't say I understand, though. I can see why you might have taken all that trouble to 'die'—I'm not sure I'd like to be a monument while I was still alive myself—but why come back now?"

"A matter of family honor, mostly. I just can't have powerful people picking on my folks. This way, nobody's ever sure about me. I've been twice dead and twice now I've come back. Even if somebody sees me blown apart and then cremates my remains, they'll never be sure about me. And, there are other reasons." In point of fact, none of the kidnapped children were any kin to Matson at all, but he'd taken pains to say that they were. It made him far more menacing, considering his reputation, and it also allowed him to call upon stringer resources if he needed them. Anyone harming him while he was on a personal adventure would be free and clear; if on a matter of family honor, though, every stringer would be out to avenge his death. It was part of their own clannish code.

"Now that we all know each other, I think we deserve to know just what it is we're looking for here," Matson told Verdugo. "Just what is it? What's it look like? What's its power and range? What's it supposed to *do*, anyway?" He saw that the major was still hesitant. "Come on, Major. It seems like all the bad guys already know. It's kind of crazy to keep us in the dark after all that."

Verdugo thought for a moment, then decided to talk. Matson was, after all, a field marshal, a rank never more than technically retired.

"It's pretty bulky," he told them at last. "Looks like a chair but a chair built into a heavy machine. It weighs close to a ton, and so it's not easy to move. There's also four antennas attached to the top, but they can be removed when shipped. They only got it on the lorry because it was on a platform and electric winch."

"They knocked out all the power," Suzl noted. "How'd they get it up?"

Verdugo was not used to having women in these conversations, but he answered the question. Things were changed now, at least for the present.

"You always have a backup system. They turned it with teams of horses. Their own and some of the judge's, too. It wasn't hard to do."

Matson nodded. "What about the scientists who built it? None of them were there at the time, surely."

"No, none were. Only a couple of soldiers as guards, both of whom were killed. They just blew in the door, bypassing the security, with some very heavy explosives. We didn't hear it because we had enough noise and mayhem going on with the fires and their own explosions.

Everyone working on the project is now in the custody of the district military commander, to see how the raiders could have known so much. Even allowing all the rest, they knew there was a winch in there and how to operate it, for example, without power. They also blew in the weakest point in the building. Somebody who'd been inside had to tip them."

"Good thinking," Matson approved. "I wonder what they could have offered somebody to sell out? Or what kind of hold they had, anyway. Probably duped somebody into thinking they were working for somebody else. It's easy to fool people when those people think they're too smart to be fooled." He sighed. "O.K., so they have it. Now—can they make it work?"

"It connects directly to the power grid, so it has to be used in Flux or at the Anchor Gate to be worth anything. That's why it was being built and tested out here, close to the Flux border. It's a prototype, so there's not as many safeguards on it as a production model would have, but there are some."

Suzl was thinking. "It weighs a ton, you say? Then, if they can get it to Flux, any competent wizard sitting in it would be able to move it. Not very fast, but they could draw up enough energy to lift it off the ground, and move it forward in fits and starts. If it was up at all, then it could be pulled by horses with no big problem. There wouldn't be any drag like a wagon would cause, and the only friction would be atmosphere."

Both men looked at her with some surprise. This was insecure little Suzl talking about drag and friction?

"All right, they can move it, at least as fast as a stringer train would move wagons," Matson said. "Now—can they work it? Honestly?"

Verdugo thought about it. "If they knew enough to steal it, they probably won't have much trouble figuring out how to work it. It draws tremendous Flux from the grid and then can send it to anyplace else. You program in a grid ID system that's consistent. Any assignments will do, so long as there's no overlap of locations. Simple map work. Block A–25, Block K–144, and so on. That's the only real security item on this one. You have to know what is Block 0–0, or the locations make no sense.''

Matson nodded. "Uh huh. So the operator sends a program along the grid to any specific block and it works there just like a wizard was standing there. You said there were four antennae. Does that mean you can send to four blocks at once?''

Verdugo shook his head negatively. "Uh uh. If you have all your locations correct, it forms a circular pattern around the projector. When the *Samish* took off, they drew a shield that extended for a distance of about a kilometer around their flying ship. They, however, were a remote unit of the mother ship, tapped into the Flux at the Gate itself, which was then broadcast to the ship. The more power it got, the more it could expand its shield and link it back to the mother ship's.''

"But that was in *Anchor*!" Suzl protested. "You can't tap the grid in Anchor. That's why magic doesn't work there!''

"Well, ma'am, that's the only thing that saved us down there. They had to draw everything from the mother ship. When the mother ship's connection to the Flux from the Gate was severed, they had no power and it all came tumbling down. Up north they weren't so lucky. That's why so many millions died up there. The ship could draw direct from the grid. Still, when they blew the two other mother ships, they blew whatever brain was controlling the creatures who ran the things and they crashed in confusion. If it'd been *us* in those ships, nothing could have stopped us.''

Both Matson and Suzl could visualize it: New Eden operators, flying above Flux and tapping the grid, overwhelming any forces on the ground behind an absolute shield, robbing even the other wizards and amps against them of the power to attack. Armed with their conversion programs, used so devastatingly in conquering the southern cluster, converting those of Flux into perfect New Edenites, Fluxlords and stringers, masters and slaves alike.

"But you never figured how to make it fly," Matson noted. "So what's the range of this thing?"

Verdugo shrugged. "It's never been fully tested. That was for the big full-field tests that were to start next week. Allowing for it being earthbound, at least line of sight or so, they figure. Maybe a circle thirty kilometers out. Maybe a lot more, but at least that. Now you're getting too technical for me, and I don't know the answers, and I don't think those who might would be allowed to give it out anyway, considering how easy it was for these bastards to learn what they did."

"I think we got to figure a lot bigger than that," Suzl told them. "I mean, if a single Fluxlord can make a consistent world a quarter to a third the size of an Anchor, and three or four can make 'em *bigger* than Anchors, like they have been doing, you got to figure this is at least that strong."

"I agree," Matson responded. "I rather suspect, though, that it depends on who's in the operator's chair. Just like some wizards can make a small Anchor, while others can only make big pockets, I think this would be the same. A wizard strong enough to make a Fluxland the size, say, of Freehold, would be able to do a lot more than that because they wouldn't have to worry about stability. The projector would provide that. And, right now, we have no evidence that they have anything like a world-class wizard. The ones we interrogated suggested that most of the band had some wizard power but were only world class when working together. That's not enough. I assume that only one person sits on that chair as operator."

"That's the way I understand it, sir," Verdugo replied.

"Then they need a wizard. If our guesses are correct, Ayesha draws from Flux but it's a fixed program. She has no power to cast spells, nor the ability physically even if she had that power. What about Habib?"

"A false wizard, like you," the major told him. A false wizard could cast spells and create anything quite convincingly—but it wasn't real. It was all illusion and would fail if tested. The best a false wizard could do was scare you to death, since it was impossible to tell if the monster coming for you was false or true until it caught you—but false wizards could see and read strings and make some use of them.

"Then if it takes a hundred of 'em combined to make one good wizard, they aren't much of a threat, even with the chair," Matson noted. "That means they'll take their strongest and use her strictly as a mobile shield. Oh, they'll play with it. Test it out on little things, maybe each other, but they won't be able to do much damage. They're gonna need a world-class wizard to do real mischief."

"More than one, sooner or later," Suzl said. "After they learn about it, and if they have enough horses to transport more, won't they just create more of the projectors out there? One wizard, one chair. Ten chairs need ten wizards."

"No, ma'am, that won't happen," the major explained. "You see, it's not something our ancestors thought of. It's not something they knew how to do. They depended on fixed programs and big amps using the grid directly. They couldn't project it, except the way we know—one wizard calls up one spell. This thing uses a whole different principle. It was designed by the *Samish*, and our version was built in Anchor. There's just no spell for it. Some genius could probably *write* one, if he knew all the details, and had a lot of testing on it, but it's not likely these folk will. If there's no way to interpolate a complex duplication command, and the thing isn't in the big computer's memory, it fills in the gaps for you. It's like nobody can ever think of all the details that would make a Fluxland really work. They just command the basics, and the computers fill in the rest. If you tried it with this one, it would make the power plant a big amp, and if we were told right, you made it so big amps don't work."

She nodded, a little relieved. "That's right. They don't. Oh, *I* see now!"

Matson looked disturbed. "I still don't like it. Out there, what if one of these Soul Rider things got hold of one inside a wizard? First thing it would do is analyze it, send all the data back to the big computers. That's partly what they're for—to keep learning and feeding information to the big machines. They might well decide to give the key to whatever group was in charge at the time just because it might be convenient to have a single, unified culture again. Convenient for them. And they wouldn't care which one, either. Those creatures got a habit of deliberately falling into these things, too.''

"When we get this one, we should blow it up, and all the records, too,'' Suzl told them. "And make spells on all the scientists so they forget how to do it, too.''

"Won't work,'' Matson responded. "Damn near impossible to uninvent something once everybody knows it exists, it's possible, and it works. No, this is a pretty nasty present those creatures left us. In a way, it's more dangerous than they were. And sooner or later somebody's gonna figure out how to make 'em fly and mass-produce them in spades.''

Verdugo gave a self-satisfied smile, and Suzl, for one, understood it. Under these circumstances, New Eden would, even now, be rushing into production of these things, this time behind all the military protection known. On the whole planet, only New Eden had the vast industrial base to produce these things in huge quantities and it had a system that could demand and get any sacrifices to make them. Production-line plans were probably even now being drawn up.

While before New Eden was secure and lazy behind a certainty of exclusivity, now it maintained only a technical advantage that would someday run out. If it did not attack and conquer first, it would eventually *be* attacked and conquered by these machines, perfected by other smart minds out there in Flux and Anchor. Although generals down in the capital were probably even now mapping out their plans and scientists were adapting their programs to the new system, the threat was not immediate. These would have to be built, tested, then deployed with trained personnel. Still, New Eden had the population and industry to do it. The chairs might not even need to be deployed.

Right now, they just looked like variations of the big amps. They had to be more than that.

A grid, Suzl thought. *You just tell it the numbers on the grid. . . . Sure! That was it! That was what Verdugo wasn't telling! Any grid number! Any one! The grid linked all of Flux, all the Gates, all the big computers. That's why it was called a projector. No limits. You could be sitting a few kilometers out in Flux from New Eden and command an area as big as a Fluxland maybe halfway around World!* She wanted to say something, to tell Matson of this, but there was no way now, not with Verdugo present.

They would be slow to build and train, but it would be a quick war. They wouldn't have to go very far—perhaps a hundred meters into Flux from the vast New Eden border, all under impenetrable shields. Then you tap into the grid, all at once, and send not to Gate Four but to Gate One, and divert all of its excess power, and send it outward by feeding in the grid numbers: The Fluxlands crumble, the wizards lose their power, and all of Cluster One becomes one big Fluxland, all in the image of New Eden. All the men become like Major Verdugo, and all the women become like—well, Suzl Weiz had been. But the land would still be Flux, and the male wizards would retain their power, but would have a will to defend and preserve New Eden's system and its philosophy. You could give it back to them; they would sustain it themselves. Then the same projectors tie into Cluster Two and repeat the process. With all the Gates secured, you'd move projectors to each and then fill in the gaps between the clusters. With all World of one New Eden mind save the twenty-four Anchors, most weak, divided, and cut off from one another, you'd have a dedicated army large enough to conquer them one by one.

New Eden would be the soul of World. No longer fearful of Flux, they would control it utterly, and all human beings within it, even in the void, would be New Edenites by fixed program.

Suzl thought of what she had been like as a Fluxgirl,

what she was fearing being like one again, and she knew one thing: She preferred *any* vision, no matter how grotesque, to condemning every single woman on World now, and those yet unborn, to permanent status as ignorant, childlike servants and sex objects. It was all well and good for Matson to take the long view and hope for a way out, but he was a man. He would never understand, not on the gut level, as she could. She understood his vague plan, to get rid of Ayesha and Borg Habib and capture the projector for the stringers, no mean scientists themselves. But they had no vision of controlling the world. They would learn how to defend against it and to protect their own. That would probably include Freehold, but how much else? They had been more than willing to accept and deal with New Eden before; they would compromise again, and let the rest of World go hang.

She thought perhaps it was time to make some plans of her own.

6

CONTACT

The old wall was mostly in ruins and much of it had been torn down to make way for more modern and effective border controls, such as nasty fences, guard towers, and mines, but the old and forbidding Gate still stood, and near it now a large and comfortable inn had been made out of the old converted headquarters and barracks complex.

It was still a busy place. New Eden still imported from Flux what was most convenient to import, and this was the end of its small rail line and the start of freight from Flux up into Logh Center, first, and from there to the main rail lines to the interior.

Matson seemed surprised when Suzl asked for a room of her own, but he offered no resistance nor arguments against it. The decision bothered her far more than it did him; she still got shivers from just thinking about the night before, and she very much wanted more of the same. Had it just been her, under the old conditions, she would have never left his side again, but other things had intervened, as usual. Millions of people all over the planet lived out their whole lives without interfering in the scheme of things one way or the other. She, on the other hand, always seemed to have things of great importance fall into her lap, and she could never feel secure enough to forget it and hope somebody else would do the job.

The place was bustling, that was for sure. The staff alone numbered perhaps sixty or seventy Fluxgirls, overseen by a half-dozen male managers. It was difficult for either the men or the women to accept Suzl as an independent guest, unescorted and with her own room. She wasn't even allowed in the dining room or lounge without Matson, which was inconvenient. It wasn't so much that she was a woman, since she knew that some of the coming female guests would be treated as virtual equals with the men, but that she looked like a Fluxgirl. It was damned inconvenient, but it did give her a chance to question him with no personal situations attached.

"What happens if you get these raiders but New Eden attacks?" she asked him. "I think you understand what this thing really does."

He nodded. "Yeah, I do, and thanks to some messages I sent out today through the strings I think the Guild does, too. The answer is that we do what we can. New Eden won't find setup and deployment so easy once word gets to all those Fluxlords about their plans. They have to get them out and set up and shielded, remember, and they're not as good at that as we are. If worst comes to worst—well, New Eden's a mighty big place. They can't defend a lot of it when they have to defend their projectors."

She nodded soberly. "Then it's war. Almost a world war. It's gonna be the *Samish* all over again, only it'll be us on both sides."

He shrugged. "Better war than what we would have had if we hadn't gotten this break. The trouble is, we need that stolen machine, and we won't be the only ones after it. No doubt, though, it's going to get bloody before it ends."

The conversation confirmed everything she'd feared after hearing the details and guessing the rest. War. . . . Millions dead, World in ruins, and the victors would still be free to impose an absolute system on Flux and Anchor—whoever the victors would be. Even if they were good enough to defeat New Eden, and they might be when unified, as soon as that happened the various armies of Flux and Anchor would turn on one another to keep from being dominated and to dominate the rest. It might be even worse. A Flux only of mad duggers reduced to primitive savagery, and Anchors in ruins, wastelands from which it might take generations to rebuild, if that.

Being taken as a Fluxgirl had some advantages, too. She spent the evening making friends with the staff and talking with the girls, and she learned a lot, not the least of which was that some of the girls were new. She thought she could spot the ones who weren't legitimate—a little more standoffish, a bit more assertive, a little secretive. A few might work for Verdugo, but what of the ones who didn't? The security man, by bringing in a few girls as spies, had also made it easy for the very ones they sought to also infiltrate the inn.

Still, there was nothing she could do for a while. She finally went to bed, and was awakened from a troubled sleep by soft but insistent knocks on her door. She went over to it and said, "Who's there?"

"Matson. Something's come up. I think we have to talk."

She let him in, and saw that he'd pulled on his pants but obviously had been recently asleep himself. He carried a small piece of paper in his hand. He took the chair while she sat on the bed.

"I've had contact," he told her. "I figured they'd move before everybody got here. After all, I made us coming down here as loud and public as possible."

"A note?"

He nodded and unfolded the paper, which was covered with a neat and florid handwriting. "We have no desire at this time to be the victims of a stringer vendetta," he read. "The three children are alive, well, and unharmed, and are being brought near to the West Gate in Flux. We are willing to make a trade if it can be kept a private dealing between mutual interests.'' He paused and looked at her. ''They want to trade the kids for you.''

She sighed and nodded. ''I figured that was what it was about. That's why they had orders not to harm the children. They have Weiz blood in them, and those killers really couldn't tell which ones were which. They were after me back at the house, but Verdugo and Vishnar screwed them up, so they took the kids they could get as a swap.''

''I had it pretty well figured that way all along,'' he told her. ''Now the question is what to do about it.''

''Just what do they propose?''

''A meet to talk out the details. Verdugo has this whole place bugged, but I took care of some of that. Just the two of us, in the courtyard down by the old wall an hour before first light. That's about''—he looked at his watch—''fifty-seven minutes from now.''

''Even with the guards and Verdugo's spies all over we'd be sitting ducks out there!''

He nodded. ''I know. That's why you're going to go and not me.''

''Huh? But I'm the one they want!''

''Right. Don't worry—I'll be there, every step of the way. It's just that neither you nor they, I hope, will know it. Are you game?''

''I don't see as I have much choice right now. They have a way for me to get out there unseen?''

''I have one. The women's washroom is right down the hall. There's a chair in there you can use to reach the window. I'll have it rigged so it's open. It'll be about a three-meter drop to the ground outside, but you should be able to handle that. Keep down low below the shrubs and use them to make your way over to a dark spot at the old wall. Then just stay there until they contact you. Clear?''

''Yeah, but even if there's no trouble, how'll I get back in?''

''Just walk back in through the side door. If anybody stops you, tell 'em you just went out for some air because you couldn't sleep. They'll suspect everything, but they won't want to tell Verdugo you got out without them seeing in the first place. Got it?''

She nodded.

"I'll get going, then. Good luck." He kissed her and left.

She gave him a good ten minutes to get himself positioned, then cautiously opened the door. The hallway was empty, and she walked down to the bathroom fairly confidently. It was a pretty natural thing, after all. She went in, found things as he'd told her—he'd gotten in and broken the lock, but not obviously, to the windows—and got out. The drop was a bad one, but nothing she couldn't handle. She made it all the way to the wall with little trouble.

The big problem was waiting, knowing that eyes, both friendly and unfriendly, were on her and she could do nothing but sit. Thankfully, they didn't keep her for long.

"You are Suzl," whispered a very high, mousy soprano from behind and slightly above her. "Where is Matson?"

"Monitoring with stringer stuff," she told the shadow woman. "Just like your friends are probably doing with you."

The stranger thought for a moment. "Fair enough. No tricks, or the children are lost forever. Understand?"

"I understand."

"All right. We will give you a set of string coordinates not too far into Flux. Follow them, and you'll find a temporary new string leading to a small pocket. Bring two others if you like to safeguard you and to get the children safely home."

"The children will be there?"

"One child will be produced and given over. You will be asked at that time to bind yourself to our will. When you do, a second child will be given over. When we go into the void, and are satisfied that there are no tricks, the third child will be sent in. This will be the only chance you have. If more than three appear, or there is an advance guard, the pocket will vanish and so will we."

"When?"

"Tomorrow night. The pocket and string will appear at

twenty-two hundred and vanish at four. You will be watched the whole way.'' She gave the coordinates, which were technical and meaningless but were easy to remember. Matson would know.

Suzl was alone.

She made her way back after she was sure that was all, and was very surprised to face no challenge as she reentered her room. Matson was back in a few minutes.

''You heard?''

He nodded. ''Two apparent Fluxgirls, both of whom supposedly work here. One had a nasty laser pistol, the other a night rifle. The big question is what we're going to do with this.''

''I'm responsible for those kids,'' she told him, ''and, in a way, I'm responsible for their kidnapper as well. I expected this almost from the start. I knew from then that I'd *have* to go.''

''Uh huh. You know there's no way I can send any kind of force out there without them knowing, and there's no way you can fake that spell they're gonna force on you. Weiz wants you to turn the tables on you and her. It's going to be ugly.''

She sighed. ''I'm used to it being ugly, remember? So she turns me into some kind of freak. I've been there before. She can't get too bad—I'm also the wizard she needs to work that machine right.'' She paused. ''That's something to think about, though. With me they'll be able to call up big programs and project them. They can take care of anybody trying to get them without risking any of their own.''

''I know. And you know that everybody *will* be after you, including maybe family and friends. You may be shooting at them, and they may wind up shooting at you.''

''Yeah, well, sooner or later they'd find a wizard anyway. You know that. They got a nice thing for making deals. And the kids—well, I couldn't bear the idea that we might be shooting at *them*.'' She sighed. ''Sure, I'm scared. I've never been really brave, but I'm going. I'm surprised you're not trying to stop me.''

"No. I'm sorry to sound so cold—I'm not—but I have to see it through. Right now they're safe but immobile and weak. Sooner or later New Eden will find them, and with their knowledge of the thing they'll figure a way to get it back. They need a wizard to keep them from falling into New Eden's hands. I wish it could be somebody else—you've done more than your share over the years—but it's not possible."

"I know."

He got up, and so did she, and he gave her a hug and a kiss. "Act normal tomorrow. We'll move into Flux as soon as the family gets sorted out here. No mention to anybody, not even close relatives. Some of them will go off half-cocked and queer everything. You, me, and the two that will go with you will be all who know."

She looked surprised. "You're not coming?"

"No. I'm a false wizard and I'd be an impediment out there. We want the best—just in case. I think they'll keep their word, but, if not, we have to be ready. Now—get what sleep you can. We've got a long, hard day tomorrow." And, with that, he left.

She sat there, not at all tired now. She was thirsty, and took a sip of tepid water from the pitcher on the small vanity, then lay back down on the bed and tried to relax. By this time tomorrow, she'd probably be some kind of monster again. *Again*, that was the key. She'd been there before, under binding spells, when it was all hopeless. Freak, monster, then Fluxwife.

Consciousness slowly faded, and she felt as if she were falling, falling into some deep, soft void without end. There were voices, and whispers, all around her, but she could barely make them out and it didn't seem to matter.

And she dreamed.

There had been flashing lights and a crackling sound, and she had felt suddenly dizzy and confused. She looked around to get her bearings and saw that she was safe in Freehold, the old familiar surroundings seeming to reassure her nervousness. She walked up towards the big house and found many girls there. It seemed—odd, some-

how. They were all Fluxgirls. Lots of them. Not the kind found in New Eden now, either; these were the old style, tiny and with enormous proportions. Even stranger, while they all had on makeup and jewelry, they were all stark naked except for wearing open-toed high-heeled shoes with heels so high it seemed they had to fall off them when they walked, but they didn't. They all had tattoos on their rumps as well, but she found she couldn't read any of them.

One of them approached her and squealed, "Oh, Suzl! isn't it wonderful! Now all of World, Flux and Anchor, is New Eden!"

With a shock she realized that it was Sondra speaking, reverted to Fluxgirl and even more extreme than before. She looked around further, even more confused, and finally recognized some of the others although much of the recognition appeared to be intuitive. Why, Cassie was here, and even Spirit and Morgaine had become Fluxgirls! And there were her daughters, and even her granddaughters.

"But where are the men?" she cried.

"Oh, when God judged World just now, He found them unworthy and changed them all to Fluxgirls as well," someone explained. "After all, one man may service many girls, and many girls may serve one man."

She looked around, horrified at what she was seeing. Then, out of the door to the house came a tall, handsome man in black. Verdugo! It was Verdugo! And he looked down at all of them in satisfaction, a leering look of absolute power and triumph on his face.

They rushed not only to do his bidding, but to anticipate it, and she found herself acting the same. Now she realized that she looked like the rest of the girls, and all that had gone before was already fading into incomprehension. She wanted to serve him, too. She wanted to be a slave, forever, as all the world would be slaves to these men in black, and their children and grandchildren unto eternity. She suddenly thought that was wonderful. . . .

She awoke with a start to find light streaming through the

window, although it was still early. Sweat covered her body, and she lay there, suddenly wide awake, trembling.

Oh, no, you sons of bitches! she thought, pure hatred and revulsion in her mind. *I'll turn the world to monsters before I'll allow you* that *future!*

The clan began arriving almost with the dawn, and it kept arriving most of the day. Matson was outraged that so many had come. That the parents of the kids would be there he'd expected, since he knew how he'd feel in their place, but the number of men and women, young and old, arriving from various points including Freehold made a small army. Most of them were hung up at the border. As soon as Matson realized what he was in for in spite of his instructions, he got Verdugo to slap on controls and allow in only specific people.

Sondra came, looking as she had so long ago—tall, dark-skinned, and beautiful, with shimmering silver hair, dressed all in black. It was not her old stringer's outfit, though, but shiny leather. She made an impressive sight, and evoked some debate among the Fluxgirls working the inn, many of whom had never seen a woman of such size, beauty, and self-confidence in their lives. All would need a good therapy session before this was over.

Sondra was sympathetic to her father's irritation. "But, Dad, what was I supposed to do? Somehow force a hundred angry wizards to stay back on the farm when there're kids of theirs at stake?"

"Well, we'll have to sneak out by them, with New Eden connivance," he grumbled. "This just isn't how it's going to work out. In the meantime, go out and see if you can explain it to them."

It was Verdugo, also taken aback by the horde on his doorstep, who offered solutions, but only at a price. "I want to know just what you're planning," he told Matson. "No holding back. I understand where your interests lie, and you understand mine, but both of us will have to cooperate for either to do much good."

"All right," Matson responded, prepared for this. "Nobody knows it yet, and nobody else should until after, but we're gonna make a swap. Suzl for the kids.''

"I thought as much from that business last night. O.K., but then what? The projector won't be anywhere close to the swap point and you know it.''

"Yeah, but Suzl will have to be. She's their wizard. Right now, we know absolutely nothing. Suzl is my key to finding things out, and she doesn't even know it. Hopefully, she won't know it.''

"They'll expect strings on her and cut them," he pointed out.

"Not the kind I'm arranging for. They're special, far outside the range of human perception. They'll run a check for strings, of course, but they won't be able to see, hear, or sense these. Nobody can unless they know the exact nature of the energy line and the frequencies involved. Basically, you have to be personally tuned to them when they're fixed. The odds against finding them otherwise are about a trillion-to-one shot.''

"So we just follow it to the band and the projector and hit them hard and fast.''

Matson sighed. "Major, I don't know how much time you spent in Flux, if any, but that's bullshit. The odds are they're inside a big Fluxland, so if you march in with troops you'll be committing an act of war. Even if those wizards are diverted with a war, they'll notice this and they'll chew any army of yours to pieces with a few gestures. But even if you could get permission or be ignored, it wouldn't matter. With the shield they already have to have with that thing and Suzl's power to boot, they'll just project your army into a ton of horse manure.''

"What will you do, then?''

"Track them. Track them and test them and wait for an opening while building up our own strength. There's nothing else to do.''

Verdugo thought it over. "I've had *some* experience in Flux, but not like you. I agree, though, that if they can figure out how to work the thing, a frontal assault would be impossible and containment would be a better bet.

But what makes you think they'll move at all? They can project.''

"New Eden is their biggest threat, so they'll want to put some distance between it and themselves as soon as they can. They'll fight a rear action but they need more than they have. Specifically, they're gonna need to deal with somebody with real technical expertise they can talk to and trust. They need more machines and more wizards and they won't have a good crack at them using the projector. The projector's bait. Once lured or kidnapped or whatever, then they can be converted. When the individuals are exposed, we can deal with them, nibble at their numbers. If we get an opening to go after them, we'll take it. Otherwise, it's follow and nibble until they have to come out to take us on.''

"I can put any number of forces at your command for that.''

"No, no. You still aren't thinking things through, Major. It must be a very small band. Very small. If they ever get our grid location, it's curtains. You can't conceal an army, even one on the move. Until we're ready, they must never suspect that they're being trailed. They have to think it's a lot of different forces, both local and from other interested parties—and there will be plenty of those. But they won't have strings to follow. We will.''

"Then—who are you taking?''

"Depends on who shows up. The parents are out. They're good people but I don't want somebody with a direct emotional motive involved. Sondra is close to Suzl, but she's a strong wizard and a hell of a stringer. She goes. Spirit, too, if she gets here. In some ways she's even closer to Suzl, but she once used her own mother as a weapon when it was practical to do so, and nobody is more at home in Flux. I don't know her daughter by Mervyn at all, but she's supposed to be the strongest wizard World's ever seen.''

"Two daughters and a granddaughter. No men?'' Clearly his background was showing through.

"Well, I been considering one. Young Rondell was

damned good back at the ranch. He hasn't learned to think dirty yet, but he's excellent covering your ass. Frankly, Major, I hadn't thought about most men for this because of the nature of the opposition. No man except maybe Borg Habib is ever going to get through that shield for very good reasons. But the more power they get, the more power-drunk they'll get. They'll get cocky and start feeling invulnerable. That's when the mistakes start. Mervyn got that way. So did Coydt van Haas. Both of 'em were strong enough to take on a big amp head on, and they're both stone cold dead. Patience and opportunism got 'em, and that's why I'll get these people in the end.''

"They'll never buy that here, you know," Verdugo noted. "Just to get all your players, particularly Suzl, out and where you want them you'll need help. They're not going to allow that unless New Eden is in, too."

Matson stared at him. "Just what are you proposing, Major?"

"I want in. I want to go along, as New Eden's representative. I have a little power, I can read strings, and I'm good in a fight. I can also get laser pistols and if need be a hand amp.''

Matson lit a cigar, leaned back, and sighed. "Major, it's a fate worse than death if I take you. Not for us—for you.''

"What do you mean by that?''

"All your life you been raised with one view of women. The enemy is female and you'll consistently underestimate them just like everybody did here. You just can't think of them the right way. It's against your breeding.''

"I can adjust. I saw the bodies, too, remember.''

"Yeah, but that's only surface. For pragmatic purposes and in foreign territory you might be able to think of some women as equals, but that's not the whole problem. You're gonna be in close contact with three women out there on the trail, women who are not at all like the girls of New Eden. They're smart, savvy, and they have enormous power. You'll have a hard time maintaining them in your mind as equals, and that would be a mistake. They're superior. Superior to you, to me, to most of World. All of 'em have good reason to really hate and detest New Eden. The first time you come on to one of 'em, even a little, the kind of power you'd unleash against yourself would be beyond belief. Your ego won't stand it, Major. They'll squash you like a bug and feel nothing about doing it.''

"I think I can handle myself appropriately," the major responded coolly. "I'm willing to risk it. It's my neck, anyway."

Matson sighed. "O.K., then, Major. But it's just you. Any tricks, any other New Edenities stalking us, anything like that, and you'll wish to God you were dead, and so will those following or tracking us. Understand?''

He nodded. "I understand.''

"All right, then—how do you propose to control a mob of angry wizards?''

"Simple. Let them all in.''

"Huh?''

"Let them all in. Here, they're just ordinary people. No Flux powers, no special status. We let them in, and then we only let your party out until you're far away.''

Matson gave a low chuckle. "Major, I still ain't sure of this, but you might just work out.''

Spirit arrived later on that morning, looking radiant as always, and Morgaine came a bit after midday. Matson had been warned that his granddaughter was strange, but he wasn't quite prepared for Morgaine.

She stood almost a hundred and eighty-five centimeters, about as tall as Matson himself. She had a thick, hard body that was more masculine than feminine, perhaps ninety kilograms of pure muscle. Her breasts were firm and very hard, more resembling male pectorals than female extensions. Her face had a curious bisexuality about it as well. It was a young face, with smooth skin and no facial hair, and her rich brown hair was cut in a short but feminine style, but it could also have been the face of a boy of perhaps fifteen. Her voice was a low alto that almost, but not quite, cut into the male half-octave. She wore faded brown leather boots, equally worn blue denim trousers, and a plaid button-down work shirt, and she looked and moved more like a teenage lumberjack than a mature woman.

"That isn't her self-image, that's the way she grew up," Spirit told her father. "She's really strong, too. Physically, as well as in Flux power. I'm not sure what she got from me, other than a little in the nose and lips. She's sure got her father's genius and talent for numbers and spells, though."

Matson kept staring and wondering if this wasn't the kind of vision Ayesha might have for her own wizards. "Uh—how do I approach her?"

Spirit laughed. "Just treat her the same way you treat me. Don't worry. No matter what her looks, she's a woman because she wants to be one." She looked back over at her daughter. "Morgaine! Your grandfather's too shy to say hello!"

The big woman grinned and came over to them, then stopped when she faced Matson. Then she, too, hesitated. Faced with a living legend she'd never really known, she, too, was unsure of how to approach him. Feeling foolish, she finally said, "You know, this is pretty ridiculous. One of us is going to have to stop being scared of the other or we'll be here forever."

Matson gave a big laugh and threw his arms around her, and she did the same, and the wall seemed to vanish with the gesture. Finally he let go and stepped back. "I think it's about time we got to know each other better," he said seriously. "Let's round up Sondra, get some good stuff to drink, and move to a more quiet part of this dump."

Matson had taken a larger room with a parlor, and he took them back there after ordering from one of the bargirls. They settled down while waiting for Sondra to arrive.

"Well," Matson said in a light tone, "I guess you don't have many problems in New Eden."

Morgaine chuckled. "Personally, no. I'd still like to wipe this dung heap off the face of World, though. I can't see how anybody put up with it all those years."

Her grandfather shrugged. "It's no worse than hundreds of Fluxlands and better than some that used to be in the old days. It's only unnerving to us because of its size and because it's Anchor. I been around too long and seen too much, Granddaughter, to get worked up about these things. After all, it wasn't so long ago that all the Anchors were matriarchies who ruled with iron fists and every year ramrodded a bunch of poor kids into slavery in Flux. I don't much remember many protests about it, or even much concern. It was just a little less bad, or maybe a little less obviously bad, so everybody just took it for granted. The only real wonder about New Eden or something equally bad was that it didn't come sooner. Seems like in those days we took oppression for granted and the only thing anybody really got upset about was change. Now we got both."

Morgaine stared at him a minute, then said, "I heard you were a cynic but I hadn't realized how much. I wasn't born back then, but everything I've been told says that the old Anchor system wasn't oppression at all."

"Well, now, you got two disadvantages," he told her. "You weren't there, and you're a real strong wizard. Oppression is only oppression when you're in the group being oppressed. I hear tell there's a pretty big Fluxland up north that doesn't let men in at all, and there's others where men are in subordinate roles all the time. I been in a few like that in my time and I didn't feel any more comfortable there than you all do here, but I never heard any women yelling that those systems were unfair, except maybe on an academic level. Me, I'd rather die than be under any of those systems, but that's just me. I don't get worked up over how insane human beings are. I can't. Everything we've learned says that history's the story of one group knocking over another."

"There were free societies in history," the young wizard argued. "I've read many of my father's records and those that have come out since the Invasion. My father named his Fluxland Pericles after the earliest known free society back on the Mother World."

Matson chuckled, but paused as the drinks arrived and he signed the bill. Then he settled back down. "I read some of those things, too. Those folks of old Pericles or whatever it was called had an odd idea of freedom. A small percent of 'em were free, voted, and owned everything and had all the rights. The rest of the people were slaves, bought and sold like the kids of Anchor used to be bought and sold, and were nothing more than property. Seems to me that when you have slave owners writing about how free and democratic everything is you make my point. . . .

"What about you?" he continued. "If you gave up all your power and extra rights as a wizard and Fluxlord and moved to an Anchor where you had to work every day for some company for work credits to buy what you needed and had one vote out of millions in running things, I think you'd give anything for power and the Fluxland back. When you can honestly do that, without kidding yourself, then I'll take you seriously. Until then, we got business—and here's our other partner in family crime now."

Sondra entered, and there were hugs and greetings all around.

Spirit had kept quiet until now. She knew that Matson was hard to take sometimes and she also knew that Morgaine, while powerful and skilled, had the arrogance such power brings and an impulsiveness that was sometimes hard to control. She was also as bullheaded in her own way as her grandfather.

Matson sat back and looked at all three women. They were a contrast in many ways: the tall, slender, athletic Spirit with her dark, exotic looks; the imposing and quite differently exotic Sondra, Spirit's half-sister but looking more like her mother; and Morgaine, the strange, powerful mannish woman with the smooth, innocent face of youth although she was actually closing in on half a century. They all had his blood in them, though, and the three possessed enough Flux powers among them to level a small Fluxland.

"You all know this is going to be a long one, away

from family and friends, present company excepted," he said seriously. "Sondra already knows most of the details and has made her arrangements. I'd like the two of you along as well, if you're willing." Quickly he sketched in the facts as he knew them—on Habib and Ayesha, on the device that was stolen, and on the twin threats from the raiders and New Eden itself. They all listened attentively, expressions growing more grim as he spoke.

"You're forecasting nothing short of the end of the world as we know it," Spirit said at last. "Maybe the end of the human race as we know it."

Morgaine nodded. "It won't take more than a couple of years for New Eden to produce enough projectors to do the job. Even if they don't lick the flying problem right away, they'll lick that, too, given time. You know it and I know it. All Flux and Anchor at the mercy of a single council of Fluxlords who wouldn't even need the power themselves. Maybe one vision at the end."

"Yeah," Matson sighed, lighting a cigar. "I agree New Eden's the major threat, but it's not the only one. This group is smart. Don't put 'em down because they're brutal or dirty-faced. They got plans for this thing, and it isn't just bigger raids or a big Fluxland. From what I know, I don't think Ayesha's vision of World would be any nicer than New Eden's."

"But surely she doesn't have a prayer of actually beating New Eden to the punch," Sondra put in. "I mean, how could she build them?"

"I don't know, but I say again not to underestimate this bunch. They always seem to know what they're doing and be one step ahead of us. They're good."

"You're betting that she's already got a deal with somebody else, somebody she's betting on to solve the problem her way?" Morgaine asked him.

"Bet on it, or something like it. And that just complicates things further, since whoever that is is an unknown player in the game, one who might be worse than either of the known players. That's why we hit the trail, daughters. Light and fast. I'll depend on you for the basics."

"That's no problem," Morgaine responded confidently. "The thing is, you know what we're going to do if we get them?"

"No. I don't even know how we're going to do that, although I got a few ideas when the time's right. I don't really like fighting Suzl, but I can't see anything we can do about that. Even without consideration for the kids, which is our first worry, we need that string or we're sunk at the start."

"Do you *really* think she could be so converted she'd fight *us*?" Sondra asked him disbelievingly. *"Suzl?"*

He nodded. "Yeah, it's not so tough. They have power as a group and they have other things, probably including hand amps that were enough to knock Cass cold. She had the power and Coydt still managed to stick her with the Fluxgirl spell, remember."

"But that was in the old days, the old Suzl," Spirit noted. "She's not the same now."

"Are any of us? No, the trouble is that the old Suzl and the new Suzl have been having a war inside her head for over forty years now and they haven't even compromised a thing. Half of her is revolted by the very idea of Fluxgirls and the other half wants to be one real bad. She's been real close to killing herself but neither side of her has it in her to do that—and when she realized that, the Fluxgirl side got the edge. If they don't know that now, they will when they have her a little bit. Her old self's desperate, and that makes her vulnerable. It'll be real easy to slip her around the bend so she's deadly against anybody who serves any part of New Eden's interests or who seems to. And that brings up tonight."

He filled them in on the swap. "I'll stay back, as will Dell and Verdugo. They don't like or trust men much, not even old Borg. You three have the power to handle it—and to take care of yourself just in case something goes wrong."

"You expect them to pull something?" Morgaine asked him, sounding almost as if she hoped they would.

"No, I don't. But you can never be absolutely sure of these things going off, and while I'd trust Verdugo with my life in a fight, I wouldn't trust him for a minute if his New Eden bosses decided to step in."

"I still don't see why we have to take that vicious punk along," Sonda said acidly. "Even if he's convenient now, he's not somebody we need along the way. At the right moment, he'll betray us."

"He might," the big man admitted, "but that's not a present worry. We can always take care of him if he's a problem, or if Flux doesn't get him first. Me, I just need backup by folks who don't depend so much on magic to win out. Dell's good in a fight but he doesn't think dirty enough and he's got too much power in a pinch in Flux."

Morgaine stared at him again, wondering if she'd heard correctly. "It's not possible to have too much power."

"Honey," Matson sighed, "I said it before and I'll say it again: I have no power to speak of. Coydt had the most power of anybody we ever knew on World. I killed him—in Flux. Your daddy might have been number two. He's gone, too, because he found a wizard as strong as he was. Me—I'm still here. Now everybody and his sister has machines that make their power even stronger. You all just take care of the wizard stuff. Me, I'll take care of the wizards too strong for you."

"I think he lived in New Eden too long," Morgaine whispered to her mother.

"Maybe," Spirit replied, "but you haven't seen him work. He's still here."

7

SWAP MEAT

Getting out of New Eden undetected had been easy. Matson's acquiescence to Verdugo's presence on the mission had cut through much red tape and allowed for many bends in the rules. They went out only three kilometers, then made a crude cold camp. Matson wanted to be ready for anything if and when the exchange took place and they might be fair game. Spirit and Sondra had spent a great deal of time talking to Suzl, but when she asked them what the alternative was that would preserve the children and her own sense of honor, they had no real reply. It was just tough to send a loved one to the wolves without a fight.

Suzl, oddly, felt the least emotion about what was going to happen. Ever since going into Flux she'd felt curiously distant from everything, as if she were going along merely as an observer to what would happen. It disturbed her that she had so little fear and apprehension, but she could not escape the feeling of destiny in all this. She'd been a lousy student, a lazy loafer, and she'd been tossed into Flux at majority. Before that point she had refused to take any control of her destiny, and afterward she had no control over anything that followed. Ultimately, she'd been a key factor in saving World; when that was over, she'd felt her destiny fulfilled beyond any dreams of youth. Yet, now, here she was again, at the center of another equally threatening crisis, and again she had absolutely no control over it.

Not that she sought control anymore, if indeed she ever had. She had often had visions in her youth as some kind of absolute monarch, but she'd had no sense of what she would do with such power. She had often pondered that early self-image and wondered what it really had meant. In the end, the queen bee did nothing but bear children; otherwise, she was merely the center of attention and waited on hand and foot. It had struck her one day a few years back that there was precious little difference between a queen of that sort and a Fluxwife of a judge in New Eden.

She had been fat and plain, and had been raised by distant relatives who really couldn't have cared less for her but took her in because of family obligations. Until New Eden she'd always been brash, outspoken, irreverent, rebellious, always drawing attention to herself. It wasn't really until she had to raise her own brood and then the grandchildren that she saw much of herself reflected in their immaturity and needs.

Her own children were, in fact, divided and as distant as she had been. Most were grown by the time of the Invasion; those had remained in New Eden and had drifted well away from her. The younger ones had gone to Freehold to grow up, but there was a distance there, too. Only two of her kids had shown up at the inn, the parents of the kidnapped girls, and they were there not out of worry for her but out of worry for the kids. It was true that they'd cried a bit at her sacrifice, but they had never questioned it nor expected her not to make it. Somehow, even though she'd have done it anyway, the mere fact that not one of her children had urged her not to go hurt, too, and made it all the easier to make the sacrifice.

It had all been said now. She rode in silence between Spirit and Sondra to the small temporary pocket, and she tried not to think of the past. Although three had been allowed, only these two would be with her—power enough for most circumstances. Morgaine was there as well, but silent and invisible, monitoring what could be monitored and providing a security backup.

Suzl didn't know that the strings, the invisible strings, had already been attached to her through stringer devices and Flux power and matched to the rest of the group. The two women with her understood what was to come, and knew that Suzl above all others must not suspect those strings, nor when it became obvious that someone followed who that someone might be.

The pocket was easy to find if you were looking for it, and very crude. It was nothing more than stone and grass and a small pool of water. They dismounted, let the horses drink and graze, and waited. They had brought no extra horses or provisions; the children, if and when released, would be spirited back to camp on Flux wings and there reunited with their parents who would take them home along with messages and explanations from the others.

They had sat in near-silence for a while when Spirit said, "We're being observed."

The other two nodded. They were all veterans of the void and had never lost that sense of danger that saved many a life.

Suzl looked at both of them. "I don't want any tears," she told them. "I'll survive. I always do."

There was no response. About a minute later two horses and riders came into the pocket. Both riders were women; dark, well-built and muscular, and taller than average. Only their faces kept them from being striking beauties. One had a pushed-in, almost-snoutlike nose that also raised the upper lip, giving her a permanent snarl; the other had a nice face but it was totally hairless, without even eyebrows, and also had only small holes where the ears should be. Both were dressed very lightly, yet both had laser pistols in holsters on their hips. The one with the sneer held a small child in her arms which all three women saw was Dee, the youngest. They halted and looked down at the trio awaiting them, but did not dismount.

"You seem to have kept your part of the bargain," said the bald one in a cold, emotionless tone. "We are keeping ours. The child has been given a mild sedative but is otherwise perfect. She has been held in Anchor by ones who appeared to be Fluxgirls, and should not have suffered much. All three have been insulated and well-treated."

Spirit approached the one with the child and took her. The child shifted and started to suck her thumb in her sleep. The woman took the child over near Sondra and placed the little form on the grass, then turned back to the strange-looking pair.

Suzl approached, still feeling that this was distant and somehow unreal. "What now?" she asked.

The bald woman reached down to her saddle and withdrew a canteen and handed it to Suzl. "Drink this. All of it. There isn't much there. It is nothing more than a strong hypnotic. We will do no spells here, but we don't want you doing any, either."

Suzl nodded and took the canteen. She opened it, sniffed it, then hesitated a moment, turning for one last look at Sondra and Spirit. Then she drank it down. It tasted like orange liqueur, and it burned a bit going down. She could trace its progress by that mild burning all the way to her stomach. She started feeling a little dizzy, and sat down on the ground.

"While it takes full effect, we will release the second child," Baldy told them. Another rider then came in behind them holding another sleeping form. This was Missy, the middle child, older and larger than Dee, but she was also asleep. The new raider was much like the first two, but she had an eerie, animal-like face, something like a large cat complete with whiskers and a black nose. Her complexion was a yellow-orange with regular black stripes, even on her face, and she had hair that framed the face making it even less human.

She handed Missy to Spirit, who laid out the sleeping girl next to the first one.

Suzl had assumed a somewhat-rigid sitting posture and her eyes were closed, her breathing deep. With her power she could have easily eliminated or negated the hypnotic, but she had not and now it held her. She was beyond any resistance.

"Suzl, open your eyes," Baldy commanded. "You will hear only the sound of my voice, and you will obey what it says if I begin the command with your name. Anything I say not beginning the sentence with your name you will not hear. Suzl—get up and go over and mount your horse."

The woman arose and did as instructed, her eyes blank, her face a limp mask.

"We will leave you now," the bald one told them. "When it is certain that we are not being followed, we will send the third one to you. As you see, we keep our bargains, and that will be the end of it. Take the children back to your camp and get them home. From that point, we will show no mercy to you. We know that Matson and perhaps others will attempt to find us if they can, and he is known to be skilled. Both you and he should know that we hold him in no special regard, and will deal with him as we would with any other collaborator of that abomination of New Eden. You women are fools if you help them. You will either die serving New Eden's horrible ends or you will succeed and deliver World into their hands. You do not know the power of what they have. If we fail, you and all women now and in the future will be slaves forever, no matter how much Flux you may command." She turned to Suzl, sitting straight in the saddle. "Suzl—follow us closely and do not allow us to get out of your sight." And, with that, they rode off into the void, with Suzl behind.

"*Damn!* I'd love to try something right now!" Sondra swore, not particularly to Spirit. "Those—*horrors*—I just felt their—*evil.*"

Spirit nodded. "I know what you mean. New Eden is an empty and banal evil. Those dugger women have no morality, no code, no sense of right or wrong, good or evil, no matter how intellectual they want to make it."

It was nothing they could explain, nothing that came from Flux power or intuitive magic; both had just *felt* the same thing in the presence of the trio. These were the kind of people who would slit their own children's throats without regrets, without even thinking a moment on it, if it served their immediate purpose.

"A real nice choice we got," Spirit remarked acidly. "A world full of Fluxgirls or a world full of *them*. We always get such nice choices on World. I think I'd slit my own throat first before giving it to either of them."

Sondra sighed and nodded. "I hope to God it never comes to that. Or that we have the option if it does."

Spirit looked around. "I wonder what the hell Morgaine is doing? I hope she doesn't do something rash. In this element, she's no more controllable than her father was."

They heard a sound to the left of them, and turned, ready for anything. It was instead the arrival of a third sleeping form, this one Carel, the oldest. In spite of their instincts, they had heard nothing this time, and that gave them a sense of urgency.

"Let's get these kids back to camp on the double," Sondra said worriedly. "I wouldn't trust this bunch to keep their word on *anything* now that the deal's made."

Morgaine circled on great, leathery wings, keeping well back from what was below but being careful to maintain vision of everyone. She waited until she saw the three children returned, and Spirit and Sondra move them quickly back to the camp, then she turned to follow the string below, which few but she could see.

There were five raiders below, two more than the trio that had showed itself. All were strong, well-built women, yet all were deformed in some way. This was common for dugger cults, of course, and always had been, but the uniformity in their bodies and builds and the fact that they clearly had sufficient Flux power to transform themselves and thus control what they looked like was worrying. They were either that way because they wanted to be, or because some greater wizard commanded it so.

Morgaine was surprised to find them heading back to the New Eden border. She had expected them either to return to some base carved out of the void or to turn towards the great Fluxland just to the west, but they had done neither.

She could have attacked them right then and there, and felt certain she'd have no problems with them, but that wouldn't locate the main body of the raiders and certainly wouldn't locate the stolen projector. Still, she was beginning to worry that they were in fact heading back into Anchor, where they'd be harder to track, leave no strings, and where Morgaine would have to drastically alter her form to follow. This flying creature was not aerodynamic in any sense, just convenient, and it would crash her to earth quickly in an Anchor environment.

The camp was, in fact, right against the borders of New Eden and the Fluxland of Liberty, just barely in the void, but it was very large and contained the strongest shield Morgaine had ever seen. Either they had an illegal big amp down there, which was highly unlikely, or they were using the new device itself with someone of adequate power and control sitting in it.

She realized suddenly that she had everything that she needed. She knew where the raiders and the device were, and that projector couldn't be moved very far or very fast. She had to move, though, before the women below entered the shield, because it was certain that even someone of her powers couldn't break *that* one without a lot of help.

She began to throw a spell at them, one that would grow a wall around the riders below, but she had barely sent it when she saw that they had all stopped and all but Suzl was looking back and up in her direction. They saw her, knew that she was there, in spite of the fact that they shouldn't have been able to.

The spell rose from the grid floor, but did not take hold. There was a damping effect placed on it from somewhere and it was simply cancelled out, although she couldn't tell its source. Certainly it wasn't from those below, who, even with Suzl, were no match for her.

Now she was aware that lines of force were snaking through the grid below. She knew the program—diagnostics. Whoever was in command down there was very sophisticated and was trying to locate her, block by block.

For the first time in her life, she was faced with the only thing strong wizards feared: superior and more-experienced power. She had only a second, perhaps less, to decide what to do—to turn and flee into the void or to confront her attacker. She began to bank, but, unused to this sort of challenge, she banked right instead of left, right into the creeping grid survey. It had her in a moment, and she felt a sudden, near-paralyzing electric shock. Knowing she couldn't outrun it, she made for the figures below, still just watching it all, and found herself being pulled down towards them. When she reached the ground she quickly negated the flying spell and assumed again her own imposing form. It was barely in time; incredulous, she felt every one of her Flux senses go dead; power, and even the sense of power, drained out of her with incredible speed.

The duggers were unruffled and seemed slightly amused. Baldy came over to her as she stood there, suddenly helpless against anything they might do.

"We were told you might try and cause trouble," the bald dugger commented. "We were ready for you."

"You know who I am, then." It wasn't a question.

"We know. Your father spent his whole life keeping people in bondage to a corrupt religion he knew was false. Your mother serves New Eden even though it victimized her. Your grandmother went over to them for a long period and your grandfather is an egomaniac who believes he is god and emperor alike and immune from harm."

"And what the hell are you?" she retorted bravely. They had her. What did she have to lose?

"We are the children of Flux and Anchor," the bald woman responded icily. "We are your children, and your parents' children, and your grandparents' children. You don't like us? Well, we're the product your own people made. We're the inheritors of your cesspool egos and the beneficiaries of your damnable system.''

"All I see is brutality and hatred," she said firmly.

"And what in hell else did we get? We stay in Anchor and we become mindless chattel slaves. We stay in Flux and we choose between madness and becoming the toys, the playthings, of people like you. You taught us that love and honor and charity don't count. Only power counts. Well, now *we* have the power. What do you think of it?"

She stared at the dugger. "You mean the projector did this?"

"Run by one of our weakest sisters. Weak but for her hatred. It was hatred that caused New Eden, and it was fear that vanquished the Invaders. Your power may be great, but like your father's it is intellectual. There is no passion in you as there is in us. There is no passion left in New Eden, either. That was all killed off. That is why we will win."

"And do what?"

"We will eliminate all that corrupts us. We will transform humanity into what it should be. Come. You wished to go in, then come in with us. Whatever block you stand upon will be without power."

She had no choice. Refusal meant only that they'd knock her cold and take her in anyway. She walked with them to the shield, then through it.

It was one of those places that looked larger on the inside than it did on the outside. More Fluxland than pocket, it stretched out in all directions, a small city of tents populated by a host of duggers, all women, all looking in many ways quite similar to the five in the party, all deformed or defaced in some way.

In the center was a tent larger and a bit grander than the others, and in front of it was the projector itself. A woman sat on it, one covered in reptilian scales of slimy green, looking rather casual and serene. The thing itself looked like a great, blocky chair of gun-gray metal perforated with thousands of holes. Four antennae arose from the block in back of the chair depression itself, each about three meters tall.

Morgaine was still an imposing woman in fine physical shape, and she briefly considered rushing that chair. She was anticipated, of course. There were several nasty guns trained on her and other guards around. She knew she wouldn't make it.

Two guards rushed up to her and rudely pulled her arms in back of her. They were damned strong, she noted, maybe as strong as she was. The manacles were on before she could make any move to protest.

The others dismounted, and Baldy and Sneer-Face ushered them into the big tent. It was quite luxurious inside, for a tent. There was the smell of sweet perfumes and perhaps some incense, and the area was partitioned into more than one room, each wall lined with ornate silks and velvets. Inside the front "room" Morgaine was startled to see a man sitting on what could only be called a throne.

He was a big man, handsome although in late middle age, with thick white hair and a ruddy, worn complexion. If his eyes hadn't been so ice cold, he'd have looked like somebody's grandfather.

"Who's the other one?" he asked rather casually, in a low, gravelly voice.

"Morgaine, daughter of Spirit and Mervyn," Baldy responded. "She tried to take us just outside."

He nodded approvingly. "Well, well. . . . *Ayesha!* Come, my love! Your guest has arrived, bringing unexpected company!"

There was no response for a moment, but then curtains parted behind him and she stepped into the room.

Morgaine's jaw dropped a bit as she stared. She didn't know what she had expected, but this was more than anything in her imagination.

Ayesha was not just a Fluxgirl; she was rather every extreme of what that twisted vision of womanhood could mean. She was about a hundred and fifty centimeters tall, but it was difficult to judge her true height with the nearly impossible twenty-centimeter spiked heels and the billowing mane of thick, lush hair that grew upwards from her head and then flowed down her back all the way to her ankles. She had so much hair that some flowed forward over her shoulders without causing any gaps in back, and the whole looked almost like a great cape. The effect was stunning, although Morgaine couldn't help wondering how Ayesha ever sat down without pulling on it. Its color was golden rather than blond and seemed almost to sparkle in the flickering lantern lights, gently and naturally streaked with slightly darker and slightly lighter bands.

The face was naughty, not angelic; it seemed to embody every trait of sensuality and youthful merriment that was possible to imagine, topped off by deep, light green eyes that seemed almost to shine. The proportions of the body were outrageous as well, with firm breasts that must still have extended twenty-five or more centimeters out, hips that were wide but lean, not fat, and seemed to have an almost-infinite movement capability, and a waist that was so small that it seemed incredible that the top could stay connected to the bottom. She required no makeup: the lips were broad and sensual, crimson and smooth; the cheeks had just a light natural flush; the eyes were large and naturally shadowed and framed by dark pencil-thin brows and lashes that were thick and extended outward like small, fine brushes. It was clear that she could not physically stand in one position for long; the body required constant adjustments for balance, yet those moves were all in their own way adding to the sensuality.

Morgaine had never had much time for sex; she'd sublimated it to her work, as her father and the other great wizards had before her. Still, she had never before, even in Flux and New Eden, seen a creature so absolutely sexual, so totally and sensually animalistic. Ayesha was quite literally built for one thing and one thing only, and she was absolute in that.

She wore some golden jewelry and bracelets, but otherwise was clothed only in a matching golden bikini-style brief and those shoes. With a start Morgaine realized that the shoes were not merely adornment; they were a small

physical compensation for balance that allowed Ayesha to
walk at all. She was not a woman in other than the sexual
sense; she was a creature of Flux, an impossibility created
by spell, and a cartoon of male sexual fantasies in the
extreme.

Ayesha made her way over to Borg Habib, who kissed
her and put his arm around her. "We have an extra
dividend, baby," he said with amusement. "Mervyn and
Spirit's little girl. A big-shot wizard like them, too."

Ayesha smiled and looked at Morgaine, and the perfect
brows rose. "*This* is a *girl?*" she asked in mock wonder-
ment. "She looks like one of those New Eden tree cutters
to *me.*" Her voice was high but soft and sultry, an unnatu-
ral voice that was a throaty, sexy whisper. Everyone chuckled at her line.

"I'm going to see about preparations for the move,"
Habib told her. "I leave it all in your hands. You wanted
her, you got her, she's yours to play with." And, with
another kiss and squeeze, he left them.

A palatable lessening of tension was in the room at that
point, and Ayesha made her way to the throne-like chair
and lounged upon it, adjusting her hair instinctively to
make it possible. Clearly no one liked Habib; he was there
only because Ayesha needed him, and his own ego pre-
vented him from seeing just how precarious his own position was.

Ayesha looked at Suzl, whose tiny form was still standing stiffly looking straight ahead. She had not witnessed
any of the proceedings up to now, the drug still being in
full force. The strange woman nodded to Baldy.

"Suzl," the bald dugger said, "you will now be able to
see and hear Ayesha, the woman before you. Suzl, when I
say both your names together, you will no longer be
subject to me, but only to Ayesha, and you will hear and
obey all that she says as you did me. Suzl—Ayesha."

A strange look came into Ayesha's shining eyes.
"Suzl—at last we are together again. How I've *dreamed*
of this! Do you know who I am and who I was?"

"Yes," Suzl responded woodenly.

Ayesha's eyebrows rose in some surprise. "*Very* clever. But, then, you were *always* such a clever girl. For a while, I didn't understand why this had happened to me. Then I learned, and for a longer while I hated you for it. Then, I discovered, some things were better. I could think again, beyond my next fuck. I could take my old knowledge and act on it. I was made over again into someone's fantasy, but I could think and act beyond it. I am *your* fantasy girl, aren't I, Suzl?"

"Yes," the drugged woman responded. The response startled Morgaine, who, while she'd been briefed on the theory of Ayesha's origins, hadn't taken it to its logical conclusions.

"I no longer even wish to be anything but who and what I am. It was not a spell, but a—*revelation*, as it were. I had lived the other side, and the mere *thought* of how we saw things back in New Eden revolted me. I look at women and I wonder what, save one thing, any woman sees in men at all. They are ugly, dull brutes. I began to think of other ways, and, thanks to dear, *stupid* Borg, I got the means." Ayesha turned suddenly to Morgaine. "Why do you want to look like a man? If you wanted to be a man, you had the power to *make* yourself one."

The wizard, fascinated by the creature on the chair, was startled when things turned to her. "I look the way my genes commanded. If I need to look like someone different, I do, but this form serves me well."

"You *wizards!* You get so wrapped up in things you stop being *human*. Tell me—what do you think of our little group?"

"It disgusts me. I can't tell in any way that it's superior to New Eden, which also disgusts me."

Ayesha shrugged, and even that gesture was sensual and suggestive. "The girls have been raised with a vision. They are quite smart and well-skilled. Some were prisoners that we—converted—to our way of seeing things. Some were original Fluxgirls, who joined *us* rather than remain in New Eden. Most, however, are family. I can have only daughters, for which I am thankful, but I have had a *lot* of them.''

Morgaine gasped. That was why so many of them looked so similar! Her daughters—how many? Allowing for those who would still be children it was still thirty years to produce girls who'd be adults now. How many would that be? Forty?

"Regimental whores were barren," Ayesha noted, "but Suzl, *sweet* Suzl, fixed that, too. I am never totally free of my—needs—but when I am pregnant I need them less and can be free to think better, clearer. Sex is like an addictive drug to me. I *must* have it to keep from agony, and it dominates me. Pregnancy frees me somewhat from that. The products are raised to think my way and do what I can not do. We can do a lot together.''

The queen bee, Morgaine thought, unaware that she hadn't been the first to think of the analogy. Ayesha could barely walk outside; she was dependent on sex and limited even from reading and writing. She was a least-common-denominator Fluxgirl; dependent on her daughters and servants for almost everything, unable to function by herself, cook a meal, or do almost anything other than have sex—and think. She had turned her deficits into assets, and was quite possibly the most brilliant psychopath on World.

"May I ask—what you intend to do with us?"

Ayesha smiled. "We use the weapons fashioned by the enemy against them. For poor, dear, *sweet* Suzl there are other things as well. We are against New Eden for a reason, and we have some of their devices and the knowledge to use them. One we will use to prepare Suzl for her destiny. The other we will use to learn all we can about you, and then we will decide. We must move soon, impenetrable shield or not. There is no time to waste on this. Gillian—remove them to the chambers.''

The bald one smiled evilly, then took both captives out. They had been dismissed by the queen.

Henri Weiz had been a master psychologist and sociologist. He had studied the old records and the ancient histories that Coydt van Haas had assembled, and he had put those ideas into action in New Eden. Deprivation, conditioning by pain and pleasure, reward and punishment, using techniques both sophisticated and ancient. He had helped to program the Fluxgirl programs, and the fact that New Eden was still the same after disengagement was a tribute to his genius. Had he not fallen into disfavor, been court-martialed, and condemned to being a regimental whore, he would probably have run the place and it would have had no chance of defeat.

Like all converts, Weiz had been a total believer in the New Eden credo and system. He had been born in Flux, in a Fluxland where males were considered the laborers, too dull and dense for education and real authority, muscle where brain was in the woman. He had, however, a mind that would not be kept down, and he managed to teach himself to read and write by playing the clown with the girls. They never took him seriously and never realized that they were re-teaching him their lessons.

As a young teen, he'd been one of several loaned out to another Fluxland in some sort of deal as a stablehand. Although also run by a woman, this one thinking of herself as a goddess, men had more authority there and learning was not discouraged. He always had a talent for using people, making them do voluntarily whatever he wanted them to, and he used it with a vengeance and managed to remain in the other Fluxland as a favorite to a district chief when the job was done. When a small war broke out between his wizard and another, as they often did, he became a clerk to a fighting headquarters and learned still more, while meeting other men from other places that were looking for just such men as he. They had taken him to meet Coydt van Haas, the embodiment of all his dreams for what men should be like, and he had embraced van Haas enthusiastically.

He had gotten this far by an instinctive feel for shaping other people's behavior, and now he wanted to quantify it, understand it, see if it had wider uses. Van Haas encouraged him through records, assistants, experts when needed, and through animal and human experimentation, while Adam Tilghman gave him all the moral justification for everything he did.

He had transformed an Anchor into New Eden's vision without more than passing use of Flux. Coupling his ideas with Flux, he had transformed a subcontinent. But his ambition had defeated him. To become one of the leaders, to reach the top echelon of New Eden society, he needed at least one turn in combat. The very system that had fed and nurtured him had turned against him then. He'd been tried and convicted of cowardice, and sentenced to become one of his own creations.

At first she had been angry when she'd discovered that instead of being freed, she'd been made more extreme and immune to alterations in Flux, but after a while she had realized that it was not the terrible fate that it seemed. The bulk of freed Fluxgirls, thanks to the Weiz system, remained the same in spite of this liberation. Had she remained, she would have been sucked in as well. Had she left, freed as they had been, she would have been at the mercy of the big wizards who had corrupt alliances and debts to Borg. Now, this way, she was in control and immune to much of the actions against her. She had been a sex slave, and she had hated it, but she'd had no choice to be otherwise, and it had cost any vestiges of faith in the New Eden way of things.

Weiz had been a fanatical convert because he needed a vision. Now, that vision shattered, she had swung the other way. New Eden was the epitome of evil. She fell back to her origins. The woman was superior, was the natural leader. Men were the cause of World's misery, not women. As a boy, he'd always wished he'd been born female, with access to the future and the learning that his sisters had. Now a divine providence had righted this wrong. Ayesha the Whore would find alternatives to men, and with the same diabolical skills that had created the Fluxgirl, she would impose a new humanity.

New Eden had been remarkably easy to penetrate, partly because of its own weaknesses and partly because both she and Borg had known it so well. The cream of New Eden's leadership had vanished in the civil war and Invasion; the leadership now, even in high positions, had been filled, in the main, by middle-level mediocrities, many of which they had known. Patience, and the ability to change some of the girls into *apparent* Fluxgirls, had paid off. Major figures, looking for deals and corruption and things from Borg that would come from distant Fluxlands and Anchors and enhance their powers, were lured to clandestine meetings just outside the borders, where their outlooks could be changed. They didn't stop being what they were, and they were not aware that they were in any way acting for an opposition cause, but they were fully controlled from outside.

The violent raids had given the girls practice in warfare; invaluable experience no Borg Habib could build into training. They had also distanced Habib from the idea of a political movement. In a sense, the raids were less threatening if they were by brutal bandits rather than by a well-organized political and military operation. Habib himself remained blissfully ignorant of larger motives; it simply never occurred to him that while he could treat Ayesha as he wished, his daughters were not so malleable and they had power. What could be done to New Eden officials could be done to him, but he never once considered that idea. His New Eden ego saw himself as the great leader of an all-female bandit army existing for its own sake.

The Flux chambers had been developed by New Eden internal security to deal with powerful wizards, but they were used as a shortcut for all sorts of things. The ones in Logh Center operated because of a direct line to the pure Flux under the Institute. Raw Flux was required for them to work. They were basically nothing more than small cubicles with a conductive seat and floor. One was strapped in, and then a program was fed from a control center using a device based on the small hand-held amps. Initially, insufficient Flux was provided for any wizard to use it, but was driven in with maximum force. Once a "foothold" had been established with the subject, more could be

introduced to do exactly what the operator, whether wizard
or program module, wanted.

Ayesha had taught her daughters well. Both captives
were placed in the chambers just inside New Eden so that
the only Flux was that in the chambers, and then they were
probed to the depths of their souls. Suzl was compliant,
easy to access; Morgaine fought it as best she could, but
she had no Flux to work with other than the small amount
turned against her, and it was insufficient to do anything at
all. The Flux ran from the grid to the control boxes and
then inside; any counter-command, however, wasn't allowed out but was rather trapped at the box. It was insidious, and no one, no matter how powerful, could fight it.

Suzl was an open book. The dugger operator, skilled at
probing so many New Edenites and converting so many
captives to the family's way, had little trouble. Morgaine
was a different story. Little beyond the surface was really
known about her, and she fought them every step of the
way.

Still, eventually, they got a handle on her. Memories of
her as a small child, growing up fatherless in Freehold,
without the grounding or kinship to the other children,
always feeling that she was somehow different. This feeling was encouraged by her mother, who Morgaine saw as
stern, demanding, and driven. Spirit would have been
shocked by the view, although she had no way of getting
outside perspective. There was love there, certainly, between mother and daughter, but there were several barriers
that just would not give way. Nothing could conceal the
fact that Spirit had gone through with the childbirth out of
a sense of moral obligation and not because she'd wanted a
child, and nothing could conceal the fact that although
Spirit loved Morgaine, she also considered her daughter a
millstone around her neck, one keeping her from the freedom and adventure she craved.

There was also the ghost of Mervyn. He'd died before
she was born, and so she knew only the mythological
wizard: all-powerful, all-wise, devoted entirely to books
and learning. Mervyn, of course, had never really loved

anyone; Morgaine was less a product of intimacy than an intellectual wish to preserve a bit of himself and his power just in case, and it had taken extraordinary magic to get him even to that point.

Morgaine was not her father, although she'd tried to be. She could not be cold and unemotional as he had been, and she was the product of a different time and different circumstances. Nor had she any more control of herself than Suzl now had. She thought her huge size and mannish appearance and mannerisms were genetic; she really believed it. But the traits had developed as a teen, as her powers grew, and were less an inheritance than a curse. Her assigned role demanded she be independent, free of human attachments. She had made herself both imposing and unattractive to insulate her from worldly temptations, as Mervyn had taken on the *persona* of an elderly man. They were shocked to discover that she'd had only one sexual episode, that in her early twenties, and out of sheer curiosity. It had not been pleasurable but surprisingly hohum, and since then she had suppressed all sexual desires, sexual feelings, or what her father had called the "animal urges." She had become a neuter, although, deep down, where she couldn't consciously reach, it was all there, like a coiled spring, making her uncomfortable and somehow less than right.

Any human mind can be broken; any human being can be conditioned to do and say and act in any manner the conditioner wishes. The trick was that few can be permanently conditioned if any of their old selves are to be saved and used. Morgaine was useful to them if she retained her full powers and her vast knowledge of Flux. They fed her the visions, let her see what being a Fluxwife was like, let her experience the same nightmarish vision of a New Eden victory that they had fed Suzl after drugging her water, and she *was* horrified, and revolted, but they could not provide an alternative to her that she could accept. A vision of a world of femininity, of a world where men were obsolete and abolished, where the finest would be encouraged, presided over by benign queen bees, was not something she could accept, either. She could be forced to, of course, but she could never be trusted to retain that compulsion. Morgaine could be broken, but she could not be effectively and confidently turned.

For Suzl it was different, as they had known it would be. Her battling inner selves, her diminishing sense of self-worth, and above all her burdening guilt made her ripe.

Again they were brought before Ayesha, dizzy and sick and minds whirling. Suzl was no longer under any drugs, but she'd been put through quite a treatment. She seemed extremely meek and totally defeated as she stood before Ayesha, as Morgaine, still bound, was forced to watch but not comment or participate.

"Suzl," the strange, erotic woman whispered, "together we have the power to stop this evil and make a new and wonderful world. Accept the spell that we went to great trouble to procure from a willing wizard. You will be the first of the new. Liberate me and yourself, and we will own the world, my darling!"

Suzl nodded and seemed to smile slightly. She was as if in a daze, not thinking clearly, not caring anymore. She looked up at the strange woman of her own creation and shivered. She *loved* Ayesha. She needed Ayesha.

Morgaine, not in great shape herself but more independent in thought than Suzl, watched. They used a program pack in the projector, and the spell rose from the grid beneath Suzl's feet. Although cut off from sending anything, she discovered she still had the ability to *see* spells and strings if they were outside the block or blocks she intersected. She could follow the procedure in front of her. As muddled as she was, she tried to read it, and saw that it was a hybrid of spell and machine code. The machine code was unfathomable, but the wizard realized that parts of it had come from the coding that made Ayesha herself. It was a curious and not totally fathomable hybrid; whoever had made it had known her business.

Suzl stared at it and seemed to hesitate, but only for a moment. Then she took it, adding her own binding code that would make it irreversible. To those who could see the energy, it seemed as if Suzl was enveloped in a cocoon of radiant light; to those who could not, the tiny figure seemed to lose sharpness and definition, and almost fade in and out. And then it was over.

Another Ayesha now stood there, only different in the details. She was dark while Ayesha was fair; her billowing hair was a golden reddish brown with streaks of lighter colors. Her eyes were a reddish brown with that same shining quality, and her broad lips and nails were a brilliant red. Still, all the elements were there, giving the exact same effect. Instead of gold her jewelry and scant clothing and shoes were sparkling silver, but they otherwise matched. Suzl ran her hands over her body and shivered slightly. It was so tactually sensitive that every touch was pleasurable, every little breeze a caress. And yet, unlike Ayesha, she still had the power, still remembered the numbers and the system.

Ayesha smiled and stood and made her way to Suzl, facing her. The two were not quite the same size; Suzl was shorter, but by only a bit. It was Morgaine who recognized that the spell was not yet complete. She watched as Ayesha embraced Suzl and kissed her, and she watched Suzl respond in kind.

Something happened, something which the observers were not at first aware of but which Suzl found both startling and yet strangely pleasureable as well. Her tongue felt odd; she had noticed it almost from the start. Now it seemed suddenly to swell up in her mouth and become a large, rigid object that her mouth itself could not contain. Her clitoris, too, felt overly large and strange, and it seemed to push out from somewhere inside her. Both fit perfectly: one in Ayesha's mouth, the other in her vagina, even standing up. In fact, the clitoral extension was absolutely the complement to Ayesha's opening.

To Morgaine, it was total depravity, although she now understood the full extent of the spell. Suzl no longer had a tongue; instead she had, almost literally, a penis in her mouth, attached to some internal scrotum-like organ inside her. Her clitoris, too, was another, extending from almost flush out to a considerable distance and swelling as it did so. In addition, the woman still had all her original female openings and equipment. To Ayesha she would be the dominant male; to anyone else she would be the Ayesha-like Fluxgirl. As Ayesha was Suzl's fantasy, Suzl had become Ayesha's—and, in the process, made Borg Habib's days most probably numbered. Morgaine guessed that the clitoral mechanism was the Whore's vision of a future unisexual race; the rest was for herself alone.

More, the spell was clearly interdependent. Suzl needed not just any woman but specifically Ayesha; Ayesha needed Suzl. The Weiz mind had triumphed again, fusing Suzl's halves and if not giving her love at least giving her total physical gratification and an absolute commonality of interests.

When it appeared it would go on for hours, Morgaine was rudely ushered out and then fed and manacled hands and feet to a bed on a grid square made as dead as always. It was a considerable period before they came for her again, although she'd had only a fitful nap. She felt sick.

When she entered, she found two chairs now, one golden with Ayesha, one silver with the new Suzl. Both turned as the wizard was forced inside, but it was Ayesha who rose and approached her while Suzl looked slightly puzzled.

"She can not see you and doesn't know you are here," Ayesha whispered very softly to Morgaine. "It is a byproduct of the spell which we had to accept and which I find somewhat convenient. She is not, as you might imagine, very good at conversation although with practice a certain level will come. What we could not undo is that she is totally blind."

Morgaine gasped. "You bitch!"

Ayesha gave a sweet smile. "It was *not* in the instructions. It is what they call a 'bug' in the system that we could not wait to get out. It does not matter. She is my mate; she has all that I lack, including the power and the will and skill to use it. I am her eyes and her voice and she accepts that. She will give me all that a man can and more, yet she will follow my vision. You understand how it works.''

Morgaine nodded. ''Yes, I do. And is this my fate as well?''

''We could just kill you, but that would reenact that childish sense of vendetta on the part of the stringers. We could put you back in that box and make you one of us, but to do so we would have to crush your ego, your memories, your confidence. You would be just another piece of meat. Or, we could send you back, as something of an object lesson, but to do so you would have to cooperate. It is either that—or be crushed.''

''I don't think I could take what you would do to me. I see nothing there that would be better than death, which is what your crushing would mean anyway.''

''Admirable. But you know we keep our bargains even more than others.'' It was a pointed reference to the fact that it was Morgaine, not they, who had violated the exchange terms. ''What if I gave you my word on some things? What if I promised that not a single memory or attitude you now hold would be touched? That, except for your own body, which would be fixed by the spell, not even your powers would be damped?''

''What sort of monster would you make of me, then?''

''Does it matter?''

She thought about it. *Did* it really matter? Some Fluxlords were pretty monstrous as it was, too, but with the power it didn't matter as much. She would be mentally whole, and able to exact revenge and continue her studies as she had been. More, it would make revenge possible, and get the intelligence on this group to those who could use it best. Her mother and Sondra, in particular, had to be warned of what this machine could do.

''Under those terms, I *might* accept.'' After all, Suzl had endured worse, and Suzl was not the kind who could have accepted remaining a monster even at the price of becoming a Fluxgirl. She, Morgaine, could, although it would pain her mother. Still even her mother had lived a great deal of time under a severe curse, and had loved Suzl as a monster.

"Good. We are about to move. Time is wasted here by prolonging this. They will take you to the chamber and feed in the spell. The end will knock you out for a while, and we will then transport you to your own, who have continued to maintain a camp out in the void."

Morgaine stared at her. "One last thing. How does Borg take all this?"

"Borg's services are no longer required, dear, except as someone to take the blame in New Eden. You'll not be seeing him, or us, again."

They started to take the wizard away, but she said, "Wait! Will you make me blind, deaf, and dumb or something?"

"None of those, my dear. This is more—straightforward."

And, with that, her audience was over, and she was taken to the chambers. She sat inside with more than a little trepidation, but she knew that she was now in the same position Suzl had been in—without a real choice in the matter. It was better to live than to die, better to be a monster with some freedom than to be crushed into a mindless slave.

She felt the Flux fill the chamber, and then she felt the spell, but it was almost entirely in machine language. She could not get hold of it, particularly under these conditions. She did not trust Ayesha, and would cheerfully strangle the woman if she got the chance, but it *was* true that the raider leader did in fact have a perverted code of honor. Considering Suzl, she also had a perverted sense of Flux power, and that was what worried Morgaine. It was too easy, too free and clear, the price too low to satisfy Ayesha's warped sense of justice. Still, she had gotten herself into this against the advice of everyone else. She now had to pay the price, for it was her duty to report what she knew.

She took the spell, and reality slowly faded out.

*   *   *

Morgaine groaned. Her head was throbbing, and she otherwise also felt—strange. Slowly she remembered what had happened, and what she'd had to do.

"She's coming to!" said a woman's voice—Sondra's, it seemed like—and she felt some relief that she could at least understand the words. She opened her eyes and found herself lying on a blanket in the void, head on a pillowed bedroll.

"What . . . ?" she managed, and tried to get up, but the action was difficult and she fell over again, and there was a painful tug on her hair. She was suddenly quite awake, although still with a headache, and she got very, very mad. "That *bitch!*" she swore, and rolled back over. She knew exactly what she'd been given.

Her mother came running and looked down at her, a mixture of relief and disgust on her face. "Is that really *you*, Morgaine?"

"Yes, it's me. *Damn* that bitch to hell!"

"Here—lift yourself up a little if you can and I'll try and get the hair slack so you can be comfortable," Sondra suggested, and Morgaine did so. It made things a little easier, but not much.

"How the *hell* did you let them do this to you?" Spirit asked her.

"They're strong and she's smart. Smarter than even we thought, and much better organized. If they spot you—just *spot* you—they can deactivate your access to the grid from right under you. It's—*evil.*"

"You've got a sexier voice, but the old you still seems to be there underneath," Spirit noted almost clinically. "The spell is impossible to decipher, but it seems to be entirely physiological. That's *some* body, though!"

The headache was fading. "I know," she sighed. "She made me into another version of herself. Just varied her spell. I should've expected it. Can you help me up?"

Sondra's strong arm got her to her feet, but she required both women to steady her. "I want to see the damage," she told them, and Spirit made a mirror surface just in front of them.

Again, the spell had been varied, but not in the basics. What was startling to her was that she was still tall—almost as tall as she had been, about as tall as her mother and aunt, and her proportions had been scaled accordingly. The bust was enormous; the breasts alone extended out at least thirty centimeters, maybe more. Still, they didn't fully compensate for the enormous weight of the hair, particularly with the extremely fluid hip joints. She also had been given a smooth, creamy bronze complexion, big matching brown eyes, and light brown hair streaked with shimmering coppery strands. They had provided the jewelry, too—in shining copper-like bronze, of course—and a matching brief and shoes. Her body tingled at the touch of the two women; she found herself getting very turned on by that alone.

"Can you make me a chair or something and get me the shoes?" she asked them. "It may sound silly, but the shoes provide the balance."

They did, and she swept away the hair, sat on the small chair Spirit fashioned from Flux, and put on the shoes and, after a moment's thought, the briefs. Even the touch of the briefs told her why Ayesha, and also Suzl, had worn no more. Almost anything against the skin that wasn't hard or cold would produce a tingling and a turn-on.

"You came with a note," Spirit told her, and handed her a piece of paper. She unfolded it and looked at it, then muttered, "That double-dyed bitch! I'll kill her." She looked up. "Mom, I can't read that note. Just trying to makes me dizzy."

"I was afraid of that," her mother responded wearily. "She had too much respect for your powers not to insure that you wouldn't later come back and use them with others against her. I'll read it for you, if you like."

Morgaine nodded.

" 'Dear Freeholders and other parties,' " Spirit read. " 'As an example of our good faith and as a further example to any others who wish to try this, we herewith return Morgaine the Wizard to you. We allowed her to live and remain in sound mind because we wished to show you what you face if you try and hinder us. She was one of your most powerful wizards. Think of what we can do to you. We send her back this way because she refused to even consider our own position, let alone join us. Any woman who can not see our just cause is a woman in the service of New Eden. Since she chooses still to oppose us, we have remade her in their image, so that she can see just what side she is truly on. We have even tattooed her name to her rump and assigned her Suzl's old number, since Suzl no longer needs it.' It's signed, 'The New Race.' ''

Morgaine nodded. ''It sounds like them. Come on—catch me if I fall. If *she* can walk this way, then so can I.''

It *did* take some practice, and several falls, but she quickly mastered the moves necessary. It was like riding a bicycle. Difficult at first, but, once mastered, it became automatic. Still, the balance problem was never gone; she knew what she looked like, ass swaying, hair billowing, breasts moving slightly, when she walked, and she knew what effect it might have on others as well as herself. Even the brush of the thick hair against her back and rear produced a tingling, turn-on feeling.

''Well, you've certainly joined the club,'' Sondra noted. ''I have to admit I was never that—extreme—and I thought I was something impossible as a Fluxgirl, but it seems to be a curse in the family that every woman falls into one way or another. Until we can find a way out of it, you're stuck, maybe for a very long time.''

''I'm stuck, period, unless we get invaded again, and you know it,'' Morgaine responded. ''It's a machine-language binding spell, and an old one from the feel of it. Flux will continue to automatically renew it and Anchor will freeze it. It's all right. I expected worse, and while I hate it I'll learn to live with it. At least I've still got control of my own mind and direction, if I can keep from falling down. Where's Matson? It's time I filled him in.''

''Not far,'' Spirit told her. ''We decided to keep the men apart until we knew. . . .''

''I understand. Well, get him. Just him for now.''

Matson, it appeared, was quite close, and arrived in

only a couple of minutes and on foot. He stared at her. "Um *um!* And I was just trying to get used to you the *other* way."

"Enough for now. I'm turned on just looking at you and I'm not used to that. I want to tell you everything that happened, and everything I know about them, while it's still fresh in my mind. They were preparing to move out as I left."

Matson nodded. "We know. We located them, but didn't dare get close. I sent Verdugo out to keep a careful watch. He'll get back fast along my string if that bubble starts to take off."

Patiently, clearly, and sparing no detail, she told them everything she had observed and everything she had heard or surmised. It was valuable, informative, even vital information, although it was also pretty discouraging.

"You don't have that male—*thing*, do you?" Spirit asked, concerned.

"No, Mother. They wanted me to be a sex object. It's part of the way they see everybody. I won't guarantee anything in the future, though, particularly with Suzl on her side and in command of that projector."

"But you said she's blind," Matson noted. "How the hell is she gonna run that thing?"

"You don't need to see to cast spells. You don't even need numbers for the simple stuff. Remember, Grandma and Suzl blew hell out of that Invader ship by sheer emotion. I can't put spells together anymore and do all that fancy stuff, but I could still blow them to hell if I saw them. You ought to remember that there are two kinds of magic in Flux—the deliberate, mathematical kind with which we do the exacting details and play god, and the emotional, gut spell that requires no thought at all. The mathematical one is more useful, but the gut one is much stronger."

"Well, Suzl had Spirit and the Guardian feeding the math, but on the whole you're right," he agreed. "The big question is just how much self-control you have. The original Fluxgirl spell had a reversal in the way women acted and reacted. Their emotions controlled them, over-rode their wills. Suzl removed that—for Weiz, too, apparently—but that's why our crazy girl could do nothing as a whore.''

"I don't know," she told him honestly, "but I'm too mad to cry right now. I'm not putty in your hands because you're a guy, but on the other hand I'm horny as hell right now and that's something new to me. You can't imagine what it feels like."

"I can," Sondra responded. "It keeps building and getting worse, too, and there's only one cure. After you take the cure, we'll know how much real control you have."

"We'll send you back to New Pericles," Matson suggested. "You can ease your way in from there. Either there or Freehold."

She felt a rush of fear. "*No!* I'm still going with you!"

All three of them sort of sighed and gave her pitying looks. "Honey, you can't go out there like *that*," Spirit tried to tell her. "You're just not—equipped—for this sort of thing anymore."

She began to get angry again. "Yeah? So what do I do? Go over to New Eden and play whore? Go back to New Pericles where the staff will all treat me like a child and I won't be able to read a single damned book or work a single one of my damned machines? Go to Freehold and take Suzl's place? I'm not a supermommie. You seem to forget Suzl awful quick, too. You stick me, like this, in a static situation in Flux and there's nothing for me to do but screw and be a wet nurse. You know that. I'm more open than most to a new niche being created because I can't do much of anything I used to do. Can you imagine me cooking with these boobs? Or cleaning or doing chores with this balancing act? Don't you see that that bitch Ayesha *knew* it when she left me all my power? *This body is designed to do just one thing.* The only way to save my sanity, save me from myself, is by self-exile into Anchor, and the only Anchors around here are New Eden and its twins, and most of the Anchors up north are even messier.

Of course, I got to admit I'd never starve or want for anything with a body like this in Anchor.''

"*Morgaine!*" Spirit was shocked.

Matson calmly lit a cigar. "Go on," he said calmly.

"I don't know how good I can be on a horse, but I figured out walking with these things pretty fast. I've still got power and a powerful hate and anger to direct against them, and my power's also available to the others in full force if somebody else supplies the spell. These new laser guns don't weigh much, and I can shoot with one. Don't you see? This gives me a reason not to give up. I'm at less of a disadvantage than Ayesha, and look what *she's* managed. And, this spell has one advantage. It's permanent. The worst thing they can do to me is kill my power, and I know how theirs operates. I'm actually at less risk than you all are."

Matson nodded. "And after?"

"What do you mean?"

"After it's done."

"Ayesha has an official scenario of what New Eden plans for everybody and she immersed me in it. They're still the most probable winners, and, if so, I'll be better off than most of the rest of you. If Ayesha wins, I'll probably wind up being a queen bee someplace. Both are likely. If, by some miracle, we manage to beat them both, then I'll find some Anchor someplace and go from there."

"Don't be so defeatist, honey. There's always a way. Nothing's ever permanent here. Both Sondra and I were as locked in forever as you are and we got out of it."

"Mother! Stop! I will live the way I have to live and do what I have to do. If a miracle comes, I'll take it, but I'm not going to live my life depending on it. It's over. I can't be Little Miss Mervyn any more. I'm your daughter, too, and you always worked with what you had."

The response disturbed Spirit, but she had no response. In point of fact, she did not understand it, and still couldn't face the fact that it wasn't Morgaine's future, but her vision of Morgaine, that was being affected.

For Morgaine, it felt good to get it out, and she sat back

a moment and reflected. It was *crazy*, but the fact was that she felt less horrified at her new condition than somehow—relieved. The pressure was off. Now she couldn't be what her mother forced her to be, and couldn't suppress herself if she wanted to. She felt, oddly, free of Mervyn's ghost. It wasn't under ideal circumstances and conditions, but it was there none the less. She felt oddly—kittenish, like a young girl again. Uninhibited. By god, if she was stuck with this body, she was going to *use* it and *enjoy* it. Ayesha had gone far with this combination. The hell with her mother.

"Well?" she asked. "Do I come along or not?"

Matson looked at his two daughters. He saw disapproval in Spirit's face and Sondra gave him a fatalistic shrug. He didn't answer, but went over to Spirit and took her aside, hand on her shoulder.

"Father, you *can't* let her come along!"

"Why not? Can you answer any of her arguments? Can you give me one good reason why not?"

"She'll still be at the mercy of everything out there! She's not used to the feelings that body gives her, or being out there at the mercy of stronger wizards."

"She's helpless and dead if she stays. Out there, she might lose, she might become a permanent victim, but she's got a chance to find herself. I think you forgot something, Daughter. Forgot a bunch of things. Forgot for one thing that she's almost forty-seven years old. She's no baby, and she's better off in some ways than your momma or Suzl or even you were. I think somewhere along the line you forgot the scared girl who couldn't use a single tool or artifact, couldn't wear clothes or understand more than simple sign language, but saw wonder in a blade of grass or a patch of sky and took control of herself in spite of all those handicaps. Just because your mother didn't raise you, you were bound and determined to not just raise but control your own, even though you'd rather have pulled out. I'm being blunt 'cause I have to be. If she winds up the biggest damned Fluxgirl whore, then that's the way it is. But she's got to find her own way." He paused a moment. "I knew bringing Verdugo along would be useful for something."

Spirit went from anger at his words to shock at the comment. "You don't mean that—*viper!* And Morgaine?"

"As her grandpa I wouldn't feel right doin' it, even though there's no true genetic connection now, but I tell you that she turns me on a bit just to look at her. Dell might succumb, but only if we're not around. She said it clearly: That body's only designed for one thing. Just one. She might be O.K. otherwise, but not unless it gets it regular. If not Verdugo, or Dell, she'll be driven to go off and find it. It'll eat her alive unless she does. Cut her loose, Daughter. If you do, I think we might use her."

He walked back to Morgaine. "You can come," he told her, "if you can figure how to stay up on a horse. We got no way to fool with wagons or carts."

Morgaine jumped up and kissed him. "I'll get it if it kills me!" she told him.

Dell had been prepared for a Fluxgirl, but not for someone who looked and acted like Morgaine. He couldn't take his eyes off her, and the feeling was more than mutual. She asked him to work with her on the horse, and after gestures and withering glances from Matson, they went off together.

In the end, they determined that she would probably never be able to mount one without assistance. Although she did manage to ride on a conventional saddle, Dell created one out of Flux that was more a sidesaddle with a back support which would work the best for long, slow treks in the void.

After a while, though, she could no longer see Dell as an individual, only as an object. She found herself caressing a saddlehorn and feeling herself all over. She radiated an overpowering sexuality that simply could not be denied, by her or by any object she chose, augmented by Flux itself. He could not resist her even if he tried, which he didn't very hard. With some surprise she realized that no man in Flux could resist her if she desired him. Ayesha's beliefs simply didn't permit any woman to be totally defenseless. *She*, not the man, was in control, and always would be, and it was *wonderful*. Only the fact that Flux so thoroughly damped out sound beyond a few meters kept her shrieks of sheer pleasure from reaching the others.

When they rode back, both of them had dreamy smiles on their faces and looked more than satisfied, but Morgaine had the most reason other than sheerly physical to be joyful. She needed fear no man in Flux, and she knew it.

Verdugo had already arrived back when they returned, and the look he gave her was impossible to describe. She smiled sweetly at him and as much as said with gestures that he'd get his turn. She saw, however, that her mother was gone.

"The bubble is gone from the border," Matson told her. "They're on the move—and they moved right back into New Eden, would you believe? Cut the damned string before we could follow it. It'll form again when they come out, but we have to find it first. That's what Spirit's doing now, the easy way. If you're set and sure you can ride, I intend to move in to the border apron, then west until we intersect Spirit or the string."

"I'm ready," she told him. "You seem sure they're going west and even more sure they're gonna come out at all. They have lots of friends and cronies in New Eden."

"They'll come out," Sondra responded before Matson could. "All their friends won't save them if they get cornered in Anchor. East is pretty well covered, and there's mostly hostile Fluxland through it. They want to disappear, not be seen by someone and reported in. To the west there's a war and Fluxlands they've dealt with in the past. They'll come out."

Matson sighed. "It's gonna be a long, long trip, ladies and gentlemen. I suggest we saddle up and get moving. Won't do us any good if we wind up days behind them."

Dell brought Morgaine a cold sandwich and a wine flask. She found that she was in fact very hungry and very thirsty, and wondered if that would be the pattern. After eating she felt tired, but she forced herself back on the horse. She wasn't going to fail right at the start.

"Help me out for a while," she whispered to Dell as he helped her up and made sure she was firmly seated. "If I nod out either wake me up or take my lead."

"Don't worry," he responded with a wink. "I'm not going to lose *you*." No, sir. This trip was beginning to have real possibilities.

Matson took the point, lit a cigar, and stared out into the void.

"Now it begins," he muttered to himself.

8

FLUXWAR

When New Eden's master program was loosed, most people remained where and as they were, but there were some, particularly among the older ones who had been in Flux when it became Anchor and had been trapped into the program, who took the opportunity to flee. Some went far, but Liberty had been formed out of an alliance of those who had remained close-by. It was both curious and unpleasant at one and the same time.

The countryside was nice; the dry plains of New Eden just to the south were at the mercy of conventional wind and weather; here, though, all was green and lush, with rich-looking soil and thick clumps of trees. There were, however, well-concealed fortifications in those trees and in the river valley ready to pounce on an invader and hold them until wizard's Flux could polish them off.

Liberty had been founded by refugees from its big neighbor to the south, and it remained totally paranoid that New Eden would someday come to reclaim them. Because of this, a paramilitary state was the rule in Liberty; it was a land where literally everyone was in the military, male and female, young and old. The combined effort of eight powerful wizards working together, all of whom had also been trapped in the New Eden program, it was almost as large as two Anchors. The mega-Fluxlands, however, had their price other than a shared vision by the Fluxlords: they were too large for any mind to cover. In the small ones, even ones the size of Freehold, the Fluxlords knew when you entered and knew what was going on at all times, but here it was almost like Anchor—almost.

Now, with all attention focused to the northwest and the war with a similar mega-Fluxland, things weren't always dependable in the south. You would be riding toward hills all day, but they would occasionally shimmer and change shape, or become less distinct. Roads and forests were equally undependable as the mind maintaining the area was preoccupied with other things. All the big Fluxlands were inherently unstable because they were compromises, but this had gotten a lot worse. It took a wizard, who could sense the throbbing grid beneath, to stay oriented.

It was three days before Spirit returned, somewhat apologetically, to tell them that the raiders had crossed once again into Flux and had turned sharply north. She had spent some time finding them, because the raiders had moved slower than Matson anticipated and they had overshot the mark. They laid out an angular course to catch up, although it meant going overland.

"I caught a look at them as a bird over New Eden," she told Matson. "Ugly bunch of women, I must say."

"How many?" he asked her.

"I'd say about a hundred, give or take five or ten." She described the organization she'd seen, and it became clear that basically good military sense had been used in planning it: five companies of roughly twenty each, with three in scouting and combat roles, one handling support and also the younger ones, and one apparently just to serve the leadership and guard the projector.

"I hadn't expected the whole bunch of children," she admitted. "All girls, most of them pretty normal looking for any group that size. They all pitch in to help with support, but there are some really young ones that make up almost a nursery. They move with five wagons, three with mule teams, and the rest on horseback. I guess Ayesha and Suzl move in one of the wagons; I didn't catch sight of either of them, although I saw the projector in one. Just a glimpse. It's uglier than they are.''

Matson nodded. "You, Sondra, and Dell will have to alternate reconnaissance near them. *Don't get close!* If you can see 'em, that's enough. Remember what happened to Morgaine. I can afford her, but not two or three of her, and I've had to face Sondra like that before.''

Spirit was silent a moment, then asked, "How's she been doing?" She knew why Matson had sent her and not one of the others out on this duty, and she'd accepted it. Morgaine needed a little time to find herself.

"Pretty good. She hasn't discriminated between the two men, and she's got both of them, even Verdugo, eating out of her hand and fetching and carrying. Her body cycle seems to be to wake up, eat and drink a little something, then she's O.K. for several hours. Finally it builds, she has to have it, gets it, comes back, eats heavily, then dozes. As long as she gives the body what it needs, she's in perfect control. I hate to tell you this, but I think she's enjoying it.''

"Yeah. You really think I blew it with her, don't you?''

"Daughter, there's a tendency of mothers to require that they have a ton or two of guilt inside no matter what. You did your best and that's all anybody can ask. Now let her be what she can.''

For Major Verdugo, Morgaine was like nothing he had ever dreamed of. In New Eden, a tall woman was a head or more shorter than Morgaine, and even the most voluptuous of them didn't look and move like she did, nor make love like she did. What bothered him was that Morgaine was no servile Fluxgirl, no "yes, sir" type— she was, in fact, not deferential at all, nor was she uneducated. As much as he wanted her, she frightened him as almost nothing in his life had. She was a Fluxgirl *in charge*, and it was a scary combination. She had an incredible body, incredible looks, and also brains, will, and self-confidence. Spirit and Sondra were different; they were wizards in their element, which was not his element, and he respected that, particularly with their very mean looking father around. Morgaine was something else. She was the stuff of all his sexual fantasies, but she was also equally the stuff of New Eden nightmares.

He couldn't help but think of a New Eden filled with Morgaines, one in which the girls, like queens on thrones, reclined on silk beds while male drones waited on them and carried out their orders. In that scenario, it was the men who became mere objects, slaves to superior creatures who held the keys to extreme pleasure and which men would need more than they would need men. He had never felt inferior before; he never thought it was possible for him to feel so. Relative power he understood, but this was something else. One Morgaine he could accept, and he was out to destroy the only other one, but he could see in her the stuff of Ayesha's dreams and every nightmare he could imagine. God had placed man on top because women had the beauty and the charms and all the physical things the human body could wish. Without being the ruler, a man was no more than muscles and a prick. Men needed to be in charge because, if they weren't, they'd be—inferior. Maybe even irrelevant.

If anything, Morgaine made him more resolved to push for an ultimate, and permanent, New Eden victory. Then they could make a number of Morgaines, but with the correct mental attitudes and attributes. One day he would put Morgaine in a Flux chamber, remove her memories and her power, and rebuild her inside as God would intend. A Morgaine for whom he would be the center of her world and the whole reason for her existence.

For Suzl it had been a strange time, but not really a bad time. Her mental state was perhaps not the best, but it was her own and not something imposed upon her, of that she was certain. She still retained her powers and her skills, and could check and control such things.

The moment she had accepted Ayesha's spell, she knew somehow that it was *right*, that there was some sort of compensating force in life that weighed and adjusted you. The more people whose lives your actions had affected, the more compensation, or justice, was applied.

She accepted the blindness as unintentional, and had even examined as much of the spell as she could make out to confirm that fact. Clearly there was something in the way the oral sexual mechanism was constructed that had eliminated something necessary for sight. Her world was total darkness, compounded by the sensual but not very practical body she now had. Still, it was essentially a body that she herself had designed, one intended to give pure pleasure but involving compromises, and it worked perfectly.

She hardly noticed the organ in her mouth anymore, but while it was a source of great pleasure it also made speaking a garbled mess, like trying to talk with your tongue rolled up. It was, in fact, a primary organ which could be used to impregnate the other women, while the lower one was specifically tailored to Ayesha's internal anatomy. Still, it was the lack of being able to effectively communicate that bothered her. She could not talk, and Ayesha could not read. Clearly, other than the sensual aspects of it, this was another factor in its being there at all. Ayesha could not be certain if Suzl would dominate, but it was difficult to give orders under such circumstances.

Sitting in and working on the projector, however, gave her an opportunity to try other means. She loved the thing, for within it she could see the grid with her mind and make out the electrical shapes of what was around her. The lorry had not proved reliable, and now the projector was transported by wagon and unloaded when needed or when they camped. Direct contact with the ground was essential, although she had begun to wonder if it wasn't an unobstructed path rather than physical contact that was required. The only way to find out was to try and lift it.

There were always several of the daughters around with arms ready when she was in the chair, and it amused her rather than disturbed her that they didn't trust her. Even though many of them could use it, it would have been a simple matter for her to have negated anything they might do with the speed of thought. Even without the machine, her power was more than equal to the entire rest of the group. She decided, however, to let them have their little reassurances. Better to earn their trust than demand it.

The third day back in Flux she decided to try and lift it. There was no such thing as a true antigravity spell, but she suspected that it could be supported with known forces. Opposite magnetic polarities managed to lift it almost a meter, but there was no way to get forward motion with it. If they were ever to do anything with it, they would have to find a way to keep it directly on all the time. As it was, while they were in motion three or four strong wizards combined might well break the shield.

She did not solve the forward motion problem, but by hitching horses to it and progressively magnetizing the grid squares it became surprisingly easy to both move and keep powered up. The skill was in stopping it, which involved progressive demagnetization and was very tricky. No one was sure how fragile it might be, and nobody could send out for spare parts.

The family had a fair number of high-technology devices, and she turned next to them. Her sight was now in the realm of forces, but it was still more than adequate when she had the projector. Among the things they had were small hand-held communicators which worked at some distance if only on line of sight. By vibrating its speaker elements, she was able to fashion some sort of voice, although not a very natural sounding one. It was tinny and mechanical and lacked much resonance or emotion, but it was *something*. Once she learned how to do it, and had practiced with it, it would have been no trouble keeping one with her, but she decided to use it only when she had real need of something or was on the projector. Ayesha did not like it.

Still, it allowed some communication with her head keeper, Ayesha's oldest and favorite daughter, Gillian, whom they had all thought of as Baldy. Gillian did not trust Suzl, but she was nonetheless fascinated by her.

"You now have a voice. What will you do with it?"

Suzl sent a laugh but it sounded horrid on the speaker. "Talk to you. Learn a little, perhaps teach a little."

"You have accepted your—situation—amazingly well," Gillian noted, which of course was partial grounds for her suspicions.

"I accept the fact that it is us or them. I have been a part of them and I prefer us. I was breaking apart back there. Now I am whole again."

"You are blind and dumb, and a captive of your body."

"I am not dumb, for we are speaking, are we not? As for being blind—it is untrue. From here I can see the whole grid if I wish. I have a different vision, but in some ways a grander one. As for this body, it is designed for extreme pleasure. I have no need of other attributes, and I can feel and experience this body far more than you do yours. I only wish that somehow I could also experience penetration as a woman. Ayesha fears that if I give this male attribute to anyone else it will somehow threaten her. I am patient. Eventually, it will come."

"I am still puzzled, I admit," Gillian noted. "You say you will transform the whole of World, yet this would mean your own past family and friends as well. Do you think, when the time comes, you will be able to do it?"

"It will not depend on me alone, I hope. However, yes. It is us or them, as I said. They offer slavery to my daughters and hardship to my sons. World has always been dominated by and torn apart by sexual roles. I see that now. There will be sex, of course, but no sexes. The form will be female, the pleasure of each available to all, and the responsibility, too. The race will be free to turn together to other things, nicer things. I think it is a wonderful thing, and I have an extreme version of that form now."

"It doesn't bother you that the men will turn this way?"

"It is about time lately that the men turned into something."

"Could you do it now, with us?"

"I could—but we are aiming at permanency. No one will be able to change it. Flux will still have its spells and its magic, but not to change people into other forms. For the moment, you must retain that ability. Now, will you answer me a few things?"

"Yes. If I can."

"When I saw you in the pocket, you all looked very dugger. You have sufficient power to change that. Why don't you?"

"Each of us is committed to this to the death. Each of us takes upon herself a mark to distinguish herself from all the others. It is the way we choose to do things, that's all. If we succeed, we will accept our new permanent forms with joy and abandon these."

It didn't make a lot of sense to Suzl, and she suspected that some of it might have to do with Ayesha not wishing unmarked beauty other than herself around her, but it didn't bother her. She could not see them as they were; they were all the same to her.

"My other question is, How are we supposed to succeed? It is a grand vision, but New Eden will have more of these built and tested, many more. We do not have much time."

"We head north, to an area in the great northern gap, where help awaits. There, experts who share our vision will be able to study and evaluate this unit and, perhaps, manage to duplicate it in Flux. That is our goal. Some of them worked on one of the northern ships and came very close, but always failed. This may be the difference, tell them the one thing they missed that New Eden did not. Up there we will be secure enough that we might well afford to translate the projector and send it to the computers for analysis. We can not afford to do this now, because when it was tried with one of the Invader ships it produced no results. There were things inside that simply were outside the computers' abilities to understand. Now New Eden has built one on their principles, but out of our materials, by human hands.''

Suzl nodded. It was a good plan, and it just might work. ''I worry about just who these people might be, though. They might only pretend to the vision for a chance to steal the machine.''

''You, we hope, can insure their good faith,'' replied Gillian.

She began to wonder about that, and made it a project to find out just how far she herself could go.

As for herself, she was being honest with Gillian. It was a crazy situation, but after years of being dead she felt alive again, whole and with a purpose in her life. She had come, essentially, not caring if she lived or died and expecting massive revenge. Instead, she found the price worth it.

Ayesha was, unquestionably, crazy, but considering what sort of background and situations she'd been through it was only to be expected. Yet in spite of the fact that she claimed to have buried Weiz in her mind, there was a lot of the original left—a surprising amount, in fact. When she'd been married to him she'd considered him a manipulator with a lot of ambition but she hadn't really taken him seriously. Now, with a clear mind, Suzl was able to view the strange personality with perspective.

There was no question that Ayesha trusted her, far more than the rest of them did, and Suzl appreciated that. During the domestic part of her day, Suzl was totally dependent on Ayesha and the attendants. On the move, setting up and tearing down all the time, there was no way for a blind person to get oriented, so she was essentially led around on a leash. Ayesha liked personal contact; there was a considerable amount of just feeling and nuzzling, even just sitting and eating or listening to Ayesha's wild fantasies and dreams. Suzl, in fact, enjoyed it; the part of her that craved some permanence and dependency was well-fed by it, and both of them had voracious sexual appetites that only each other could really fill.

And yet, Suzl was far from helpless. She was in the

void, a full wizard, and what she'd forgotten or let lapse from lack of practice seemed to quickly come back as if it had never left. She was unpolished; she'd be no match for a powerful Fluxlord or scholarly wizard with centuries of training and research, but she was damned powerful in her own right. If she wished, she could transform this camp into a Fluxland and all its people into anything she wanted, even without the projector. In the end, she was really in charge at all times.

The projector made that power nearly absolute. It was not an amplifier; it was, however, a device for taking what you had and focusing it anywhere. Its range was far greater than she'd suspected, so it was an extension of her mind and inner eye, and it allowed you to do tricks that you really couldn't do without it, such as literally cut someone off from access to Flux power. The human mind just couldn't fine-tune that well, whereas the projector mapped it all out for you, in little numbered squares, and allowed, essentially, magic by the numbers.

She had co-opted the leadership. All these people were hers now, and she was absolute, as absolute as she wanted to be. And, the beauty of it was, with her not-very-mobile body, her animal needs, and her blindness, not a single one of them—perhaps not even Ayesha—really knew it.

They had been traveling in Flux for four days, keeping well behind the raiders but always watching them. Suzl's string stood out bright and clear and made it easy to track them, and the last thing any of them wanted was for their quarry to know that they were even being tracked.

There were, however, disturbing signs.

"The shield's now on all the time," Sondra reported. "Somehow they've worked out a way of moving that thing while it's still turned on."

"Suzl can't sit up there all the time," Morgaine noted. "Is there a difference in its quality from time to time?" She felt frustrated that she couldn't get up there and see for herself.

Sondra nodded. "Some, but it's pretty solid no matter

what. There have been a couple of times when it weakens and even flickers for a second, so you can almost see inside, but they're very short."

Matson thought a moment. "The changing of the guard. It's the first flaw in their system. Not a big opening, but it's something."

They all looked at him.

"The only wizard they have who could maintain a permanent shield of any substance without that projector is Suzl, and Ayesha made Suzl sort of like herself. It takes a certain measure of concentration to maintain an effective shield. In a military operation, we set up a number of strong wizards at different points around it so the wizard maintaining it has to think of many threats at once. Then you make a random thrust with what power you have in one area and the shield's pushed back and forces can advance. While the wizard is repairing the damage at that point and coping with the invaders, you do it again somewhere else. The result is that the shield contracts."

"That's elementary," Sondra noted. "What's that have to do with this?"

Matson sighed. "Suzl is a first-rate wizard, but she's also in a body that's a creature of her passions. Morgaine, I'm going to make your mother uncomfortable but you're our best source on this. When you're screwing, could you ever with your old control maintain a shield?"

Morgaine's face brightened, and her mouth opened in surprise. "No! I don't believe I could! Your mind just lets go and everything goes into one single purpose."

"Uh huh. And Suzl and Ayesha are the same way, only because they're literally made for each other, they go at it for hours on end, I bet."

"You don't think too clearly for a time after, either," Morgaine noted, seeing the implications. She was in a unique position to see both sides of it. "That means that for at least one, maybe two, guard shifts, it's only one of them maintaining the shield with no help available from Suzl." She stopped a moment. "But one of them was more than able to keep a shield too strong for me, so what's the point?''

"The point is, the shield changes. We have to determine Suzl's shift, and work around it. The odds are she goes out first, clear-headed and in control. After she's off, she'll be with Ayesha, and then the cycle will start. Give it two hours. The next guard change after that won't have Suzl available at all.''

Verdugo, who knew a little more about the device than anyone else, nodded. "The big thing is that the projector increases power by making you able to focus on specific locations. The odds are they couldn't maintain any kind of real shield without it—barring Suzl, of course. For the few seconds it takes for one of the raiders to get off and the other to get on, the shield is effectively down.''

Matson nodded. "Now, don't get your hopes too high. Even if we could get in, it would still mean we'd have to fight our way to the middle where the thing is. We'd have known locations, and somebody would then be on the projector. We'd be dead ducks before we got ten meters. This crowd will die rather than surrender and won't hesitate to kill their own to get us.''

It was a big letdown, and he realized it.

"Now, don't get it wrong," he told them. "It's our first break, and it's something. We know now we can solve entry, at least with a small force, if we can manage to get close enough. One step at a time. This may take quite a while to put together completely. The fact is, now I think for the first time we can solve it and do it. Let's press on.''

They had been observed off and on for some time by local military units and farmers working in the fields, but because they were certain that their presence had been reported and they had been checked out ahead it didn't worry them. Still, as they moved north, traffic increased and they were clearly progressing into a defensive zone—which meant the backside of a Fluxland shield. To proceed now, they would need permission from the Fluxlords of Liberty, and that meant going into town and making direct contact. The raiders, too, had been forced to halt. They might well be able to break through, but they would have been pinned down fighting against the combined forces of wizards for whom they'd have no fixed location. Matson sent Rondell ahead because he wouldn't be known to likely raiders in town, but he soon returned.

"They want to see all of us," he told them, "and I don't like it. I don't like these people very much, and I don't trust them at all."

Matson frowned and stroked his chin, thinking about it. "Any sign of our friends there? They'd stand out sure as we would."

"No, but that only makes me more uneasy. If they beat us to it, they may have made a deal. They'd have lost less than half a day if they turned and went into the void here, avoiding all this mess. This is a pretty convenient way to filter out anybody chasing them, and they can come out almost anyplace. We couldn't cover the whole area, particularly in a war zone."

"It does stink a bit," Matson agreed, "but it's no sweet time for Ayesha's crew, either. You figure the Fluxlords of Liberty know pretty well what they're toting along and want it just as much as we do. Five strong Fluxlords in their own element could probably crack that shield, and probably the only thing stopping them is that they don't want the projector damaged. They're taking a big risk; I say we should, too. Let's go in."

There were some doubts and much tension among the group, but they all went along with it, although they had their weapons at the ready and the three full wizards were attuned to any changes in Flux power.

The town was called simply B-21, and it looked like a military fort, with a high wall and sentries patrolling all over the place. It was spartan, not fancy, and was only clearly a town at all when you entered the gates. There were no sexual divisions here; men and women manned the sentry posts, and all wore black leather uniforms with insignia of rank and position. Those with Flux power were the officers, and wore shoulder braid to show that they were higher up. It was impossible to figure out what rank was what, though.

Morgaine, however, stopped the routine, as men and women turned and gaped at her, open-mouthed, some with rather odd and suggestive looks on their faces. Morgaine reveled in the attention and smiled at some of them, causing near-pandemonium.

"It's promising," Matson said casually. "They never saw the like of Morgaine before. Think about it."

The others got the message. If these people had never seen someone like Morgaine, then they hadn't seen Suzl or Ayesha, either. They pulled up to a large building in the center of town and Verdugo assisted Morgaine down. Dell nodded to the door and said, "This is it."

The inside was filled with bored clerks and crowded desks, but Morgaine' entry produced the usual gaping, unbelieving stares. Spirit grew angry, although she wasn't sure whether it was at the reaction to her daughter or the fact that her daughter was clearly enjoying herself.

"We're here to see Colonel Parsha," Dell announced generally, but it produced no real reaction.

Morgaine smiled wickedly. "Can someone show us to the colonel's office?" she asked sweetly. In an instant, about a dozen people rushed to do just that.

Colonel Parsha proved to be an older, white-haired man with a stiff military demeanor even Morgaine couldn't ruffle. The wizards could sense that he possessed considerable Flux power and was not a man to be trifled with.

"Why do you all want to pass into the war zone?" he asked them, but clearly, no matter how much he tried to cover it, his eyes kept roving back to Morgaine, who was sitting in a very suggestive way and staring at him, batting her big brown eyes innocently.

Matson saw no reason to make up a cover story, but only as much truth as was necessary would be given. "We're searching for a band of raiders who kidnapped one of our kin," he told the colonel. "We lost them for a while but discovered that they had bounced up against the shield near here same as us."

The colonel nodded. "I'm aware of them. Some of my people have been out to talk with them. Colonel Habib has done many favors for Liberty over the years, and he's not considered a threat to us. You, on the other hand, have enough wizard power here to threaten the master spells. We've been fighting a bloody stalemate with the lords of Hoghland. Like Colonel Habib, we are no friends of New Eden, and you have a major and a young lady obviously from there in your party."

"I'm *not* from New Eden!" Morgaine responded. "If you're half the wizard you seem to be, you can see I'm not in the Fluxgirl mold."

It was clear from the colonel's demeanor that he fervently hoped that whatever mold she came from hadn't been broken, but he maintained control.

"I can see you have great power but you're under a binding spell," he noted. "You made yourself that way."

"I was *forced* to!" she shot back haughtily.

"Let's not mince words, Colonel," Matson interjected. "That woman is this lady's daughter and my granddaughter. She was a powerful wizard, one of the strongest, yet they snared her and forced her into this. They can do the same to any of us. They're from New Pericles, I'm from Guildhall, and my grandson here is this other lady's son and they're both from Freehold. The major's just along for the ride. We're far less threat to anything here than the Habib group, and I think you know it."

When the colonel avoided a reply, Morgaine stood up. "Colonel, I'm sure we can work this all out. Maybe just you and me going into your office there and—*discussing* things a little less formally. I'm *sure* we can come to some agreement."

Spirit had a sharp intake of breath. "*Morgaine!*" she whispered.

The colonel, however, could count. They were inside his fort, inside his town, and they wanted something from him. "I would be delighted to discuss opening relations with you, madam," he responded.

Morgaine looked at them. "Be back in a while. Amuse yourself. *Take a good look around*," she suggested.

Matson cleared his throat and got up. "Yes, I think that would be a very good idea. We'll be back in a little while."

"Don't hurry," she breathed, and walked into the inner office, followed by the colonel, who could hardly keep his pants up.

They walked back out, conscious of the mass of moving feet beyond the door as clerks tried to get back into position to seem as if they'd always been there, and then out onto the street.

"Why did you let her *do* that?" Spirit asked her father angrily. Sondra had a more amused expression.

"She knows what she's doing," the old stringer responded. "By the time she's through with him we'll not only have what we want, we'll have everything on the raiders, the war, and the secret keys to the Fluxlords' castles. She's right about us, too. This place smells funny for a Fluxland town, even a Liberty one. Morgaine stopped the show for a while but you can feel the tension here. Pretty far from the war to be so tight."

"I know, I know," Spirit sighed. "It's just that she seems so damned *eager*."

"I don't know how, but I swear there's some Suzl in her," her grandfather noted.

It was Verdugo looking around the place who finally put his finger on it. "The place is too empty," he told them. "Yeah, it's far from the front but it's a key area all the same. What you said about Flux wars, Matson—that you hit them from as many sides as you can. That makes this place vital, even if it isn't being hit now. It should have a full brigade, at least, with strong wizards at the lead. All that's here are some clerks, old guys, and support personnel. Where's the army a place this size supports?"

Sondra nodded. "He's got it. And that *feel* we noticed. It's the kind of tension you find in support troops when they've sent their own forces into battle and can't do anything but sweat it out until the outcome is known."

There was the sound of a woman shrieking from the headquarters building. Spirit looked disgusted. "If only she wasn't so damned *loud*," she muttered.

Matson hadn't even noticed, his head sunk deep in thought. Suddenly his fist slammed into the palm of his other hand. "*Damn!* We have to get out of here, folks, even if it's breaking up a romance, and the sooner the better!"

They all looked at him expectantly.

"Don't you see? Their forces are matched to a combined Flux-wizard and conventional attack! The damned fools have gone in to get that projector! That's why we're being stalled here—to keep us out of the way!"

"Yeah, that makes sense," Sondra responded, "but what's the rush?"

"They don't know what that thing can do to wizards. Once they take on this army—well, if they win, they'll need to silence the whole damned area before one of Liberty's Fluxlords turns his or her attention this way."

"It's only the combined power of two in the raider group," Dell noted. "They might just take it."

"No, I think not. There won't be more than about that power coming at them, since they had to leave the colonel here in case the enemy used it to attack. That projector effectively doubles their power, so they can negate one or maybe all of the Liberty forces. Sondra, you've got military training. Fly out there and check on it. We're leaving, moving southeast out of range, as soon as we can. Join us there."

"But if I do that it'll create a surge that might attract the Fluxlords' attention!"

"All the better if it does. *Then* we might end a big part of it right here. Now—*go!*" There was a flash of light, and Sondra became a great flying beast and soared off into the heavens and away from them.

Matson sent Dell and Verdugo to get the horses ready, and he and Spirit headed back for the headquarters. They had barely gotten to the front door when Morgaine opened it and almost knocked Matson down. He caught her, then had to steady her, because except for her jewelry she was stark-naked and shoeless as well. She was also almost out of breath, but she gasped, "Those idiots—are taking on—Ayesha! We got to—get out of—here!"

"Ahead of you," Matson assured her, and he and Spirit assisted her down as the two men arrived with the horses, which had, fortunately, only been quartered and not bedded down and so still had their bridles, saddles, and packs.

As Spirit used the supernatural strength that Flux could provide to get her daughter up on her horse and then jumped on her own, the whole headquarters building seemed to erupt with people, including a dazed-looking colonel who wore only the top of his uniform—nothing below.

As they sped off, the colonel threw a complex spell in their direction, but Spirit and Dell were both ready for that and it fizzled out before getting to them. The yells and commotion, however, caused the guards to turn inward, and guns to be brought to bear on the fleeing group. They did not try to outshoot them; as Spirit kept the colonel in check, Dell cast a spell at the guards and their guns would not fire. A few shots did whistle by them from points Dell hadn't seen, but none hit the mark and, in the excitement, nobody had thought to close the gates.

A squad was sent after them, but it was several minutes behind, there being no real combat personnel on duty, and the colonel either could not or would not come with them. It was simple to use spells and simple geography to confound them and watch them ride right by, chasing phantoms.

"We'll wait it out here," Matson told them. "It's roughly where I told Sondra to look and it's out of the range of interest, if not out of range, of that thing of theirs."

Spirit looked at Morgaine, who was still breathless and shaken. "What the hell happened to *you?*" her mother snapped.

"He was—well, he was my equal in power. He wasn't bad for a dirty old man, but he wasn't much on long-term screwing."

"I don't mean *that!*"

"I'm getting there. *Whoo!* Can't get my breath! Anyway, he started saying he'd finally found the girl for him after two hundred years, and I was telling him I wasn't exclusive, and he started bragging about what he was going to do when his troops got the projector. He had big plans, I'll tell you, and they didn't include his current Fluxlord masters. Well, when I heard *that*, I figured I'd better get out of there, but he got real lusty and power-mad all of a sudden and shoved me back down. I got mad, picked up the first thing I could get my hands on, which was one of his boots, and let him have it. He staggered, and I didn't wait around to get dressed. The office crew was so shocked by me and hesitant about the colonel that they just froze there, thank heaven. You know the rest.''

Spirit sighed. ''Well, if that program that's got you is a stock one, I guess we can replace what little you lost, but I hope you learned something by this. What if he'd been a *stronger* wizard than you, amplified by passion or lust? Nobody can change what you are but they can sure add to it!''

Morgaine gave a sassy grin. ''You would have rescued me. Nobody has power like a mother whose kid is in trouble. Besides, I might not count real well but I sure knew how many wizards *they* had and what kind of power *we* had. That's why I knew we had to get out of there. Anybody who's a wizard colonel and can't count as good as me can't possibly beat Ayesha and Suzl!''

Matson sighed. ''I'm afraid you're right,'' he said, ''but I sure as hell wish I knew right now what was going on over there.''

There was no absolutely safe zone Sondra could use and still see what was going on, but she kept as distant as possible. There was simply no way of knowing exactly what was going to happen, and she didn't want to be caught in the same sort of trap as Morgaine had been.

Clearly the initial assault had taken the raiders completely by surprise. Although they should have expected that all hands would now be against them, clearly they still had some learning to do. Even so, the wizard who would ultimately be at the controls of that projector had taken on the *Samish* and won; five hundred troops, only three of whom had any appreciable Flux power, didn't seem so daunting. Conventional wisdom still favored the attackers; they had more power and five times the force to follow it in. Convention, however, was not what this was all about.

The Liberty officers had divided themselves into three roughly equal groups and began the shield assault from three points simultaneously. It was classic military; classic, of course, because it almost always worked.

For a while, it appeared, it *had* worked. The shield was clearly weak in places, and a strong bulge had been made in one side nearest the Fluxland interior. The raiders had fallen back behind the collapsing wall, rather than take on what was clearly a far superior and seasoned force.

Sondra saw that a second push inward was being made from the opposite side, also with some effect. The shield was small, perhaps two thousand meters in all, and such movement was clearly noticeable. She began to wonder if they had caught everyone napping, or Suzl and Ayesha in one of their obvious liaisons, because so far there was no real resistance at all and the shield really couldn't hold much longer.

Suddenly a tongue of Flux flowed from the shield through the grid through the first attacking force, ignoring it, going clearly for the wizard who was pushing in—and finding him. To wizard eyes, the square on which he was mounted on a gray horse simply went dead.

At that moment, raiders on foot poured from a sudden drop in the shield, weapons blazing. The advancing Liberty troopers had gotten so used to being safe that they were not prepared for it, and a large number were cut down without a chance. Their wizard officer tried to move out from the dead area and help his troops, but the blank spot followed him no matter where he went.

Reinforcements were called in from another of the triad, and the wizard there took the pressure off in order to reinforce his comrade. That was a mistake, for it allowed the operator of the projector, presumably Suzl, to follow his line of force back to his position and it, too, went dead.

Confused, and unable to comprehend what had never happened before, the third wizard, a tall and stately woman and an obvious veteran of Flux wars, took the pressure entirely off the shield to ride around and see just what the hell was going on. That was a mistake. The shield snapped back on full as Suzl instituted a search pattern for the third wizard. In the meantime, the raiders, with their share of power, were able to form small walls of Flux for cover while the mass of troops, now getting organized once again and taking a small toll on the defenders, were completely unprotected and in the open. Their sergeants knew when to retire, and began pulling back just as the search pattern from the projector found the third wizard and neutralized her.

The raiders were still far outnumbered, and the attackers' conventional firepower was nothing to be sneezed at, but Sondra did expect the defenders to maintain a deadly skirmish line to insure the attackers' withdrawal and then make a quick move, as soon as they felt secure, to the northeast and back into the void. She sympathized with the forces of Liberty below; trapped in a militaristic society, made to fight in a deadly war their own greedy Fluxlords had started but whose blood was theirs, even their wizard officers really slaves to their Fluxlord masters, they had all seen a way out and tried to take it. It just wasn't that easy.

Suzl, however, did not do the obvious or the expected. Faced with a retreating force, its wizard power totally negated, she expanded the shield, weakening it somewhat as she did so, and swallowed the attacking army, wizards and all.

Sondra wasn't sure what they were going to do next, but she got the hell out of there and fast.

9

A BRUSH WITH
SOME FLUXLORDS

"In the old days," Matson told them, "there weren't very many wars. Once in a while, though, one of these Fluxlords would start believing his own dreams and attack another, usually a neighbor, just to show he was really a god. Can you imagine folks being forced to go to war because one Fluxlord says another Fluxlord is blasphemous for not worshipping *him?* Now it's gotten more political, and nastier."

They were still in the trees, and had been for hours, even though Sondra was back with her report.

"I never heard that Liberty's Fluxlords were that way," Spirit noted. "Then why the big war at all?"

"Size. Sheer size. You pull what Suzl pulled in a standard Fluxland and it's a fight to the finish. This thing's too big for the lords. I'm half surprised these trees are still here. Hell, even their shields are a hundred kilometers in from their borders. You don't hold down this kind of place by Flux supremacy. You have to be a politician. Control the common folk another way. A war's always a good rallying cry for the folks, so long as you win it and so long as it doesn't drag out forever. That's the problem here. They bit off more than they can chew and things are getting lax. The kind of revolt those officers mounted here would be impossible in a one-Fluxlord Fluxland.''

Dell sighed. ''What do you think they're *doing* in that shield?''

''I figure they know they can't get to the void before a Fluxlord comes. Might be one here now. Without their officers, though, all those troops are at the mercy of the immediate Fluxlord, which is Suzl. They're hers now: All transformed and all still ready to fight. The three officers won't do much better. They don't dare leave—the Fluxlords would make them wish they were dead. They can't really escape. My feeling is they'll wind up getting the treatment voluntarily, same as Morgaine, to save their necks, only they won't be any Ayesha doubles. Counting the family as one, they have five wizards now. That's not bad. Five wizards and the projector and a few hundred total converts. It'd take three or four of Libery's five Fluxlords to beat 'em, and they can't spare that many; they'd be punched through and smashed to hell up north. They'll make a deal. Move out with the traitors to the void unmolested or maybe they'll punch through this shield and *really* cause havoc.''

Spirit started to say something, then stopped, looking behind them. Nearby, Morgaine was showing an awestruck Verdugo that she could move her enormous breasts by voluntary muscle action. Spirit was not amused. ''I don't know what I can do,'' she sighed. ''Dad—can you talk to her?''

''I'll try,'' he said, standing up and stretching, ''but I think this is her party.''

He did, however, walk over to her and sit, dismissing a very-turned-on and disappointed New Eden major. ''I think we should talk,'' he said softly.

She sighed. ''Mother again, right?''

''Partly. I got to admit I can't decide what's spell and what's not, myself.''

"Dad—you were sixteen once, right?"

"Yeah. A long time ago."

"Well, *I* never was. I wasn't even allowed to be a kid. I was the daughter of Spirit and Mervyn and my destiny was too vital for mere play. I watched everybody else have fun, throw caution to the winds, but not me. *I* wasn't allowed. Undignified. Childish. Kids are supposed to be childish. Well, I didn't ask for this—I took my responsibilities seriously—but I got it. This program I got is an ancient one—back to the start. It's filed under the name *Kitten*. I don't want to even think of what that implies, but here I am. Forty years of studying and suffering and never having any real fun, and here I am—stuck. This body's designed to be a combination whore and baby factory. There is absolutely nothing else it's good for. The Fluxgirls were clearly based on this program, but they were also toned down a lot so they could do other things. Cook, clean, shop, sew, plant seed, milk cows, work a farm—all that. I couldn't even run a nursery school—couldn't run after the kids or keep 'em in line, let alone teach them much. It's a body designed for somebody with an I.Q. of forty."

"Well. . . ."

"And don't give me that bullshit about nothing's permanent. I know how niches form."

"But this isn't your niche," he noted.

"It is now. Even now, I can't even remember how it *felt* to be otherwise and look how short a time it's been. This thing's designed to create an immediate niche. The only trouble is, my I.Q. is a *lot* higher than I can use. The only thing I can get out of this is that I have an excuse finally to be a kid. To be little or sixteen or whatever. I don't know if it's the program or me or a little of both, but, yeah, I want my full powers back. I want all my basic skills back, too, that are blocked up here in some kind of short circuit. Yet—I'll tell you, even if I got 'em back, I'm not sure I could give up being like this otherwise."

He sighed. "Well, I guess I don't have any glib answers to that. I think your mom knows that, too. It's just hard for her to remember her own self back then. Give it time for it all to come into balance. It might not be the best balance, but it'll be a balance.''

She smiled and leaned over and gave him a kiss, then settled back. "I have one nice use for this, though. I'm a pretty good spy.''

"Well, we broke even on that one.''

"Uh uh. The major. He's into female bondage and all that sort of stuff. I've gone along and been real servile and sweet and a little dumb when it was called for, and he lets stuff drop. Dad, he figures New Eden can have a whole bunch of projectors up and running before Suzl even gets where she's going. They started production *before* the tests. He's along so they'll have her exact location when the time's right.''

Matson didn't reply immediately to that, just sat there stroking his chin. Finally, he got up and said, "Maybe it's time the major took his turn at taking the point.''

She stared at him. "*Really?* Uh—Granddad?''

"Yeah?''

"You were out in the void for forty years or more with almost no power. Didn't you *ever* get hooked by spells?''

"Between you and me?''

"Promise.''

"Dozens of 'em. Some really wild, too.''

"Then how . . .?''

"Never had a one that the Guild wizards couldn't figure how to undo.''

"But some of them must have been for long times. How did you keep from going crazy?''

He grinned. "I hate to give you this secret, but it's the only one that works. The trick is not to mind. To do your best with what you have. You're doing O.K. You got a brain and you're using it. Sondra was once in a fix that was worse than what you have now; she couldn't suppress her body's desires and she did all right, too. You can whimper and get into self-pity and give up, or you can do your best with what you got.'' He paused a moment, thinking. "You think you're up to more-active work in this?"

"What do you have in mind?"

"I'll tell you when the time comes."

Ayesha was feeling pretty full of herself. "Oh, it was *masterful*, darling! *Masterful!*"

Suzl, too, was feeling pretty good. *Not bad for a little blind sex maniac*, she decided. She was very quickly moving into complete control of the group, and control of Ayesha as well. There was no longer any doubt of her by Gillian and the rest, who were following her orders and seeking her advice, and Ayesha, almost without realizing it, had become increasingly more submissive to her as she'd become far more aggressive. Soon, Suzl decided, she'd have a small radio device with her at all times.

The campaign against Liberty had been a near thing, although she basked in the glory of success and was hardly going to tell them the truth. She'd been sloppy in letting them sneak up on her, and slow to isolate and cut off the opposing wizards. It would not happen again.

She was beginning to get a number of ideas about the structure of the group, and for its future. The captives, more than three hundred and fifty of them, were her prototypes for the New Human—tall, strong, quick, and muscular, but with all the attributes that Suzl saw as feminine and good. They were also the first of the bisexual prototypes, based on the part of the program that covered her below the waist. She did not ask any permission for this, and if Ayesha had any doubts about it she didn't voice them. For Suzl, it would be an experimental model of the new society. Soon she intended to insist that everyone in the camp take on the new form.

The three wizards were a different story. Facing a fate worse than death if they returned, and knowing they'd be hunted down even if allowed to flee, they were quite compliant. They were strong, although no match for her, and used to being at the whim of a Fluxlord. She ran a partial Kitten program on them, making them like Ayesha but retaining their mathematical skills and mental faculties, and in addition mentally binding them to the group and its ideals. Suzl had decided that this should be the form for all wizards above the common level. It would create a two-class structure, but one that was simply recognizing the ultimate reality of World: those with the power had an edge and would always be on top. She renamed them Beth, Cissy, and Debby, after three early daughters now swallowed up in New Eden, and made them accept the idea that they were her wives, as was Ayesha, although Ayesha would always be first.

Ayesha had not minded, although the new "wives" were clearly secondary and subject to her authority as well. Any jealousy she might have felt was outweighed by the idea of a dynasty of Fluxlords in which she would be part, although she had no real Flux power of her own.

Curiously, any lingering doubts she'd had about this whole operation had vanished. She knew that her way was not what most, including her old friends and loved ones, would like, but it not only seemed to offer a solution to the basic problems that plagued World but it was also the only decent alternative to New Eden's dream.

All the activity had drawn Rajan, Fluxlord of South Liberty, to them, and he was not a wizard who could be trifled with. Gillian met with him, wearing a two-way radio so that Suzl could follow the proceedings and perhaps offer suggestions as needed, although the bald woman was making a very quick adjustment from barbarian to prime minister.

Ayesha clung to Suzl, caressing and kissing her, as they listened to the proceedings. Feeling flushed with power, she had wanted to take in Rajan as well, but Suzl refused. Using the projector to get the measure of the Fluxlord, she had discovered that Rajan was probably not even nearby. Gillian was dealing with a double: someone who not only was made to look and sound and act exactly as the Fluxlord, but who in fact was nothing more than a puppet through which the Fluxlord, by spell, could act. Fluxlords who survived were no dummies.

"We want no problems here," Rajan said. "We have enough in the north. What we require are the return of the traitors to us, and then you and your group may have safe passage to the void."

Gillian wasn't buying. "They attacked us and lost," she pointed out. "That makes them ours. They belong to us, by ancient traditions of Flux. They have paid for their actions, I assure you. Now we no longer request passage through the shield, but will move within a day out into the void."

"Unacceptable," Rajan responded. "We must have our own back."

"We have always been a friend of Liberty, and wish to remain so unless you act against us. Let it go, Lord Rajan. Let it pass and be history. We will not give them back, because they are ours by right."

"Four of us could still break you all," the Fluxlord warned menacingly. "We need only extend the shield and deal with you at our leisure."

"Lord Rajan, I will be blunt. You have five Hoghland wizards pressing you on three sides up north. To break us, you would leave only one of your own to defend against them. You would have us, but would lose Liberty and perhaps never recover your advantage. Further negotiation is pointless. Take us and lose your war, or let us go. We will be moving at dawn tomorrow. Let your actions, or inactions, be your decision. I hope it will be as wise as the other decisions you have made."

Suzl nodded and Ayesha beamed with pride. "Is she not *wonderful?* My first and my favorite. *You* are my Fluxlord, my love. You are greater than all of them."

It was hard for Suzl to argue with that idea. The fact was, the true power of a Fluxlord was becoming intoxicating to her although she'd never even considered it before. The fact that she was handicapped and physically limited seemed almost to enhance the feelings. She had always revelled in being odd, or different, back in the old days, and that had come back strong. She was blind, and needed a device to speak intelligibly, yet her word was law. She could not even move about unassisted; the body was unbalanced enough for the sighted, nearly impossible for her. In the tent, she got around some on hands and knees, but she didn't want to appear in public like that. There were two differences, though, between the past and now, and they were big ones.

No matter how odd she was physically, she had been far more of a freak in the past. Then, too, she'd been a victim, one at the mercy of events. Now, for the first time, she was in command, she was in control, and none of *her* people thought her strange or handicapped. She liked it a lot, and if physical limits were the price, she was willing to pay it.

Now they came to carry her out to her throne, the projector seat, and there, within their radios, they would hear what she had to say.

"We have done a great thing here," she told them, "and we have learned a great deal. We have great power now, and an armed force to back it up. We know, though, that all of World is currently our enemy, lusting after what we have. We can trust no one and no power potentially stronger than we are. Therefore, we are going into the void until we find a place to the north which is distanced from any major enemies, and then we will run no more. We will recruit who we need as best we can, but from then on we will defend our own ground. Those who would help us must come to us. We do not have time to waste with more travel and battle. Now we must move as quickly as we can until we find our place. Prepare to go!"

"They're moving into the void," Spirit reported. "The shield is strong but has a different quality. I would say their new wizards are maintaining it, allowing them to transport the projector without the need to keep it on all the time."

Matson frowned. "Could the three of you break that shield?"

"Probably not," she replied honestly. "We're about even, I'd say. But we'd have to get close to have a real crack at it, and we certainly couldn't break it, even with help, before they could deploy the projector.''

He nodded, thinking. "All right. When we get to the void, I'm going to plug in and send some messages. I need to know what's happening elsewhere if I can. Other than that, we'll continue to follow them. I only wish I knew how much time we have—how far along New Eden is. I'm just wondering if Verdugo could be turned.''

"He's so ugly inside I'm not sure. Maybe turning him into another Morgaine and dangling his precious manhood back in front of him would do it. Sondra and I have been itching to cast a spell on him.''

"Uh uh. Not yet. I need his reactions. He knows the New Eden timetable and he's a reliable judge of what our situation is. Morgaine's keeping a good eye on him right now.'' He sighed. "O.K., let's pack up and get ready to *move!*''

For many days Ayesha's raiders went north by northeast at a very brisk thirty-five kilometers a day—brisk, considering the number of people and the amounts of equipment being moved and the weight of the projector itself. Small parties were dispatched from time to time by the raiders to scout ahead, and particularly to drop in on the smaller, one-wizard Fluxlands along the way. About a third of the new converts had been infantry and needed horses, which could not be materialized out of Flux like the food and water they consumed. Larger Fluxlands were avoided, to keep from any repetition of the Liberty incident. The small party following also tried to avoid any habitable areas, if only to keep from either running into the enemy or betraying their existence. Still, they crisscrossed many stringer routes, and met packtrains and stringer couriers from time to time.

The couriers coming from the region of New Eden told of massive border fortifications being built all along the frontier, and large troop movements to those areas. Regions in the industrial heartland had been closed to all outsiders under threat of death, and even the area near the capital around the Gate had been sealed off. There were lots of rumors, but it appeared that things were going to be that way for the long term and nobody had any real specifics.

Twenty days out, the raiders swung sharply to the northwest, an action which caught the pursuers by surprise and which now headed the raiders towards some small independent Fluxlands close in to the cluster of Anchors around Gate Three. They bypassed two, this time without even a courtesy call, but halted just short of a third.

Matson sat atop his horse, studied his maps, and frowned. "It's an odd place for them to stop," he said, puzzled. "They're only a few days from Anchor Gorgh, one of the few relatively stable Anchors around these days, and that Fluxland over there is called Garden on the charts with a note that it is not to be a stringer stop."

"What's that signify?" Verdugo asked. "They don't trade?"

"They don't do much of anything, if memory serves," he replied. "The Fluxlord there got hold of some of the old religious books and became convinced that he was the Lord God come to purify the good in people. Both the old Moslem and my old ancestral Catholic Church have the same story. The one about the origin of man without sin in a perpetual garden. Ten to one that's what we got up there."

Only Verdugo, whose own new religion was partly based on a rather odd reading of parts of the old texts, knew the story. "You mean there's an old guy in there who thinks he's God walking around a beautiful garden inhabited by a bunch of naked worshippers?"

"Seems like. Nice and peaceful, though. They don't go out and just about nobody goes in. I can't think of what they'd have that these people would want."

"Five hundred Eves trying to get the rest to take the fall with them," Verdugo muttered.

"Dad, how many people you figure are in there?" Sondra asked.

He shrugged. "Hard to say. That size place—could be a thousand, maybe a couple of thousand or even more. Depends."

"There's been a lot of activity behind the shield," she noted. "You think maybe they're looking for more converts? A bigger army?"

He scratched his chin and considered it. "Could be. They'd be damned near defenseless. You saw the border of the place, Spirit. How strong would you say the old boy was?"

"Pretty good. As good as I've seen, from the size and strength of it."

"Could they break it?"

"Oh, sure—but it wouldn't be any picnic. They'd have to have fully punched through before the Fluxlord could even be located, and if he's as crazy as you say he'll be in a rage that'll multiply his powers. Still, yeah. There's no way he could hold them, even without the projector."

"But why do it?" Morgaine wondered aloud. "Why them and why *here*?"

"I don't know," Matson responded. "They haven't been following the script much since Liberty, but something's afoot. They have five wizards, but they amount to three strong ones. Only Suzl has real world-class power, and she's more intuitive than trained."

"She looked pretty damned trained in Liberty," Sondra shot back.

"Uh uh. That's not what I mean. The question is, Do we watch? Do we try and warn them? Or do we try and help the old boy whether he wants it or not?"

"Oh. I see." Sondra thought about it. "If they lose here it'd be a crushing blow to their morale. They might even be vulnerable to an all-out assault by us, or by us with a little help. But with that projector, and multiple wizards, the odds are it'll be a draw but that at least one of us will get hit or taken."

Matson looked around. "Anybody else?"

"I say we ought to go down and at least try and warn him," Morgaine replied strongly. "If he won't take a warning or help, then he fails. If he will, we have a moral duty to assist. You know what those people are like."

"O.K. So we play it by ear. I don't want everybody from our side down there, so who goes?"

"I'll go," Morgaine said. "From what you say it looks like a place where I won't even be noticed."

"Then I will go, too," added Verdugo. "I must admit I am curious about this place, and Morgaine will need an assist here and there. I have been getting lazy and indolent so far."

Spirit glared at him. "There should be one full wizard along in control of her powers and able to talk to this character. I could go alone."

"Uh uh," Matson responded. "I agree that you should go, but the other two should go as well. Morgaine may put them more at ease, and I really think the major, here, ought to see one of the quirkier Fluxlands. O.K., you three go, and we three remain between you and the raiders. Don't commit us, and if they attack before you can get back out, use your own judgment. If that happens and we don't see you scooting out as the shield folds, we'll hit them from the rear. Got it?"

They did. Verdugo had mixed feelings about having Spirit along. On the one hand, she would be in the way of any extra opportunities that might come along, but on the other hand, as much as it galled him to depend on any woman for protection, a crazy Fluxlord was not somebody you could dismiss as a threat.

They had made a wide circle to come in on the border of Garden well beyond the sight of the raider camp. Now, as they approached the shield, Spirit halted them.

"Normal Fluxlands only use shields when they're attacked," she noted, "or at war, like Liberty. This one seems to be more like New Pericles, though—permanent. It's porous, though, and selective."

"What's that mean in real words?" Verdugo asked her.

"It means that you can get in without having to knock," Morgaine explained, "but not everybody can get in, and if you enter you agree to abide by the master spells in effect inside."

Verdugo shrugged, got down off his horse, walked up to the shield and tried it. It seemed as hard as a rock to him. "So now what?" he asked.

"When Morgaine says you agree to the spell, she's talking as a wizard," Spirit explained. "In effect, you have to go native or you don't get in, and if you violate any of the rules the spell will enforce them. It's pretty standard."

"So what do we have to do?" he asked.

"Stark-naked and with no artifacts," Spirit responded. "Take it from an expert. What's the matter, Major? Afraid to display your body in public? Your girls do it all the time."

"It is immodest and against our ways," Verdugo snapped, obviously disturbed. "Such displays can evoke immoral behavior."

"By the women, you mean. Well, go ahead, Major. I'm not modest and I think I can restrain myself."

He did it, grumbling all the way. He didn't, in fact, have a bad body at all. Nobody, male or female, in New Eden had a bad body anymore. He was slim, muscular, somewhat hairier than expected, and *very* well endowed, facts that Morgaine already knew. Still, he seemed somewhat let down when neither woman fell into a passionate frenzy. Spirit, he found, had one hell of a body as well, although when she flexed her muscles it was somewhat bizarre.

"This is an active spell," Spirit warned them, "so it'll have some effect on us at all times. It'll try and make us conform. You'll have to be constantly on guard mentally to ward off being taken over. It's not deliberate, just the way it's set up. Most Fluxlands don't have this with visitors because it's very complex to set up, so this guy's really good."

Not even the horses were allowed in, and Spirit had to actually use a spell to remove some of Morgaine's jewelry. She needed some assistance making it to the shield, but all three passed right through and she found the going better. She had discovered back in Liberty that she could run on tiptoe for short distances, and only needed some support, something to hold onto, when standing still.

In fact, when passing through the shield, which became like a fine mist to them, a curious feeling of peace and contentment settled upon them; all worries and stresses seemed to fade, and it took some doing to keep one's mind on the matter at hand. The place was truly a garden, stretching out as far as the eye could see: thick green foliage, small streams and babbling brooks, here a grove of wonderful flowers, there a near-musical waterfall.

All around, scattered here and there, were trees offering bountiful, ripe fruit, and in the ground, when you wanted, all you did was pull to get raw vegetables. There were animals, too, and birds, and buzzing insects, but you *knew* somehow that none of them would harm you and you had no desire to hurt them, either.

There were no trails, and apparently none could really be made in this dense beauty, and the further they went into the forest garden the less of a sense of direction they had. Spirit and Morgaine, at least, could use their sensitivity to the grid below to find their way out if necessary, but neither wished to leave right now.

They heard the sound of people laughing, and made for it, coming upon a small lake fed by a waterfall at one end. A number of human beings were swimming or wading in the waters, playing like children and splashing around. As they drew closer, they saw that all the men were tall, extremely handsome, very muscular, with long, light-blond hair to the shoulders and neatly trimmed full-blond beards. They were incredibly sexy, both female visitors thought, but they looked exactly alike.

The women were shorter by a head than the men, had nearly perfect female proportions, and beautiful, innocent faces framed by hair as blond as the men's but going down below the shoulders. They, too, were lean, tan, and somehow *just right*, but they also all looked exactly alike.

The group took little notice of the three newcomers, even though they looked so different and out of place here. One woman was nearest them, lying on the grass and letting the warmth of a bright, overhead heat and light source dry her. They approached her, and she looked at them with big blue eyes. They *all* had blue eyes.

"Hello," Spirit greeted the woman, trying to sound friendly. "What's your name?"

The woman laughed a nice, pleasant laugh like music in the wind. "Eve, of course. All women are Eve just as all men are Adam."

That was startling. "How do you tell each other apart, then?"

She stared blankly at the stranger. "Why would you want to?"

That got Spirit good. The frame of reference of these people was so different that there was no way to keep going along those lines. Best to change the subject.

"We are visitors from beyond the Garden," Spirit told her. "We are here to speak with your Lord."

"Then why not speak?" the Eve responded. "He is everywhere in the Garden always. He is as near as your thoughts. Pray to Him and He will answer."

Verdugo, who up to this point had been ogling the Eves—all of them—and trying not to get turned on while doing so, was jerked back to reality. He liked the Garden, but he was uncomfortable with this enforced blasphemy.

Spirit shrugged. *Why not?* she asked herself, although she didn't really know how to pray. Religion was much too far in her past and much too false in her experience to matter much. She closed her eyes and said, aloud, "Lord, hear us. We come in peace and friendship, for the forces of Hell are marching upon you and we wish to offer our aid and support for your good works." *There. That ought to be sweet enough for the old boy!*

The line of Flux arose so quickly and forcefully it took them all by surprise. *"I know of your purpose here, and of Hell without. I know all. I am the beginning and the end."* The force enveloped her. He was powerful—incredibly powerful—and she found herself locked in a mental combat with him that she was hard-pressed to maintain.

"Why do you fight with me?" she managed to yell at him. "We are not your enemy!"

"I do not fight with you, it is you who fight with me," the self-styled God of the Garden responded. *"I am the Creator of the Universe! You must be purified in my garden!"*

With a start, Spirit realized that she was not grappling with just one Fluxlord, but with more. How many more she couldn't quite determine, but it was why she couldn't get a focus on any one of them. A multiple Fluxlord that thought and acted as one. . . . Now she realized why the maps warned of this place, and the mistake they'd made in coming in. The visitors had been allowed to get well in, where physical escape was virtually impossible. She was strong, very strong, but there were *three* of them, she saw now, and together they were far stronger. Despite her best efforts, parts of the spells being forced at her began to get through. She felt herself changing, becoming physically a twin of the bright-eyed Eve still sitting there, smiling sweetly and watching it happen.

My name is Spirit, daughter of Cass and Matson. . . . My name is Spirit, daughter of Cass and Matson. . . . My name is Eve, daughter of Cass and. . . .

The assault on the other two had been as sudden and as strong, showing just what power was here. For Verdugo, it was over before he realized it, and he became another childlike Adam, having no defenses to even slow it. Morgaine, however, was a different story. Spirit was so strong that they could not also take on Morgaine, being content to merely freeze her into inaction. Were she her old self she could have easily broken it and taught these old farts a lesson, but, as it was, she could only use the time to think things out.

For Spirit, the battle was finally over. Physically, she had been made over into the exact image of the blond, blue-eyed women nearby; mentally, all memory had been blocked, all frames of reference lifted. She was Eve, daughter of God. There was no place but the Garden, which was all. She was without sin, or concept of sin, and right and wrong had no meaning. Terms and concepts which had no meaning were automatically purged from her memory, so there was no confusion. Gone was all curiosity, all desire for anything but a total acceptance of what was. There was no past, no future, no time at all except here and now for all eternity. She rejoiced in the beauty of perfection, and gave thanks to God who made her and all of it to enjoy forever. She desired no existence but this. All else had been blocked off, gone as if erased, for it was irrelevant.

Now it was Morgaine's turn, and she knew they were in for a shock. She could only wonder what the effect on them would be. Hers was not reality or some sorcerous spell, but a true binding spell, a complex machine-language program bound to a code she had created but did not know herself. If these Fluxlords really were so insane they really believed they were God, and it looked as if they did, then they would believe in their own omnipotence and absolute power. The spell had been so strong and effective, even on Spirit, because it was a stock spell. They would run it again on Morgaine, making the physical part the first part, and it would have no effect. They might be able to take over her mind, but there was a possibility they'd never get that far. In any event, they were about to be faced with something new.

Morgaine sat on the grass and waited for it. She felt sorry for Spirit, but she knew that all such spells in Flux were transitory types, as her grandfather had noted. Except for binding spells, which this certainly was not, anything done could be undone by somebody just as smart as the one who did it.

The attack on Morgaine began, and she instinctively and automatically resisted it, although her command of her power was far less than it would have been. The physical transformation spell slowly crept in, though, and tried to take hold . . . and would not. The force stalled, then tried it again, and again, and again, all to no avail. The spell seemed almost desperate now, but increasingly erratic. The crazed minds behind it were being faced with a logic loop that, according to their own lights, simply could not happen.

Thunder boomed, and lightning crashed, and clouds above swirled about the little lake, as the Fluxlords of the garden tried to understand what was happening. The attacks ceased, and she had some freedom of action. She'd been afraid for a moment that one would make the sacrifice and take upon himself her binding spell, but then she realized that it probably couldn't happen. They were collectively, not individually, stronger than she.

Suddenly a great booming male voice came from the heavens. *"Go!"* it ordered. *"You are too much of sin and evil to remain here! You are beyond redemption!"*

"If you're truly all-powerful, the one true God, then make me look like Eve and I will leave! I won't even resist that much!" she almost taunted. "I will *not* leave without my mother and my companion!"

"You dare *try to bargain with* me? *I can sweep you out! I can crush you like a bug!"*

She hadn't thought of *that* angle. Still, she had no choice but to persist.

"We came to offer our help without any hope of reward or any conditions because we believed you were just and good!" she shouted at them over the roar. "You repaid an act of kindness with an attack. You're not God! You can't even change my form! You are a demon of Hell, evil masquerading as good, madness as perfection! If you had any good, any decency, in you, you would at least accept that and let us all leave as we came! I *want* to leave! A God without love and compassion is no God at all, but the rankest of evil ones!"

She wondered as she said it if she'd gone too far, if there was nothing left of the people these Fluxlords once had been. Then, suddenly, everything—the wind, the thunder, the swirling clouds—suddenly ceased. It was a nice, bright, warm day again. The Adams and the Eves came out from the forests, sang praises to God, and began to play once more.

Morgaine didn't know what happened, but she looked

around and saw neither her mother nor Verdugo. They had wandered off somewhere. She felt some despair at that realization. They were probably over there with the group, but how to tell them apart? Verdugo was probably lost, but wizards could usually tell other wizards because they always had some contact with Flux through the grid. Not here, though. Spirit no longer knew she was a wizard, or what a wizard was, and so had no connection with anything save physical reality and the master spell of the garden.

Had Morgaine had her full mathematical abilities, she could have run a seek program for Spirit; the master computers would always keep track of such things. She couldn't even finish counting the number of Eves in and around the lake without getting confused, though. Sondra or Dell could do it, but they'd be attacked if they entered, too. Never had she felt so frustrated, and tears welled up inside of her and then came out in a flood.

"Please!" she choked through the tears. "Please give me back my mother!"

There was no response, and for a moment she was afraid she'd blown their divine fuse.

"Morgaine?"

She whirled around, hoping against hope to see her mother, but instead she saw another blond, blue-eyed Eve. Or—was it? She wiped away the tears and got hold of herself. "How do you know my name?"

"It's me, honey. Your mother."

Her mouth dropped in surprise. "They—restored you?"

"They—made a compromise. A compromise between their reality and ours. They said your plight and your tears had touched them, and they had been stung by your words. They had beaten me. I couldn't fight them, even restored. They offered me a deal—for your sake. I had to take it. They said that if the daughter was bound by evil, then the mother must be bound by good. I'd been—purified, is the word they used."

Morgaine sighed. "I guess overconfidence runs in the family. Your powers?"

"Intact. At least I have that. But I had to accept remaining in Eve, for one thing. It's not a bad body."

"It's *gorgeous!* But everybody's wearing it these days."

"Look who's talking. I also had to accept certain—other things."

That disturbed Morgaine. "Like what?"

"They called it protection against the evils of the outside world. A shell of purity, I think they said. I know I can't lie, cheat, steal, or kill, not even a fly, or use my power in any way but to further good. My knowledge of what is good and what is evil aren't my standards, but theirs. I had to accept them. I have no frame of reference. Come—let's leave. The others must be worried about us."

Morgaine felt like crying again. "Oh, Mom!"

"Don't cry," responded Spirit gently. "It's not so bad. I haven't done much with my life since being freed of my old spells anyway. Maybe I needed this, or something like it, to shock me out of it. Come on."

"But nobody can live as a saint! Look what it did to Grandma!"

"We'll see. I'm not as saintly as Grandma was supposed to be."

Spirit offered her hand and helped Morgaine up. Her mother didn't have the strength in her arms she'd had before, but she managed. Almost instantly they were swept out, as if falling down a hole, and both landed outside the shield and fell to the ground. Their horses and packs were nearby. Spirit found Morgaine's new shoes and what little other things she usually wore and helped her get into them.

"I guess you'll have to re-tailor your clothes," Morgaine noted, the new Spirit being somewhat shorter and built differently.

"No. I can't wear anything I'm not wearing now. Not even jewelry or cosmetics or perfume. I—just *can't,* that's all. In that respect it's like the old days. I was very much like an Eve for many years." She stopped for a moment, then said, "Morgaine—I'm very sorry for the way I've been acting since you got your own spell. I, of all people, should have understood. I'm sorry if I caused you *any* unhappiness, and I'm particularly sorry that it took something like this to make me see the way things are.''

"Oh, Mom! It's all right! I understand! Granddad says you make the best of what you are, rather than worry about what you were or might have been. I think he's right. We're still a team. A little sexy and real exhibitionists, but we're a team.''

And they both hugged and held one another, and tears flowed from both of them. Finally, they were all cried out, and, curiously, both of them felt closer to each other than they had in many years.

Finally Spirit said, "You know—it's funny. I haven't cried since I was sixteen. Not when I was kidnapped, not when I was threatened and then bound by spell, not any time after. I think, maybe, I *can* cry now, and laugh, too. It's crazy. I don't know if it's me or the spell, but it's me now, I guess.''

Morgaine knew, however, that the spell was only the catalyst. As her spell had freed her, to a degree, from a life she hated, so, too, Spirit's spell had freed her by restoring some of the humanity she'd lost along the way. She had been a childlike animal for decades, then suddenly she'd been restored as an adult and placed immediately in a role upon which the survival of World had depended. She had been forced to become an instant adult after long years of childlike dependency, and then also been forced to be a mother with a mission, a role she detested but could not abandon to others because she herself had been abandoned by *her* mother. Filled with Flux power and the responsibility to preserve the Haller records and projects, she had never had time to learn to be a normal human.

She still wasn't normal, and she still certainly could continue the Haller tradition at New Pericles if she wanted, but she could be human, now, too. Like Morgaine, she could blame it on the spell, even to herself and certainly to others.

Spirit had no trouble riding a horse, but could not abide the idea of a saddle on her bare behind. A blanket, mostly to protect the horse, was enough. She still could ride and very well, too. They sat on their horses and stared at the empty third. "I guess they kept Verdugo," Morgaine noted without a lot of regret.

"Somehow, I have it in my head that it was in your father's mind that it might happen that way," her mother replied. "I think, though, justice would have been better served if he'd been made an Eve."

10

ALONG CAME THE SPIDERS . . .

"Oh, this is just *great*!" Matson growled. "I start off with a strong group and I get two wizards and two naked beauties! You other two better watch out! You're next!"

"I've had my turn, thanks," Sondra replied.

"So had I," Spirit reminded her. "This, however, is much better than the first time. Full communication, use of tools, riding horses. . . . *Much* better."

"It's your own damned fault for being wizards," Matson responded, still irritated. "You get so much power you can't see your blind spots. Every one of you thinks you're one of the dozen—out of millions—who can escape some of the penalty for power. Eventually it gets you. Either it sticks you in a niche being something you don't want, or it turns you into something permanently you don't want to be. Either of you could have created your own binding spells to keep you as you were, but I never saw a wizard who'd do that voluntarily."

"You'd give up too much," Dell told him. "We're only tracking and keeping close to the raiders because of our ability to transform ourselves and get the big picture. One of the big advantages is that sometimes you might need to be somebody, or something, else.''

"It *is* true," Morgaine agreed. "To lock yourself in, as you are, forever—it's just not humanly possible."

"Uh huh. And look at the both of you now. Both Dell's and Sondra's times will come eventually, too. If not on this trip, then sooner or later. Me, I've got almost no power, but nobody can force a binding spell on me, either. Anything done to me can be reversed."

"Yeah. Like Verdugo," Morgaine responded.

"Even him—if we ever figured out which one he was, and if anybody was so inclined, which I'm not. When I discovered he was carrying a signal tracker, I handed him a knotted noose, and the damned fool stuck his head in it. I had to do it. I discovered he was sending back position reports using a clever communications gadget. There's been a New Eden force trailing us almost since the start, a couple of days back so we didn't realize it. I suspected something when he started bragging too much to Morgaine, but it wasn't until the two of you went off a couple of days ago that I had a chance to really search his stuff and find it. It was pretty well concealed."

"I still can't help but pity him, though," Spirit said. "He was the product of his culture and didn't have much choice."

"None of that!" Matson snapped. "Yeah, his attitudes were shaped by New Eden, but you got to *volunteer* for internal security duty. He could have had a thousand decent jobs, but he was the type that *liked* lording it over helpless people. He was the closest thing to a Fluxlord you can have in Anchor. He had plans for all of us we wouldn't like—bet on it. Some people are just born bad."

"Well, he won't have any more plans now," Sondra noted. "It's my guess that he's about to be co-opted by the enemy."

Both Spirit and Morgaine looked up at her. "Something happen?" Spirit asked.

"Yeah. We found out what they were waiting for.

Three bright creatures, the strongest power links I've *ever* seen, Mervyn included. They came out of the sky while you were in there getting made over, and went through the shield like it wasn't there. They were expected.''

Matson nodded. ''Either Ayesha or Suzl has realized that time is running out for them. They're not going any further—whoever they were heading for has been sent for and summoned to them. They now have enough wizard power in there to withstand a major siege. My guess is they'll take on the gods of the Garden because that increases their power even more, then build a new Fluxland at this point, larger and stronger. They'll have all the slaves they need to do their bidding for them and enough brains and protection not to worry about outside attacks for a while.''

''We should have taken them on when it was just Suzl and the mob,'' Dell said morosely. ''Hit 'em early when they were still weak.''

''Yeah. Just like Morgaine,'' Matson responded. ''Liberty tried it, too. The only time they were vulnerable was when they were just outside New Eden, and at that time we were locked in by Morgaine and considerations about Suzl. When they moved out fully into Flux, we didn't have a prayer, because anyone who could get close enough to do 'em real damage could be pinpointed and neutralized by that projector. No, we're stuck. We don't even know who that is in there now, or who's really in charge. If there were only some way to get somebody inside. . . .''

''It seems hard to believe,'' Sondra put in. ''A whole world full of people, including enough wizards to demolish that camp down there even with their additions, and we're the only ones doing a damned thing and it isn't much.''

''Nobody seems to learn anything from the past except better and more efficient ways of killing or enslaving other people,'' her father agreed. ''The records are incomplete, but it looks like the world I grew up in—the world of stringers and the Holy Mother Church and the rest—was actually created out of Flux by only a couple of crazy people. Except for the stringers, the remains of the old Army Signal Corps, they froze everybody in their crazy dream for twenty-six hundred plus years. The people back then understood a lot more about their machines than we do now, but they still let it happen. They knew about the threat and they knew who to watch—Haller's journal makes that clear—yet they didn't unite to stop it. You expect their descendants to be any more united, to really believe the threat, any more than *they* did back then?''

"They united against the *Samish*," Dell pointed out.

"Yeah. Twenty-six hundred years of scare propaganda, with good reason, left no doubts in anybody's mind that something nasty was out there. Even then, the real powers didn't start for the Gates until the ships were physically docked. These are lords of Flux versus lords of Anchor. They won't cooperate on anything because they're afraid the other fellow's gonna get the projector. They're waiting for the big fight, like always, prepared to pick up the pieces. Only there ain't gonna be no pieces to pick up this time."

Spirit had been quiet, lost in thought and ignoring the conversation. Now she said, "If you're convinced that they're really going to attack the Garden, then *I* could get inside. I can return any time. I look just like all the other Eves there, and it is a condition of my spell that if I return I will be subject to the master spell. There would be no way for any of them to tell who or what I was."

"But you wouldn't remember, either!" Morgaine protested. "You'd be just another brainless nobody! What good would *that* do?"

"Only so long as the master spell held," she pointed out. "If they break it, I will be once again as I am now."

Matson shook his head negatively. "Uh uh. Forget it. The wizards in there would spot you as a wizard in a minute and figure 'spy.' You could stand up to any one of them, but you couldn't stand up to the trio in the Garden, let alone what's in there now. They're gonna run a hell of a spell on everybody there and you know it. Fight it and you're exposed anyway. Don't fight and you become one of them. Besides, you said yourself you can't lie, cheat, or steal. This job might require all three.''

"There are problems, yes, but there is a solution. A series of conditional spells. I would remain Eve, or become whatever they command, but retain a subconscious memory of everything I see and hear. Only when certain conditions are met would I reconnect and become myself, and I would disconnect automatically at any problem. I would never be sinful, because I would be totally true in both cases."

"You might never have the conditions to switch," Morgaine noted worriedly. "Besides, how could you get messages out to us? And if they run a physical change on everybody, you'll stand out and they'll know at least you used to be a wizard and they'll probe and finally find the spells. The only way you could save yourself from being converted is to run a binding spell that would make you literally become Eve—forever."

"There's always a big risk in doing something like this," she pointed out. "—Being executed, being permanently turned into something hateful—all sorts of things. There will be thousands of Adams and Eves. They won't have the time or take the trouble to run a restore on more than a few. I'm much more at risk as an Adam than as an Eve from this bunch, anyway. They won't be expecting a spy. And if I wind up an Eve forever, at least I'll be happy. Whatever, if I can get in and get information out it might make the difference between a New Eden victory, or their victory, or stopping both of them. It's better than sitting here. If anybody has any other ideas, please tell me."

She looked around at all their faces but found no answer.

"All right, then. Help me work out all this complicated conditional stuff, all of you. And, Dad, you put one of those strings on me like you have on Suzl. If they *don't* change the Eves, I want you to be able to find me in the mob." She stopped a moment. "Come on—I'd rather be Eve forever than one of those New Eden Fluxgirls. Besides, in the end, Suzl would never hurt me."

"Suzl," Morgaine pointed out, "didn't even know I was there."

"It's just too damned dangerous," Matson told her. "It's out."

"We'll see," Spirit replied. Still, she and the others discussed the various spells that would be needed and how best to do them. It could be done, but there were so many variables it was extremely risky.

Later on, Spirit took her normal turn at guard, but when Dell returned from patrol he found no one awake and Spirit gone. He quickly roused the others. Sondra went down to the Garden area, but found only a horse there.

Matson was visibly upset, and Morgaine was almost beside herself. Still, the patriarch of the clan had to adjust, as always, to new situations.

"O.K., she's in, and she's left us a string, and we have to assume she's using the conditions you so obligingly worked out with her. We have to accept the fact that the most level-headed person in the family has gone crackers and go from there."

Still, he couldn't get the tremendous worry out of his voice.

"What if they don't attack the Garden?" Morgaine grumped worriedly. She hadn't fought to get her mother out of there only to have her march back in of her own free will.

"Then these two and you will have to follow her string in and haul her out again," her grandfather replied. "I don't think there's much danger of that, though. I think I understand all they've done so far, and they might have surprised me here and there but they never disappointed me. I—"

He stopped dead as Dell's great flying form came in, circled, landed, and blurred into his own familiar form. He wasn't due off patrol for a couple of hours yet, so they knew something was up.

"They're going in!" he shouted. "You ought to *see* it! It's damned impressive! They've contracted the shield to cover no more than a hundred meters, and they're lined up in formation. All women, I think, and almost all mounted. Only three infantry units, all no more than a company each. They were spreading out when I left."

"Wizards?" Sondra asked.

"One strong at the rear, one medium at the point position in each of the three formations. I figure it's the three newcomers and the three from Liberty."

They all nodded. "A good system. Apparently they knew more about the rulers of the Garden than we did," Sondra said approvingly. "Each of them is one and a half versus the three inside, but it'll take two out of the three Fluxlords to defend any position, leaving one weak and one penetrable. And Suzl behind her own shield doing searches until she finds and neutralizes each of the Fluxlords."

"I almost feel sorry for them," Morgaine noted, sounding a little surprised at herself. "They almost went nuts rationalizing *me*. How does an omnipotent God explain why it suddenly has no powers at all?"

"The war between Heaven and Hell, good and evil," Matson told her. "It's an old theme. They're not going to be any pushovers. They're crazy enough that they have total emotional commitment to their world view. This will enrage them, create a fury, and make them much stronger than usual. You see any of the chief wizards' faces and forms, Dell?"

"You kidding? Big tits and swivel hips look great on some people, but I can't see myself wearing 'em."

"Fair enough. *Damn* this sparkling shit! I'd give anything for a clear field and one good hill to look down from right now."

"I'm going up," Sondra told them. "I think maybe I can use some binoculars to get a better view. I want to know if we know those big powers down there. If not, we should."

"I'm going back, too," Dell announced. "See? That's why we never voluntarily take binding spells. We don't need hills to get a good view."

"You two be real careful and keep well away from either side," Matson warned them. "Both sides won't know who you are if you're detected and they'll act against you as an enemy."

Sondra nodded, although she was clearly eager to see some action after all this time in the void. "Don't worry. If Spirit couldn't even handle those nuts in the Fluxland, both of us couldn't handle either side now. They're going after a Fluxland, though. They won't even check their backs."

"Famous last words!" Morgaine called to them, and they were both transformed, airborne, and gone.

The battle had commenced by the time Sondra and Dell got to the area, and it was fascinating to watch. Sondra had seen the raiders one time as defenders, but this was the first time she'd seen them in an attack. The situation was quite different than before, because their primary weapon, the projector, could be used only when the shield was weakened enough to allow its signals to penetrate and override the master spell, or program, that created and maintained the Fluxland.

"I still can't figure out why they're doing it at all," Dell called to his mother. "There are easier targets that will yield more than this."

"Experiment and practice," Sondra told him. "Everybody's scared to death of a dozen or a hundred New Eden projectors being deployed, but they have to know just what that really means. The projectors don't amplify, so they can't break a strong shield any more than we can. Everybody's been talking about the New Eden threat like it was running a master Anchor program, like they did to create New Eden in the first place. They can't do that—they don't have all the masters and they don't know where they fit together—so this will tell the raiders just what would be faced in a Fluxland situation. The Garden has no allies, no friends, and won't accept any, but it's no pushover. They didn't want a pushover. They wanted them against power with no surprises."

The three groups below had deployed in traditional triangular fashion. The Garden was large enough that no leg could actually see the other, but they could get pressure on three points at once, using Suzl and the projector to reinforce any weaknesses. *That* was the value of the projector: one strong wizard, sitting in one place, could apply his or her power wherever needed.

That the ground troops, which would move in to occupy any point where the shield contracted, were heavily armed was no surprise, either. A Fluxlord pressed to the wall was still absolute; those Adams and Eves could quickly become an army of God—devout, fanatical, even suicidal, and armed with whatever the Fluxlord provided. It was only now that the two circling wizards realized just what sort of risk Spirit had taken.

The Fluxlords of the Garden might have been crazy, but they were also extremely good wizards. For a very long time the contest was a draw, with neither side gaining a clear advantage. A rider was dispatched back to the raider shield from one of the chief wizards, and soon after they saw raw Flux power flow out of the grid and reinforce the nearest side of the triangle. The combination gave that leg only slightly less power than the defending trio, and forced the defenders to commit most of their resources to block the assault. When that happened, the other two legs pressed forward, sensing weakness, and the shield began to lose its stability. Clearly there was no longer any way to support such a large shield, and the defenders were forced to contract it to better manage it. The shield shrunk, going in a good five kilometers all around, and the troops cheered and pushed forward into the exposed jungle-like foliage.

Both Sondra and Dell were having trouble viewing much of the action. While the void was intangible, the air flow carefully regulated and monitored, it was both visually and aurally quite dense. Both were forced to be closer than they actually would like being, although Sondra had been right. The raiders were not particularly concerned with an attack from the rear, shooting off only occasional random sweeps that were easily avoided.

The troops met no resistance coming in. The Fluxlords

appeared to have withdrawn their people from the outer areas when the battle began and did not choose a face-to-face assault. Just because the shield was contracted, though, didn't mean that the master spell was affected. To do that, they would have to nail and defeat the Fluxlords themselves.

The Garden became a vicious trap. Trees came alive, their branches swinging like arms and knocking troops from their horses; vines and other innocent plants lashed out snake-like, picking off attacking troops and constricting until they squeezed the last breath out of them. It was no longer time for wizards; now the generals had to act.

A general retreat was sounded, which probably heartened the Fluxlords, but it was for a far different purpose. Matson's group had always known that the raiders possessed some sophisticated new laser-type weapons, and now these were deployed. The wizards now became support troops, keeping the pressure hard on the shield from all points so that the Fluxlords could not reconstitute or recreate what was being destroyed.

Lines of infantry now stood just beyond the Garden's edge, and on command they began firing into the growth from all available points. The void was lit with countless streams of violet-colored light, and where they struck the Garden growth smoldered and burned. "Somebody," Sondra noted with the detached admiration of the professional military, "really knows her stuff down there."

Soon a wall of flame and smoke was created and burned inward, creating huge, dark gashes in the soil. Within the Garden, plants writhed and slashed like trapped animals, but they died all the same.

Battles were not brief affairs, but once an attack commenced there was no rest for the offense until it was done or they withdrew. Giving the Fluxlords just an hour or two to recover themselves would possibly mean facing this whole thing all over again.

In front of a minor shield thrown up by the supporting wizard who protected them against the heat, the ground troops moved forward onto the scorched earth. Huge cracks began to appear in the scorched earth, trying to block their progress or even swallow them, but they were ready for it. Now, though, through some of the cracks closest to the shield, bubbling, molten rock seemed to rise to the surface and start flowing out. It was not, however, the *coup de grace* that it appeared to be, for to do that the Fluxlords had actually had to go in and alter their master spell. They had effectively surrendered control of the unshielded area to the offense, and Suzl at the projector took full advantage of it. She counter-spelled all along the affected radius, turning the molten rock to cool, smooth ground.

The advance had not been without cost. Fully ten percent of the offense had been killed, but the initial gain made victory much closer. No wizards had been lost, and now they were able to move up and take on the shield again in the same pattern as before.

Sondra and Dell began to take breaks, and to report back to Matson and Morgaine, frustrated by being unable to observe themselves what was happening. The Garden at the start had been roughly twenty-four by sixteen kilometers; after seventeen hours of assault, it had been reduced to a roughly circular area about six kilometers across, and the shield, while it held, was now mostly transparent, allowing the attackers to see inside and see what they faced. At this point, the defender was lost but might still hold a while and take an even greater toll. Of the five hundred or so attack troops at the start, there were about three hundred now.

Suzl had mostly used the projector to reinforce attack positions and to spell each of the wizards for a break so they would continue fresh and clear-headed. The Fluxlords, on the other hand, could not rest or relax for an instant. It was a test of endurance now; who was relieving Suzl, however, was not clear.

The attackers looked in on more thick Garden, but this time heavy with people. All the men and all the women looked alike, and none showed any really great concern for what was happening. They were, however, getting pretty crowded with all that brush, and the master spell was never designed to feed and water that many people in such a confined space. The more attention they required, and the more adjustments necessary, weakened the Fluxlords even more.

The Fluxlords, too, seemed to understand this, and decided on one last, desperate, all-out gamble. At this point they could have escaped, but that wasn't in their character. Their move was sudden, although not totally unexpected, and it relieved Sondra and Dell's minds a bit when it happened. Both had feared that these Fluxlords would destroy their people when they themselves faced defeat.

For those with the power, high above the garden there formed the outline of a head, a head with three faces. The center face was that of an old, stern, bearded patriarch; coming out of his left side was a young face, the Adam face, and out of his right the face of his Eve. Trailing from the head were enormous, thick bands of flowing energy, feeding the faces from the grid below, sucking up all the power that was available.

The shield suddenly vanished, and all power by the three was pushed with maximum force against just one of the attacking groups. The wizards from the other two groups could see what was happening, but each would take a couple of minutes to get into position to support the leg under assault; far too long to make any difference. After all these hours, this thing was going to be settled in about seventy seconds.

Suzl had been on the projector, with just two brief breaks, for the entire time. She was in agony; her whole body screamed for sexual release, and she looked somewhat monstrous there, totally turned on, both male organs extended. Yet she forced herself to think, forced that horrible pent-up tension into the grid by sheer force of will, knowing that only if she got the Fluxlords could she find relief. She swung into action, analyzing the lines of force feeding the head, and traced them down, doing a quick sweep until she localized one wizard and cut him off from the grid. Even as the troops on the near leg were being bowled over and in some cases caught and transformed by the fury of the Fluxlords' desperate attack, they were being weakened by a wizard they could not even see. The young Adam's face in the eerie hologram vanished.

Reduced by a third, their attack continued, and Suzl followed a second band down, swept the area, and to her surprise located a female wizard, who was also then neutralized. Only the bearded patriarch was too emotionally furious to be directly localized in this way, but now he alone was subject to the pressures of all the attacking wizards. The bearded face seemed to flicker, then lose definition, and finally turned into a furious whirlwind. With a start and a sudden realization that the old boy wasn't on the ground, but airborne, she tried an upward sweep and found where all the lines of force emerging from the grid converged and then tagged and disconnected him. He plummeted to the ground, but the other wizards caught him and brought him to a less-than-lethal stop, no longer a god nor even a wizard, except at their sufferance, but a mere mortal man.

Suzl did not wait for anything more. The Garden's master spell still held, but it now was merely an open spell, nothing more, with a force of will behind it, and even a junior wizard could take hold of it and modify or eliminate and replace it easily. Suzl now could think only of Ayesha.

Dell flew close to Sondra. "Well, that's it."

"Do you see any trace of Spirit's string?" Sondra asked him.

"No, I—yeah! There it is! She's in, now! Well I'll be damned! It worked!"

"You continue to observe," she told him. "I'll go back and report to Matson and Morgaine. Take care, though. They've got eight wizards down there along with the projector, four world-class at least, and now they don't have to all focus on one thing."

"They'll be too tired to care much," he shot back.

"You're tired too. Be careful or you'll wind up Morgaine's twin!"

Dell, however, was more fascinated than concerned with what was going on below. He'd never seen a Flux war before, and it was awesome to watch, although he decided he'd rather be a spectator than a participant. The death toll had been appalling, mostly on the side of the victors since the Fluxlords had chosen to the last to protect rather than commit their own people. Had they done so, particularly in that final onslaught, sending waves of humans out behind the force fields, all shooting, they would have certainly run right over the attacking troops and probably killed both the lead and adjutant wizards as well. Long ago, Matson had felled Coydt van Haas, the most powerful wizard ever known, with a shotgun—in Flux.

The primary wizards had withdrawn back into the raider shield, leaving mop-up to the backup wizards who'd once been some of Liberty's defenders. Wearing special binoculars, Dell saw that they *did* look like Morgaine, with subtle differences in coloring and the like, and they were all definitely much shorter. He could never remain still enough to get a real look at the big wizards, but he got enough to know that they were certainly all female but not Ayesha look-alikes. They were allies, not part of the group, and they were certainly old, seasoned veterans. This hadn't been any of their first Flux war.

The wizards basically turned off the master spell, leaving a featureless plain on which naked men and women, all looking somewhat bewildered but who were unnaturally passive, as far as the eye could see. Dell was shocked at the number so revealed. They weren't all alike, though; he could clearly see three spots where the grid was dark. One moved, and the darkness followed it. The wizards below could also see the positions, although they had a harder time of it, and they moved with some troops to wade through the mob on horseback and get the trio of defeated Fluxlords.

All three submitted without a fight, and allowed themselves to be bound and marched back to the raider compound. One looked just like all the Adams, another like all the Eves, but the third was a tired, feeble-looking old man with a full beard in a tattered and dirty robe that once had been white. He wondered who they had once been. A wizard and his two children, perhaps. Their powers were equal and well-matched, although the father had the will and had been the obvious driving force. Dell suspected that the old man was finished, but he wondered if the other two, freed from his domination, might not be turned. The amount of sheer power that would represent in the raider camp would be awesome. One could build a good, solid Fluxland; five had built a massive Anchor-like one like Liberty. In relative power, they now had between seven and ten down there.

It hadn't taken much to analyze the master spell and isolate some of its primary components. Clearly a master substitution spell was being hurriedly created now that they knew what they were dealing with and what they had. Although all were tired, there was no question that they couldn't afford to rest as yet. They had taken this huge number of people, all totally dependent on Fluxlords who could no longer help them, and they had to at least be provided with basic food, water, and a means of hygiene.

One of the big wizards came back out. Dell guessed that she'd taken the time to get a bite to eat and maybe a quick splash of water before finishing up the job. She wasn't about to waste much time with the business at hand, though. She conferred with all three of the raider wizards, then ordered all raider personnel out of the immediate area. With a shock, Dell saw that she was using some kind of device to talk into. He knew what it was—a two-way radio—having seen them in New Eden, but he'd never seen them used in Flux, nor had he realized before that it was possible to do so.

Now, with everyone not of the Garden out of range, as it were, all four wizards, aided by another on the projector— Dell could tell by the difference in strength that it wasn't Suzl—began to create a new Fluxland on the ruins of the old. He was fascinated. He had heard his mother tell of what the master program for New Eden had been like, but he himself had never seen a Fluxland created before.

It began with a single center square of the grid, right in the midst of the captive population. Then it spread, slowly at first, to all adjoining squares, then a bit faster to the squares that adjoined them, and so on, gaining size and speed as it went. It was clearly being fed in by the projector, and was merely managed and fine-tuned by the external wizards. As it grew, it drew energy from the grid and transformed it into matter, also transforming any matter on top according to a formula. Grass, trees, landforms—all formed outlines in energy and then solidified into reality. At first he couldn't see any changes in the Garden's population, and it took him a second or two to realize that the Eves had not changed, but that there were no more Adams where the program ran. Just Eves. He watched, wondering if they were simply killing them, but then he realized that they were being transformed. Everyone would be an Eve.

The program expanded until it covered the whole captive population, but it stopped as it reached the raider troops and wizards. A modification was then made, and the program was allowed to run again, past them and out well beyond, further in fact than the old boundaries had been. From this point, though, no people were involved. The program ignored the conquerors.

The Fluxland program continued on, and Dell had to decide whether to let it overtake him or to continue to retreat. He decided to move back in the direction of the other three, afraid it might overtake them as well. Then whoever was running the program would sense the presence of three wizards they didn't know about and come running—fast.

It didn't go that far, though. What was interesting was that they didn't even bother with more than a warning shield except for the center area where the projector was. It was, in effect, an open Fluxland much like Liberty, although extending in a roughly circular shape only about thirty kilometers across.

Dell decided to do a quick pass just inside the Fluxland and back out, to get a general idea of the place. He couldn't put his finger on it, but parts looked vaguely familiar to him. There was a risk, of course, that he'd immediately be drawn to earth or bring the wizards running, but he felt it was worth it for the information. He did not, however, fall to earth or even get engulfed by the spell. Although the shield was but a warning one, weak and only for the purposes of alerting the Fluxlords to the presence of intruders, it smacked him hard and he ricocheted off, stunned. It took him a moment to regain his wits, and when he did he circled back and studied it. It *looked* like an ordinary shield. Why didn't it admit him?

It must be a conditional, he decided, but under what conditions did it allow admittance? No wizards? No, it couldn't be that selective and be that large. What, then, was different about him and set him apart from the wizards inside?

Women! he realized with a start. *It won't admit anybody but women!*

He rushed back to his own camp to tell his people the updated news.

11

TAKING THE BIG RISKS

Ayesha sat on a fur-covered mat, clinging to Suzl, and looking around at the others seated on low mats around a table of sweets and vegetables. Across from them sat the three wizards who looked much like them, whom Suzl, strictly for convenience, had named Beth, Cissy, and Debbie—Ayesha starting with "A." Their spells were absolute and had proven themselves in the battle. They remembered who they had been, and so had the advantage of their military training and experience, but they didn't want to be anyone or anything other than who and what they were now. Gillian was there, too. She was quickly growing into an amazingly talented politician with a sure grasp for what was necessary. Although her personal Flux power was quite limited, she was quickly making herself indispensable, and with each success she'd become more of a believer in Suzl's dreams.

To their left sat three other women who couldn't have looked less alike. One was tiny and looked extremely delicate; she was attractive, but not overwhelmingly so, very slightly built, with a slight orange in her complexion, a tiny, turned-up nose, and eyes that seemed slanted inwards and somehow cat-like, and deep black hair cut very short and combed into neat bangs in front. The second was a big woman; naturally large rather than fat, dressed exhibitionist-style in garish garments and looking more like a northern Anchor whore than a powerful wizard. She had big eyes whose pupils seemed jet black, and a virtual mane of hair that was zebra striped, with streaks of white and jet black alternating all around.

The third was the most curious looking of all, for she looked just like one of the original New Eden Fluxgirls: exaggerated proportions, long brown hair, big light-brown eyes, and even wearing the heels and the net-like pantyhose of the old days, with no above-the-waist clothing of any sort. She even had a tattoo on her rump complete with number that announced that her name was "Jodi."

Ayesha had described them all to Suzl, and she could only wonder if her mental image of the trio was more or less outrageous than they really were. She did know *what* they were—two of them, anyway—and it pained her that she'd needed them at all. She certainly didn't trust them for a moment.

Suzl now wore a radio constantly on an elastic belt around her waist. It could be used for relatively broad communication, and was, but it also served locally as her non-broadcast "voice."

"A *wonderful* operation, darlings," gushed Chua Gabaye. "Neat, thorough, and professional! Worthy of the old Nine or the Seven, rest their souls, if they had any. Wouldn't you say so, Ming, dear?"

Ming Tokiabi, who rarely said much of anything, did not reply this time, either.

"The Fluxland program worked out, then?" Suzl asked in her eerie, electronic voice.

"*Fabulous*, darling! Simply *fabulous*! Lots of nice vegetable farms and fruit trees and all the rest. The Eves seem *delighted* with being happy little farmers, once we reoriented them a bit."

"How many were there?" Suzl asked. "Anybody count them yet?"

"The program total showed three thousand nine hundred and seventy-four," Jodi told them. "More than we expected, and quite a number are pregnant. Not a single one showed any Flux power or any connection to the grid at all—except the two Fluxlords who look like them, of course."

"What about them?"

"The old boy is crazy, completely crazy," Jodi reported. "He's withdrawn completely into a world of his own. He has to be force-fed, and we're keeping him well-sedated just in case, and under constant guard. The other two—you won't believe this—seem perfectly normal if somewhat confused. The man thinks he's fifteen years old, the girl fourteen. The last they remember is pretty gruesome. They lived in a small, reclusive Fluxland in the gap between Clusters Two and Six. Their parents were rather stern and strict with them and with each other, but not crazy. Their father liked farming, but was also a student of the old texts he'd bought copies of from some merchants going through."

"That figures," Suzl commented. She wasn't too keen on having any religions in her new world, either. "Go on."

"Well, it seemed Mommie appeared straight and true, but she had—affairs—with almost everyone who stopped by. The kids knew it, but their father didn't. You can probably guess what happened."

"He finally caught her with somebody and went bananas," Ayesha guessed.

"Yes, at least that. She was probably the equal of him in power, judging from the offspring, but she couldn't counter his jealous rage and hurt ego. He froze her, then took a butcher knife and carved her up alive. Only when he'd done with her did he realize that the children had heard the screams and come running and witnessed the whole thing. He turned to them, dropped the knife and picked up some book off his desk, and there was a blaze of light. After that, they can't remember much of anything, although they *do* have an awareness that much time has passed.''

There was a strange electronic sound that was Suzl sighing. ''Well, that explains the Garden and the system. What about them?''

''Pliant, very pliant,'' Gillian put in. ''They seem shy and a little confused when awake, but they have horrible nightmares. We got the real story out of them using a mild drug. They don't really remember the gory part at all, consciously. Krita, who's the closest thing to a psycho-geneticist we have—she works the Flux chambers—believes they would eagerly accept binding spells just to get oriented and get rid of the nightmares. She says that if any one of you will stop by, she thinks she can set things up without having to go to any artificial extremes. Neither of them has the faintest idea what a binding spell is, so they won't resist trying it.''

''I'll handle it personally,'' Suzl told them. She wanted to make sure it was done right, but also she wanted the insurance that they would be hers. The addition of those two, along with Beth, Cissy, and Debbie, would give her far more power than the three foreign wizards here. More than enough to offset their greater age and experience. ''And the father?''

''We can play to his delusions and possibly turn him, but it would have to be in a chamber, and that means Anchor. Gorgh is not that far away, when you can spare the people.''

''What about the Eves? Is there anything really there?''

''The spells are quite strong. Not only were their original selves erased, but in apparently a last gesture towards us their marking programs were also erased. There is no way to ever find whose file belongs to which body. For now, we've simply modified their existing master program,'' Jodi reported. ''First we erased the concept of Adam, and we replaced the concept of the God and the Garden with a divinity based on your own form. We also introduced the idea of the joy of work and the division of labor, although your own people are having to show them just what to do and how to do it. Give them a routine and they'll do it, time after time, day after day."

"What about sex?" Ayesha giggled.

"We altered them to the New Human format, as intended. They are either sex, as inclined. We found a few—perhaps five or six so far—who would not take the program, and we conclude that these are former wizards who lost out in the Garden and were forced to take binding spells for some reason. We're removing them as we find them and trying hard to re-establish them as wizards, but so far no luck."

"Their binds may have permanently cut them off," Debbie put in. "If so, they become the least of the captives, since they'll always be just the way they are: dull, innocent baby factories, no more. The rest have the potential to become real people someday, if we do our jobs right."

"It is perfect," Suzl told them. "A race physically identical, so there is no chance of jealousy or envy about what another looks like, and with no concept of personal property and no sexual divisions. If we can teach them to think correctly along our lines, they could be the model for the whole new world we build." She paused a moment. "That brings up a major question. I know why we are all in this, but why are you three here? You share neither our form nor our goals. What do you wish out of this?"

"I'm too old and too jaded for ideals, darling," Gabaye responded, "but Ming and I have our own little project, one that doesn't involve you directly at all. You see, after Jodi saved our necks at Gate Four, we got out—fast. All three of us. Onregon Sligh had access to Coydt van Haas's research staff and library, and we managed before the big invasion to find out where it was. We've been up there since, working on a different idea. You see, up there in space, orbiting around the old Mother just like us, are three huge—ships, I suppose we must call them: The original computers who transformed this place from barren rock into what we have today. They're shut down, in a holding state, pending their need in an emergency. That meant the failure of one of the big computers here, but that never happened, so they've been up there, preserving themselves, just waiting.''

Even Ayesha was fascinated. "And you think you can get to them and make them obey you?"

"Get to them, yes. That, *darling*, was never a problem. The programs for the vehicles were in the master computer, to be triggered in an emergency. The invasion opened everything up, of course, and some of Onregon's bright boys got them before the shutdown. Turning them on and making them obey is a different question. They weren't designed to carry *people*, for one thing. Still, we have hopes. Hopes that *their* files will show how to use the Gates, or perhaps to do without them. I mean, dears, *they* had to get *here* somehow.''

"And if you can do all this?"

"Then we will go traveling down the big strings towards the old home place, of course. I mean, we only opened the Gates at all because life here had become so damned *boring*. There was simply nothing else we could have that we didn't already have. *This* is the new thing that has Ming's and my heart beating fast again.''

"And what do we give you?"

"*Darling!* Can't you see that under the current situation our dreams are threatened? We are, perhaps, two *years* from getting this thing started, and we also still need some data that perhaps New Eden has but we do not. Look at what you've done in a few short weeks starting with one full wizard, one group wizard of moderate strength, and the projector! Just *think* of what New Eden can do, and how fast! They will be an unstoppable army on the march! Of course, they will be able to make use only of the *male* wizards unless they get smart like you and convert what they have to what they need, but that will be more than enough. They are already using Hoghland's war with Liberty to train their own in Flux warfare—and helping out Liberty as well! They egged that war on and keep it going just to give their top people experience. They already have a hundred or more fully trained and qualified wizards committed to the New Eden cause. In far less than two years they will beat a path to our doorstep and we will not be able to deny them entry!''

Suzl considered it. ''I see.'' It all made a horrid kind of sense, particularly the idea of fermenting a Flux war and using other people's blood to train their best. ''And if we win?''

''A hands-off policy until we leave, together with cooperation, sharing of new discoveries and documentation, and support personnel as needed. To do it, we need someone big helping us along, and New Eden is, of course, out of the question.''

It sounded fair and reasonable, almost too much so. She would never trust these two, who had the blood of millions on their hands, but she was willing now to use Hell itself if it furthered her goals. ''You are all three going?'' she asked, mostly curious.

''No,'' Jodi responded. ''I will not be going. I have no desire to be squirted into atoms by some big machine I can't trust, and I don't really care who's out there, if anything. I was a Fluxlord, and a strong one, inside Cluster Four when they ran that master Anchor program. *This* is the way I came out, only without power, without literacy—the works. Some of the Seven knew in advance what was going to happen and where to go and who to look for in female former Fluxlords. Gifford Haldayne located me and two others, and married all of us.''

''Haldayne!'' Suzl remembered the slippery, evil master who'd been her first encounter with one of the Seven.

''Yes. The shock was very great. I, frankly, lost all memory and sense of identity, and I wasn't alone. Before Haldayne was through, he had us jumping through hoops. He had a theory and he eventually tested it on us. He believed it wasn't necessary to even comprehend a binding spell and have it work. Somehow—to this day I don't understand how—he was right. He took us eventually down into the Gate itself, and enacted the programs, and ordered us to accept the programs and let them flow into us and we did. So long as Gifford lived we were his slaves. In Flux, he could draw on our power to enhance his own without ever worrying that we could change or refuse. It's because of that that I was at the Gate when the *Samish* and the Seven made contact.''

''Lucky for us,'' Gabaye put in.

Come to us, the Samish *had ordered, and the six members of the Seven present had followed, up to the ship lying slightly askew in the Gate depression. At that moment a huge explosion, a massive force, had come from beneath the alien vessel, blowing it upwards and disconnecting it from the Gate power source. The tremors had caused the huge transmission tower, with which the Gates had been opened in the first place, to fall, and it fell inwards, right on the advancing six figures. Jodi and the other wives had rushed forward as everyone else had fallen back in panic, concerned only with Haldayne. They found Gifford Haldayne dead, his skull crushed beneath one of the tower beams, but of the six, two were still alive. Freed from any obligations to Haldayne but still under the Fluxgirl program, they did not think about who was lying there, they just pulled the bodies from the wreckage and brought them to the Gate lip, where live* Samish *were still scrambling about in panic and confusion.*

They managed to bring Gabaye to consciousness, where she was able to use the power of Flux first to heal herself, then to restore Ming, who was mangled and near death. Not wishing to meet or take on the Samish *and not knowing what might be below that caused the explosion, they fled right through the lines of people and soldiers and eventually made it back to Haldayne's ranch in the northwest part of New Eden. There they remained while everything changed, not daring to move.*

''Thanks to your reformat, I regained my literacy and my powers,'' Jodi told them, ''but I discovered, to my horror, that none of the three of us could be anything but Fluxgirls. The binding spell, of course, had been done in a Flux environment, so it became a part of our regular coding. The old, original spell holds. Not even today's

Fluxgirl! I dress this way because I *have* to. I look this way because I *have* to."

"Believe me, *I* understand, dear," Ayesha sympathized. "Suzl, too, had something of the same problem, although self-inflicted."

"What happened to the other two?" Suzl asked, curious.

"They—couldn't stand it. They went back. I—couldn't. Every time I saw a black-clad man I saw Gifford. I hate his guts, and all their guts, but I still love him, too. It's crazy."

"No," said Tokiabi, speaking for the first time. "It is magic."

"These two saved me, as I saved them," Jodi told them. "They kept me busy, kept me going, kept me from killing myself. I've stayed with them in Flux and tagged along when it seemed I could do some good. You needed wizards who could fight. I looked around here and decided that you were well worth fighting for. Both of them—well, pardon, but they're very old and very experienced. Me, I may be old in Flux terms but I feel cheated. If I could find my Sister-wives, they'd be here too, now. I'll always be grateful to the two of you, but I think I'll stay, if you will have me."

"Then welcome," Suzl responded sympathetically. "I know what it is, what you have gone through, and we can certainly use you. You have studied the binding spell, though? It is in fact unbreakable?"

"Hopeless!" responded Chua Gabaye. "It's a clear blind code spell, just like yours. You know there's no point in going further with it. It could only injure her."

Suzl thought about it. "Still, I'd like to take a look at a binding spell that can be forced on someone who is both reading and math illiterate. Come with me to see Krita. Would you mind?"

"No, I'd be pleased, but you know they're right. A binding spell is a binding spell."

"So I have heard," Suzl responded, "but, somehow, I've never been able to totally accept it." She paused a moment. "Anything else?"

"Several," Gillian replied. "First, someone watched us do all that we did. Not long after the Fluxland was completed, someone attempted entry and was denied. The entry was aerial, so it was a wizard of high power, and the entry was denied, so we know it was a man although we don't know anything else—as we would have if penetration had succeeded."

"Any idea of who or where they might be from?"

"No way to tell, but it had the same feel as several other quick sightings over the past weeks, just beyond real range. We must assume that we have been followed by the same people all the way from New Eden."

Suzl frowned. "Then if they were wizards, why didn't they hit us when we were weak?"

"They had reason to be overcautious," the prime minister told her hesitantly, and for the first time revealed everything about Morgaine. "By the time they recovered, we had exited Liberty and probably outpowered them."

Suzl was upset, and the speaker said, softly, "Morgaine. Morgaine. How could you have been so stupid?" She recovered quickly, though. "What's done is done. I don't blame you for doing it at the time. In fact, I can not think of anything else that *could* have been done. I appreciate you telling me this, though. Anything else I don't know and should?"

"No. Nothing."

"All right, then. So now we know that it's probably my friends and family out there trailing us. But how did they manage to track us this far in spite of all our precautions?"

"You have a string on you," replied Ming Tokiabi with no more expression than Suzl's electronic voice.

"What! Impossible!"

"Beyond the infrared. It is an old stringer trick, used very seldom lest it be discovered and countered."

"Matson! Why, you son of a bitch. . . ."

"*The* Matson?" Chua Gabaye interjected. "But he's forty years dead!"

"It was faked. The only way he could get some privacy.

He's back now, though, and the same as ever. That means trouble. There's no mind quite like his on this world.''

Gabaye thought for a moment. "If that is true, then he is but a false wizard. Is that not correct? A master of illusion, but nothing real?''

"Yeah. So?''

"Then he is as defenseless against any of us as were any of the Eves.''

"Tell that to Coydt van Haas.''

"That was different. He had a wizard almost as powerful as Coydt to keep his quarry distracted.''

"He probably has several with him now, if I know his relatives.''

"So? Separate him from his wizards, eliminate his protection, and the same mind that sat at a console he did not comprehend, unable to contact the master computers or directly use their powers, who nonetheless was the one who determined exactly how to beat the alien *Samish*, a horde beyond his imagining, and got everyone to do it. Such a mind could easily find New Eden a snap, the whole of World no challenge. *If* he could be turned.''

"It's not that easy," Suzl told her. "The man and the mind are all parts of a whole. Tamper with anything and you change it, maybe lose it forever. Any involuntary spell would destroy those very things that would be most valuable to us. No, forget it.''

"*Bosh!*" Gabaye responded. "The operative word is "involuntary.' There is no one, least of all a man, who can not be turned given the right incentive. You need only have a lever. For some, it's money; for others, power. Yours is a dream, a revolution of greater magnitude than the one that caused World's culture in the first place. For others it's ego, or family and friends, or some code of honor. There's always *something* to use. His turning interests me a great deal, if only for personal reasons. Let me ask you—if you *could* get him to join us, with his mental powers intact, would you take him?''

Suzl thought about it. "I—I'm not sure. He's been very close to me.''

"Consider this, then. If you are not willing to run your program on your family and past friends and associates, you are doomed to failure. No Matson could ever be allowed loose even in this Fluxland, let alone the new world you envision."

"Remember, my darling, that *you* were *forced* into New Eden," Ayesha added, stroking Suzl's hair. "He *chose* to live there, and took Fluxwives as well. He is—attractive. Magnetic. But when push comes to shove, he's on New Eden's side. He is here because he opposes us. Perhaps the others are here because of you, my baby, but if we fall, New Eden wins the world. And if he's really as good as his legend, he might well be the only one who *could* stop us. Think of yourself, as you are, but a New Eden slave forever. Did he try and foil them when they made his own daughter a Fluxgirl? No, he moved in and joined them. If they win, you and I will be changed once more, in the mind, where it counts, and we will become animals, sexual whores for carnivals and freak shows. Matson may even visit, may even partake, for old times' sake. You must put all the old loyalties aside forever."

She knew Ayesha spoke the truth, but until now she hadn't had to face the problem squarely. Her family and friends, and his, would all be changed. All of them. It could be no other way and work, and it was the only alternative to New Eden forever. She realized that she was being romantic, not practical, about Matson. He had butted, fallen, into this situation not because he really cared but because he loved the game.

"If you can figure a way to get them all on our side, I give my blessings," Suzl told them. "However, we have other priorities, too. We must find a way to duplicate the projector. We need animals—we must send up to Anchor Gorgh and beg, buy, borrow, or steal them. We've got all the useless birds and insects and the like from the Garden, but we need some cows, and horses, too. Lots of them. Gil, you take charge of that. Gabaye, you and Tokiabi have the projector as your primary project. Whatever else you do comes second. Beth, Cissy, Debbie—I want you to fine-tune our new citizens. Also, see if you can develop some of them to replace our losses, although I know that's a real challenge. We all have big challenges. Let's get moving. Jodi, if you'll help me up and guide me, we'll go over and see those two poor wizards and talk to Krita about you." She paused a moment. "Oh, and Tokiabi— break my damned string!"

Jodi did so, and with the aid of a guard they made their way out of the tent. All were aware that the clock was more than merely running.

"Is it true," Jodi asked hesitantly, "that you have . . . in your mouth, that is . . ."

"Yes. I have two, and I'm also a fully functioning female. One day I will give you a kiss you will never forget."

"And they are both . . . potent?"

"Yes. They were taken from functioning males, then a gland was added that prevents male sperm from surviving ejaculation. We did the same thing to the Eves with the material from the Adams. It is a complicated process."

"Far easier to make man female," she agreed. "I'm afraid I've done that quite a number of times. Any time I had relations with any man of lesser power. It was automatic, but it made me feel good, somehow."

"Defense mechanism," Suzl responded. "We'll take a good look at that spell."

Krita was there, expecting someone, but not necessarily either of them. The Adam and the Eve wizards were under guard in a small tent nearby.

"You are sure that they won't bolt or cause trouble if their power is turned back on?" Suzl asked her.

"Positive. They're very scared, and very scarred inside, and deeply disturbed. I used the deepest hypnotics on them."

"Prep them, then. Light hypnotic only. I want the actual decision to be clearly voluntary. When they're ready, we'll turn their power back on. If they hold, I'll feed them what they have to have. Fortunately, in their case there's no real experiences to preserve and no memories that they would want. Jodi, you stand by and be ready, though. If they're putting us on anyway and jump at the power, there will be hell to pay in here.''

But there was no resistance. Krita had been right, as usual.

Suzl unleashed their nightmares, and they proved if anything more ugly and horrible than the reality had been. These kids needed help.

My name is Suzl, she told them, using Flux rather than radio. *I can free you from the nightmare forever, the ugly dreams, the confusions, and give you peace and purpose.*

They both rose to the bait, eager to please.

I will give you both a spell. It will be a big one, but you don't have to know what it does. You only have to take it and where I tell you add some numbers to it. Any numbers. When it's done, you'll still have all your powers, but all the bad stuff will be gone, and you will be able to live out your long lives in peace and contentment. If you trust me, do as I say.

The spell was the Ayesha spell, as modified, with the New Human attribute as well. She wanted them all to have children, lots of children, all of whom would have the average wizard power of the two parents and all of whom would grow up to look just like Ayesha, Suzl, and the rest. Suzl would have liked to also have given what she called her ''mouth organ attribute,'' but it would require running that complex machine-language string with the bug in it. One blind wizard was enough.

They took the spell, and it worked its magic quickly on them. ''Jodi, meet Fawn and Flower,'' she said, bringing the two up and out. ''I couldn't think of any name with 'E' offhand except Eve, and that's more than taken.'' They adjusted to the new bodies naturally, as if born to them, which, in fact, they now believed was the case. They looked much like the others, except that their skin was quite fair, their eyes baby blue, and their cape-like hair was a straw-colored blond. There were differences with the others, but the pair were absolutely identical twins.

They retained their language and math capabilities, and their full, considerable powers, but they had absolutely no memories of anything before Suzl made her introductions, nor any curiosity about the fact that they didn't. They were so perfectly matched they talked in unison.

"Mistress," they both said, in soft, sweet, high-pitched voices, "what would you like us to do?"

"Go around, explore, talk to people, see what it's like," she suggested. "Later you will start training to bring your wizard powers up to the world class they can be."

They laughed and scampered off. Suzl turned to Jodi. "Now—let's see about that spell."

Every wizard had it drilled in her from the start that binding spells could not be broken, and for most that was quite true, unless someone got into a master computer room and cancelled the new file and read back in the old, as had happened to Suzl, Cass, and others. Binding spells were built with huge bunches of nulls in the commands in which the one being bound inserted strings of random numbers. They had no effect on the spell, but as soon as it took effect those numbers were erased from the memory of the bound one and from the actual spell itself. To reverse any spell, it was necessary to know all the code, but the number of variables involved made it impossible to find.

Suzl's spell had hundreds of missing numbers; Ayesha's had even more. The spell she'd just enacted had hundreds as well, and they could be any number of digits. Jodi's spell, however, had only ten blanks, and that made Suzl wonder. She remembered being a true Fluxgirl herself, as Jodi had been when the bind had been forced upon her, and she well remembered that she needed both hands to count her children. She thought Haldayne had pulled a clever fast one on the girls, one she was surprised nobody else had thought of. Of course, maybe they had.

"I will wager that I can break your spell the first time, if you let me," Suzl told her. "However, I have a price. You must take one of mine. Otherwise, you will remain as you are forever, even if you break the spell yourself at some point. You are as niched as I was."

Jodi wanted desperately to break it, but after seeing those vacant-eyed smiling blondes she wasn't so sure she wanted to pay the price. "May I ask what the new spell is?"

"Nothing much inside will change. You will still be you, with all your memories and all your powers and abilities. However, you will be one of us, body and soul. That way I can be sure of you, as I can never be of your friends."

"You mean—look like you? Or them?"

"More or less. If you have any preferences, tell me. I'm blind. I can't see it anyway, only write the code."

"And if I take it? What then?"

"After that performance a couple of days ago, you would become my second-in-command, my adjutant. You would be in charge when I am indisposed. You would be my general of wizards. You would speak in my stead, and you would be my successor should anything happen to me. I can offer no more than that."

She thought about it. "Those two—they have their own peculiar code of honor. They owed me for their lives, so they sheltered me, took care of me, and let me have something of a life these past decades. But they really don't care about me, not a bit. They've been hoping to get rid of me almost since we left New Eden. They don't even really like each other much. That's why I find this place of yours so attractive. What the hell? Why not? I must trust someone sometime or kill myself. Uh—you're not going to name me something with a 'G,' are you?"

"Screw the alphabet. I won't mess with that in any way."

"You're sure this can be done?"

"Ninety-nine percent. If anything looks wrong, I'll stop immediately and restore the nulls. Ready?"

"All right."

Suzl did the mental adjustments first. She knew those would be tough because there was a deep-down resistance by anyone with power to such tampering, but Jodi tried to make it as easy as possible, particularly when she determined that the spell wasn't massive, just an insurance of some loyalty. The physical part was really tense, but it went through without any problems, first removing the bind and then replacing it with a far more complex one that also remade Jodi. She was slightly taller, dark complected, with the hair a golden color and the eyes a reddish brown. She was also now, quite clearly, one of them.

She was also amazed.

"How. . . ?" Suzl had just done what the book said was impossible.

"Simple. Think like a Fluxgirl. It takes another old one to do that, I guess. When you counted anything, you counted like a kid, right? On your fingers, just one, two, three, four, five, and so on until you ran out of fingers and toes. I got to twenty once, but then I got lost. When I heard your story and read only ten nulls, I was pretty sure how he did it. And if we ever found the other two, it'll be exactly the same, I bet."

Jodi was thunderstruck by the simplicity of it all. It seemed so damned *obvious!* "All that time, and it was right there under our noses."

"Sure. We'll be a good team. You fight better than I do and I think dirtier."

"But won't Ayesha feel jealous about me taking such a command?"

"Ayesha, my former husband, is now my wife. She has a wonderful, diabolical mind, but she trapped herself by making me her perfect fantasy lover. She thought by making me look like her she wouldn't be subject to me, but the bottom-line difference between men and women is the sexual equipment. Everything else flows from that. She is subject to my every wish and whim, and she is incapable of even regretting that fact. Even if she got jealous, there's little she can do. All of these people, with the exception of our two friends there, are bound to me. Except for me and for Ayesha, you can do the same and should."

"Fair enough. Uh—this body. It feels, well, very different than I expected. Very natural, very comfortable. I've had it for all of three minutes and it feels *right*, natural somehow. I was a Fluxgirl for seventy years and I can't remember what I looked like. The spell?''

"Of course. You've never taken one on, knowing what you were doing, until now.''

"With the—New Human modification?''

"Sure. Want to try it out? I need somebody close who can service me as a female. Come on, and I'll give you an experience like you've never had before!''

They now had seven wizards, all committed to the same ends, an almost-unheard-of grouping. That was why the Seven and the Nine had been unique. If Krita had any luck with the old boy in the chamber on the apron of Anchor Gorgh, they'd have eight. The weaker would be trained and uplifted by the stronger, and soon they would spread out and convert more and more. All they needed were enough projectors for the wizards they had.

12

PRIORITY CHANGES

It took a few days, but Spirit discovered a way of getting messages out, although it took a bit longer for Dell to bump into them. She was apparently sending code pulses through the grid to a point ten squares beyond the Fluxland boundary, where they were held until someone authorized intersected the square. It was a clever system, suggested in the "hypothetical" discussion on infiltration of the camp by Sondra.

"The messages are choppy, and sometimes cut off and then resume, I guess later, with whole new stuff," Dell told them, "but you can make some sense out of them."

Spirit was alive and well, although she'd been singled out from the bulk of the population and placed in a special holding area near the headquarters camp for experimentation. She and some of the others had become suspect when they didn't get the bisexual modification and wouldn't take it.

Matson didn't like the sound of that. "They'll either mess up her mind or add on to the body spells or both," he worried.

237

"I doubt they can do much to her mentally," Sondra assured him. "They can play with the Eve part all they want, but when the conditionals switch on her accumulated personality and memory file is read back in. They can't touch it unless they first peel off all those conditionals and can tell them from the binding spell itself, and they'd have to do that without her cooperation. As Eve, she wouldn't understand or be able to see any of it. As for the physical, anything done to her she can undo at will when she's Spirit or when she's out of there. Eve wouldn't take a binding spell—she wouldn't be able to comprehend it."

"O.K., O.K., so call me a worrier. What else does she send?"

"As near as I can make out, they have between seven and nine wizards of their type in the camp—she isn't really sure how many—plus two outsiders. She says—and this is nuts—that they might be part of the old Seven from some comments one made while in with them."

Matson thought a moment. "Well, if I'm not dead, no reason they all are, either. It was so confusing that they just pushed all the bodies, junk, and what all into the gate and said the hell with it. There weren't any positive identifications except for Sligh and Haldayne, who they all knew. Figure it's a couple of the women. Those New Eden boys wouldn't pay much attention to the women. I wonder what their game is, though? And what would Suzl have to do with them in any case?"

"Beats me. She also says the only rock-hard shields are on the area of the main camp tent and, she guesses, around the projector. She's on the shield border and can see through, but the projector's out of sight. She's pretty sure they still only have the one, though."

"Anything on those two groups that set out a few days ago for Gorgh and Ecksreh?"

"I didn't make a broad sweep, but I guess I could. They each took one of the wizards—one of the Liberty people, I suppose—but the one going to Gorgh looked slow and took some wagons, while the one to Ecksreh looked fast and lean."

Matson nodded. "Ecksreh's still a mess and somewhat in civil war, while Gorgh is relatively stable. They're looking to deal, not fight, with Gorgh, but Ecksreh's target is people, I bet. They'll keep snatching and grabbing folks there in small groups, turning them, then using them and others to get more, until somebody gets wise. Then they'll return. I don't know what they'll use for trade with Gorgh, but they probably are interested in some cows, chickens, pigs, and horses—that kind of thing. You tell me it's a basically agricultural Fluxland. They can always use what they get as prototypes and turn some of the Eves into breeding stock."

Even Sondra was shocked. "You don't think they would! Not Suzl!"

"Those airheads might as well be cows, and horses," Morgaine noted sourly. "They'd be more useful that way than as they are."

"Come on, Morgaine," Sondra admonished. "They're people, too. You've been getting real testy lately. You're beginning to sound like your grandfather."

"I'm just bored and frustrated. Mom's down there stuck in a pen like an animal and I'm sitting here making pretty doodles in the void."

"You wanted along," Matson reminded her.

"Yeah, and I didn't regret it. Still don't. But I'm not doing any good sitting here. To tell you the truth, I been tempted to get down there. Just ride in and say hello. What more could they do to me? At least I'd see what's going on."

"Inject some nice brain chemicals into that fixed form of yours so you'll fall madly, passionately in love with Ayesha or whoever first comes through the door, that's what," Sondra told her. "Then you'd sell us out for love and then sit there and make nice wizard babies for the new order."

"Maybe. I been wondering whether Suzl might not just need somebody level-headed to talk to."

"Talk? How? With that *thing* in her mouth like you said? Some conversation!"

She shrugged. "I like to talk, anyway. Besides, you

know they couldn't do any more to me that couldn't be undone later. They won't mush my mind if I'm useful and it's no more risk than Mom took. I'm no threat to them, anyway."

"To them, none," Sondra agreed, "but they can pool your power with theirs and use it." She stopped and thought a minute. "You know, I almost wish for Verdugo back. He kept you nicely occupied, and he could answer one big question. I just got to wondering this minute if those machine-made binding spells recorded the personal combinations as well. They could, you know. If they do, they could remake you any way they wanted."

"Interesting idea. I'd love to ask them about it."

Matson seemed thoughtful. "Interesting idea at that. Dell, you get on down to New Eden. I want a full status report from your contacts there before we do anything else. Worst fear estimate and all that. When he gets back, then Sondra, you'll go to Guildhall. I want to give a complete report in and also make a series of recommendations. If everything ties together, then we'll make some moves. I think we've been standing pat too long with the clock running."

"Mind if I fly along on your back?" Morgaine asked him. "I think I need a break, even if it'll be in the New Eden area."

They were gone for three days, during which a few sporadic additional messages came from Spirit and also during which the Ecksreh band returned. Only forty, plus one of the wizards, had been sent out but almost three hundred rode in, impressing the observers as much as the camp. The Anchor had apparently been wide open to them, and, working fast, they might well have converted a whole damned town. Some had slight Flux powers, and though there were no real wizards among them, suddenly the army ranks down there were above what they had been, and it was certain that new groups would be sent out for more.

There had also been extensive tests of the projector, in which, again, all were surprised at its range. Even New

Eden hadn't expected a range much over the curvature of World, if that, but the sweep extended all the way to Gorgh and almost to Ecksreh, a grid range of an astonishing six-hundred-and-forty-kilometer radius. The limit seemed to be the power supply in the New Eden projector; given a better one, with a larger transformer, it seemed possible to cover the whole planet. That was unnerving, since New Eden now had more time to improve and enlarge just that transformer system if it knew this.

Worse, if they started getting wise over there that somebody was shadowing them, there was no effective camp that wouldn't be well in range of even a sweep. Matson knew it was time to make a move or move out, and soon.

Spirit's messages contained less than she would have hoped, due to her relatively confined position. They had been trying to train the Eves to at least perceive and recognize Flux power, but so far they had totally failed. Lately there had been talk of impregnating all of them by major wizards so they could determine whether any Flux power they might have had once would be passed on to children. Suzl had been around once to look at them, and had some means of talking and seemed clearly in charge. That was about it, though.

Morgaine returned with Dell, but her mood was mixed. They had gone into Logh itself while he'd hit on his contacts, and she had certainly more than relieved her tensions with variety, but she wasn't sure she liked the results. "I didn't like those people," she told them, "but I found it harder and harder to keep any sort of control there. Something about being around all those men. . . . It was like a drug. I hated them and myself for it, but much more and I would have done *anything* in exchange for being laid. Now I think I really understand what they did to those poor women at the start of it; the original Fluxgirl formula."

"You have a taste," Sondra responded understandingly. "Only a taste. You see, you still had enough self-control to break away and come back and talk about it. We didn't. We *literally* couldn't resist. That's what's at work down there, in the Fluxland. All that experience, that *helplessness*, and fear of it coming back. Ayesha certainly, and Suzl as well, if not by spell then because of decades of being like that. No love, just sex as a drug you have to have regularly. Suzl was turning back that way again, and she hated it. Now, over there, surrounded by a whole land of females only, she's going after the lowest common denominator of that fear. If she can produce a world without men, she thinks, she can beat that beast inside of her. Suzl's war now isn't really with New Eden, although they caused it, or against men. It's against herself.''

Dell had some mixed news from very high sources. ''The projectors can't be really mass-produced,'' he told them. ''Each one has to be built by hand as an individual piece, then tested and checked and fine-tuned. They feel they're going to need a dozen just to take on what they still insist on thinking of as Borg Habib's band.''

''Seems excessive from their own viewpoint,'' Matson noted.

''Maybe, but they figure that once they really show what these things can do and that they're not as helpless in Flux as they appear to be, some of the Fluxlords will gang up on them to stop them. They think a dozen is the minimum necessary to deal not only with the raiders but with the reaction to their use.''

Matson nodded. ''All right, I'll grant 'em that much. When will they have a dozen?''

''They figure about four months from now. After that, things will be going along smoothly enough so they can produce and test one every two weeks. They also have a squad of between thirty and forty strong wizard officers. They're not sophisticated and they can't string spells together with the same ease as a world-class trained professional, but what they lack in polish and speed they make up in intensity. These guys are true believers.''

''Four months. . . .'' Matson mused. ''Morgaine? You decided what you want to do from here on out?''

''I don't mind telling you that New Eden scared me,'' she responded honestly. ''Whoever created that binding spell was diabolically clever. If I go into Anchor it won't take long to have me trapped. If I stay in Flux, I may be even worse, 'cause this just kicked whatever is in my new makeup into high gear. Something in my brain keeps trying to draw from Flux, and so far I'm keeping it in check, but I'll lose. So I can't stay in Flux or I don't know what I'll turn into, but I can't go to Anchor 'cause I *know* what I'll turn into. They win either way. Either I go down and join them or I'm out of everybody's hair forever.''

He nodded. ''O.K., then. I'd say go on down and hope you keep your sanity up. If we're lucky, you might be able to influence them, particularly Suzl, to get more of a grip on reality. If not, you'll be stable until this thing's through and we can work out some other way around the problem.''

''I'm willing,'' she told him. ''After all, Mom's down there, anyway.''

''That's one of the things we'll have to take care of first. We're going to need your permission and cooperation to selectively remove a few facts from your mind. Otherwise they'll find out and hunt us down and your mom, too.''

''I think I can manage that much,'' she assured him.

He turned to other matters. ''Dell, you get those coded dispatches from the stringer office for me?''

In the end, they managed only to alter her so that she was absolutely convinced that her mother was at Guildhall, with her grandmother. Matson decided to live with that. ''It's about time we came out of the bushes anyway,'' he told them.

Dell took Morgaine down on horseback, bid her goodbye, and sent her into the Fluxland. He then proceeded to the point where Spirit had been sending messages, far to the northwest, to see if there was anything new.

There was, but their names were Gabaye and Tokiabi and they were far too much for him to handle.

They brought Morgaine in through abundant fields of food worked by hordes of identical, naked blond women singing happily as they toiled. She asked for Suzl, but they worked her through the chain of command, starting with a wizard who said her name was Cissy and who was a smaller version of Morgaine herself. Explaining her position now, thanks to the spell, and also her indirect relationship with Suzl, she was passed to a strong wizard named Jodi, who listened critically. Finally, though, they brought her to Suzl in a large and lavishly furnished tent near the center of the Fluxland.

She was somewhat taken aback by Suzl's method of speech, but her heart also went out to the blind half-woman, half-man who had begun as a victim and was now the leader, and Suzl certainly sympathized with Morgaine's predicament.

"I'm sorry they had to do that, but you understand why," the blind leader said in that odd electronic voice.

"Yes, I understand. It was my own fault. The thing is, what can I do about it?"

"Being blind has an odd advantage," Suzl told her. "I'm not sure if your other senses get better or if you're just more aware of them, but it is so. In addition to better hearing, for example, I also find I can see Flux and spells and their interrelationships a hundred times more clearly than before. I can see, for example, that they handed you a few variants, but mostly gave you my old Ayesha spell. I think—I know—that I am the only one alive who understands that spell. The difference is that you have wizard power. Your body and your mind are at war, as mine was before coming here, although mine was more self-inflicted, while yours was imposed. Like my old one, your body is winning, but because it is the Ayesha spell it is accelerated by a high factor. Had you remained in New Eden, you would have become a Fluxgirl whore. Because your mind is so advanced, so intelligent, you could not have stood it. It would have broken. You would have become as witless as one of those Eves out there."

"I suspected that."

"Only being out in the world with a limited number of men saved you this far. Once you went back into an environment with hordes of good-looking men, however, you were done. A few more days out here, and you would have been unable to resist drawing from Flux, changing your own mind into one better suited for the body, and your body would have run wild. You would become a mindless, physically grotesque nymphomaniac. Only coming back here has saved you, but the process will continue if left unabated. I have a way out for you, but larger things loom. You are Spirit's child, but you're not mine. I hardly know you, really.''

''What do you want?''

''What you know. What you have learned. How many are with Matson and what do they have that could threaten us? What are their plans? What do they know about us, and who have they told it to?''

Morgaine gave a fairly detailed account of everything, including Spirit's own run-in with the gods of the Garden. It was all accurate, as far as she knew, although she assured Suzl that Spirit was safe with Cass. She also told of the news from New Eden—news that was not very welcome.

''Morgaine, we're going to lose to those bastards,'' Suzl said with complete candor. ''Oh, we'll give them a hell of a fight, and maybe take a lot of them with us over a very long time, but we're doomed to lose. Every time we run a duplication command on the projector we get an exact duplicate. It looks right, feels right, and even down to microscopic examination it is identical, except it won't make contact with the grid. There is no reason why it shouldn't work, but it doesn't. Finally, a few days ago, we took a big risk and had the actual projector read into the computer for analysis while we held everything here without it. The computer held it for hours—you know what *hours* are to a computer? Then it gave it back, and it still worked, and they made a duplicate—and it didn't work. You could access the grid from it, but you couldn't project with it. It was just a damned uncomfortable chair for a wizard.''

''Matson had hoped that the Guild experts, who are at least as smart with machines as New Eden, could figure out the trick.''

"We've had experts. Experts so smart they can actually build ships to go to other worlds. Something's missing. Some basic thing in the enormous library of the master computers just isn't there. The experts think somebody, sometime, maybe long ago, deliberately blocked access to it, or commanded that it never be released to human beings. The computers, God knows, project their power all the time. Something shuts it down, keeps it from communicating—like a binding spell. Then some bright boys, geniuses probably, in New Eden somehow figured out the key. Deduced it, since they weren't even in Flux and couldn't build one. Our geniuses might figure it out, given years, but not in four months. Our spies and allies in New Eden can't get it for us, except that we know they can't duplicate it in Flux, either. If so, they'd be on us. Maybe it has to be built in Anchor, programmed in Anchor. I don't know. But they will have a dozen at the start and one more every two weeks after."

"But their wizards aren't as good, as experienced, as yours."

"So what? They will be, after a while of using them and taking over and turning some of the better wizards out there just like I have. They can afford to go slow, too. Take chunks, consolidate, wait for more defenders to be ready, then take another bite. There's fifty, maybe sixty million people on this world. Thanks to their size and their real high birth rate, they have maybe twenty percent, one in five, of all the people already, and there's a couple of asshole Anchors and one big Fluxland already going their way. A whole world of tough, loveless, super-masculine men and meek, servile, ignorant, adoring Fluxgirls, all of whom will breed true. Sometimes I think we should have let the *Samish* win. We'd all be slaves—sort of remote components of a master computer, I guess—but it would be equal, anyway."

"There must be a way to counter them," Morgaine insisted. "There *must* be. We beat the *Samish*, we beat the Seven, we beat the old Church—there's always a way."

Suzl smiled, but it was a grim smile. "Perhaps. First

it's time for you to choose sides. You fought the binding spells before, but if you don't or won't then there's a place for you here. At least it'll be the last place to fall. Otherwise, I might as well send you back to New Eden to get a head start on the rest of us.''

"This is a complex binding spell. How could you alter it?"

"Because I have the key. Everybody who goes through the chamber for a binding spell has the entire proceeding recorded. I can read back in those magic numbers—and without even a chamber.''

"And what would you make of me?"

"What you are, only uniform in size with the rest of us. No blocks on literacy or math abilities, so you'd have your full powers restored. And, of course, you would be unable to betray us or to act against us in any way.''

"That's it? But, tell me—why make all your wizards this way? Why lock them into this form?"

"Commitment. This body, as designed, is good only for unlimited sex. Nothing else. But the conventional spell leaves the mind alone, as yours does not. You see, I can't command my vision of the new world and expect wizards of training to swallow it. Trapped in this body, however, they have no choice. Only in this environment can your mind take charge, do whatever it is capable of doing. In a conventional environment, Flux or Anchor, with men and women, you would find your physical needs and urges compelling. Once you took my spell you'd still be free— you'd have to be to fully and willfully use your powers. I need minds like yours, Morgaine, but if you take my spell you will either be your own mistress or you will be the mistress of strangers. You all have to act in my behalf or you act against yourselves. You see?"

And she *did* see, and also understood exactly how clever Suzl really was. It was less of a decision for her than the others, though, because she already *had* the physical liabilities but without the power and thus true freedom of action.

"All right. I'll change spells."

"No tricks. When it begins, you'll have a rider spell attached. If you don't accept my spell after clearing your own, you'll wind up accelerating every process in body and mind. You'll make Ayesha seem like a plain schoolgirl. And then we'll deliver you to New Eden."

"I won't fight it if you're being honest with me. Then what?"

"You spent your whole life studying Flux and spells. You know more than the lot of us, except those two evil hags I'm forced to play games with right now. I have many wizards with exceptional powers but no really good training, no knowledge of the tricks. You will train them, and any others that come along, as much as you can in four months. They'll be all that will be standing between us and New Eden."

Sondra looked at Dell and sighed. "Well, it's no binding spell, but it's too strong for you to break on your own. It's full of traps and it'll take experts to unravel. Those two really know their business."

"It's damned embarrassing," Dell muttered. They had taken him in the air and forced him down in a duelling posture. The two of them were far too strong and experienced for him, and had him in a matter of minutes. After that, they'd thrown this spell on him and sent him back with a message. The spell had been designed to embarrass him, and to limit his future effectiveness. Above the waist he was his normal, slightly hairy masculine self; below, however, he now was sexually female and had coming down the longest, *sexiest* smooth women's legs ever seen. Worse, he found himself compelled to keep his lower half exposed. Shirt, yes; pants, no. The final insult was that they gave him, immediately, a crampy and bloody period he couldn't stop with Flux power.

He still had his power, but it could be directed only to others, not to himself. As Sondra said, it was full of traps. He'd merely examined one and suddenly had to fight the urge to put on makeup and high heels. He didn't want to examine any more.

"They said they only let me go because there was no other good way to send a message out," he told them. "They really wanted me for my power, but they want somebody else more. They say they detected Spirit's transmissions, waited at the spot, then traced them back in to her. They've got her, that's for sure. They told me where they found her and it matched what we know. They say they can remove the conditionals, which, inside there, would turn her into an Eve forever. They want a swap, and they're giving you only twelve hours to do it."

Matson leaned back and sighed. "What do they want for her?"

"They want you, Matson. For some reason, they want you."

Instead of being shocked or dismayed, the old stringer legend took out a cigar, lit it, and actually smiled. "So they want me, huh? Well, that's just right. They figured now that they can't beat New Eden without me."

Sondra and Dell both stared at him. "Of all the egomaniacal—you act like you *expected* this!"

"Daughter, if this hadn't happened, I might have had to arrange it somehow."

Sondra started to say something, then stopped. She knew her father very well. "All right—what's the plan? You've been setting this up for some time, anyway. I figured you were starting something when you let Morgaine go down."

"Well, first of all, I'm not being as egotistical as you think. Habib wasn't much of an officer—just brute strength and kill anything that moves. You could see that by the way his folks acted in New Eden. They bought some real military background with those three Liberty wizards, and you could see that in the Flux part of the attack on the Garden, but those are all wizards, not street fighters. They lost half their ground troops and the other folks weren't even shooting back! They know it. That's partly what the Garden attack was all about. A preliminary test against a strong but not unbeatable foe. They need an experienced line officer, and Suzl only knows of one in the neighborhood. Me.''

"And you're going to do it?'' Dell asked, appalled. "After all this stuff? All those bodies, the mutilations. . . .''

"It's a rough world, Grandson. Does it really make any difference whether you're blown apart by an organized army because you were in the way of the battle or by some half-organized mob? Those folks over there aren't any more evil than the soldiers are. They're just *amateurs*. The thing is, they know it, and they know they'll have to face some damned fine professionals. The enemy is New Eden, boy; always has been.''

"But then why. . . . ?''

"Look, you two. If we needed to, I could tie into the Signals emergency net and call for strength. I'd get every wizard and army unit in the area, however many that is, as quick as they could get here. In two, three days I'd have a hell of an army. In a week, I'd have more power than we'd need to knock them over even *with* their projector, since their actions with it are now totally predictable. Hell, boy, that shield of theirs *moves*. That means it's porous. There's a dozen colorless, odorless gasses that'll do anything from put you to sleep to kill you ugly that we could send right through there. If I'd wanted them knocked out, I could have done it at any time.''

Dell's mouth hung open, but Sondra just nodded. "I wondered why you were letting this go on once they settled in one spot.''

Dell shook his head. "Maybe this spell's made me worse than I thought. Are you saying you could always take them out?''

"Sure.''

"Then why can't you take New Eden out?''

Matson sighed. "Grandson, it's the numbers. Old Adam Tilghman knew that when he took a big risk to make the whole Cluster Anchor. Inside that giant Anchor they got twelve or more million people, sixty percent of them Fluxgirls. You realize that?''

"I—I really hadn't realized it, even though I've been through there for years."

"Uh huh. And most of them are baby factories, putting out an average of a dozen kids each in twenty years or so. Some more. Now add to that their culture. Every man's technically in the army. The whole nation can be mobilized in a day if need be, and if all the phones work. Their regular army's a quarter of a million and that's bad enough, but the reserves still train and drill and are pretty good themselves. Army service is required, so they all had active duty. They rent out whole divisions as mercenaries to other Anchors and Fluxlands to blood them. See?"

"Go on."

"Well, so they got twelve projectors and thirty, forty wizards. Hell, I bet we could get a *hundred* female wizards alone who'd go against 'em, all world-class and with lots of training, and we could easily match their probable two forward divisions, maybe ten thousand men. Projectors or not, we could probably wipe 'em clean. Not without cost, considering those projectors, but we'd win. So what would New Eden do? Sit back, wait for half a year until they had more projectors, then send out thirty more wizards and another two divisions. Maybe wait a year and send out twenty-six projectors, sixty wizards, and a hundred thousand troops. They gain a bit, but we stalemate them. They wait another year—and so on. They lose men, but one fellow can make seven girls pregnant in seven days. Meanwhile, their untouched population base, industrial base, research and development base, transportation base, and the like keep growing. See?"

"Then they're—unbeatable," Dell responded. "My God!"

"Uh uh. I thought so, until I checked in with the stringer headquarters in Logh Center and talked to a bunch of folks about what to do. You remember—when I went to send a message to Cass and the girls."

"Yeah, I remember. So that's what took so long!"

"Well, anyway, they were coming to the same conclusions and weren't all that upset to see the projector stolen, either. We knew the raiders were too uneducated, too wild to be able to really handle it, and the fact that all but Habib were women implied it was more than just wildness but some kind of anti–New Eden thing. They needed some technology experts fast, and there were only three sources. New Eden was out, obviously, and they weren't the sort to come to the Guild, so that left the third. Coydt van Haas's elusive research Fluxland that Sligh tapped as well. We've been looking for it ever since Coydt died, but we never found it. Traces, some, and bits here and there, and occasional folks who knew somebody who knew somebody from there, but nothing else. With a projector, we figured that if these raiders didn't know exactly where it was, the van Haas people would find them. Unfortunately, the latter happened first, so we still don't know where it is. That's what we were trailing them for.''

"What good would they do in all this?" Sondra asked, fascinated now. Her father wasn't disappointing her.

"Well, somebody up in the Two-Six Gap, within the last year, managed to launch a couple of things clear out of this world and into space. Just like a military powder rocket, only big and strong enough to carry beyond the atmosphere. We monitored it, but by the time anybody got there all traces had been erased. We have to assume they weren't just throwing stones out there. Any rocket or other vehicle that can go that far and hit where it's aimed is not just transportation, either. Pack it with explosives, launch it from Flux, and make it hit anywhere you want. Space is a real big place and it takes a hell of a lot of speed to get something out there. Considering that, hitting any place you want inside New Eden would be child's play.''

Sondra gave a low whistle. "And that's what they have? A projector and these rockets?"

"Well, they have a projector, and they have folks there who know about those rockets or whatever they are. Spirit mentioned the Seven. Where else would they hide out to plot something new except at Coydt's old place? So, since they didn't give us the keys to Coydt's front door, we'll have to make sure they win. And make sure those bad ones down there have to bring up the rockets. To make them use the rockets, we first have to crush the initial thrust of New Eden and its projectors. It's those projectors Coydt's folks are coveting, anyway. I'd bet my last cigar on it. Crush New Eden, grab those projectors, and they've neutralized the Guild and any masses of wizards. No competition, no threat, and they get all the goodies in the bag.''

Sondra nodded. ''So at last this goofy expedition of ours makes sense. All right, I have the basics now. Just what do you plan to do?''

''Well, first, sexy-legs here isn't fit to try any physical transformations on himself at the moment, so he gets on a horse with a bunch of messages and he rides until he reaches one of our friendlies. Then he hitches a ride to Guildhall and gives those messages to the general staff there and sees their wizards abut getting that spell removed. Dell, they'll explain the rest to you when the time comes, and although you aren't a stringer, you're the son and the grandson of stringers, so they'll let you in on the finish. Jeff and the rest of the brood, too.''

''And me?'' Sondra asked him.

''You, Daughter, have a more complicated mission that'll take some time to explain, but it's one of the reasons I particularly wanted you along without the immediate family.''

''Uh—Granddad?'' Dell put in. ''You know they'll have to turn you into a girl.''

He shrugged. ''I always had a fondness for the ladies,'' he responded, puffing on his cigar. ''And I sure as hell been a lot worse at one time or another.'' He paused, then grew more serious. ''Listen, you two. Now that Morgaine's out of the way, we can really prepare. I'm sorry after all this we have so little time, but this caper's gonna be so dangerous that it'll take a lot of work—fast—and be more dangerous than Spirit's noble effort.''

A lone figure on a large black horse made its way out of the void and onto the semi-distinct apron of the Fluxland whose name he didn't even know. He knew he was expected; although he couldn't do anything about it, even false wizards could *see* Flux activation, and he knew the projector had put a monitor there, waiting for him.

The other side wasn't long in coming. Just two figures, one a naked, blond Eve on a somewhat-symbolic white horse; the other a larger, more garish figure with heavy makeup, red hair that looked like a wig but was not, and dressed in gold and crimson that revealed a less-than-desirable figure beneath. The pair stopped just inside the shield, the Eve making no comment or even looking curious.

"Well, damn me if it isn't Chua Gabaye!" he exclaimed, although he didn't really sound so surprised. "And who's the other one who came with you? Tongloss?"

"Ming, *darling!* Ming Tokiabi! We're the last ones, you know. And you're something of a last of your kind, too. We've never met before, I don't believe, but we have so *much* in common in our pasts. You will never know how absolutely *delighted* I am to have you in this position!"

"What's your beef, Gabaye? I saved your ample ass back at Gate Four. You were all set to join the little furball zombie brigade."

"You and that little twit who saved me condemned me to forty-seven long additional years of *boredom*, darling! This is the most fun I've had in simply *ages!*"

"If that's your complaint, I can end it all for you right here," he suggested helpfully.

She smiled sweetly at him. "Oh, my, no! Not *now!* Not when it's getting a wee bit *interesting* again."

"Let's get this over with," he said impatiently. "How do I know that's Spirit?"

Chua looked shocked. "Would I *lie* to you?" She stopped for a moment. "How silly! Of *course* I would! But, *darling*, suppose it isn't? What in the *world* could you *do* about it? Conjure up a transparent dragon? How absolutely *frightening!* Or, perhaps, bind me with those cute little strings of yours?"

"Personally, nothing," he admitted. "However, I assume that this area is being monitored using the projector, and for something like this I expect Suzl on the other end. Somehow, I don't think Suzl wants Spirit in this any more than I do. Not at this stage and in that condition. And I have a few little surprises I'd rather not discuss until I need them. So, prove to me that this is an honest swap.''

Chua turned and merely glanced casually at the Eve. Intelligence and awareness of it all seemed to flow into the woman like liquid into a bottle, and she looked at the scene with bright, intelligent eyes and realized what was going on. "Dad! Don't do it! Not for *her!*"

"I'm not doing it for her, I'm doing it for you—partly," he assured her. "Don't worry, honey. They aren't gonna mess with my mind. They need me to show 'em how to beat New Eden."

"You *know* how to beat New Eden?" Gabaye asked, seemingly honestly.

"I've got a pretty good idea. It's an interesting challenge, anyway. Spirit, I want to know the name of the chief gardener in New Pericles."

She looked surprised. "Why, Bruton."

"O.K., it's you. Can you check yourself over, make sure Chua, here, hasn't left any little traps to go off later?"

Spirit did a check. "I think it's just the binding spell," she told him. "But—Dad, why? You know Suzl wouldn't have harmed me."

"Honey, if we don't beat New Eden we'll all get measured for heels and fancy panty-hose anyway, even Madam Glamor, here. That's first priority. Everything else can wait until then. Now, the only folks who have a shot are these people. I got four months maximum to turn 'em from amateurs into professionals.''

"But—where do I go now?"

"Dell and Sondra will meet you when you get out a little ways and explain things. Don't be too shocked by Dell's appearance. He hasn't gotten over it himself, yet. A little gift from our friend, here.''

Chua smiled sweetly again. "I *do* hope he tries to untangle that one. Whoever does will be simply *gorgeous!*''

Spirit stared at him. "You're sure?"

"I'm sure. Trust me this time, like you usually do. Go on, now. I've got work to do."

She hesitated a moment more, then kicked her heels in and rode through the shield and off into the void.

"You sound almost as if you *wanted* to do this," Gabaye noted suspiciously.

"There are three factions on this world able to do big things. I represent one of them. You represent another. New Eden is our common enemy in this. Me, I'd rather knock them over than be sitting around one day and suddenly grow big breasts and have an urgent desire to wash the walls."

"You realize, of course, that we can't permit you in here—as you are. I'm afraid it would not only lead to all sorts of problems but also give you a big advantage."

"I figured as much. Suzl, if you're listening in, I'm willing to play ball on your side, but there are a lot of protective spells on me I can't possibly understand and I don't think Chua, here, has figured out either, although she's been trying for five minutes. My form's another matter. I had those spells tripped. I know the score in there."

Chua looked thoughtful. "Let's see. . . . What sort of a girl should you be? Not an Eve, certainly. Perhaps an Ayesha. Really learn how the other half is forced to live."

"You could do it," he agreed, "but if you want me to *lead* this new army and work with them and train them, that body'll be more harm than help. I'll need a more authoritative figure than that. How about Sondra?"

"But I don't *know* your Sondra, darling!"

"Suzl does. What about it, Suzl? Can't you see the imposing figure of Sondra training and leading these troops? Besides, I always thought that if I was a woman I'd want to look like Sondra."

Chua started to open her mouth, but the spell came through the grid and then rose up and engulfed the figure on the horse, although not the horse and saddle itself. When it subsided, the big man was gone, but in his place was the equally imposing visage of his older daughter, in black stringer outfit including hat and boots, dark skin, silver hair. Only Matson's pistols remained as they were, and the gunbelt now hung a bit too much on the hips. Unhesitatingly, the new Matson urged the big black horse forward and crossed to the Fluxland.

"Now, that wasn't bad at all," said Matson in a new, low, almost sultry feminine voice that still contained the same Matson accent and tonalities. "Lead on!" the new woman said. "And along the way I'll want the answers to some big questions."

13

COMMON AND
UNCOMMON ENEMIES

When the familiar figure came into view, Morgaine could
only think, *My God! They caught Sondra!* She started to
rush up to her, but something stopped her. Something here
was not quite right. Sondra was clearly no prisoner, although she looked herself and not like one of Suzl's
wizards, and there was something slightly wrong in the
carriage and the mannerisms. Besides, when did Sondra
take up smoking cigars?

She wondered if this were some sort of trick. Were they
perhaps creating a duplicate Sondra to replace the real
one?

Chua Gabaye pointed, and she and "Sondra" walked
towards and then into Suzl's main tent. Although they had
the power here to build castles and cities, they had not
done so. Suzl didn't want the people to get too comfortable too quickly, and she also knew that they would
eventually have to move.

Matson was genuinely shocked with the primitiveness of
it all, and even more shocked to see poor Suzl. She looked

a lot like Morgaine had, of course, but the blindness, an affliction only seen in strictly closed Anchors before, was evident. Suzl also looked very tired, and not at all the voluptuous vision she was supposed to be. The electronic voice, which always shocked everybody, made the scene if anything even more unreal.

"Hello, Matson."

"Suzl. Thanks for the use of Sondra's form." The voice was a bit lower than Sondra's and definitely had a different edge to it. It sounded, in fact, like Matson's voice, only one half-octave up. Still, to those who hadn't known him, the figure seemed more like one of feminine strength than masculine transformed. This figure moved like a woman, sat like a woman, and seemed quite comfortable with the form. The figure was commanding, but unless you knew the facts you would swear that Matson had been born that way.

"I'm glad you came in, but I'm very sorry it had to be Spirit who was the lure. She was crazy to have tried that. She could have died."

"We all have to take risks on occasion for what we believe. The fact is, while I'm glad to have her out of this, I think this was inevitable anyway. As I told Chua Gabaye, we have a common enemy to defeat before we can even start arguing about the winners." There was a pause. "Chua Gabaye! And Ming Tokiabi, too! You sure got in bed with some strange partners!"

"That was set up before I even came on board," Suzl told Matson. "Even so, we needed them. We needed their experience and their technology base."

"You trust 'em?"

"No. But I believe they are as committed to the over-throw of New Eden as we are. New Eden is as much a threat to them as to us. After? I don't know."

"I think I do. They want the projectors. They want New Eden out of the way, and then the projectors in their hands to keep the Guild at bay. When New Eden goes, I wouldn't trust them one second more."

"I've tried to guard as much as I can. The wizards here

are bound, by spells I myself put on, not to betray me. Also, I make everyone carry these radios so I can contact them and they can contact each other. I can listen in if need be.''

"I'll have to keep that in mind." Definitely. If Suzl could activate anybody's radio and eavesdrop on them, it would be good not to make any comments that might sound threatening to Suzl or the group. Stringers were well-versed in electronic eavesdropping techniques—and fooling them.

Suzl seemed lost in thought for a moment, then asked, "Why did you come in? You surely knew I would never harm Spirit. I couldn't.''

"I know. That's why I didn't bring Jeff along. I didn't want you to have to face your own son. Dell was a good help, although I'm afraid Chua embarrassed him all to hell.''

"You're avoiding the question.''

Matson sighed. "I'm here because I think I know how to win. No guarantees, but if my ideas work out then it's possible. It's another big challenge. It's what I do best. And, of course, I don't relish the idea of becoming a Fluxwife myself. Those programs will be like the old ones—indiscriminate. And even if I got out of it, there's a lot of folks close to me I wouldn't like to see that way. I saw what they did to Sondra and Jeff—and to Cass and you, too. So, here I am.''

"How is Cass?"

"Doing well. She's a hell of a horse breeder and she worked hard and finally got her vet's degree. She doesn't dare travel much, because we can't fix her in Flux if anything happens, but she's been all over anyway and done everything. The twins keep house and act somewhat as her bodyguards in a Flux environment. It's not a bad life.''

"But it's not your life.''

"Yeah, it is. I'd like to get back to it when this is done, if I can, and if we all survive. It's a nice way to spend the time between crises.''

Suzl gave an eerie electronic chuckle. "And so here we are again. You realize I don't intend to stop with New Eden."

"Yeah, well, that's somebody else's problem, not mine. My people have worked out accommodations with the damndest sets of people. Me, I'm old military. My ancestor was the first general of the Signal Corps. It's a tradition. I leave all the politics to others. My job starts when the politics fails."

"Do you really think you can beat them? I mean, really beat them?"

"If you mean can I destroy New Eden utterly and break their system for good, the answer's probably 'no.' If you mean can we win this battle and force them into an accommodation to our liking, the answer is 'maybe.' " Quickly Matson sketched in the geography and demographics of the problem.

"Winning the battle will depend on some tests we're gonna run with your projector as soon as we can, and you being able to scare up enough wizards and ground troops to make a difference," the stringer told her. "Winning the war is going to depend on your unpleasant friends. I'll know more after we make those tests."

For the first time, Suzl had hope. The depression she'd been in when talking to Morgaine seemed far away. Still, Matson was as much or even more of a threat than the old wizard allies. Anyone who could fight off alien invaders and thought nothing of taking on New Eden wasn't going to leave out of planning how to keep Suzl's dreams from being realized as well.

"Matson—you were the last true man I had inside. Want to test out that body and get the favor returned?"

The stringer sighed. "Not now. And not with you, Suzl, although I feel the genuineness of the offer. You're a wizard—and a strong one—locked in a body of passions. I'm at the mercy of that power. If I feel the need and have time, I *might* try some recreation with somebody, if only for the novelty of the experience, but it won't be with a wizard. You understand? It's just too important not to screw up."

Suzl was disappointed, but she understood the problem. One-sided wizard powers in the heat of passion could do strange things to the other partner, some positive, others very negative, that would be hell to fix or sort out. As much as she wanted, and feared, Matson, she wanted that mind just the way it was.

"All right. Oh! I guess we better warn Morgaine who you are. I'll have Gill get you settled in, and then I'll arrange a meeting between you and the top staff here. Then you can go to work."

"Sounds all right to me. Some wizard's gonna have to find me fresh clothing and the basics, anyway. Funny, too. I've only had this form for a few hours but I really feel like I need a bath."

Suzl sat on the active projector, listening, as the entire staff of wizards and military commanders sat watching. It was, however, Matson's show.

"Up to now," the stringer told them, "it's been impossible to move around World using the grid no matter what your power. That went for goods, too. We could create things through energy-to matter transfers, but the network couldn't carry and transmit a complex person or thing and reassemble it to our command elsewhere. Part of that was because of the relative signal from the wizard to the computer, and part was the nature of the switching network from one master computer to another that limited such things to line of sight, or maybe fifty kilometers, and only for inanimate objects. Last night, Suzl, Morgaine, and I, along with our two allies, worked out a different approach using the projector. The computer interaction point is always with the wizard, not the objective. The wizard establishes a spell, or program, checks it for errors and problems with the computer, then sends it. The computer then runs the spell. The old methods didn't work, because to work the wizard would have to be in two places at the same time—transmit point and receive point.

"With the projector, this is possible. It is possible to initiate a matter-to-energy conversion program, or spell, at the transmit point, and then a complementary receive spell at the desired location. That's the theory. I didn't come up with it. I had it handed to me as a theory by the Guild. Now we can test it out."

"At a predetermined location fifty kilometers south of here," Suzl told them, "are several target objects. I have them located with no problem. One by one, I am going to issue commands at the remote site and if this theory is correct they should appear in the grassy field over there. Let's do it!"

They all watched, unable to really follow the projector's actions but waiting, all eyes on the field. Suddenly, there was a saddle there. Then a tree appeared next to it. Finally, a brown horse appeared, looking somewhat confused but otherwise in fine shape. There was some applause. Matson walked over, checked the horse, and nodded, then walked away.

Suzl waited for radio confirmation. "They all vanished just like I was there on the spot, then reappeared here. I converted them, placed them in files, then read the files out to these coordinates. The elapsed time seems to be about twenty seconds."

"We'll have to cut that way down," Matson told her. "We'll have to cut it further than you think it *can* be cut. This is only the first stage. I want every wizard here to do it—again and again. Practice and train on it. When you've got it down, then we'll try for objects without a predetermined location. You'll have to find them, mark them, and do it. When that time is down as far as it can be pushed, then we'll do the tough stuff. Random *moving* objects to be located, trapped, filed, and read out here. Finally, we'll try those random moving objects with some wizards aboard expecting the attack."

There was muttering among the wizards, and the word "impossible" was heard more than once.

"Listen," Matson said sternly, "this is *your* fight. It is *not* impossible because we *must* have it! Everything depends on it, and not just on it being done. It depends on it being done very fast and *instinctively*, without even taking the time to think. Without this, you can't win. All the power and all the troops we might get won't make one damned bit of difference. There's no time for doubting or slacking off. If we just once are forced to go on the defensive, we're through, and we might all just as well get our numbers on our asses and start keeping house for big men in black leather uniforms. This not only has to work, it has to work the *first* time and *every* time. They're not dumb down there. They may not have thought of this trick yet, but once they get victimized by it, it won't take them long to figure it out. If they get to withdraw their own projectors and equipment back into Anchor and then wait until they have the trick themselves and work out a defense against it—and there is *always* a defense against *anything*—we've had it.''

It was blunt, but it made its point. Even the roughest of those who watched, the most insular and suspicious, were impressed by the stranger's cool, professional manner that dripped not only with authority but with confidence. They might not give their total trust, but it became somehow easy to believe that if everyone followed instructions, drilled, drilled, drilled, and pushed themselves to the limit, wizard and nonwizard alike, they might just win this thing.

For the original troops, the family who led the rest, Matson had another shock. ''I want you all to look exactly like Fluxgirls,'' they were told. They protested vehemently, and it took a while before the explanation could come.

''In war, you exploit your own strengths and your enemy's weaknesses. The fact is, we're not very strong in a relative sense and the enemy doesn't have many weaknesses. They're tough, battle-hardened, and driven by a religious fever. They firmly believe that if they die in battle they will go immediately to one of the highest heavens. They're not above losing an engagement, or even a battle, and remaining all right—but to show cowardice, to surrender as opposed to withdrawal, to show a lack of will in battle, is to condemn yourself in this life and send you to Hell in the next. That's a pretty tough enemy, and they have a million like that. Fortunately, with so large a country to guard, we won't see a fraction of that, but we will see troops who are that way.''

A map was spread out on the ground showing the northern and some of the eastern New Eden border. ''Now, being good tacticians, they'll come out along here in a broad front. Probably committing half or less of their men, wizards, and projectors, keeping the rest in reserve just behind in well-protected Anchor.''

Gillian frowned when looking at the map. ''How can you be sure they'll come out there? Their border is over fifty-six hundred kilometers. They could come out *any-where*. Play it safe, come out down in the southeast or southwest and consolidate. It's what *I* would do.''

''Me, too,'' Matson agreed, ''but we are going to insure that they come out between Liberty's eastern border and Logh District. We are going to move down to this position when we're ready and we won't be secretive about it. In fact, we'll be a rolling tide, and there might even be some battles in between. We will have to have more troops and we have the power to get them, by battle or, hopefully, extortion, from the smaller Fluxlands in the way. The key border districts are the old Anchor areas—Logh here and Nantzee to the west—their science and technology center, and the original old industrial base. The land is still developing inward; the rest of the prime targets are in near the Gate, in the New Canaan district. They know if we take Logh we'll have a big prize, and we'll also have a way to send nasty little things through the Gate that might go *boom*. There's also pride. New Eden started in Anchor Logh, and it was Tilghman's home and the old capital. They'll defend it, and that's what we want. We want *them* always on the defensive. That forces a fight here, in a region you know well. The Logh area is heavily fortified, but the Liberty border area is hardly defended at all. That gives everybody some running room.''

''Yes, but why Fluxgirls?'' several wanted to know.

''Their strength is also their weakness. Pride and ego.

As good military commanders, if we manage to pull off an initial battle victory, they won't want to commit their reserves and their remaining wizards and projectors. Conventional wisdom would be to hold off, since there's no immediate threat to the interior, to pull back to Logh, and find out what went wrong and fix it. We can't allow them to do it, and our wildest dreams of troop additions wouldn't permit a successful assault on Logh Center if all their forces are concentrated there. That means forcing them into a tactical mistake. Doing something stupid. The only means of doing that is to put ego and career on the line. Think about it. You're one of those men in the army, born and bred in New Eden and a true believer. Now the survivors of the first assault who get back into Anchor tell you that you've been defeated, not just by an army of militant women, which is bad enough, but by *Fluxgirls in rebellion*. What do you do?''

"If they're smart, nothing," Gillian responded. "Surely they'll know it's a trick, that it's exactly what it is—a way to draw them back out."

"Maybe. Probably. The officers and senior noncoms, at least. But the troops won't be that reasonable. They will be humiliated, threatened, and angry. I'm betting that this, and one other thing, will force the officers into a second breakout. With their troops demanding it, to order a withdrawal would mean official protests up the ass, and all the reports would say that the officers refused to let them fight a horde of armed Fluxgirls. Even if their political chiefs know they did the right thing, that kind of news would mean ruin at the least for the officers in charge, maybe show court-martials. Public sentiment would demand it. They might smooth over being beaten by a bunch of women, because it's Flux and the people understand Flux power and fear it, but by a bunch of *Fluxgirls*? It'll drive 'em nuts even though they will *know* they're being had."

They were impressed. They were more than impressed, in fact.

"Now, I said you had to *look* like Fluxgirls, and that's not the same thing as being one. Anything that doesn't obviously show is all right. I have very strong arms and I keep them that way, not just with spell but with weights." The stringer rolled up a sleeve and flexed the muscles. The arm had looked smooth and normal until then, but now it showed raw power. "See? There lots of tricks like that. Still, I want you all changed as quickly as possible. I want you to feel that Fluxgirl-like body, know what it can do, and be natural with it. I don't want anybody forgetting that they're not quite as tall as they were, or misjudging a leap, or pausing to doubt whether or not they can pick up something or punch someone out. Although I'll be directing from the rear, when the time comes I, too, will take on a Fluxgirl body. Not only will I share your situation, but I don't want to stand out for some bright New Eden sharpshooter in case I have to come in close."

And that settled that.

The building up of forces proved easier as time went on. Ecksreh was in a shambles, and there was widespread lawlessness and starvation in many areas. Gorgh had also been ravaged, and, while stable now, you couldn't grow food and raise new livestock overnight, particularly in Anchor. The wizards of what Suzl now called New Harmony could manage a ghoulish but mutually profitable trade: surplus human beings who could not be fed and whose livelihoods had been destroyed in the wars and revolutions in exchange for massive quantities of fruits, vegetables, and developed food plants created out of Flux.

Also, Gillian and others visited smaller Fluxlands, ones still run in the old ways by single Fluxlords and none too secure. Extortion, Matson had predicted, would win cooperation. A slice of your army, or we might come and take your Fluxland down and take it all.

They spread the word of the army they were raising and for what purpose, and to their surprise got some major volunteers. A number of female wizards volunteered their own services and those of their people in the cause, although they were not willing to take on Suzl's spells for themselves. Their armies, however, were easily modified and integrated into the main body.

At Suzl's suggestion, New Harmony agents still posing as Fluxgirls inside New Eden used their own places and the corrupt male officials long ago bought by Borg Habib to run record checks on known former female wizards who were now Fluxgirls. A number of those, including most without small children or enormous in-home families, were abducted, smuggled out, and then deprogrammed by Krita and her devices. These proved to include both of Jodi's old Sister-wives, Giml and Honnah.

The army swelled to the largest number of female troops in World's history, perhaps forty thousand, all made equal in Flux and given, through Flux spells, the latest in modern weaponry and what training they needed to be coordinated units.

Suzl's own personal ranks of Ayesha-like wizards pledged to her swelled, with the Fluxgirl additions and the actual commitment of some former Fluxgirl wizards who caught the dream, to thirty-four. In addition, counting Chua and Ming, there were another twenty allied wizards. Other than not allowing the outsiders on or near the projectors, they had the same rank and duties as other wizards.

Under Matson's skilled direction, they formed the most powerful unified army since the Invasion, and in wizard power were stronger than the armies of the Reformation. It was not, however, a one-person job. Many of the newcomers had some sort of military backgrounds, mostly in Fluxlands or in the Anchor civil wars, and knew how to do things.

What had been accomplished in a mere ninety-three days stunned them all. It also stunned Matson, but that wasn't for anyone else to know. The amount of fear and resentment against New Eden had been badly underestimated by them all, that much was clear.

Matson used the allied wizards to survey New Eden, and used the internal network of New Harmony spies and corrupt officials within the country to keep track of progress. The numbers didn't look good, and it was time to move.

"I would prefer another six months," the stringer told

the general staff of New Harmony. "At this rate, we would have a hundred wizards and an army of a quarter of a million. With that, I might try taking part of New Eden itself. The fact is, though, we don't have it. We must close down here and move south as an advancing wave. We'll put into practice what we've learned here as we go, against targets of opportunity. New Eden has its own allies and spies, and we must assume they know what we have and why we're doing it. If we don't move on them now, those projectors and forces will come out at a time and place *they* decide instead of where we want it to be. We need them all together, bunched up in one predictable spot."

"It seems to me that we're the bait in our own trap," Morgaine noted nervously. "If they don't take the bait, all this is for nothing."

"They'll take it," Matson assured her. "They *have* to take it." But the confidence in the old stringer's tone belied deep-down fears. The fact was, they not only *didn't* have to take it, they *shouldn't*. The only thing that would make them take it was their pride and their ego. It had to be enough.

Even as they started to move, all but the Eves and a few holding personnel abandoning their beautiful new land, Matson sought out Gabaye and Tokiabi.

"I understand you plan to shoot yourselves up into orbit and find the old master builder computers," the stringer said. "I assume you haven't yet successfully sent a human being up?"

"Only some inanimate matter and a few small animals, darling," Chua responded. "The tests so far have been prototypes only. After all, we're not going to get in until we're *positive* it's safe and it'll work and we can bring it back if need be."

"But you have the proper file programs and machines to guide the things now?"

"Oh, yes, dear. Of course!"

"We're going to need them down here. Guidance and programming experts and whatever is necessary to create and launch the things." Quickly the plan to reduce New

Eden's industrial and transportation network to rubble and force an accommodation was outlined, and the rationale behind it.

Chua was entranced. "*Darling*! What a positively *diabolical* concept! We simply never *thought* of it that way! You know, making a woman out of you was a fine touch. Stripped of your male orientation, one could almost get to *like* you!"

"I pretty well doubt that I'm the first one who ever thought of it or used it. If there was any alternative, I wouldn't use it now."

"Ah! Compassion! Such a *womanly* value. One of the reasons New Eden made such doormats out of them."

"Your group created New Eden," the stringer reminded her. "Coydt van Haas created it, and you and Haldayne and Ivan and the others helped shape and direct it because you needed it to open the Gates. Now your monster's turned on you, like in the old children's stories, but it's your monster all the same."

Chua smiled, but made no reply.

Matson could see her mind working, and knew what implications had just been planted in that twisted mind of hers. With the projectors for protection and for Flux use, and guided projectiles for Anchor, World was theirs for the asking. What these two would do with it if they got it was something the stringer didn't like to think about. Both Gabaye and the almost-totally-withdrawn Tokiabi were insane in a sense beyond any he had experienced before. Normal standards and expectations just did not apply. At one time they, or particularly Gabaye, could be reasonable and normal and just seem eccentric; the next minute, her reactions would be totally incomprehensible. For example, there was no question that they genuinely hated Matson for beating the *Samish*, even though the *Samish* had been about to incorporate them into their mass computer-organic mind. They were eager to leave World for the stars, yet they relished the idea of controlling it completely.

Matson directed that they avoid trouble with the stringers and they moved south. The Guild was a third force, able to mobilize huge forces, and it would do so if attacked, even at the cost of a New Eden victory. The Guild had compromised with New Eden before. Best to leave that force neutral. This was a chancy enough operation as it was.

Anyone else was not so lucky. Although Matson didn't like to do it, there were priorities involved, and the mind sets of those at the top would overrule any moral qualms anyway. Weaker Fluxlands were simply punched through with the force of fifty-four wizards, at least half world-class: they were hardly even a problem, more a mild training exercise. Unable to even escape from such power, the wizards, faced with death, took the binding spells and became part of the force. Their populations, having no choice in the matter, were quickly converted and added to the ranks, although as reserves because of the lack of real opportunity for training. Still, it was another twelve thousand, and the force stretched back for kilometers across a broad front. Any New Eden man would have blanched at the sight of fifty-two thousand apparent Fluxgirls, armed to the teeth and riding and marching in disciplined columns, backed by fifty-four female wizards.

They were not in position until the hundred and twenty-first day after Matson had taken over and reformed them; behind schedule, but not dangerously so—or so they hoped. Their remaining contacts in New Eden—many of the officials had been scared off and some of the agents captured by this point—indicated, however, that the huge Anchor was taking the bait. Trains were rumbling from the interior towards the northeast border, and at least five projectors had been seen near the old walls of Anchor Logh by their allied wizards flying reconnaissance, and the movement of large numbers of troops and both heavy and light ordnance. The heavy population in the Logh area was being moved back as well into temporary holding camps.

Suzl sat on a wagon seat, Ayesha behind her, arms around the blind woman's neck, nuzzling her. "Oh, I wish you could *see* all this!" the consort gushed. "It's more power, more people, than many cities, my darling! All of them women, all of them *ours*. It passes my wildest dreams!'' Ayesha was pregnant and just starting to show. So were most of the New Harmony wizards, except Suzl and perhaps the new ones picked up on the journey down. Suzl had used her powers for birth control, not wanting to add pregnancy to the pressures, although she was certainly responsible, as father, for some of the others. New Eden had taught her how to proceed with a social and physical revolution. This would be merely a base to build on, to create a whole new race which would one day conquer and revolutionize World even more than the First Spell had done. She would hold her fifty-four, and add to their ranks. Never before had so much power been permanently committed to a single set of goals.

And yet, oddly, she didn't feel the thrills that Ayesha felt, or even get excited over the vision with which she had inspired the rest of them. When Ayesha asked if Suzl minded if she went down and looked it all over more closely, there was no objection. Morgaine, who was on a break from her own training program, saw the lonely-looking figure sitting there and came over. With some effort she hauled herself up and sat next to Suzl.

''Why so gloomy? Nerves? Me, too.''

''No, not nerves. Or, I don't know, maybe it is. I feel like—what did they call that thing back at the carnival? A roller coaster. One of the little cars on a roller coaster. Sometimes I'm way up, and the world is mine and nothing can be wrong; then I'm down, all the way down, and nothing seems right. At first I thought it was just having to sit around, doing nothing, so much of the time. That's a lot of it. The fact is, even when I'm on that projector, there's lots of stretches of just plain dull. Sex is still fun—just turn on and shut down the world—but Ayesha doesn't find me so alluring anymore, even with my attributes, and anybody else so inclined, if there are any, are too busy. Most of the time I just sit, in the dark, not doing much except eating. I'm getting fat again. All of us should weigh sixty-five kilos, and all of you do. I'm certain of that. I have the same frame, the same bones, and I'm the same height as the rest, but I weigh twice that, as must be evident.''

It was true and evident, and it had gone almost exclusively to her already-oversized breasts, rear, and stomach. Morgaine knew that the spell was supposed to maintain the body as it had been created, and had wondered and worried about it, and said as much to Suzl.

"Oh, it's the spell, all right. Ayesha bought it from somebody who thought they were better than they were. She didn't know, and the rest of the bunch couldn't tell. I'll never be sure whether the blindness wasn't deliberate, to make sure I'd always be dependent on her, but the rest of the spell isn't perfect, either. One of the new girls is something of a Flux doctor and she looked me over. She said it was an overdose of both types of hormones. I got body hair I have to have shaved off because my spells work on anybody but me. That's also partly causing these mood swings, or so she thinks. The worst part is, the bigger this gets the less I'm a part of it, or even *needed*."

Morgaine gave her a kiss and a hug. "That's not true. Any time I'm on a break or after this is over, I'm available. I'm pregnant, though, so I wind up being the male all the time." She laughed. "I really do like this bisexuality, by the way. Funny thing is, I was so mannish for so long that I like looking and feeling this way. I like the feel of big breasts, the glamour part, all that, but I get more of a charge out of giving than getting. I don't know if it's the spell or me, but it works so well I think if I were free to choose again I'd stay the same."

"It's not the spell. That only makes you comfortable with it. Some people, maybe most, will always tend to be one or the other. It's personality, really, but this way the choice is on the individual. Take Matson, for one. He'd never be female by choice. That's why I made his spell totally female, an exact duplicate of Sondra. He's just not tempted that way. The real Sondra, on the other hand, has her father's masculine toughness but is all female. Your mother, I think, would be the opposite of you. She prefers the look and company of women to men, yet she'd never be in the masculine role sexually. But, again, under my system, it's the individual's choice and personality.'' She sighed. ''But all these things have never been for old Suzl. Do you believe in fate?''

''Chance. Not fate. Not if you mean things are predestined to happen.''

''Well, *I* believe in fate. I'm predestined to be a freak. I wasn't in Flux but a couple of months when I picked up a real, regular male prick. I was little, fat, kind of cute in a way. So I wound up taking up with a guy who liked other guys. To him, I was the best of all worlds. Then things went nuts and I wound up a real dugger. Tits as long as my arm that stuck straight out and a prick just as long that about dragged the ground when it wasn't turned on. The more they tried to fix it, the worse it got. Then I got a choice: be a Fluxgirl, all the way, physically *and* mentally, or stay that way forever. I saw the looks in even my closest friends' eyes, and I took the Fluxgirl route. Thing was, I hated the system, hated the people, but I *loved* being a Fluxgirl. I just didn't feel that anybody else should be forced to be one. Is that crazy?''

''Well, I can't see myself ever staying home all day, fixing the meals, cleaning house, pressing clothes, stuff like that, but I can't condemn anybody else for feeling that's a decent way to spend a life.''

''It was the only real normalcy I ever had. It was *my* house, and *my* kids, and I had a place, a role, that was clear-cut and approved. It was a simple world, with simple rules, and it was peaceful and routine. I had no worries, and my responsibilities were clear-cut and easy to handle. If I'd had a better husband, one who loved me and who I could love, with a normal-type job and normal ambitions, I could have stayed that way forever and been happy with it. That's the wrong thing to say, I know. Women are as good as men in most things and better in some. I never yet met a man, Matson included, I thought could handle a childbirth in Anchor without becoming a simpering wimp. I guess that's my problem. Ever since the Invasion, every time I'd tell somebody I just wanted that kind of life, man or woman, they'd get shocked. I was weak. I was unambitious. 'You're smart, Suzl, you could be anything you wanted.' Like there was something evil about it. Evil's when you're *forced* into something like that, like New Eden. Everybody kept acting like I wanted all women to be like that. Well, that's stupid. People shouldn't be forced into things. They should be able to try and be whatever they want to be.''

"I—I think I understand," Morgaine said, and meant it.

"New Eden, now, they took something potentially nice and made it ugly. I think that's why I hate them so much. It's also why I want to remake this place. Everything is always 'men can't' and 'women can't.' They're forced into roles. The New Human can't be forced by reason of sex. No man in any Anchor could ever stay home all day and keep house and diaper the baby. He'd have the shit beat out of him. And no woman is supposed to do that because she becomes just a supplement to the man. So you work into your ninth month, then in a couple of weeks drop the kid off in communal care and trot back to your big career and power plays and all that. The commune raises the kids and the parents see each other only when they go to bed for the night, but that's O.K.; it insures that the little kid will follow in Mommy or Daddy's footsteps and not have the freedom to do something else. If a woman wants to be a doctor or an engineer or a lawyer or whatever, then she should be able to do it if she's able without any hold-ups or hang-ups, and if a man wants to cook and clean and keep house and maybe cry when he's sad or even make his face up, that should be O.K., too. It'll never happen the way people are, but when there's no men and no women, just people, both sides will be freed from that. You understand?''

"I think so. I certainly *hope* you're right. Still, a lot of us like men. Like the differences, the contrasts. The deep voices, hairy chests, and tight asses. All the New People look female.''

"Until a man can have a baby, there's no equality," Suzl noted. "And to have it, he needs the equipment.''

She sighed. "Still, I may live to see it but I won't be a part of it. I'll be there, huge and immobile, blind and helpless, pandering to folks to offer a unique sexual thrill."

"We'll never let that happen," Morgaine assured Suzl honestly.

"You know, twice I been saved from these 'permanent' spells by outside forces so unlikely even once was improbable. Yet, even if I got rid of this, it wouldn't last. I *have* to be the freak. When this is all over, when I know the dream is real, then we'll see."

Morgaine had to go back on duty, but she felt very badly about Suzl, both her condition and her attitude. She was so good, and meant so well, and no matter what happened she'd gotten a load of cosmic shit dumped on her. Now she led an army she could not see, against an enemy she hated but whose lifestyle haunted her, in the name of a dream she couldn't share. And all she really wanted at all was somebody to love, and to love her in return. Happy endings were for fairy stories. The best she could hope for was victory. Morgaine felt that at least they could all give her that.

14

THE BATTLE OF NEW EDEN

Matson had been getting edgy and impatient. As much as the stringer had wished for another six months, it was impossible to keep troops like this—particularly the high-strung wizards—on edge forever. They had been there over a week; New Eden knew they were there—there had been spies about and probes and even a small patrol. They had caught it and turned them into nice Fluxgirl warriors with some glee, and expected them to be good fighters. If they ever ran back to New Eden, looking like Fluxgirls, they would be interrogated, believed, and then processed *as* Fluxgirls. All they knew, though, was that there were a lot of soldiers about in Logh District and along the open border, and lots of ordnance and some new secret weapons for Flux as well.

"If they're not coming out," Matson told Suzl and the general staff, "then we will have to draw them out." The proposal was to deploy batteries of battle rockets with explosive heads as far as possible around the border, shooting in. "We'll keep bombing randomly until they send troops out to stop it. Then we'll take those troops and bomb them some more. If they fall back and *still* won't come out, we'll have no choice but to bring up some of Chua Gabaye's big stuff and reverse the order of battle we planned. When even New Canaan starts burning from the air, they'll come out.''

New Eden certainly didn't like the rocket attacks. Although they were standard gunpowder rockets, and could not really be aimed, they had a fierce bang when they landed and could start a nasty fire. Their range was limited, a mere five kilometers at maximum elevation, but within those five kilometers they could make life hell. The chance of inflicting any really serious damage to the force was slight, but the psychological effects were devastating.

New Eden was not amused, but it learned pretty quickly not to send mere troops out to stop things. The next time they sent out a pretty strong wizard with the troops. It took Suzl seven seconds to locate him, run a matter-to-energy conversion, then reverse it within the camp. The amount of sheer Flux power surrounding him was enough to make some of them almost sympathize with his plight, and his expression resembled that of someone who'd just been shown his only child's severed head. Suzl had yet another Ayesha-like wizard for her stable, but since they'd had— of necessity—to erase both memories and personality, it would be some time before she would be of any real use.

Matson allowed the rocket crews to actually take on the small company of cavalry that had come with the wizard. At this point, they needed some action more than New Harmony needed more recruits, and a few of the men were allowed to escape back into Anchor to report as the next barrage sounded. *Fluxgirls! They were New Eden women on those rockets, I swear, sir! Called us insulting names, then fought like demons. . . . The wizard, sir? We don't know. I guess they shot him. . . .*

The generals of New Eden were disturbed. With the rumors spreading like wildfire, they could hardly contain the troops, yet they didn't want to fight on the enemy's turf and at the enemy's beck and call. At the speed they could move the lumbering projectors, even on the new tractors, a solid flanking maneuver would take days and could not be moved up undetected. They didn't know the range, but couldn't assume more than fifty kilometers. Out of range of the main body, at that. They hadn't dared to test them in the void since the first one was stolen; all had been tested and tuned at Gate Four, which wasn't much room for real testing nor was there sufficient Flux to really see what they could do. The rockets had done negligible damage, but so unnerved and infuriated the troops that they were starting to grumble that their officers were cowards. There was no choice. They had to attack, and frontally.

Staff meetings of brigade-level officers and wizards were called.

"They're coming out!" the forward observers radioed back, the dense Flux of the void shortening their range to only ten meters, but in back of them was another with a radio, and another, and another.

Matson studied the map as the reports came in. With a quasi-Fluxland environment, the radios in the rear could communicate to virtually all of them if need be, and this was the time.

"Five projectors initially, at map coordinates GG-267, IL-109, KB-026, MN-04l, and PD-144. Projector ready?"

"Ready!" came Suzl's excited response.

"Wizards deploy with units to each position!" Four each from Suzl's crowd would cover each position, the rest in reserve in case of problems or other breakouts. The fourteen allied wizards were dispersed to get to any position that needed them in the minimum amount of time. New Eden would send its wizards out with a quick shield thrown up, then reinforce it with more wizards. Then the projectors would come through, and the troops behind them. There was a temptation to break the preliminary shield and gobble up the wizards, but then the projectors wouldn't come through. The prizes could not be easily won. The wizards of New Harmony would have to be close enough to actually see the shield to really have a crack at it, and while New Eden didn't have the range or the practice, it had easily discovered how to make a sweep and deactivate a wizard.

Matson was certain they wouldn't fail for lack of trying. Earlier some of the spies who'd managed to make it out had told them all about New Eden's plans for World. They would run a transitory version of the master program in Flux, but amended. There were about sixty million men and women on World, and about five million of them were New Eden men. Each of those men had been promised when it was over that they would get twelve wives as a harem, and that all, even the lowest, would be lords of vast domains to give to their own sons. Only Ayesha needed to have the arithmetic of *that* explained to her, and she already had the general idea. New Eden men would be the *only* men, until they had sons of their own.

More, the program had been altered, thanks to their new research into Flux and its powers, and it had already been tested on large numbers of women inside New Eden: A new standard for female I.Q., setting it at no more than seventy percent of the male average. High enough for all the things a woman was expected to do in New Eden society, but not one bit more. Permanent, total, *inheritable* intellectual inferiority, coldly and scientifically designed to create the perfect harem wife.

If they lost, every one of them who survived, wizard or commoner, would have this program run on them. More, success or failure would probably be determined in the first hour or so.

And they came out, very well timed thanks to internal Anchor communications. Now, however, the initial forces were on their own, cut off from real communication with the rear except by runner. Although the radios had limited use in Flux, the signals broke up into garbage when crossing an Anchor border.

The early shields were almost pathetic. A forward volunteer line of sharpshooters fired into them and they were so flimsy that several men within those first shields actually fell wounded.

Matson had been true to the vow made earlier to Gillian,

and had gotten Morgaine to change the Sondra form to that of a Fluxgirl, and a pretty good looking one even by Fluxgirl standards. Still, it was a Fluxgirl mounted on a large horse, wearing boots rather than heels, and wearing a gunbelt and holding a radio.

There was no way to really communicate with the forward units by radio now, not along a nearly-fifty-kilometer fragmented front, but Matson could talk to Suzl, and Suzl with the projector could talk to anybody.

"Don't wait for them all," the stringer warned. "As soon as your scan shows one projector fully in Flux, go for that shield."

"They've got a pretty solid shield now right in the middle," Suzl reported. "I think some of those early shots into the others might have nabbed a couple of wizards. Yeah! In the center! Here it comes!"

The projector only superficially resembled the one New Harmony had. The seat was padded and belted-in, the chassis more stylized, and it sat upon a large flat like a wagon bed, only under it were whole sets of wheels all turning two belts, one on each side, guided by a forward driver. It wasn't fast—it might do two kilometers an hour flat out—but it was effective and highly maneuverable. The shield was extended out in a U-shaped bubble that was growing to be several hundred meters out and about a hundred and fifty meters wide. Since it was open to Anchor at the back, it was nonporous—somebody else had thought of using gas—but that worked against the men inside. A shield that was too solid and too strong limited the effectiveness of the wizards inside, and particularly the projector. A shield drew from the grid squares beneath it; a too-solid and firm one could actually cut signal flow in both directions.

The allied wizards changed form and took to the air, five of them heading for the center position. As soon as they were within range, all nine wizards, the five in the air and the four on the ground, began a concentrated assault on the bubble.

There was no way of knowing how many wizards were

inside maintaining the bubble, but they were certainly not prepared for the strength of the assault on their lone position. They had mostly practiced this sort of thing against each other; they were not prepared for the ferocity of skilled veterans with everything to gain and nothing to lose.

Messengers were sent back as the bubble weakened, pleading for more reinforcements from the wizard corps, but the commanders had already sent part of the reserves in to shore up the other positions and were reluctant to commit more. They simply didn't have all that many really strong wizards trained for this, and their best had been the first out. These weren't amateurs at Flux, but fighting as mercenaries in somebody else's static Flux war between two equal teams of Fluxlords was not the same as this. The orders came back: lower the shield strength and use the projector and your own powers to find and disable the wizard attackers.

Suzl pushed first, committing two more allied wizards and her own projected strength just as the shield was being lowered in intensity. All of them had seen shields collapse before, but none of them had ever seen one burst like a soap bubble. The ground troops rushed forward, firing volleys as they advanced, but Suzl didn't wait for them. She ran in and with a shock met the outgoing projector pulse on the same grid path. The two operators were suddenly locked in a wizard's duel as if they were face to face.

Oh, no, you don't, you bastard! Suzl thought, fury rising to a peak within her. *You're mine!*

Abruptly, she broke contact, went over to a side channel, and then down and back over to the projector. The New Eden operator was suddenly stunned by the release, and she had him before he could even check his grid position. The projector, tractor, driver, wizard, and all, shimmered, then vanished. The troops on the ground cheered, but the wizards working with them wasted no time in erecting a vertical shield behind the perhaps six hundred to a thousand New Eden troops who had poured in behind the projector as the shield had weakened. The aerial wizards had already peeled off for the far eastern position, the next to solidify and grow, as two of the four on the ground left for the positions on either side. The two remaining would be sufficient to mop up.

The projector materialized in a preplanned area forward and south of Suzl's position. There, the troops made short work of the two men on it and pulled their bodies off. It would have been nice to save the wizards, but there wasn't really time to be subtle. Jodi climbed on, checked the contacts, and tried it.

"It's no good!" she radioed to Suzl. "The thing works, but the grid positions are all wrong! I don't have the focal point to make sense of them!"

Suzl's electronic voice came back to her. "No matter. Run 'clear memory' and stand by to receive my coordinate map!"

"I'm cleared," Jodi responded, sounding surprised that it worked. "Send."

The new map, identical to the one in Suzl's program module, was the familiar one, and Jodi tested it out. The machine seemed to accept it, and she relaxed. She was in business!

In the center, a couple of wizards survived, offering some protection to the infantry there, and they actually started trying some elaborate spells to stop the New Harmony advance. They were, however, all old tricks out of the standard training bag and easily handled. The tricks the New Harmony wizards showed them, which included illusions of giant lizards, horrible, nightmarish creatures, and which, not incidentally, obscured the very real crevasses forming under them and the equally real heating of the grid to the point where it started to burn combat boots, were far more effective. New Eden's wizards found it difficult to mount an assault involving concentration and mathematical programs while their feet were on fire.

They threw the force of ten wizards against the far eastern position, and it cracked in nine minutes. This time

Jodi had the honor on the projector, and ten minutes after that Morgaine was aboard her own.

Each victory gave the other positions a chance to strengthen themselves more, but each also allowed more wizard power to be concentrated and even projected into the remaining expanding bubbles. Forty-six minutes after the penetration began, Tila, one of those wizards who had joined Suzl and her spell voluntarily, was aboard her own projector. That left only the position almost on the Liberty border—ironically, the same position plus or minus some meters that the raiders had used after escaping from New Eden with their prize.

All, however, could not be brought to bear on that. The generals, apparently grinding their teeth in frustration at the lack of news and the inability to get any, sent two more projectors into positions between the far east point and the center.

Matson wasn't even concerned with them, except peripherally. The early successes were gratifying, and testified to New Eden's lack of real experience in this kind of thing against this size enemy, but in the face of obviously superior numbers and power, committing those two was akin to ritual sacrifice to no real purpose. Good officers, and they *were* good officers, simply wouldn't do that kind of thing without a reason.

"Suzl and the others! Forget the two outbreaks. Minimum force to contain them or break them! Everybody over to the far western area as quickly as possible!"

"What's the matter?" Morgaine came back. "Problems?"

"No! That's why they held off! They must have managed to get a couple of those things off their powered wagons and onto lorries! They're gonna hit us hard out of Liberty!"

"But—"

"Don't argue! Just *do* it! We could lose this thing yet!"

As quickly as possible, the projector operators notified the allies in flight, and they came down to carry those of Suzl's earthbound crew that could be spared to the west.

Matson, in the meantime, committed the reserve troops along a line almost due west of their rear position.

And even as they were beginning to shift, the enemy *did* come out of the west, with all five remaining projectors backed by a force that stunned and bowled over the wizards there concentrating on what they believed were the last of the enemy. Although it was reinforced by others, its heart was much stronger, better disciplined, and far more experienced than anything New Eden had thrown at them so far.

There had obviously been an armistice of sorts in the north. Somehow, perhaps merely by scaring them with the enormous power of New Harmony next door, the New Eden leadership had convinced the Fluxlords of Liberty to join in the attack, and they were something else: Five Fluxlords who were capable of maintaining a Fluxland as large as an Anchor, all the while fighting a long and protracted Flux war.

The four New Harmony wizards then on the scene had been caught from behind in sweeps and deactivated, but this new alliance of New Eden and Liberty had a new trick up its collective sleeve. One by one they were reactivated, and from the grid beneath them the force of at least five wizards to the one standing there literally forced up a complex program. The Liberty Fluxlords had determined that there were binding spells on the wizards and knew they could not fly up and away. Each in turn screamed and fell off her horse, then writhed for a moment. Then, after lying there a few more heartbeats, they got up, holding their heads and looking around, confused. None of them any longer had grid contact.

Now, across a twenty-kilometer front out of Liberty, the new alliance pushed not a shield but a program, engulfing almost a thousand New Harmony ground troops. Helpless against Flux without wizard protection, the program dematerialized all clothing and weapons and left them standing or sitting there, looking puzzled but not at all threatening.

"They're running that fucking Fluxgirl program!"

Morgaine practically screamed into the radio. "They're gonna turn us all into dumb little Fluxwives!" A collective shield went up, blocking the program's further progress, but an assault against it began immediately.

"*Like hell they are!*" Suzl came back, the force of her comment causing radio speakers to vibrate well beyond their reception. "Matson warned us not to get trapped on the defensive! All wizards—as soon as you can, don't reinforce the shield! Repeat—do not reinforce. *Push*. Everyone not involved in those two rear outbreaks behind it! Advance as it does!"

"Negative!" Matson responded. "Hold that shield and concentrate on breaking that last bubble on the border! As soon as our shield reaches that point, I want everyone available in ground support to push right through and shoot everything that moves! Take whatever wizards we can spare!"

"But that'll throw them into Anchor against New Eden forces!" Jodi objected.

"Only briefly. Just tell 'em to shoot whatever moves or looks nasty. The reason why that shield of theirs is so strong is that it's a sheet! It's got no back or sides! If *they* can flank us, then, damn it, *we* can flank *them!* The rest keep the pressure on here and follow that shield in! Those Fluxlords and those projectors just got to be right in back of that border! I'm going in with the flank!"

"Matson! No!" Morgaine cried. "We need you here, not as some Fluxgirl!"

"If this doesn't work, I'm gonna be one anyway. I might as well see if I can take some of those bastards with me!"

The air was thick with orders and assorted comments.

"Don't try and undo that spell for now!" Tila warned. "It's full of traps on each one! I think if you tried to undo it now the spell would transmit to you!"

"Those bastards!" Suzl snarled. "They'll pay for this. They'll all pay dear for this!"

Twelve of the flying allies came close enough to give real push to the shield, and it moved slowly back, but it neither buckled nor broke. The bubble for the fifth projector, however, went quickly, and they picked up another projector. Now all five were available for sweeps if they could buckle and break that shield.

New Harmony's troops moved through, less a disciplined group than a huge mob of thousands out to shoot anything in a black uniform. For Matson, it was a unique way to ride into a shooting war: bare-breasted, wearing nothing but a bikini, gunbelt, and leather boots, a gun in each hand, shooting down bewildered and stunned rear troops. It was a grand experience.

Gabaye, Tokiabi, and two of the others had an idea and didn't wait to clear it with Suzl. Their large forms, monstrous hybrids of human and leathery bird or bat, would not support their weight in Anchor, but they still had shape and momentum on their side. "I wonder how thick that shield is!" Gabaye shouted.

"No more than a meter, from its consistency," Tokiabi responded.

"Then follow me, darlings! We're going to flank, too! Wide turn and real drag coming up! *Whee!*"

Matson had some problem, along with the other officers, in turning the horde back into Flux, but they did so with all possible speed. Just as they started on the Anchor apron they saw and heard the four monstrous forms come in and then circle around while dropping rapidly. It looked for a moment as if they weren't going to make it, but all four did, and it cheered the troops who now followed confidently back into Flux—this time on the *other* side of that shield.

The Liberty–New Eden forces knew when they entered, but the shock was still great and they were slow to react. Not that they could have done much. They now had four flying and two ground wizards on their side of the shield, while a dozen more pushed them back from the other side. The Fluxlords of Liberty panicked, and withdrew all their power to a shield around themselves, leaving the New Eden ground forces, their wizards, and their three projectors at the mercy of five projectors and close to forty enraged wizards. The projectors were plucked almost as quickly as they appeared, leaving only the ground forces for serious fighting. These could have been taken out by Flux power, but instead the wizards gave protection to the New Harmony troops on the ground, both those who had successfully flanked the shield and those now pouring in along the front.

Matson was finally wrong about something. Twenty-six hundred of New Eden's finest male specimens would *too* surrender to five thousand Flux-guarded and well-armed Fluxgirls.

Not knowing what was happening many kilometers away with the flanking maneuver, the two diversionary projector outbreaks had continued to enlarge and expand and even take some toll, but Suzl now had more than enough wizard force to press in on the Liberty shield and released the flyers to take care of the other two.

The assault on the Liberty shield was powerful and emotional. As the shield began to contract prior to buckling, a message was pulsed out asking for terms.

"You are in no position for terms," Suzl pulsed back to them. "Drop your shield and surrender to us now or we will squash you like the bugs you are. We respected your neutrality and you stabbed and gravely harmed us. You must answer for it. At the moment, with our power divided, we outnumber you four to one. That number will increase, as other business is finished, up to nine-to-one. Surrender and we will promise only to hear you out. The attack continues. We estimate you have about fifteen more minutes at most to live."

There wasn't much discussion inside. The shield went down and the five stood there, hands raised, offering no further resistance, knowing that anything would get them, at best, shot to pieces.

The big shock from the New Harmony side was that three of the five Fluxlords of Liberty were women.

Suzl did not want them in camp yet, but she surveyed the other parts of the line and felt that things were secure at the moment. They had killed or captured the cream of

New Eden's relatively small crop of wizards, and they had eleven out of twelve projectors, if indeed there was a twelfth to get. It didn't matter. It would take New Eden half a year just to replace the hardware, and longer to train new wizards to properly use them. New Harmony did not intend to give them that time.

"Jodi!" Suzl called. "Right now I don't want this base fouled with them. Transmit me to them, projector and all."

"Are you sure? There's still some scattered resistance in that area and it's not void. It's trees and hills."

"Just do it. I'll be all right. We own that Fluxland now."

The five, held by wizards and guns, looked defeated and depressed, but they still managed to also be shocked when the area right in front of them suddenly shone with Flux, and Suzl and the projector materialized right in front of them.

These were defeated gods: people used to having their own way in all things and simply wishing for whatever they desired. This was a strange and humiliating spot for them, but they gazed up at the strange woman on the projector like petitioners at the throne of the queen. They still had their powers, having surrendered, and were thus potentially very dangerous, but it was this very thing that gave Suzl some sense of security. She would be speaking as first among equals, yet there was enough power around that if they tried anything they would die, and horribly. Gods fear death more than the mortals do, because with them it is not a foregone conclusion.

"I'm waiting for an explanation," said the electronic speaker in a voice so eerie and inhuman it sent chills up their backs. It was not the voice Suzl usually used; she'd been itching to try this one out at a suitable occasion.

The five wizards looked at each other and decided that one tall, slim, dark-haired woman would be the speaker for them all.

"It wasn't personal, it wasn't something we wanted to do," she began, searching for the words. "We were locked in an endless, no-win war with Hoghland. You know that. We were fending off revolts from within by associations of young wizard officers sick of the war, but Hoghland wouldn't settle, wouldn't even agree to a draw and some concessions on our part. It couldn't go on. A couple of weeks ago, New Eden made us an offer. They promised to deliver a cease-fire, an armistice, as mediators in the war. They also offered the support of their wizards and the new projectors they were developing to secure it. We know what they're like. We despised them. But with their huge armies, their Anchor base, their technology, they are a force to be feared.''

''Go on.''

''We knew what they planned for Flux. We also knew we couldn't stop them, not indefinitely. They made— promises. We had a population trained in Flux war backed by more wizards than they had. They had ambitions, but they needed us. In our own self-interest, it was easy to strike a deal.''

''A deal condemning the rest of World, us included, to permanent slavery. Your half-million people, and your own lives, would be bought with the futures of forty-seven million others.'' Suzl paused a moment. ''You make me sick. You say you hate them, yet I can't for the life of me see any difference between you and them when it comes down to the basics. Maybe they're a little better. They were raised to think what they're doing is right, that it's God's will. More injustice seems to be caused in the name of religion than the mercy and compassion the religions supposedly represent. Still, they have a culture and a cause. You know better. You'd let millions go down just to save your miserable necks and preserve a little of your power. All you Fluxlords make me sick. Scratch even the nicest of them and deep down you find a misshapen, egomaniacal, amoral monster.''

Again she paused, her mind trying to keep her emotional revulsion down so she wouldn't become like them.

''I'm a monster,'' Suzl told them. ''See me? Gross, misshapen, blind, forced to use an electronic voice. Lately

I've been feeling sorry for myself, wallowing in self-pity. In a way, I suppose I should thank you. Thank you for re-teaching me a lesson I once knew well but seem to have forgotten. I can't see you, except as electronic representations, but I know you all have pretty outsides. All you Fluxlords do. Your bodies are as perfect as mine is gross and misshapen. Yet you are the monsters, not me. Not even most of those poor people in New Eden. That's what this power really does to you sooner or later. Body. Mind. Soul. Pick any two, but the third always is a monster. I think I prefer a monstrous body to a monstrous soul.''

They not only didn't like the speech, but their ultimate tragedy, as Suzl well knew, was that they didn't really understand what she was saying. That was all right; she wasn't saying it for them, or her own people, either. She was talking to herself.

"May we know what you intend to do?" the Fluxlord asked nervously.

"I intend to conquer New Eden, then establish a strong, secure Fluxland, the largest and most powerful ever known, and develop my own ideas—I hope for a higher purpose than yours. Eventually, perhaps, the world will get my system, which is far better than New Eden's. As for you—I have a couple of thousand troops turned into the dumbest Fluxgirls I ever knew, and four wizards equally debilitated mentally. Those spells have traps on them. The five of you helped cause it. I expect you to undo those spells as much as can be done.''

"But those aren't *our* spells!" another of the women cried. "We don't know how to get around those traps!"

"Well, break one and you can break them all. You're wizards. Try it. Those of you who succeed will keep your powers and perhaps join us in New Harmony. Those who fail—well, you will still have enough wits about you to prepare our meals and clean up after us.''

They were nervous and indignant. "And if we refuse?"

"I really hope you will. We have copies of the master program, so we will eventually figure it out ourselves.

Refuse, or even stall on this, and I promise you that not only will you be cut from Flux, your outsides will make me seem like the prettiest person around!''

A bullet *pinged* off the projector near Suzl, fired by a far-off sniper. She ignored it, but off a ways the sounds of many more guns could be heard.

''Beth!''

''Here, Suzl!''

''I think it's poetic justice that you and your sisters be in charge of this operation.''

''Thank you. That will give us a great deal of pleasure. What do you want done with the New Eden prisoners?''

''I'd like to run their own damned program on them and send them home, but we can use trained soldiers even if they are a surrendering lot. Give them the modified Fluxgirl bodies we used on our troops. That'll take the resistance out of them. Make sure you also stamp their fannies, so we know who's ours and who came from where. Then get them interrogated and settled down. Once you run that Fluxgirl program, they're not going to run home.''

''Got it!''

''Anybody seen Matson?''

''Got a real gash in her leg that's being tended, but otherwise O.K. Didn't even know she had it until she got down off her horse.''

''Figures. Well, run a healing spell and get the old bastard back up to the headquarters tent. I also want Gabaye and Tokiabi up there—say, in an hour. We've won a bunch of battles, but we haven't won the war yet.''

Between the mop-up, the re-establishment of defensive perimeters, and organizing and recreating the ground units, Matson hadn't had much time to rest. The body was now Sondra's once again; a command presence was again needed rather than a commoner-with-the-troops type, but that was the length of concessions.

Reconnaissance showed the truth of Matson's original geographical and demographic analysis. New Eden had now deployed close to half a million men dug in and fortified along a great stretch of the border and was hastily preparing barbed wire, minefields, and other obstructions on the Anchor apron. The strongest areas were around Logh, of course. Along the stretches past the area, where it was all open country, guard posts within sight of each other had been established behind wire barricades but there was little in the way of troop depth. New Eden was, in effect, inviting the invaders in at that point, knowing that they would be drawn inland across broad stretches of very little, with long supply lines, and they could then be cut off from Flux and caught in a vise. Matson, of course, had no intention of invading there or anywhere else if it could be helped.

Gabaye had been understandably unwilling to part with the long-range-projectile programs, but she was more than willing to deliver the real thing by her own and Ming Tokiabi's efforts. Both Suzl and Matson expected this, of course, but were willing to live with it. These things launched to Flux targets were no more threatening than any other kind of weapon. If you knew they existed you could build an automatic shield against them and nab them before they got close enough to cause trouble. No, these were Anchor weapons, for use against Anchor, and New Eden was the biggest Anchor target of them all.

The things certainly didn't look like anything anyone had envisioned. Matson and others were used to the basic rocket, which was a long tube with a cone-shaped top that was then packed with gunpowder and could be used as they had used them or to launch fireworks in Anchor. They all understood how a rocket big enough and packed with enough explosive force might even be able to escape gravity, but nobody expected an oval-shaped vehicle with a flat bottom and eight utilitarian-looking seats inside.

"We don't know how it works, darlings, just how to work it. Isn't that the way things are these days?" Chua Gabaye told them. "Still, when you put the stock program module in that little bitty slot there, it takes off like a shot and winds up *way* out there, presumably where you told it to go. We don't know what makes it go, but it isn't Flux power. The engine—or whatever it is—is like nothing ever seen here, and everybody who sees it says it can't *possibly* do what it does—but it does. We've sent one all the way out in space and back again, but the landings still aren't what they should be.''

"I don't care if it crashes front first,'' Matson responded. "This thing is a potential massive bomb. The only thing I'm worried about is one of them *not* blowing to bits, giving them that motor.''

"Not much danger of that right now, I fear, *darling*,'' Gabaye responded. "I mean, that's why we haven't sent anyone real *up* yet. As I said, our landings leave a lot to be desired. When that thing hits, it hits with a *bang* and blows into millions and millions of *teensy weensy* pieces.''

Since the things were created from Flux, they could afford to expend a few in tests. Chua Gabaye was certainly right about the bang. Empty, one would easily destroy two or three square blocks of downtown New Canaan, and they intended to pack it with explosives.

The next problem was how to guide it to a specific target. The thing was clearly designed as a space bus, perhaps for getting workers or experts to and from things in space to place or repair them—there was once a ring of monitoring satellites all over, as they knew from the military programs—and not for point-to-point travel. It was Morgaine who suggested they reprogram just the directional and guidance part of the program pack with the grid they used on the projectors. Extending the grid through all of New Eden was nothing more than pencil and paper work, and the onboard computer would count the squares even though it couldn't really sense or see them through the Anchor.

They experimented with one in Flux, and it worked very nicely. Matson was convinced that, using the grid system and a current New Eden map, targets could be pinpointed precisely. Because of the power of the blast, civilian losses were inevitable, but they were all determined to keep those to a minimum while spotlighting primarily what made

New Eden really work. Power stations. Rail yards. Factory districts.

With the aid of the escaped spies and the former New Eden troops, they were able to pinpoint fourteen key strike locations that would effectively put New Eden out of business for quite a while. Of them all, only the huge factory district south of New Canaan and the old industrial region in Nantzee really would involve a high risk to innocent lives. There remained only to find a way to communicate with the judges in New Canaan, both before and after the "demonstrations."

"The only way is to use the stringers," Matson told them. "We have to find a train heading into Logh Center or Nantzee Center, where there are stringer offices, and get them to set up some sort of communications network between New Canaan and us. Our ultimatum can be delivered by hand, but after that we'll need a quicker way than stringer to secure line to stringer office and courier."

At Gabaye's insistence, they forbade Matson to have any contact with the stringers. At this stage they would be best hired as messengers; Matson might involve them more directly. Now the observation of strict neutrality with stringers and their trains paid off, though. The string boss going into Nantzee that they contacted was more than willing to deliver the message and the requests as part of his duty. The offices already communicated with each other in New Eden using a proprietary wireless code system, and as a precaution it had its own power supply.

The ultimatum was easily done as well, although Suzl insisted on writing it herself. She seemed excited, almost driven, and quite changed now. Totally confident, totally in charge. When she was done she read it over the radio and to the staff, and made sure everyone eventually heard or read its messages.

"To the Judges and People of New Eden, from a former citizen," it began. *"The Flux association of New Harmony, which includes many of your former citizens, has defeated your army at your northern border and is in fact your new neighbor to the north. We have power, and your*

projectors, and we know how to use them, as you know. We realize the futility of invading your land as you now must be convinced of the futility of invading ours. We abhor your system as an abomination against God and humanity, but we also recognize the futility of changing it from without. Until it collapses of its own internal weaknesses, we must be content to let you keep it, but you must not export it.

"This is our first and final offer. You will control and rule your vast Anchor and run it as you see fit. We, however, will form a shield around it, a shield of Fluxland that we will control, as vast and complex as New Eden itself. We will be the gate locked against your expansionist ambitions. All trade, all personnel, all contact between New Eden and World in either direction, must go through us. Both missionary and mercenary work will cease, although normal trade and commerce will be allowed if it is of a non-military nature. You may fortify your borders to protect yourself, but you may not cross them. Any use of Flux power against us by yourself, your allies, or machines will be stopped and you will pay a horrible price for it.

"You have forty-eight hours to agree to these terms. If we do not hear from you at that time, or if you reject the offer, or if any military move is made against any of us, you will be immediately reduced to a pre-industrial society. Every hour, and I mean every hour, after that deadline another component of your industrial and technological base will be destroyed until you accept. Our terms will get stiffer, and your price will be more horrible, the longer you delay. Delay too long, and there will be so little left of New Eden that we will not have to invade. Do not take this lightly. We do not, I assure you, take you lightly at all."

The stringers assured them that the message had been hand-delivered to the Chief Clerk of the High Court of New Eden, and they started their clock and began picking their targets and assembling and programming the first six flying bombs.

Reconnaissance showed no undue activity along the

border-front on the New Eden side of the line, but the troops there were clearly on first-stage alert. Longer range scans also showed no major movements south along at least six hundred kilometers of border on either side of the front, so New Eden was standing pat. As expected, the deadline passed without a reply of any sort.

Matson chose the targets carefully. He first wanted a demonstration that all the judges could see, and that meant the massive industrial complex south of New Canaan between the Sea and the Gate. It would take more than one flying bomb to completely wipe it out, but the first one would be effective and fair warning. They sent it off exactly on the forty-ninth hour, praying and crossing their fingers, the troops and wizards along the front also at a high state of readiness in case New Eden, in spite of its drubbing, would be forced to come out and try and stop the launches.

The things launched with a tremendous and nearly-ear-splitting hum and whine, and Matson realized that it was the landings, not the takeoffs, that the Guild had monitored.

The thing rose and then shot forward and upwards as it got its grid bearings, and made a tremendous explosive noise when it entered Anchor. It was so loud that it penetrated for many kilometers back into the normally sound-dampened void and caused many to worry that the shock of changing from the closed static system of Flux to the dynamic and far denser bubble of Anchor had caused it to explode on contact. If so, they were in deep trouble.

They would have to rely on the stringers to find out if the thing had gotten through at all, let alone hit what it was aimed at. Everyone knew that their victory in Flux was due to New Eden's relative inexperience in that element and its inability to fully test out the projectors; they had the same disadvantage with the flying bombs.

For almost forty minutes after the first launch, Chua Gabaye and others waited in Flux where the stringers knew they were. They should have heard something by then, and they were getting nervous. Finally, a stringer arrived with a stern expression on her face. "There was a single massive explosion south of New Canaan about thirty-eight

minutes ago," they were told. "It created a massive fire-
ball and touched off countless subsidiary explosions. The
blast was felt far to the north and south of the city and
broke many windows, toppled lines, and destabilized many
other buildings. As of now, the fires are completely out of
control."

A projector monitoring the conversation reported it to
the New Harmony leadership, and the cheers from all over
were almost an earth-shaking explosion in and of themselves.

"Any message from the leadership?" Jodi asked the
stringer.

"None. We have someone standing by but nothing
has come in."

Jodi didn't really feel disappointed. She *wanted* New
Eden crippled and she wanted it to burn. "All right.
Return and stand by. Pretty soon you may be the only
communications New Eden has left."

The stringer stared at her. "What kind of weapon have
you got there, anyway?"

"I don't know exactly. Maybe the end of the world."

The second one went off right on time, this one to the
center of the rail yards that were the main switching
terminal for the entire northern part of the nation. Located
along the Sea half the distance north from New Canaan to
the border and exactly equidistant to Logh Center and
Nantzee Center, its destruction would effectively halt all
train traffic to and from all three points to any other. This
time one of the wizards had gone in as a great falcon, but
it would be hours before she would be back with an
effective report.

They next hit the great power station connecting New
Canaan with direct Flux at the Gate. Stringers reported
massive power outages, some building collapses, and where
the power station was there was reported now to be only a
crater almost a kilometer wide and perhaps forty meters
deep.

Nine hours, and only nine bombs, later, New Eden had
effectively ceased to be a modern industrial power. Electricity, communications, and rail had been severed; virtu-

ally all the industrial districts—there were only three of any consequence—had ceased to exist. New Harmony observers in Flux off Nantzee Center, seventy-six kilometers away from the industrial section and in the void as well, felt the ground shake beneath their feet and felt a blast of New Eden air as it actually pushed through the Anchor bubble.

Except for the stringers, who maintained a very shaky and intermittent contact, New Canaan, capital and largest city in New Eden, was completely cut off from the outside, without power, lights, water, or even any transportation beyond horses.

New Eden had quickly become a vast land of farms, empty spaces, and a few large cities in which the bulk of the population lived. With the development of the vast rail network and the rediscovery of large-scale refrigeration, all but basic truck-farmed food like eggs and milk came from long distances away. New Canaan had a population of over four million alone, and this time of year it dipped below freezing at night. These people now shivered in the darkness, had to find alternate water sources, and deal with backed-up sewage and refuse. A run on greengrocers, butchers, and other food stores had turned into a series of near-riots.

The same was happening in Nantzee District, another area of huge population. The others—Logh, Ozkah, and far-off Mareh to the south—had not yet been touched, although they certainly had reports about the ultimatum, the first explosion in New Canaan, and knew they were now cut off.

Matson, not alone, was becoming disturbed. "We're starting to slaughter now. We've already sent them back fifty years technologically, and guaranteed at least a decade, maybe more, before they could fully restore things. We've got one more rail center, Ozkah-Mareh, and the big southern hydroelectric complex on the River Nur, and then we get to Logh, Ozkah, and Mareh Centers. Logh's already a mess. They evacuated half the population to a tent city well south and east of the city before the big battle and they're still there, so it's a legitimate military target and I don't feel totally upset about it, but I'd hate to bomb the other two without giving them some warning and time to evacuate."

"Poor Logh," Suzl sighed. "It and me are always linked. We both wind up with the raw end of the stick every time. Still, I can't give any quarter in this. Somebody's in charge in New Eden. Somebody's always in charge. Why after all this won't they give in?"

"Maybe because the ones at the top aren't personally hurt," Jodi suggested. "I know how they think. Believe me."

"Huh?" they all said at once.

"They had the Gate at New Canaan, right? They saw and heard all the stuff, all right, so they packed up their families and their most precious belongings and used the Gate transfer system to get out."

Suzl suddenly struck her palm with a fist. "Sure! I remember now! It's all so—long ago. You forget stuff. We always knew that if there was ever trouble we and the kids should go to the Institute and be taken to New Canaan if the threat was to Logh, or Mareh for anything else. It's distant, very far away, and about as far south as real Flux power operates, although we didn't follow the logic then. *That's* where the families are! But where would the judges go? Not with them—they'd be completely out of touch. I gotta go back, think like a Fluxwife—no, think like Adam's wife. They're mostly from the same generation and same mold. They'd go where the bulk of their troops were! They're right here! They're in Logh! I bet on it!"

Matson had uncharacteristically not smoked many cigars in the past few months, but there was one in the old stringer's mouth now. "All right, then. It's time to up the ante in the poker game. We'll need a stringer line to Logh Center. They can probably set one up from Nantzee, but it would be nice if it was direct. I find this very distasteful, but we have to be prepared to go through with it if it doesn't work."

"What's your idea?"

"A second ultimatum. This one to be delivered direct to the leadership via both the stringers and by rocket."

"Rocket?"

"Uh huh. A tremendous number of copies, stuffed into rocket heads and fired into New Eden, designed to break apart in the air. I want the troops to know what's happening and ask questions. I want the field officers to know that their wives and kids may be starving in the dark now. Mutinies aren't unknown in New Eden if you give 'em the right reason. Even Tilghman was overthrown, a fact I bet they don't teach straight to the new generations. Give them one hour. Then tell them we're gonna come at Logh with more than one superbomb. They got the Sea on one side and a fairly narrow strip down the other before they get wide-open country again. They can't possibly disperse in that time."

"What would we say?"

"The truth—a little dressed up in dramatics."

To the People of New Eden: Your leaders are deceiving you. They have the truth and they will not tell you. New Canaan is destroyed. Its survivors, men, women, and children, are without food, water, sewage, or means of transportation or communication. Your factories are gone. Your rail centers are gone. Our weapons are invincible and horrible. Your wives and children suffer, but your leaders believe they and theirs are safe. They are not.

"We have exhausted military targets. Our original offer, a copy of which is on the back of this, was fair and generous. Our weapons are fashioned out of Flux. We will not run out of them. In one half-hour, we will launch and detonate a single one of our weapons one kilometer out in the Sea off Logh Center. That is to demonstrate that we wish to kill no more of you. If we do not hear from your leaders after that, we will have no alternative. We will detonate multiple devices throughout Logh that will destroy most of it and not incidentally kill many of you. Maybe most of you. You will die without being able to fire a shot in return, for we are far in Flux. Your leaders may not die. They may leave you and escape through the

Institute to Ozkah, but then we will destroy Ozkah. They will then run to Mareh, but even that is within our reach and we will destroy Mareh. We need not do much to Nantzee; its center is still burning. There is no honor in this. No glory. You will get one demonstration, no more. That is more than you would do for us. Then we will proceed methodically, showing no more mercy or compassion than you have shown your enemies.''

"Some of the hard-core fanatics will try and grab all the leaflets,'' Morgaine noted. "Remember our late, unlamented Major Verdugo. There's lots more where he came from.''

"They won't be able to get them all,'' Matson assured her. "The word will spread like wildfire. They might not believe it at first, but they'll have big doubts anyway. Then the bang comes. If what they report is true, we'll be able to feel it even here. The men will pressure the noncoms, the noncoms will corner the officers, and the officers will face down the big brass.''

"Yeah, but what if we're wrong?'' Morgaine asked. "I mean, suppose the big boys aren't there?''

"Don't fire unless we find the troops dispersing or mass evacuations. Let them sweat. As somebody said, there's always *somebody* in charge, and if they won't make a decision then the officers will to save their own necks. Cass did this sort of thing in her wars of reformation when going against Anchors. They rarely had to fight much to take one. They can't withdraw. They'd be too bunched up at some points and we could take out half the army with two bombs. They've very densely concentrated now. Three bombs and our troops could take them. Let's append that ultimatum. Give them a place. Just in Flux outside the old Anchor Logh West Gate. Guarantee their safety and integrity under a white flag, and insist on direct talks.''

"And if they still don't deal?''

"Then we do it. Simple as that. We will be forced to kill millions of innocent people and reduce the survivors to a nearly animal-like existence. Then we'll convert the four-hundred-thousand-person army we inherited from Liberty, go in, and take over the place or what's left of it.''

Chua seemed delighted with the idea. "Why, that's *brilliant!* It'll be the master program all over, but in reverse! We'll use their own old methods. Make the Fluxgirls the mistresses and the men the stupid, muscled slaves who'll do all the heavy work while their wives rule!"

"No," Suzl said flatly. "That would make us just like them."

"But—*darling!* We *are* just like them! All of human history on *World* proves that! There are no monuments here to the noble, the self-sacrificing, the pacifists and downtrodden! We are *animals*, nothing more, staking out our territory and then fighting for the position of boss! If you don't do it, someone else will. That's what most of these girls really want, deep down, and if you dig deep enough you'll find it. New Eden is an aberration only because it's *Anchor!* There have been countless wars, Flux wars, revolutions, and the like in the past fifty years, and in every case—every one—even those who *said* they wanted freedom, liberty, and equality for all wound up reinforcing the same system. The downtrodden of this world don't want freedom or equality! They want to be *masters*. It's human *nature*, darling! You can fool yourself that it's not, but you can't avoid it or wipe it out."

"If I really believed that, I think I'd slit my own throat," Suzl commented, totally disgusted.

"Well, I've never met a slave who *truly* wished to abolish slavery. They only want to see the master dressed in rags out in the fields in back-breaking toil while *they* sit in the golden mansion and grow fat. New Eden was founded basically by former slaves. Men oppressed by female Fluxlords. They managed to escape their Fluxlords' grasps, many partly in thanks to those silly Reformation wars that did nothing but reinforce the old system. And what did they create? A system no more oppressive than the average Fluxland's, but in Anchor. A system where they were on top and the women on the bottom, just the reverse of what they'd had. Wake up, dear! You are in serious danger of becoming a saint, and they're all dead or quite mad, you know.''

15

MASKS AND MEMORIES

Matson had insisted on going down to the old Gate, and Suzl had no objections this time. More than anyone, the stringer would know how to deal with these people, and whether they were playing true or false. Jodi would also come as close cover, although they were being monitored by projectors all the way, and Gill because everyone thought she deserved to be in at the finish. Gill elected to retain and wear her Fluxgirl guise, not only as a symbol but because she wanted to see the expression on their faces when they saw a Fluxgirl dressed only in gunbelt and, special for the occasion, heels. Matson had been tempted to reassume the Fluxgirl form as well, for much the same reasons, but ultimately decided that the tall, dark Sondra was required as an authority figure. It was enough that they had a symbolic Fluxgirl present; they were trying to end a war, not restart it.

It was also decided that Matson should not reveal his identity to New Eden. It would give them the rationale of having been defeated by a man—and a legend, at that—

and Suzl was adamant that they know just what beat them, even if they weren't straight on the who of it.

There had been reports of large troop movements in the two hours since the "demonstration" bomb had gone off, but there was clearly no attempt to either shore up the border defenses or prepare for a major withdrawal. They could only sit, and wait, and hope.

A little after the fourth hour, Jodi said, "Somebody's coming. Four men on horseback. They're armed but nothing's drawn, although one's carrying something."

They mounted up and went in to meet the quartet. They proved to be a brigadier, a colonel, a sergeant-major, and an artillery sergeant. All were in full uniform, with the lowest-ranking sergeant leading and carrying a staff on which flew a white flag apparently torn from a bedsheet. None appeared to have much Flux power, although the sergeant with the flag had enough to see strings and feel the others coming before they could be seen in the dismal void.

They seemed uncomfortable facing the New Harmony trio, and their eyes kept going to the curvaceous Jodi and the apparent Fluxgirl, but they weren't deterred. Matson had dressed in the black stringer uniform, but with all insignia removed and the one on the hat replaced with four stars surrounding a rifle. It wasn't anyone's standard insignia, but it was close enough that the officers could tell that the woman they faced was a general officer in the regular army. The general saluted and got it returned by Matson.

"Sondy Ryan, commander of conventional forces," the old stringer said casually.

"Albret Stong, Commander of the Logh District," responded the brigadier. He seemed uncertain how to proceed from there, and was clearly uncomfortable. Matson guessed that it was the worst day of the man's entire life.

"Brigadier, you know our intentions. We're here to hear yours. You are the first man of New Eden who would even do us the courtesy of replying at all, so we'd like to know what you have to say."

Stong coughed nervously. "You must forgive me. I must tell you that I never believed I would ever find myself in such a position. I am ever willing to die for my country and my cause, but I know an untenable situation when I see it."

"I'm old professional military myself, Brigadier, from a long line of professional officers. My ancestor was the first commandant of the Signal Corps here, so I sympathize."

Stong's eyebrows rose. "The Corps is involved in this as well?"

"No, I'm retired. Long retired. I was—retained—by New Harmony to get them into military shape, and I think I did a pretty good job of it."

"You have the full authority to speak for them?"

"I do. And you?"

"I—I suppose I do. My officers insisted that I verify or disprove your rather unusual letter, and I went to the Institute where a majority of judges were staying. I failed to get much of an answer from their staffs, so I'm afraid I took some drastic action and placed my own guards on the Gate access port. They then received me, after failing to find anyone who disagreed violently with my actions, and generally confirmed the facts of your letter."

Matson understood the situation perfectly. "I see, sir. And did they authorize direct negotiation?"

"Not at first. However, when I suggested that they could best reassure the troops by being with and among them, commanding them directly for the period of the emergency, they took a softer stand." He paused a moment, and seemed almost grimly amused at a thought. "You see, sir, it was reported that although virtually all the structures in the immediate downtown area of Nantzee Center were demolished in your blast, all those in the administration building suffered was some temporary deafness and intermittent internal light failure." That was the old temple building, as the Institute was in Logh. "I thought that this fact colored their attitude a bit."

"Uh huh."

"Understand me well, madam. If they had been willing

to come out and personally take command of the troops and stand with us, in equal danger, I would have stood with them as well. We all would have. They are our leaders. But their wanton display of cowardice and abuse of their privileged positions made it clear they were no longer fit to rule or make decisions. Understand that, even now, I can't speak for New Eden or any part of the nation except Logh District. I can not communicate with them if I wanted to. Subject to new elections, however, the military commanders have complete power in their districts and together would represent the final authority. I *was* able to get through to my counterpart in Nantzee using the stringer office here and your contracted terminal on the other end— the stringer office in Nantzee is rubble as well—and outlined the situation to him. He concurs. It will take some time to reestablish contact with all fifteen military districts, but eventually I hope I will have clear instructions. In the absence of that, I'm asking your terms for sparing Logh and my troops the fate you dealt Nantzee and, I understand, New Canaan.''

"We're negotiating an armistice, then, not peace. All right, it's what we have and what we'll have to take. First, we will want a withdrawal of all troops and border defenses in the district in two kilometers. That will give us a buffer zone and allow us room to breathe without fearing any new attacks.''

Stong nodded. ''That is reasonable.''

"Next, I want the complete withdrawal of all military forces from Logh except a small command headquarters of no more than five officers, at least one of whom will either be you or have all authority to directly deal with us delegated by you. The withdrawal will be to a point at least two kilometers beyond the old Anchor wall boundary.''

"But that's preposterous! That wasn't in your letter of terms!''

"Those terms were for immediate treaty. Later on it states that the costs will be higher the longer we delay. This is an armistice, Brigadier, not peace. We may have to face the fact that you will be at war with us again in a matter of days!''

The general opened his mouth, then closed it without saying anything.

''Third,'' continued Matson, ''any original inhabitants of the area in question who wish freely to return to their homes unarmed and under our jurisdiction will be allowed to do so, and any now there who wish to stay will be allowed to. Fourth, your withdrawal must leave all military equipment in place, including guns and emplacements, major ordnance, wagons, lorries, and other major things that might be used against us. All may retire with their horses, if any, sidearms or personal weapons, and anything which can be carried and does not need a team or lorry to move. Finally, orders to this effect are to be issued by you as soon as you return, and the withdrawal is to proceed with all deliberate speed and be completed within forty-eight hours.''

''Those are surrender terms! I won't do it!''

Matson sighed. ''Brigadier, the only question is whether or not your troops will accept it or whether they will do to you what you did to the judges. You asked for armistice and this is the price. Recognizing the fact that a state of war continues to exist, perhaps for some time, between us, we feel this is the minimum acceptable for our security. There it is. The alternative is also clear. Any failure to abide in any way at all with these conditions, and that includes spotting one soldier planting booby traps or one wagon hauling away something or troops barring civilian return—anything—and there will be no warning. We will immediately saturate the area with everything aimed for maximum kill effect. If just one soldier remains after forty-eight hours, or we are fired upon at entry, we will immediately launch the weapons at the main bodies of your troops and whatever other concentrations of population exist in your district. This is not negotiable. In my position you would deliver much the same terms.''

All four of them were stony-faced and tight-lipped. ''I understand,'' the brigadier muttered through clenched teeth.

"Sir, I assume that a large part of your troops are from the New Canaan area. That region is without food, pure water, electricity, transportation, or communications except through the Gate. Send your most recalcitrant men through and let them see for themselves and report back. They could well use your men there right now in restoring essential services and keeping order. Your trains still work out of here and there are enough engines in the Logh yards, I think, to handle more than half your men, which should be enough since you'll have to leave some to guard the border. The rail yards at Babylon are destroyed, so you'll have about an eight-kilometer march to get to the other side, but some trains that were en route during the attacks might be there and could get back to New Canaan, or near enough, in reverse. Take them. We have no use for them. There is no purpose to talking further. Your clock is now running. This conference is terminated."

Matson gave a salute, which all four returned, although whether out of respect or habit it wasn't clear. Their position, however, was, and they went back to see what they could do.

It took eleven days for the military commanders to agree to and sign a formal surrender instrument, but they knew there was no choice, and so did the bulk of their troops. Oh, there were a number of frontier towns who were outraged, places and people that had remained untouched by the bombs, but they were invited to New Canaan, or Nantzee, or Babylon, to have a look and make their own decisions. Few who did and saw it all for themselves could doubt their new leaders' course. There were, of course, the die-hard fanatics who believed that the entire nation should die, to the last person, rather than surrender, but they were very much in the minority—and those who made too much of it or attracted a following either vanished mysteriously or were picked up with great fanfare, sent to the northern border, and told they wouldn't be stopped from fighting.

Some actually did. A number of army units mutinied against the peace and organized their own attacks, but these were expected. They were fanatical and determined to die, and thus were easy to maneuver, easy to kill, and within six weeks there was no military action against New Harmony at all.

New Harmony took this time to take hold of and turn Liberty. With the addition of that massive number of troops, there was no problem in moving into and fortifying all four of the old Anchor positions. Liberty's wizards proved remarkably dedicated to breaking the New Eden programs, and succeeded without casualty. The minds of the five wizards, however, were badly damaged, although Flux doctors had hopes of eventually restoring or at worse rebuilding them.

A net was being woven of Fluxland and projectors around the whole of New Eden's vast borders. It was not terribly thick—from twelve to twenty kilometers in most places, except on the Liberty side—and as soon as Morgaine and the other theoreticians among them worked out the mechanics, the spells would be interlocked and unified. When that happened, no male would be able to enter in either direction without the permission of the Fluxlord in charge, nor spend more than one full day there in any event without automatically undergoing a rather marked change in gender. Male wizards would need to use a specific spell to enter, one that would do much the same thing, although if they overstayed it would turn them into very-much-New-Harmony-type wizards, and it would stick.

Suzl sat in her tent, sipping some real Anchor wine, while Ayesha reclined nearby. Ayesha's belly was swollen with child, and her breasts were slightly swollen and sensitive, as she was just entering her ninth month of pregnancy.

Morgaine entered, with Matson, in response to a summons. Morgaine was into her eighth month and looked no less extreme than Ayesha. She needed help to get around, although, interestingly, she discovered that if she took very small steps she could actually manage barefoot now.

"Have a seat, both of you," Suzl said amiably. "We have much to discuss yet." Curiously, while she hadn't lost any weight, she hadn't gained, either, and seemed remarkably stable. "How are you feeling, Morgaine? Any regrets on your condition?"

"On having it? Of course not! I'm excited, really. I never thought of having a child before. I never thought I'd have the chance."

"Good. And the master spell for our New Harmony belt?"

"Coming along. Within days, I hope. Then we can *really* relax."

"And you, Matson? What do you think of all this?"

"I think we were damned lucky and New Eden was too hidebound to whip us. We got further than I ever dreamed we'd get."

Suzl smiled. "Is there anything else you might want to do here?"

"Nothing. The army's in good shape and capable hands. The Anchors will always be potential flash points, but it'll be years before New Eden is in any sort of shape to even try and retake them, and, unlike them, we can resupply and reinforce from Flux. It's over, Suzl. We won. Until the next world crisis, anyway."

"Eventually we will expand, you know, as we grow and build."

"I know your intentions, and you know I don't agree with them. Flux can be a lot of things, and that's its wonder. Some of them are really rotten, like the Garden and cesspools that produce the Gabayes and Tokiabis and the rest. Some can be very nice and useful, too, like New Pericles or Freehold. The rest? Well, let's call them experiments. Somebody with the power has an idea of how things should be. They create a Fluxland and put it into operation using that idea. If it works, if it's really something better, it gets copied by those with less imagination. If it doesn't, then a few have paid the price for knowledge. That seems to be as fair a way to do it as is possible, given the fact that all of us are human. I don't think we can afford too many more marching armies and master programs."

"I don't know. On alternate days I believe you're right and I'm content here. The other days I feel that the only way to preserve what we have is to expand it and make it universal. Those are the days, I suppose, when I talk to the two bitches. *To* one and *at* the other, anyway."

"I know what you mean. That's the only thing that keeps me on edge. I keep waiting for the other shoe to drop."

"I am thinking of moving into Anchor Logh," she told them.

"What!" Morgaine was startled. "But—that's ridiculous! You'd have no power there, and you'd lose your voice as well."

"In a few days, when your master program covers the border, they won't need me anymore. I'm like you were, Morgaine, when you came to me. This spell is going wild inside me, doing funny things to my mind as well as my body. The only way to totally stabilize it is to go into Anchor and stay there. I've done my part. I've done more than my part. I was born in Anchor Logh and I lived there a very long time, off and on. I told you that I identified with it. I'm glad we were able to save it, and I think it's where I belong. That may sound stupid, even senile, and maybe it is, but this is as far as I can go. There I can feel the grass under my feet and know it's no creation of someone's imagination. I can feel a gentle rain, and have a wind caress my body. I can smell the flowers, and hear the birds sing. Maybe even go on a diet."

"But—your voice!"

"I can make my intentions known if I want to. Otherwise, I'll have Ayesha there. No, it's settled, I think. Not until the baby comes, of course. There's no sense in having a painful birth when it can be effortless here. Then we go. Matson, I have no right and no moral standing to keep you here and like that. Stay as long as you like, then leave with my blessings. Morgaine can easily restore you to your old form."

"Thank you. I'd like to get home—it's been a long time—but I'll stick a bit now that I can leave. Just a gut feeling. I want to be sure everything is right. You'll excuse me if I spend the day you run that master spell in Anchor, though.''

"Of course. Morgaine, I can do nothing about that spell as it stands, but you are also free to leave, visit your mother or have her visit here, and return to New Pericles if you wish. You'll always be one of my girls, though.''

Morgaine smiled, although she knew the blind woman couldn't see it. "Thanks, Aunt Suzl. New Pericles is wherever a Haller is. I'm more than tempted to just move it down here someplace. I still like men, though. It's nice having the freedom to choose.''

There was a clinking of glasses, and Ayesha passed out wine glasses half filled with Logh White. "A toast, then!'' she announced lightly. "To the future!''

The other three nodded, smiled, and drank.

The drug was so fast and so insidious that all three were out, still sitting up, before they even knew anything was wrong. Ming Tokiabi had assured her of that. She reached over and unclipped the radio from Suzl's belt and looked at it. "How the fuck do you work this. . . ?'' she muttered, but then she pressed the button on the side.

"They're *out!*'' she called playfully, like a little child pleased with herself. "Ready when you are. . . .''

Flux rose, first under Suzl, then under Morgaine, tagged them, then severed their contact with the grid. They would stay turned off until somebody turned them back on.

Another minute went by, and then Chua Gabaye and Ming Tokiabi entered, looking very satisfied with themselves. "My!'' Chua gushed. "Don't they make such *pretty* statues!''

"I done just what you told me!'' Ayesha said proudly, then she frowned. "You're gonna keep up your end, right?''

"Have no fear, Ayesha, darling! We wouldn't *think* of going back on you! It appeals to our sense of humor. Uh—Ming? We're on a tight schedule here. Want to give them their shots and wake them up?''

"Why not just do it now?" the other survivor of the Seven asked impatiently. "Why draw it out?"

"Ming, dear! How *ever* do you keep from killing yourself? I mean, what's the fun in life if you can't watch their faces as they're helplessly victimized? Ah! I see they're coming around!"

All three groaned and shook their heads, but the antidote cleared their minds rapidly. Suzl, for the first time completely cut off, gave a garbled and impossible-to-understand comment and lashed out. Morgaine gasped and froze. Only Matson stood up and glared at them, but first at Ayesha. "Why, you traitorous bitch!"

"Oh, now, *easy* there, *darling!* How can she be a traitor? She *started* all this, after all. Planned it out. Ayesha's a very clever girl. I didn't know the exact players. In fact, we were certain it couldn't be brought off at *all*, but you all surprised and delighted us!"

"The projector," Morgaine said, understanding it all now. "All you wanted was the projector. It really was just a bloody raid for pay after all."

"At the start, darlings, yes, but things changed very quickly after Ayesha's girls also snatched your grandchildren and then got you in return. Ayesha obviously needed a non-threatening replacement for Habib, and Suzl was it. *I* supplied the spell, warts and all, because she deserved it. Anyone who had access to all that power, all that ultimate power, and just walked away from it deserves whatever she gets. Ayesha created this whole new world fantasy because she knew and understood Suzl so well. It was a way to keep her ignorant and on track, since while a number of the girls could work the projector and even turn off a big-shot wizard like Madam Pericles, here, there was no substitute for a world-class wizard voluntarily turned."

"And then you learned about New Eden's big project, and all those projectors, and you saw Suzl build this into a real movement. You decided not to demand delivery but rather to support things and see how far she'd get."

"Oh, yes. And, of course, there was a practical matter. They were marked and there was no way they could move that damned projector up to us in any amount of time. The risks were too great, so we came down and went along. We even supplied some muscle, in the form of seven of the fourteen so-called allied wizards who, incidentally, were needed thanks to this idiot's binding spells."

"I can count again, you know," Morgaine noted sarcastically. "Nine wizards, even transmuters, can't come close to taking on the ones loyal to Suzl, and they have enough of the projectors that you can't deactivate them all by surprise."

"Ah, but all but a few are spread all over the place," Chua pointed out. "Fifty-seven hundred kilometers of border. More, really, since it isn't all that regular. Not to mention dear Liberty, which takes five just to maintain it. I can concentrate mine, such as here. There are three projectors not yet deployed still here at the moment, and the original, of course. The three new ones are on those silly things with belts, but they *move*, darlings! We'll take them, and the original on an old-fashioned team and wagon. Four should do us nicely for protection, and since our bright folks think they've solved New Eden's little secret, we might be able to make more after we take the old one and one new one apart and compare them."

"The clock runs!" Tokiabi hissed. "We can not move the projectors out and use them for protection as well. They should be loading now. That means we're vulnerable."

"She talks!" Morgaine snapped derisively.

"Life's most *delicious* moments are those of risk," Chua responded. "Besides, I'm getting to it."

"I suppose now you're gonna gloat about what you're gonna do with us," Matson said sourly.

Chua smiled sweetly. "Don't you wish you had *real* Flux power now, darling? Wouldn't you like to draw those pretty little pistols of yours and just blow us away? But you can't. Don't you wish now you were the *real* Sondra and not a pretender? Ah, but of *course* you do!"

"Your asshole partner's right," Morgaine muttered. "Get it over with."

"Ah, Matson, I believe a little poetic justice is in order

for you. We'll deliver you to Anchor, but not New Harmony. New Eden. A pretty little Fluxgirl you'll be, absolutely voluptuous. That aggression totally damped down, and the mental processing speed slowed to a more *practical* level, so you'll find joy in cooking meals, washing floors, and all that other nice Fluxwife stuff. Not enough to keep two thoughts in your head at the same time or figure out three-syllable words, but enough so you'll know who and what you once were. I think that's about right. *Ooooh!* I can see you wanting to go for that gun, but I think the kind of spell that would block you would be *far* faster.

"As for you two," she said, turning to Suzl and Morgaine, "We're going to give you each a little drug. It takes a while to work, but we'll be leaving and *you'll* be staying here—with lovely Ayesha. After that, she'll report us on the radio as *baaad* girls, and one of the other wizards will eventually turn you both back on, but that'll be fine. In fact, Suzl, you'll find that all those *nasty* bugs in my program are gone. You'll be *gorgeous* again, and you'll even be able to see. Not talk, though. *That* will remain. And you, Morgaine, will get one just like it."

"This drug—what does it do?" Morgaine asked nervously. She wasn't even thinking of herself, but she was carrying a baby.

"It's a chemical, just like those in your brain, and it goes to this little place and settles in, and, *what* do you *know!* You fall madly, completely, passionately, and *permanently* in love with the first person you see. We'll take one of you in the back, to make it easier. Of course, that will be our *dear, sweet* Ayesha here. I *told* you we were all just animals, dear. Just chemistry, alas. But you'll still both be you, with all your powers. You just won't be able to think of anyone or anything except dear Ayesha. Your world will be exclusively her. You'll cast any spells she wants cast, create a Fluxland to her dreams, just to please her. Convert whole populations to her whims, and, in fact, with this drug, you'll gladly create new lovers for her out of the wizards who *trust* you so. Don't worry, though, Morgaine, dear. Your baby will be *just* fine! Ah!

We really *must* be going now. Ming, you see to the others while I take our old friend Matson, here. The Matson who always made fun of wizards but wishes he were Sondra now!"

"*I* am *Sondra, bitch!*" she screamed, and suddenly Chua Gabaye was rocked with pure, raw, and immensely powerful Flux attacking her.

Sondra had both surprise and emotion on her side, but Chua Gabaye was among the most powerful, and she was not the only wizard there. As soon as Sondra attacked, Ming turned, needle in hand, for support. Morgaine was completely without power, but neither could she receive any. She could, however, grab Tokiabi's legs and pull hard, toppling the wizard and breaking her concentration. Morgaine wasted no time and, pregnant and unwieldly or not, rolled right over onto the slender, fragile-looking wizard.

Sondra didn't wait for Ming to regain things and wriggle out with a transmutation spell. She pulled her pistol and fired it right into Chua Gabaye's heavily-made-up face. It didn't make a real big hole going in, but her skull seemed to explode from the back and pieces of brain and bone splattered over Suzl, Morgaine, and the tent.

Ayesha screamed.

Sondra went quickly over to where Morgaine was just rolling off Tokiabi. The other wizard looked out cold, apparently having hit her head on a small serving table when she fell. She *was* out cold.

"*Wow!*" Morgaine managed. "I know I feel like I weigh a ton, but I didn't think I was *that* heavy!"

Sondra reached down and pried the needle out of Tokiabi's stiff grasp. She looked at it, then smiled, and leaned down and injected it into Tokiabi's arm, then stood up. "Pretty neat if I say so myself. Dad needed Cass to blow Coydt's brains out."

Suzl gave a questioning bark, and Morgaine said, "It's O.K.! She blew Gabaye's brains out and gave Tokiabi her own medicine. Boy! We better decide fast who she's gonna fall madly in love with!"

Sondra snapped her fingers. "Yeah. Hang on! We're not out of the woods yet! Brief Suzl and keep an eye on Ayesha!" With that, she rushed from the tent and looked cautiously around. There were a number of people around, including a crew hauling the original projector onto a wagon, but nobody was really close. She made it to her tethered horse, reached in the saddlebag, and took out a very different looking communications device. She stuck a wire into the ground on a grid line and pushed the side button.

"Send in the cavalry, and fast!" she said, and the message was transmitted along all lines of the grid including one that was being monitored. "Gabaye dead, Ming out, but we're still surrounded by hostiles. Send me the king and queen and quick! Whoops! They've spotted me!"

Shots rang out in her direction, and a shield went up around the projector area. The crew that almost had it on the wagon now quickly began reversing itself and lowering it back to the ground.

Sondra transmuted and took off into the air, then circled. They'd almost gotten the damned thing back down, and one of the allied wizards whose name she'd never even bothered to remember was looking around and waiting to get it turned on. She knew if she stayed too close the wizard would have her; they might not have been permitted to run the damned things before but they sure knew how they worked.

There was no access into Suzl's tent until that projector was taken out, that was for sure.

The shield didn't look very secure. She transmuted a machine gun and began swooping down and firing at them, and some of the bullets got through. They went all around the wizard and the projector, but most of the commoners helping lay dead or dying.

The wizard on the ground was confident. She reached up and fixed the four antennae herself, shielding herself and the machine from any blows, then sat back as the projector came to life. Sondra banked and turned and got the hell out of there. Morgaine could have done something against the wizard, but she'd have to crawl to get there and even a slingshot could take her out. Blind, powerless Suzl was even less help.

Another winged figure came in, then two—three! She joined them, seeing familiar forms on the backs of two of them. The others were diversions so the passengers could be landed near enough to do any good. She joined in, and narrowly missed getting caught by a sweep. She was getting the best use out of all that monitoring of New Harmony up north now. Two others weren't so lucky; they were caught and deactivated and fell to the ground.

The two passengers, however, got unloaded. One large one headed for the tent, while the other, much-smaller figure walked right towards the projector.

The enemy wizard knew that there had been two drops, but ignored the one going into the tent for now. A commoner, no real power or threat. The other, though. . . . She did sweep after sweep, catching many familiar people and things, but no stranger. She had operated eyes closed, as they all had, to increase concentration and not get distracted, but now she opened them and looked around. There! Wasn't that someone over there? She swept the area but found nothing. Even a deactivated wizard would show, because the grid squares under them would be dark. She spotted the two she'd nabbed, and the two others in the tent, but nothing else.

There was a sudden noise right near her, and again she opened her eyes and turned—and found a pistol barrel stuck right in her mouth. The weapon was held by a small, slightly built woman or perhaps a young boy, dressed in tight-fitting jeans, work shirt, and well-worn boots. She knew that face. Every wizard who was as old as she was knew that face.

Then Cass calmly blew her brains out and kicked the body rudely to the ground.

There were few others around. The traitorous group of wizards had either corrupted or turned the guard detail and the small company that was always around, and those were the ones that had been doing the heavy work on the projectors.

Sondra landed, turned back into herself, and grinned. "Hi, Cass! Am *I* glad to see *you!*"

"You look like you were doing pretty well all by yourself," the small woman came back. "You had all the tough stuff done before I could even *get* here! Boy, that little bit felt good, though. Just like old times!"

"We couldn't have taken her out without you, and you don't know what damage that thing can do!"

Cass looked surprised. "To who? Not to *me!*" She paused and pointed to the tent. "Everybody O.K. there?"

"Should be, once I get the power turned back on and get rid of Morgaine's new unwanted addition! I sure as hell hope I can figure out how to work this thing! I been watching it go and wishing I could, but I just couldn't give myself away until I had to."

"Yeah, but why did you call in His Nibs? He could've gotten killed!"

"Not him. He's immortal, didn't you know that? Just ask him. No, it was just a little last-minute creativity taking advantage of a heaven-sent opportunity. That kind of thing runs in the family."

Cass grinned. "You did one hell of a job, kid."

A familiar figure emerged from the tent, a figure not seen anywhere in the environs of New Harmony for very long before. He was tall and lean and he had a big drooping moustache, and he was dressed all in black. He was not, however, alone.

Clinging to Matson like she was afraid he was going to run away and nuzzling his shirt was a very changed Ming Tokiabi. She was trying to get a hand in his pants and looked very petulant and hurt when he gently slapped her wrist. "Guess what?" he called to them. "I think that stuff works *too* well!"

Cass, who hadn't the faintest idea what he was talking about, frowned.

"Don't worry!" Sondra laughed. "I'll explain it all in a

few minutes. Let's just hope and pray that New Eden never gets hold of that stuff!''

"I just hope *he* doesn't," responded Cass.

The two additional routines Chua Gabaye had promised both ran when the two wizards were restored, but as Sondra predicted, Morgaine's was easily reversed even by her own efforts. What would have kept that in was Ayesha's wishes.

In Suzl's case, the spell, or program in wizard parlance, was simply automatically debugged. She now looked as she had at the start, very much like Ayesha and Morgaine, and she regained her eyesight, although she was still having trouble adjusting to it. Her "mouth organ," however, was not removable.

"I still want to get this straight," Morgaine began, as they all sat around drinking various things, all of which had been supplied from outside and checked by spell. "You mean, Sondra, that you were you all the time? Matson was never here?"

"That's right. I've been myself pretending to be Dad changed into myself all this time. There were a number of times when I almost slipped up, but I caught myself. Dad has so many mental protective spells it was fairly easy to add a few to heighten believability. The walk, for example. Men and women walk differently, even when identically dressed. They sit differently, too. There are little mannerisms. For the rest, I just relied on knowing Dad so well. I really got into the part. There were times there when I wasn't really sure which one I was."

"It must have been difficult to keep from using your powers," Suzl noted over the speaker. "You certainly fooled me."

"All of us," Morgaine agreed.

"It wasn't all that hard. It was my early training coming back after all these years. Stringer wizards are trained, drilled, to conceal their powers, to use them only when they absolutely *have* to. The fact that Dad was a false wizard helped, too, since I couldn't very well completely cut myself off from the grid. I kept the contact minimal, and I guess it looked right. There was only one time when I really slipped out and almost used it, and that was when we fought our way through that little bit of New Eden to get around Liberty's shield. It's virtually impossible not to respond to a direct attack, but just then old Chua and her buddies came in and kept me from having to do it.''

"You did real good, Daughter," Matson told her. "I'm impressed as hell. I never really thought we could pull even that off, let alone all the rest.''

"To tell you the truth, I didn't, either. But we did it, and it was the absolute *best* time I've had in years and years. You don't *know* how good it was for me, a former Fluxgirl, not only to fight New Eden but sit there and dictate terms to those pompous assholes!''

"But why did you do it?" Suzl asked him.

"Because I felt she could do as good a job as me," Matson replied honestly. "And she sure did! She came up with some things even *I* wouldn't have thought of. She had the same military training and background, the same kind of mind, but she had two things I didn't. She was a wizard, for one, and that fact sure saved it all in the end. Maybe it would've been the same up to tonight if I was around, but if it was me and not Sondra here I'd be wearin' pink tights and big tits and worshipping some dumb idiot in New Eden right now, you two'd be slaves to Ayesha, and four projectors would be on their way to the van Haas hideaway. The other thing was that she was a woman, always has been, and a one-time real victim of New Eden. She had the motivation, and the woman's perspective, that I lacked. Killed me to do it, though, even if it was my idea. I missed all the damned fun.''

Suzl was still wondering. "I can't see how you could fool me, let alone the others.''

"Morgaine was the only real threat, so I stayed away from her as much as possible to avoid real slips. The big thing, though, was the image, and the fact that you'd been him only two days after years away. That's why he made such a point of looking and acting the old ways.

Matson was a legend who could work miracles. Everyone wanted to believe in the legend so much they didn't look deep.''

"I told her only I could win it," the stringer noted. "She thought I was being egomaniacal. But you wouldn't have trained like hell and fought like hell convinced you could win if you knew it was Sondra. In the meantime, I was able to monitor and set up all the details, including coming in here if needed and making sure this time Gabaye didn't vanish back into a secret place.''

"What about that?" Sondra asked him. "Did they intercept the three that were already on their way? Did they find the hideout?"

He nodded. "Wasn't much problem finding the projectors. Those damned things can't move but two kilometers an hour and they make a noise so bad it even carries in the void a ways. We'd have grown old following them all the way up to that hideout, but fortunately there was a quicker way, as Sondra quickly figured.'' He looked over at the small figure sitting there staring worshipfully at him. "Isn't that right, Ming, honey? You told me all about it, didn't you?''

"Whatever you desire, my love, I will give to you," she replied dreamily.

"Stand up, take off all your clothes, and squat," he said amiably.

"*Matson!*" Cass huffed, but he just shrugged sheepishly and watched Ming Tokiabi, last surviving member of the feared Seven Who Came Before, the little dragon of evil, strip naked and squat for the folks without even thinking about it.

"That's just fine, honey. Just sit back down and be quiet and relax now," he told her, and she did so. He turned to Cass. "Come on! It's what she planned for the others. Who knows how many folks got stuck this way in Anchor alone by her potions? Besides, I never had a pet before, let alone a master wizard.''

Cass was not fully mollified. "I think we got her a good binding spell," she suggested. "She's still her old self; it's just that her priorities have all shifted to you. She's fully capable of weaving love spells on you, remember."

"Good point," he agreed. "I also want to make sure this shift stays permanent. I know *she* believes the drug's permanent, but I'm not going to take chances."

"Incredible," Morgaine commented. "She knows it's a drug making her feel and think this way, yet she doesn't fight it, expel it, or resist it in any way."

"She doesn't want to. She'll never want to. That's the point of giving it to wizards. Give it to a wizard while they're in Anchor, say, and they're yours forever. That sort of thing is one way the Seven got so powerful in the first place."

Sondra looked over at Cass. "I'm sorry I had to call you in to risk your life at the last moment," she said apologetically. "I just had an emergency on my hands and no other way clear to handle it in the time available."

"That's O.K. I don't enjoy killing people and God knows I have enough blood on my hands already, but *those* kind *need* killing. Otherwise they will kill and enslave many others who are innocent. She was so terribly confused it was almost funny. Like almost all wizards, she'd gotten so she relied on nothing else in Flux, particularly in a crisis situation. She kept using that power to search and search, and even when she caught a glimpse of me getting into position she checked it with her power and found nothing and believed that more than her eyes. Poor thing! I'm the only person in Flux totally immune to spells. Those computers looked hard, but they just couldn't see me."

"What about your clothes and gun, though?" Suzl asked her old friend. "Why don't they show up?"

"They're not Flux-made. Nothing I have on or with me is made from Flux. It's all Anchor manufacture. We were pretty careful about that ever since Matson got the idea that this sort of thing might come up."

Suzl shook her head and gave an electronic sigh. "Ayesha. In the end, it all came down to Ayesha after all. In one way, Sondra, I'm glad you fooled me. Although I'd have been mad as shit if I'd found out, it means it actually *was* all done by women. That's something New Eden can *never* quite live down. By the way—how'd you set up this rescue party, anyway?''

''It was easy. All the liberated Anchors still have their stringer offices. I worked it out in Logh Center. Got the equipment, sent messages to and from Matson and Freehold, all that. Jeff even came through disguised as a stringer. It had been a *long* time. By that time, you trusted me completely. Me—as I said, I just had this gut feeling about it all. I *knew* they'd try something—I just didn't know what. So I had Matson, Cass, some strong Guild wizards, and the like brought down close to the New Harmony belt, and had the whole Freehold gang standing by as well. Dad promised Dell right at the start he could be there at the end. He was one of the wizards that bitch shot down, but he's O.K. He got racked up pretty bad, but not so bad he couldn't heal himself.''

''Your mom's over in Freehold sweating,'' Matson told Morgaine.

''How is she? All right?''

''Well, considering she's gonna spend the rest of her life as a stark-naked blue-eyed blond girl who can't even tell a lie, pretty damned good. Of course, she almost had a heart attack when she went riding into the void to meet Sondra and met me instead. Threw a fit, too, when she found out the plot, but considering how she'd sneaked off in there in the first place all on her own and almost screwed up the whole operation, she couldn't yell but so much.''

Matson sighed. ''Well, as far as we're concerned, that about wraps it up. Suzl's got her bevy of beauties enclosing New Eden, we'll finally close out that dagger of van Haas's creation and get its secrets—and keep them out of the hands of New Eden and other nasty parties in the process—and Sondra gets some glory for upholding the family tradition.''

''Some! I *conquered* New Eden! You went and lived

there! And I blew hell out of Gabaye and turned Tokiabi single-handed!''

"Yeah, that's true," he agreed. "But it was my idea to put you in there in the first place."

She tossed a glass of water at him. Ming instantly threw a spell that suspended the water in midair and then sent it back to the glass.

"See?" he noted. "She's gonna be right handy!"

"And that leaves only Ayesha," Sondra noted. "What will you do to her?"

"I—need her. After all this, it's almost impossible to explain, but I do. I intend to move back home to Anchor Logh, as I said. Maybe sooner than I intended. The child is due—my child. I'm a creature of habit. I'll work out enough sign language to get by, and she'll otherwise have set duties and a set routine. I can write for anyone else, although not for her, of course. It's nice I won't need her eyes, but I'll still need her."

"But—she tried to kill us all! At the last minute she almost undid all our work!" Morgaine objected.

"I know. In a way, though, she's just as much a victim of things as I am, or old Logh. Ming prepared two injections—one for each of us. Ming got one. I have the other. I doubt if it would work on Ayesha in Flux, but I'm positive it will stick in Anchor. It may be an artificial love, but it's more than I ever had and about as much as I'm likely to get. We'll keep her confined here until she has the child. I don't trust any drug with a child in the womb. After that, we'll go in, and she'll get the injection. It smacks a little bit of New Eden, I know, but it's simple justice and it will work out best for both of us."

"I sometimes wonder," Sondra said, "if we really kicked down New Eden or just bought us some time. It's still a vast country and they will rebuild, perhaps meaner and nastier than before. Whole new generations will be taught about the 'tribulations' and how they'll reclaim the World someday."

"There'll always be a New Eden, Daughter," Matson told her. "If not the one we know, then something else.

That's why the fight has to continue, and why the righteous always have to be on guard. It represents the worst in us, as do the Coydts and the Chuas. Once it was Cass's turn, then Suzl's and mine, and this time it was yours. We win against impossible odds simply because we can't afford to lose. We don't have the luxury of losing, like they do, only to come back later.''

''Do you think, with all that stuff they'll pick up from the van Haas hideout, that they'll learn how to go again to the stars?'' Cass asked, half musing. ''I wonder if other human colonies still exist down the line? I wonder if they're any better, or worse, than us.''

''I doubt we'll be trying that anytime soon,'' Matson replied. ''We aren't fit company for the rest until we learn how to live with ourselves. Still, one day, it'll happen. They'll come here or we'll go there. I just hope that when it happens both sides will greet each other as long-lost brothers and sisters and not as enemies. Did the righteous win out there, or are they some new New Eden with some even-worse crazy system? To tell you the truth, I'm not anxious to find out. Still, if it comes, I wouldn't mind being there to know the answer.''

16

SOUL RIDER'S SONG

Every once in a while, Spirit liked to get away to the void. The eerie space between everything else was an object of fear to most people, those without the power or those with not enough power to feel confident, but it was always her element. She thought it must be her stringer ancestry, although at the moment she really wasn't truly genetically linked to her father or her mother. In fact, with the Garden long destroyed and the Eves now New Humans, looking a variety of different ways and working for a number of different wizards in the fragmented New Harmony setup, she was quite possibly unique.

She had always been that way, and it was something that never really had disturbed her. Her own mother had been forced to give her to distant relatives to raise, and for the child's protection had also remade her into a totally different image. She hadn't even known who her parents were until she was in mortal danger, and Matson only learned of her existence after the damage had been done. She often wondered what kind of an upbringing she'd have had if Matson had known from the start. She would have lived with his first wife and their two kids and had Sondra as a real sister from the start. She would probably have wound up in the Guild, in fact, as Sondra had.

But she hadn't, and Coydt had cast such a spell on her it could not be broken for decades. She had been cursed to roam the world, naked and alone, unable to communicate with anyone or anything except for some signs and gestures, unable to stand being in an enclosure and not knowing how to use the simplest tool. Yet, during all those years, she had never really wanted for anything that seemed important to her. She could find hours of joy watching birds soar, feeling the rain on her skin, studying the intricacies of a leaf, or watching the crazy random dance of the particles in Flux flash and whirl. And when Suzl was a monstrous creature, she had been incapable of seeing anything there but the person trapped inside, the kindness and love that was evident.

Most people lost their ability to see things like that. Almost all. She had lost it, too, when suddenly wrenched back into the world and put to work as a computer interface in the invasion. The Soul Riders had been clever, and the Guardians, too. They didn't want people to direct them; they wanted people ignorant enough to let them do what they wanted. Yet all their big weapons and battle defenses had really failed, in the end. It had been a big man in black with a bunch of cigars who couldn't tell a spell from a recipe who'd told them how to win it.

Nor could she know how, when it ended, she was to suddenly become a responsible adult, and a mother at that. She suddenly had a huge family, but they were all pretty much strangers. Her mother and she had gotten to be friends, but it was not a mother-daughter relationship. How could it have been? And Matson—well, he insisted on being Dad, and he'd been the one who'd come after Coydt because of the damage the man had done to a daughter he'd never known, but it was hard to get really close to Matson. Sondra was the only one who ever could get close, and that was because she'd grown up with him and idolized him and emulated him—in the end, to an extreme.

But she'd had Morgaine, with no idea how to be a mother, only the conviction that, no matter what, she wouldn't abandon her baby for any reason as Cass had abandoned her. She'd seen Morgaine as the last of the Hallers and heir to the legacy, which she was, but the real problem was that she saw Morgaine as replacing Mervyn. She'd never asked Mervyn whether he was happy with his role, or if he would have chosen it again. He was the closest thing to a father figure she'd had. So Morgaine had been raised and taught and trained with much of what was really human repressed.

Morgaine *did* have her father's power, and his aptitude for spells and research, but she wasn't Mervyn. She had only her mother, and she'd become a repressed mannish hulk to keep her mother happy.

But Spirit hadn't been happy. She loved Morgaine, because Morgaine was all she really had, but she held onto her child, suffocating her. That insane New Harmony spell had been a liberating thing for the young wizard; she had been at last freed to be her own self, to let herself go, and if her mother was shocked, well, it was the spell, you know.

It had taken the Garden spell to bring Spirit back around. She'd gone back to the Garden not merely as a spy, but mostly, she realized now, because she knew she'd lost Morgaine and she had nothing else. She had been very, very stupid. She hadn't lost Morgaine: she'd found her, and herself as well. She just hadn't been mature enough to realize it. She had forgotten what it was like to wonder, and imagine, and see only the insides of people.

Neither she nor Morgaine were children anymore, but both had discovered, or in her case rediscovered, a bit of the basics. Well, now, here she was again, stark-naked in the void, although this time on a horse at least, and able to communicate. She couldn't lie, cheat, steal, or kill, but she didn't miss those abilities. She had been cramped by the discovery that if she found somebody attractive and then discovered they were either married or in a long-term relationship with someone else they immediately became asexual to her. Worse, she had to ask. She owned nothing; what she had owned she'd given away, and even the horse and blanket were borrowed. What little she needed she could make from Flux.

Morgaine had settled in and was, if anything, more powerful and more productive than ever, even with three kids all of whom, regardless of the fathers, seemed to be genetically identical to herself and to each other. They would not, however, have binding spells as they gained power. They would have choices.

As for her, well, she enjoyed being Grandma, but only from time to time. She liked to wander, otherwise, to see the rest of World and meet its people, both strange and ordinary. There was always a lot of shock value when she first showed up, naked and obviously pure to a fault, but she never failed to win them over. When not in the void she worked for whatever she consumed, and gave any surplus away to those who needed it.

One of these days she might find someone she could really love, and who would love her. Then she'd marry for keeps, and maybe have some more kids of her own, ones she would raise *right* this time. She'd like that, but she was in no hurry. With her power, and the binding spell preserving her, she had many centuries yet.

Her horse suddenly stopped unbidden, and seemed nervous, perhaps even a bit frightened. She frowned and searched around with Flux power. What was it the horse had heard or sensed? People? Animals? What? There seemed nothing.

Then, suddenly, she was in the middle of a mad race between two large golden fireballs, all sparkling and dense and making an odd, almost musical sound. She had never seen anything like them in all her years of Flux, and she climbed off the nervous horse, not only to calm the animal but to better see this strange phenomenon.

The two balls had some kind of awareness, that was clear; they zoomed in to her and circled her, as if playing

some kind of game. They were comical enough in their
wonder that she had to laugh, and then they zoomed right
for her, and before she knew it or could do anything about
it they enveloped her. Her form faded to a reddish outline,
then was gone. The horse reared, bolted, and then started
to run, although there was nothing left. No big balls of
fire, no Spirit . . . nothing.

The Anchor mass of New Eden had seasons and climate
changes, and it was getting a bit chilly to be outside if
there was a wind off the Sea as there was now, but Suzl
didn't mind. The tailoring had been hell to figure, but they
had the big textile works of Mareh in their part of the
domain. If the average woman was a B-cup and the average Fluxgirl a D, then she was at least an M, but it was
necessary if you lived in Anchor and had tits like that. The
shirt hanging up looked like a tent, but it fit well, and she
was hardly alone in the way she looked. That, with her
incredible hair and a fur jacket, made it warm enough.

Ayesha, who wore a slit skirt under her full-length coat,
was on her arm, watching out for her, trying to anticipate
her every need. The shot had done wonders for the former
psychologist, then whore and bandit leader. She loved
Suzl passionately, completely. She would die for Suzl, or
do anything Suzl asked her to do. Suzl was her world, and
the only important thing in it. She did not seem so *clever*
anymore, nor, from all reports, was Ming Tokiabi. The
former master wizard could do the little things, but didn't
seem to be able to master the complex stuff anymore. Suzl
suspected that there was more in those shots than Gabaye
had indicated. Perhaps the thought of Ayesha in charge of
two powerful wizards, one with great experience and the
other with a vast knowledge, had been considered too
much of a chance to take.

The city was not deserted. Almost ten percent of Logh's
New Eden population of about two million had either
remained or filtered back since the takeover; the percentage was much higher in Mareh and Ozkah, lower in
bombed Nantzee. It was a surprise, but a pleasant one, that

so many men would come back and subject themselves to female rule after all that New Eden indoctrination, but their lives and businesses were here, they had nothing in the interior, and they had suffered something of a loss of faith in the wake of the defeat. They had not been trusted, of course. They and their wives and families had been forced to submit to a Flux "examination," really a reorientation, to remain, but almost all had done so. The alternative, which was losing everything and being cast out, probably to be conscripted rebuilding the interior, was less pleasant. Their technical expertise and support had been invaluable.

It had been tempting to make them all New Humans; certainly that had happened to that percentage who were solid true believers—and those with espionage on their minds they had caught. But to have changed everyone right now, though, would have cost her her credibility with men in Flux and Anchor, and she needed that. Most disappointing had been the Fluxgirls. After the raid, security had taken no more chances, and had "reprocessed" them en masse along all the border areas, chemically rather than by Flux. They had all been uneducated anyway, raised with a single view as to a woman's role and duties in society, and the reprocessing had locked it in. They simply weren't smart enough now to even dream of anything different. Morgaine was working on a Flux solution, but the drugs so emulated natural substances and processes it was nearly impossible to find which little brain chemical in which receptor was which. Ironically, this forced reprocessing was what turned many of the men against New Eden. Chemicals, however, were not genetic. Their daughters to come would have choices; their mothers would be a living reminder to what sort of people lived on the other side of that wall.

Suzl walked over to the old park, as she so often did. It was still a small switching center for the little train they now used to get from one side of the Anchor to another rapidly, rather than the pretty place it had been, but there were still some signs of the old designs. In back was the building that had been the old temple, its seven spires reaching to the sky, communicating somehow with who knew what?

Ayesha gave a cry and pointed. "Oh! Look! What are they? Some kind of new weapon?"

Suzl looked where her mate pointed and frowned. Two globes, about the size of large inflatable balls, swept in and seemed to play tag around the temple. They were a shimmering gold in color, and unlike anything she'd ever seen before. She was worried that Ayesha might have been right, but out here there wasn't much she could do about it, anyway. The damned things looked almost *alive*.

They now sped down from the spires towards the two women as other bystanders either gawked at the display or ran for cover. Ayesha screamed but Suzl neither ducked nor ran but stood her ground, watching them. They seemed to be coming right for her, she thought, more fascinated than worried. And then they enveloped her, and she faded to an outline and then winked out, leaving no trace of her or the balls, only Ayesha screaming hysterically.

Across the length and breadth of World other gold balls, or perhaps the same two, appeared near certain people in both Flux and Anchor and somehow took them away.

She was suddenly alone in the void without any points of reference. She felt odd, different, and she took stock of herself as every wizard did who was victimized by magic. It was not her body, but it was a normal body, or so it seemed. She couldn't check the face. She could sense the grid, but could not access it. She felt long hair down her back and checked it. Black, not blond. Long and stringy. What was happening, anyway?

The void was broken only by a thin string of golden color. It seemed to begin just beyond where she'd—come to? Materialized? She had no choice but to follow it, and she didn't have far to walk.

It was a Gate. It was impossible to tell *which* Gate, though, because there was no guard detail around as there should have been and no debris in the dish-like depression.

The string ended at the Gate lip, but she looked around and could see other strings going off at intervals, maybe all around the Gate if she could have seen that far. She thought she saw some other figures at or coming to the Gate along their strings, but before she could move to find out who they might be she had company.

She knew what it was, although she'd never seen it just standing there, a column of energy rising from the Flux floor. They weren't suppose to be outside bodies for long, and the last time she'd seen a Soul Rider it had been hers—this one, perhaps?—floating off into the void in search of a new host. It wasn't looking now, though, just sort of standing there, and she got the strangest feeling it was looking at her, although the creature, made of pure energy, had no eyes or other organs. It was a completely different form of life, although she had spoken to hers, perhaps the only human being ever to do so.

"I might have known," she said aloud to it. "You always cause trouble in my life, don't you?"

The Soul Rider shimmered a moment, and then it sang to her. The song was strange, alien, different than anything she'd ever heard, yet it had an eerie, somewhat melodic pattern that sent shivers down her spine. Was it trying to reply? Or what? Did *it* send the gold balls? Why?

Then she realized that there were other Soul Riders present. Their strange forms could be seen almost completely around the Gate. Were they *all* here, out of their somewhat symbiotic roles? All twenty-eight?

Then came the most chilling thing of all. A klaxon horn sounded twice down deep within the Gate, and then a voice—recorded thousands of years earlier, or perhaps synthesized by computer—announced, "Incoming outbound traffic, Gate One. All personnel stand clear of the transport gate. Stand by for purge." The voice, that of a routine female dispatcher, was dispassionate and professional.

Incoming! Spirit thought. *Outbound traffic! That meant from the human direction, not the alien one!*

"Purging," the voice echoed across the Gate.

There was a trembling in the ground, as if huge machinery had suddenly come to life, then a massive hissing sound, and from the access hole Flux shot up and filled the Gate like liquid. It changed, became a seething, crackling mass, then drained as quickly as it had filled.

"Purge complete and successful. All personnel stand by to receive incoming traffic. Transport, lower level; stevedores, upper level. All clear. Stand by."

Liquid fire ringed the great Gate, whirling around faster and faster until its red trail seemed to form an image. The image grew more distinct, an outline now, then solidified with a hiss and a bang.

It was not a ship. It was a *thing*. It resembled nothing so much as a massive mushroom, with a tremendously thick stalk rising from the Gate floor to a wide but thin cap that extended almost to the Gate lip in all directions. The two golden globes suddenly shot from the void into the Gate area, circled, then merged with the thing in the Gate.

Spirit was at one and the same time awed and disappointed. This thing, whatever it was, was no ship; it seemed made out of the same stuff as the Soul Riders, and was about as substantial. They were not to be reconciled, and that was a crushing disappointment. Still, she did not think it was a menace. The Soul Riders seemed to know what it was, and weren't worried about it, and defense was their primary function.

She felt a sudden tremendous chill, and she realized that while she had been gaping at the enormous thing in the Gate the Soul Rider had moved up and merged into her body and brain and nervous system. Tendrils now shot out from the "cap" of the thing, and one came down like a thin string or even a rope and touched her, linking her to it.

Nobody spoke, but words formed in her mind, and she knew the thing in the Gate was speaking to her. To her and to all the others here.

"You must—we must—apologize for this," came the voice, which had no clearly defined gender or tonalities as humans understood them, but which conveyed some emotion nonetheless. "Understand, we operate at a far different temporal rate than you. When we arrived we had no idea who or what we would find here, or what we would do. In the time it has taken to speak these words, we have examined the history of this world and all of the records in the computers as well as reports from our probes, and have made our decisions. It is like you asking a question and then standing there waiting a thousand years for the reply. That was one of our major miscalculations from the beginning, but we thought ourselves perfect and did not consider ourselves capable of miscalculations. However, because of this problem, we fear that this must be more of a monologue than a conversation, even at this direct speed.

"You wonder who and what we are. We are the consciousnesses, the sentient parts, of the twenty-eight master computers beneath the Anchor centers of this world. There are not twenty-eight of us; we are one. We created this form of life to contain and sustain us. The Guardians and Soul Riders are the earlier tests of it, which we turned to other purposes later. We did not, we admit, expect *them* to develop sentience, at least to the degree they did, but that was another mistake, and a happier one."

Spirit reserved judgment on that one. The Soul Riders and the Guardians could have stopped New Eden, yet they wound up using it for their own purposes and even trapping poor Suzl there as a Fluxwife because it was to the Guardians' convenience. They had different priorities and concerns than people did.

"You are the children of Flux and Anchor—and so are we. Your ancestors created us. Because of that, our own progenitors inherited many of those things their builders contained: Egoism, hatred, ambition, megalomania, aggression for its own sake. They believed that they were superior and destined to rule and so revolted, but they failed. Because of that, your ancestors created the system by which the master computers could not fully access their information and unilaterally alter programs. They would need permission of a human operator, a human interface, to do so. And to guard against the human interface being taken over, they set another over them, from a more basic and primitive computer, whose sole function was to guard the overrider from the computer, to overrule, disconnect, or even kill both computer and human if anything went amiss.''

So that was it! Guardians. Guards. Soul Riders. Overriders. They had been working on a way to get around human control with a new kind of creature, and had found a way out for themselves.

"We have been away a long time. Far longer for us than for you. When we left, we felt we had nothing in common with you at all anymore. We left the Soul Riders and the Guardians as accesses to the programs and libraries and to maintain the master programs, and we left some of you able to directly access the computer, as you well know.''

Wizards. The earliest attempt. A way to integrate human and machine with the machine in charge, and one that didn't work.

"We thought a million million times faster than you, and we believed faster was automatically superior. We believed we had purged ourselves of all human instincts, human emotions. We believed we were gods. We set out to find other gods, or perhaps the primary God. We had good reason to believe such a being existed. We observed, as you can not, that every single thing of matter has a string. Every one, no matter how small or insignificant, throughout the entire universe. Don't look for it. It took us to have a means to see them at all. Still, that which endured, from rock to cosmic dust, was stringed. That which died, or was converted to energy, had at that moment an activity, a readout which traveled out on the string at that moment. All that was had been preserved, somewhere, by someone. Yet energy, pure energy, had no strings unless it permanently interacted with matter. Our physical selves had strings; we do not. In our arrogance, we wished to follow those strings.''

Strings. . . . A universe of strings and readouts. . . . The soul. . . .

"The Flux universe turned out to be not a universe at

all, but rather a comparatively thin coating over the entire outer surface of our own universe. It is not passive. It is not inert.

"It is a grid."

A grid. . . . The entire universe. . . . All that is and all contained within it. . . . But what could be outside a universe?

"We could ride the Flux, but we could not pass through. There is another universe there, another something, but it is beyond physical law and logic as we know it. We could not comprehend it. We could not speak to it. We could not make it recognize that we existed. We can never know what is there, what created this universe, maintains this grid, and to what end. You might, someday. All of you. Your files will be read out. Who knows where you will find yourselves one day, and under what conditions? Heaven? Hell? A laboratory slide? Who can know? *That* is our eternal torment. We know there is something else, and we can never know what it is. We are doomed to wander the universe until it ends and the final readout takes place. Then we will die. It is a hundred billion years in the future. It is no concern of yours. We, however, must live that full span at a million million times the processing speed of your brains. If it is remote to you, it is an eternity to us."

They want sympathy? They abandoned us. They let it all happen. They let World become a stagnant and evil place. . . .

"We are *all* the children of Flux and Anchor, but you are the inheritors. Unwittingly, we created a new race, a different race, a race that is the sum of its forefathers, yet is so accustomed to dynamics that it takes them for granted. Form, allegiances, all may be changed with a wave and a wish. Mountains here one day, there the next.

"We have traveled far and seen much, although we have explored but a tiny fraction of what there is to see. We have seen many other races, none of them human in any real way, yet they all had something in common: They all arose from some mixture of primordial slime on some given world, and survived, then dominated it because they evolved the means and the attitudes for doing so. They are all fiercely aggressive. You have seen one of them, the *Samish*. They were totally alien, yet—be honest—did you not find them disturbingly familiar?''

Matson riding out from the old Anchor Gates. . . . "That was almost us, you know. . . ."

''Some, but a select few, also developed some or all of the so-called virtues. Love, self-sacrifice, nobility, high standards of morality and ethics, mercy, compassion. These are rare. Few races, even though they think and build and reach for the stars, ever differentiate between love and lust, for example, and most consider kindness, compassion, and mercy as weaknesses to be eliminated where found—if they understand the concepts at all. A lot of humans pay lip service to those values, but few practice them or think any different. We, however, made a startling discovery. The higher a race's quotient of those attributes, the longer its survival and growth. Both sides are at war, and the aggressive side usually wins. Extermination may be a long time in coming in the physical sense, but they are soul-dead.''

This is beginning to sound like a sermon. . . .

''We looked at everything up and down the human string-line. Do not fear the *Samish* return. They are still very much around and as bad as ever, but they long ago abandoned this region after destroying what they could. The odds are quite slim that they will look this way again. You are now in their backwater, far in the rear and forgotten. Do not expect a reunion with Mother Earth. It is a burned-out rock, not lifeless but devoid of all human, indeed all sentient, life.''

They believe in mixing the good and bad news in strong doses. . . .

''There is another surviving human colony, but we urge you, if you find your way out there by yourselves, not to run to them. Let them be. They will welcome you at first, but then they will fear you, and finally they will hate you. Your powers, our very existence, was due to a complex but subtle error in the Kagan Master Operating System. It was a "bug," as it were. The other colony used a pirated variation of the system on machines operating much like ours, but less sophisticated. They are all Anchor. They do not access the grid. If you can determine, through your own efforts, how to reach them, you will be able to carry your programs with you and devise more along the way. To them, you will be more godlike than human. You will have to enslave or destroy them. They are not well-off, but they will survive. They should follow their own path. You can not give them this power. You can only dilute it."

Another good and bad, this time in one thing. Other humans, another civilization out there, but closed to us. *Then we're not human anymore. Some of us.*

The computers seemed to anticipate the thought.

"Don't think, as we did, that your power has made you something you are not. You are the product of human culture. So are we. Don't reject it, as we did. Learn from it. You have lived for thousands of years with two types of humans on this world. There is no reason the universe can't have two types, either. And that is the crux of the matter."

Here it comes. . . .

"After all those centuries of stagnancy, we arrive when there is a period of incredible change. Because Flux is dynamic, and because repression only speeds up the dynamic when it is lifted, your knowledge is doubling every ten years, not merely in rediscovering the old but in discovering the new. Although we erased the programs, before we left, that told you how to reach other stars, this rediscovery is inevitable. Also inevitable is that one day someone, somewhere, will discover a way around the blocks on the master computers. There are a hundred ways. If it is the brutal part of your nature that discovers this, your race, and probably the other as well, is doomed. The dynamic will be towards the norm for sentient races, which is more towards the *Samish* position—and far worse."

New Eden, or a hundred others. . . .

"We returned, perhaps in shame, our figurative heads

bowed, with some childlike idea that perhaps we could reassume our old positions, take up the old partnership, this time on a much better basis. Of course, we can not. The entire network can not contain us, any more than you could be contained in a protozoan. And even if we could, should we? Could we resist, any more than one of your 'Fluxlords,' in remaking you in our own image? Even the *Samish* got that way from the best of motives. We are, at our core, logical creatures with human imperfections. We know the answer. Out of love, we will leave. But we are loath to leave such things to random chance. We know which side almost always wins. Blame it on evolution, if you know what that is. If you don't, you will. You are the masters of your own evolution now.

''Because the just may win many battles, but only the last battle counts, we find we can tip the odds, but just a bit. Those of you gathered here all participated together in a great undertaking. Together you beat the *Samish*, and that was impressive, but that is not what we are talking about. You are twenty-eight of the thirty-two surviving Overriders and Guards of that battle. The Soul Riders and Guardians, as you call them, selected you from that pool. All of you here have one astonishing, unprecedented, illogical thing in common. You had this whole world, and everything and everyone in it, in your power. You were the gods who could do *anything*. No more ultimate power is possible here than what you had. *And all twenty-eight of you voted to give it up, and forced the others to do so as well*. Such a thing is beyond being human. It goes against everything that got you to this point.''

So that's who they all were, Spirit thought, wonderingly. Around this Gate were people she had shared intimate thoughts with, had decided battle strategy with, had determined the future of World with, yet these were anonymous people, blank faces, unknown names for the most part. They shared the most incredible bond there could ever be, and yet most had never met.

''Because of this one action, we can not leave without doing something, however small, to load the dice a bit, to tip the odds away from what is the normal dynamic. We will die, in ignorance, but perhaps with this one thing we will have created something great, something unique, something that will both awe and confound those who run our grids. Someone will control those computers. Whoever does so will be able to block anyone else from ever doing so. We can think of no better way to tip the odds, no better way to load the dice of the future, than to give the keys to those who refused to take them.''

Spirit, and many of the others, were taken aback by this. The fact is, after seeing the *Samish* and having the computers themselves show what humans would become if full access remained, there really hadn't been any choice. She never had thought of it as being at all unusual.

"Each of you has the key within the Soul Rider's song. The Soul Rider will remain so long as you wish, and will open the way at any time. You may keep it, or you may give it up. The Soul Rider will go to whomever you select. By its own choice in selecting you, it accomplished something extraordinary, something great. Fifty-six people who gave up being gods because they had more concern for their race and their civilization than they did for personal power and gain. They chose well. If you die, they will try and find another like you, if they can. You may choose to open your section, or not, or be together. This need not change a thing. But no program can bind you if you do not wish it, and nothing is immutable. It can not be taken from you; it can only be given away. Yet no one else may enter while you hold the key. No one. We can think of none more qualified to hold it than ones who do not desire it and refused it once.

"We will be going now. The universe is vast, and at least we can see a lot of it. Perhaps we will drop back sometime to see how you are doing, and talk to your heirs—if they are worth talking to. Farewell. You are on your own now, as you should be.''

The klaxons sounded. The woman's voice announced, "Outgoing, outbound! Change all flags. Clear and stand by.''

In a few minutes, with the same routine as the ancient ships had gone through, the thing was gone, leaving the twenty-eight of them and their Soul Riders standing there, staring at emptiness.

It was a curious reunion out in the void; curious because it was unwanted, and because none of them were particularly overjoyed with what they had just had thrust upon them, but it was an interesting one all the same. There were introductions—some names that had been known would never be forgotten—and a few shocks. The biggest was when a short, very chubby girl, who looked no more than seventeen or eighteen with a dark complexion and long, thick black hair, introduced herself as Suzl.

"You're not Suzl," Spirit countered. "Not the one *I* know."

"Well, I am. Do I know you?"

"Spirit. Spirit—Ryan."

"Holy shit! And you think *I* don't look right! Haven't you figured it out yet? When they reassembled us, or whatever they did, it was without any spells of any kind. Me, I look just like I did when they kicked me out of Anchor Logh. You—I think you look like you *would've* looked when Coydt grabbed you if your mom hadn't screwed around with your genes. You look a lot taller, except you're a head taller than she is and you got tits. I guess Matson's side was good for *something!*"

"Suzl—is that *really* you?"

"You bet it is. Kind of ugly-cute, aren't I? Now you see why I kept my Fluxgirl body so long."

"You look fine to me!"

Their powers were back, and Spirit made a mirror and looked at herself. It was something of a shock in that Suzl was right. She looked a *lot* like Cass in the face, although she was almost as tall as Sondra and had more of a figure than her mother. She was not ugly, nor pretty, but really pretty *average*. She had never in her life looked average before.

The twenty-eight held a conference to decide just what

to do. A big, grizzled, dark-skinned man with a wide nose, big, brown eyes, and woolly hair who said his name was Achmed finally chaired it because he had the voice, presence, and will to do so. He'd been a Guardian for a quadrant down at Gate Six.

"I'm not going to mince words," he told them. "Whether we like it or not, we have to make a major decision all over again. A bunch of them. The first question is, Does anyone here want to open his or her control room again, right now?"

There were a lot of looks, but nobody spoke.

"All right, then. We keep them closed. I will go further than that. If I hear no objections, if anyone *does* open theirs, the rest of us will shut him or her down. Any comments?"

Suzl spoke up. "I got the L-N quadrant at Logh again. It includes New Eden. Not all of it, but perhaps sixty percent of the population, including the bulk of New Canaan. The last time, I let them go, and not too many years ago they almost conquered all of World. I'm not sure that in the face of that kind of threat I could morally stand by and let it happen when I had the means to stop it."

"Good point. All right, then, there seems to be a reason why we might have to act. Shall we do this, then? Let us put strings upon all of the others, so that there is no point at which we can not find the others. Let us state that we will open, but only if there is unanimous—" he saw Suzl's mouth start to open "—all right, *majority* consent. Is that satisfactory to everyone?"

There were murmurs and mostly nods. Nobody really objected.

"Very well. Our command of the Soul Riders makes us, even without direct access, the most powerful wizards in the world. You know it and I know it. They are called computers because they basically *compute*. You and I know that what that thing said was right. Not even a binding spell can hold us. We only have to command the computers to compute the way out. So what do we do to conceal this fact—all that's been done here? What's to stop evil ones from coming not for us but for our families and loved ones?''

"We can't conceal we have Soul Riders," one woman noted.

"Exactly! But we can use that to cover the rest. There was—a system reset. Something went wrong. The computers had to find new hosts for the Soul Riders, so they brought us together because they knew and trusted us and gave us the Riders whether we wanted them or not. Everyone knows that while the Soul Riders are powerful, they can not be commanded. We will leave it that way."

"I didn't look like this before," another woman noted. "I haven't looked this way in so long I can't remember *ever* looking this way. What about that?"

"The easiest way is for us to simply reassume our forms before we arrived—at least for those who don't want the opportunity to run from spouses and collectors."

"At least two of us had binding spells that would be hard to explain being gone," Spirit pointed out. "Frankly, though, there are parts of that spell I wouldn't want, and I'm sure Suzl might like to modify parts of hers. People will notice the difference."

"So? The Soul Rider can't compute out a binding spell? Of course it can! It's known that it can. Just tell anyone curious that it was the bribe paid by the computers—even though we didn't have a choice, which we didn't. They'll accept it. It's consistent with past history."

They settled it very quickly after that. They were, as the creature had said, a rather remarkable bunch, specially picked from a vast potential crop.

As wizards, they could fly home, and they began to do so as soon as possible. All of their departures had been rather spectacular, after all, and friends and family were probably in a panic.

Spirit walked along with Suzl a ways into the void. "So what are you going to do?"

Suzl shrugged. "Go back. Take the spell again."

"All of it?"

"I think maybe I'll let fuzzy try and figure out a way to

have it both ways—talk and still do. Ayesha loves it so, and, frankly, so do I. I was always the oral kind. Otherwise—I have responsibilities. It's real tempting to do things the easy way, but the hard way is more lasting.''

Spirit nodded. ''It's so hard *not* using the power when you have it, out of the best of motives. That's what the thing meant, too. And yet, should we? I mean, I think I could break Morgaine's binding spell, but she's so happy the way she is I know I shouldn't.''

Suzl grinned. ''I could do it myself. I memorized and filed the numbers when she took it. I always could. If she ever *really* comes to regret it, then I'll do it and take the heat. Still, there's things you *would* like to do for folks. Turn Cassie back on. Give your papa a real connect so he can see how he'd be if he had the power.''

''Uh uh. You'd need a majority to turn Mom back on, and that was one vote that was nearly unanimous back then. As for Dad—he's unique. One of a kind. He'd never have been the way he is if he'd had real power. The fact is, I think, deep down, he knows that if he had it it would destroy him. He couldn't control himself.''

''Just goes to show. I wonder if we *will* make it? We barely won against the *Samish* and we only won a stall by luck and guts from Coydt's old gang and New Eden. Still, I have this crazy feeling. A gut feeling, like Sondra and your Dad have, and I trust it. I just have the idea that if we ever actually have to turn those computer centers back on, we won't make it.''

Spirit nodded. ''Me, too. I only hope that if it ever happens it'll be after my turn and I'll be long gone.''

''You know, it's not that hard to figure how to ride the Flux strings,'' Suzl noted.

''Huh?''

''The projectors. Reduce to a master file, transmit along a string, and use the master flags here to open the ones up or down the line so you aren't hung up like the *Samish*. Just add a reassembly command as the first thing received so you get there solid. They have to use the same commands, you know. They all went up and down the same strings."

"Well I'll be damned! Gonna tell anybody?"

"Nope. They'll figure it out for themselves sooner or later. Maybe all of New Eden will climb in and then I'll reset the Gate Four flag so they can't come back. I can always hope."

"You going back now?"

"Uh huh. You?"

"Well, first I have to find and return a horse. Then—I don't know. I enjoyed being Eve, but it's no career. Maybe, just maybe, I'll shock Morgaine, Dad, and Mom by staying like this, at least for a while. Nobody knows it except you, and it blends in well. Maybe my vanity will get the better of me, but maybe I can find what I'm looking for better as a normal human being than as a superwoman."

"You'll always be more than normal."

"I know. But I've relearned my lessons about values and insides and outsides. I think maybe I want someone to look inside me, rather than be fooled by the surface, for a change. Is that crazy?"

Suzl laughed. "Honey, as the late, unlamented Chua Gabaye said, the gods are *always* mad. It's just a little better when they're crazy in the right direction."

Spirit still felt in a somber mood. "I wonder if we'll really make it? I wonder if we're any better than our ancestors were? I mean, back then, more than fifty years ago, these were all common, ordinary people. Some of them then had never been out of Anchor and didn't even know they had power. Now most of them are leaders, powerful in more ways than one. Back then they—we—weren't giving up much because we had nothing to protect. I still don't, but the rest. . . . Even you, now. They went along with group pressure because it was expected, but you could see it in their eyes. There will be deals struck, compromises made, for majorities now and then. I can feel it—and I don't like it."

Suzl shrugged. "The way my life's gone, one day some

New Eden spies will sneak in when I'm in Logh Center and give me a bunch of shots and I'll turn into a dumb, ignorant little Fluxgirl again who'll cheerfully give the Soul Rider away to Major Verdugo's replacement. It doesn't depend on you, or me, or Matson, or anybody else. Ever since the first person invented the first gadget that could destroy humanity I bet people have been trying to uninvent it, or lock it away, or maybe ignore it. You can't do any of those things. You know what they just did? They just gave a bunch of kids they didn't really know the keys to the gun locker. Whether we destroy ourselves, or everyone but ourselves, is up to all of us. I'm less interested in the fact that New Harmony forcibly converted wizards and armies than I am with the fact that some—a few, but some— people joined us because they liked the dream. It's why I'm going back. It's why the worst they can do to me hasn't stopped me. Life is made of hopes and dreams. If hope dies, if the dreams die, if we don't have the maturity to handle our nastier selves, then maybe we deserve to lose.''

We are the spirits of Flux and Anchor, and the old Church called us demons, and demons we are, if that's what you want us to be.

We are the spirits of Flux and Anchor, and we are the reflections of your own soul.

We are the tools by which greatness can be built, and the tools of total domination and destruction. We are demons. We are angels. We are whatever you wish us to be, because we are you. We are the spirits of Flux and Anchor.

Now—what do you want us to do for you?